Wolf

at the

Door

CHRISTINE WARREN

St. Martin's Paperbacks

WOLF AT THE DOOR

Copyright © 2006 by Christine Warren.

Excerpt from *She's No Faerie Princess* copyright © 2006 by Christine Warren.

ISBN: 0-312-93962-0
EAN: 9780312-93962-5

Printed in the United States of America

St. Martin's Paperbacks edition / March 2006

St. Martin's Paperbacks are published by St. Martin's Press, 175 Fifth Avenue, New York, NY 10010.

10 9 8 7 6 5 4 3 2 1

Thanks always to my parents,
who told me to write anything so long as I wrote.

And thanks also to the Pack, for being fabulous;

to R, who made sure I did write;

to G, of course;

and to S, K, and J, who help me into as much trouble
as they help me out of. Now that's what I call friendship.

One

Honeysuckle.

The idiot attorney in the gray suit continued to natter on about something useless—the most beneficial way to structure a retirement portfolio or some such rot—but Sullivan Quinn had long since tuned it out. The hair on the back of his neck bristled to attention. His muscles tensed and his nostrils flared as he drank in the tormenting fragrance. Somewhere in this snugly elegant club, among these rooms full of werefolk and vampires, witches and magic-users, in the middle of a January cold snap, he could smell the sweet, elusive scent of honeysuckle vines.

And it was driving this particular werewolf out of his bloody mind.

". . . lost it when the dot-com bubble burst," short, bald, and boring continued. "Really knocked me for a loop. I didn't have a bite for nearly three days."

Quinn made some sort of not even remotely sympathetic sound and breathed in deeply.

To the left.

His head snapped around, light brown eyes no doubt glowing in reflection of his intensity. He scanned the area thoroughly and tried to suppress a growl when he didn't see an obvious source of the fragrance. It called to him, a sweet heady beacon of femininity, fertility, and fuckability. His three favorite f-words.

Maybe he'd been too long without a lover, or maybe his family was right and his hormones were telling him he was getting too old not to have a mate. Then again, maybe he'd just been sent round the bend by the corrupting influence of New York City. Whatever it was, all he knew was that he wanted that honeysuckle.

What he wouldn't give just then to be back among his own pack, where he could order the bright, intoxicating flowers brought to him like tribute.

Okay, so maybe that was a bit much. As *guth* of his pack, Quinn lacked the ultimate authority of Alpha, but he made up for it with a freedom and respect enjoyed by few others. Whereas Lupines deferred to the Alpha because of his power, they looked up to the *guth* because of the scope of his responsibilities. After all, in addition to being the pack's ambassador and negotiator, the *guth* was the keeper of its traditions, its histories, and its stories. He was the pack's living link to its past, as well as their insurance of a favorable future. So they might not have brought him the honeysuckle as tribute, but they would at least have let him end his current conversation without giving the impression of terminal rudeness.

"Oh, I got over it, of course. Drank three pints straight from the bags before I was fit company again," the charisma-less wonder said, peppering his delivery with a few smug chuckles. "That'll teach this old vamp a new trick or two. You'll never catch me on another starvation diet!"

Quinn ignored the man's forced joviality—which, coming from a vampire who looked like Oliver Hardy, frankly creeped him out—and continued to search. He had to find that honeysuckle. In the last forty seconds, it had become the most important goal in his universe. Never mind that he'd flown from Ireland not two days ago to represent his country at a critical international meeting of Others, staking the honor of himself and his pack on his abilities as a diplomat. Bollocks to that. He needed those flowers.

". . . portfolio had been cursed by some old Cuban woman I bumped into at the market. Cost a fortune to have a witch break the spell, but since then things seem to be picking up steam. I've been quite pleased."

The small part of Quinn's brain that hadn't been commandeered to join the search team allowed him to respond with an eloquent grunt. Then Quinn inhaled another hint of honeyed blossoms, and that last holdout joined the search.

The Emperor of Ennui paused for breath and swirled his glass of watered-down bourbon. "But that's enough about me—"

"Yes," Quinn agreed. The hell with good manners. He had more important things to concentrate on, like giving in to the compulsion to follow his nose and leaving Sir Stultifying to yammer away at thin air.

He wove his way through the crowd of people gathered to welcome him and his fellow European representatives to America, ignoring every single one of them. Right then and for the first time in his life, he didn't care about his standing in diplomatic circles, about the long history of his family as ambassadors among the Others, about his reputation as a man who helped ease the way of his people into the future while keeping alive the stories of their traditions past.

Bugger all of that. He ignored the men who knew him and the women who wanted to and the important figures he'd come all this way to meet. He kept his attention focused straight ahead and followed the beckoning tendril of scent like a man in the desert followed a mirage. Single-mindedly. And hungrily.

He forgot about being a dignitary, forgot about being a guest, even forgot about being an Irishman. Christ, what had gotten into him? He knew the very thing that made him good at his job was that he always kept his cool, no matter how provoking the circumstances. He'd never have made an effective *guth* otherwise. Yet here he was, and there his cool went.

He continued to wonder about it even as the lingering scent drew him like a ring through his nose among the crowds that milled in the hall. There seemed to be folk everywhere, walking in and out of rooms, talking, laughing, and interacting with a tranquillity that the uninitiated might have found astonishing. After all, in a room full of predators, someone usually had to be the prey.

At one time that might have been true, and on more than one occasion Quinn had longed to return to the old ways—usually after settling a mind-numbingly unimportant dispute between packs. But just as the humans had evolved from Vikings to crusaders to frantic missile-defense builders, so too had the Others of the world evolved. They'd learned many centuries ago that to fight among themselves merely gave the humans an advantage in fighting them as well. For some, a common enemy made for as solid a truce as a common goal.

For once, though, Quinn's mind was not on the politics of truces or enemies or common goals. It wasn't on the advice his father had given him the day he'd taken over as *guth*: Always keep his wits about him, no matter what the distraction, no matter how strong the temptation. No, every brain cell he had, be it manly or bestial, had fixed on the sunshine yellow of honeysuckle flowers and the sweet taste of their nectar. He needed a sip. Now.

The mysterious scent maddened him, strong one moment, fleeting the next. Bloody hell, less than forty-eight hours in the country and he'd already developed an obsession. No wonder his pack had jokingly told him New York City would drive a good Irishman mad. They could be right.

Up.

Upupup.

His gaze shot toward the ceiling, as if he expected to see leafy green tendrils twining their way down from the chandeliers. Instead, he blinked up at lovely, white plasterwork like a drooling moron.

"Quinn."

He grunted something unintelligible—well, unintelligible to all but another Lupine—and continued to stare.

"Quinn!"

The growl in that repetition got his attention, and Quinn lowered his gaze from the ceiling of the main hall of the Vircolac Club to the curious face of Tobias Walker, a master of bad timing and representative of his host pack, the Silverback Clan. From the moment of their first meeting thirtysome hours before, they'd fallen into the easy and insulting rapport of good friends or bad brothers.

Tobias raised an eyebrow. "If you're looking for the security cameras, buddy, you're not going to find them. Logan Hunter installed them himself before he moved up north. The security here is top-notch."

"Fascinating, I'm sure," Quinn said, closing his eyes and inhaling deeply. "But I'm really rather busy at the moment, Walker. I'll buy you a pint later and let you bend my ear as long as you please. Now, if you'll excuse me—"

He had barely turned toward the stairs before Tobias caught his shoulder and spun him back around. "Not so fast, Quinn. I didn't come over here to chat about the weather. I'm playing messenger."

Quinn barely paused. "Then tell your message-giver that I'm unavailable for the next little while, will you, boyo? I've more important things to see to at the moment."

"Afraid I can't do that, *pal*. This is business."

Shite.

Quinn bit back the curse. Of all the bloody times for someone to remind him of his duties. It served as yet more proof that God must hate him.

"What type of business?"

"The type you came here for."

Just then, Quinn spotted the stairway, half-concealed around a corner, and wanted to howl at the injustice. He knew that was where the honeysuckle was leading him, and he couldn't get to it. In a minute, someone was going to dangle a raw porterhouse in front of his nose and then tell him it wasn't time for dinner. He just knew it.

He rounded on Tobias, eyes blazing with frustration. "D'you think you might be a tad more specific, lad?"

"Lad? What the hell has gotten into you?" Tobias

paused only long enough to hear Quinn's snarl before he snapped back. "Whatever it is, don't bite the messenger, Cujo. Adele Berry has asked to meet you."

The name pierced Quinn's distraction. "Berry? She sounds familiar, but I can't—"

"She holds a seat on the Council's Inner Circle."

"Shitepissbollocksfuck."

"That's the spirit." Tobias clapped one hand on the other man's shoulder and turned him back toward the club's enormous ballroom. The room he'd just left. Because it was in the opposite direction of his honeysuckle flowers. "She's holding court near the champagne fountain. You're just gonna love her."

Grinding his teeth to sand, Quinn shrugged the hand off his shoulder and headed resentfully in the indicated direction. "Certainly I will. I can tell from the sugared tone of your voice that I shall treasure this experience for all time."

"You'll certainly remember it for all time. No one forgets their first meeting with Dame Adele."

"Dame Adele?"

Glancing briefly backward, Quinn caught the uncomfortable expression that passed across Tobias's face.

"Yeah," the American said, "you might not want to call her that . . . you know, to her face."

"Why, thank you, Tobias. I'm not certain I would have worked that one out for myself."

"I'm here to help."

"And why don't you help yourself to a silver suppository, you supercilious Yank bast—"

"Good evening, young man."

If Quinn clenched his teeth any harder, he'd wind up having them removed from his sinuses.

Turning his back to the Lupine he'd like to strangle, he blew out a slow breath and pasted a charming smile on his face for the small, elegant woman seated before him. After all, she might have bad timing, but business was business.

"Ma'am," he said, taking her frail, soft hand in his and evaluating her at a glance. She had the look of an aged Audrey Hepburn and the bearing of Queen Victoria. "Sullivan Quinn. I'm honored to be making your acquaintance."

"Indeed, Mr. Quinn, I know quite well who you are." She had the imperious tone used only by royalty or three-year-olds. Even he would be hard-pressed to match her for arrogance. "I am Adele Berry, one of the organizers of this little soirée and of your visit here to the United States. I know everything there is to know about you."

Quinn straightened to his full height and fought to keep his hackles from rising. He had been brought up to respect his elders. Right up until the day he could best them in a fight. "Now that would be an impressive achievement, ma'am, and one I'd be curious to know the trick of."

She stared at him from surprisingly dark and canny eyes. "I didn't get to be where I am by revealing my tricks, Mr. Quinn. Nor did I ask the Silverback to introduce us so we could make small talk about your ignorance."

His breath hissed in so loudly, he knew she must have heard it. She just chose to ignore it.

"I required an introduction," she said, straightening her impeccable posture even further, hands folded delicately over the handle of a silver-hilted cane. "I required an introduction because I want to know if the rumors I've heard about your planned speech before the Council might possibly be true."

Quinn bit back an impatient retort and searched for a conciliatory answer. When that didn't work, he searched for civility. "As I'm not privy to such rumors, having only arrived in New York two short days ago, I can't speculate on the truth of them, ma'am."

"Kindly do not play word games with me, young man. I asked you a question, and I expect a direct and concise answer."

At any other time, he would have been amused by this old woman with an attitude from hell and the manners to match, but not tonight. His nerves were on edge, his trousers were tightening, his mind was distracted, and his beast was yanking at the reins in an attempt to get free and get to the source of the floral sweetness in the air.

"No, you didn't, ma'am. You issued a command, which I'm sure is something you're quite accustomed to doing, but to which I am not accustomed to responding."

He watched those dark eyes narrow and struggled to keep the snarl off his face. No matter what his instincts screamed, this woman was not issuing him a challenge. He couldn't let himself treat her by the rules of Lupine society, even if Lupine society would have allowed him to pin her to the floor and clamp his teeth around her jugular.

"Young man, I am a member of the Council of Others."

She fairly radiated elegant outrage, but Quinn remained unswayed. The anger of being torn from his flower hunt helped sustain his resistance.

"I have been weighing the fate of the folk in this city for more than fifty years, be they shifter or vampire, witch or changeling. I am an elder in this community, and I am entitled to an answer. I am entitled to know if you will announce to the Council that your delegation is planning to reveal the existence of our kind to human society."

"With all due respect, ma'am, you will have that answer the minute I give it before the Council."

"I am not inclined to wait!"

"And I am not inclined to humor old women with inflated senses of entitlement!" The reply came out as a roar before he could stop it, though his teeth clacked together in the attempt.

That quite likely hadn't been the wisest move of his political career. He had spent a lot of time before flying to the United States finding out everything he needed to know about the Council of Others, and he'd read several indications that Adele Berry and the Council were twined together tighter than braided silk. For more than four decades, her voice had influenced the body that governed the activities of every nonhuman citizen of the greater Manhattan and tristate areas. She was not a woman to dismiss lightly.

Quinn took a deep breath and tried again. This was not one of his pack, he reminded himself as he attempted to pry his jaws apart. In fact, she wasn't even Lupine; he could smell that much. Actually, he thought, pausing to inhale, she smelled—

"Young man . . ."

—like rose and earth and the faintest trace of warm honeysuckle vines.

Honeysuckle.

Quinn froze, nose locked on target like a dog on point, and breathed in deeply.

Fresh, sweet honeysuckle. Ripe and rich and ready to be fucked—

PLUCKED, he corrected himself, *ready to be plucked.*

"Young man, I demand an explanation of this discourtesy!"

Adele's voice rang brittle and strident in his ears, and he couldn't have cared less. One more deep sniff told him his honeysuckle flower had been here before she disappeared. She had been near this woman, maybe even hugged her, and her scent led directly away from the grande dame and toward the hallway stair.

"Pardon," he growled, already turning and moving toward the door. "It's the Irish in me. Not a civilized bone in our bodies. Ask a Brit."

He didn't stick around to see her jaw snap shut, but he wouldn't have cared if he had. He was too busy licking his chops and grinning the grin of a big, bad wolf.

A wolf with a taste for honey.

Two

I am so going to pay for this, Cassidy Poe scolded herself as she pushed open the door to the roof and peered out. *And I so don't care.*

If she had to endure one more minute at the party downstairs without a break, her control would snap and she'd end up doing something really stupid, like throwing her champagne in some vampire's face. Then she'd be in big trouble. They had no sense of humor about that kind of thing, so she was better off sneaking up to the greenhouse garden here on the roof and taking a few minutes to regroup before she returned to the fray.

She figured she'd better finish the champagne, too, and disarm herself. Just in case.

She made a face as she drained her glass. You would think by now that she'd have the whole obligatory social event thing down pat—after all, her grandmother had lectured her on their importance since she was six—and in a way she did. She knew the right things to say, the right gestures to make. She even knew exactly which fork to use under every conceivable dining circumstance. She descended from something like ten generations of diplomats and ambassadors. Her some-ridiculous-number-of-greats-grandmother had been one of the negotiators at the end of the Fae-Demon Wars all those centuries ago. With a history like that, she should be a natural at this sort of thing, right?

Too bad she hated it with such a fiery passion.

Making a face, Cassidy forced herself to admit that "hate" might be a bit too strong of a word. In reality, she found parts of it fascinating. The way people and races and species interacted had always held her riveted. If it hadn't, she never would have become an anthropologist and made a living studying cultures and how they related to each other. It was just the political side she couldn't stand. Politics always reminded her a bit too much of nights spent with a babysitter while her parents were off negotiating with the head of some vampire house, or the representative of some obscure order of magic-users. And that reminded her of their deaths, which just made her want to cry like a little girl, so she interpreted her feelings for the entire world of Others diplomacy as hate and felt better for it.

Except that her grandmother refused to take no for an answer, even from Cassidy. Especially from Cassidy. When Adele issued a command invitation, you didn't refuse, and a blood relationship was no protection against the mighty grande dame's wrath.

Take tonight, for instance. Cassidy would have preferred to be out somewhere having a root canal than mingling with the elite of Other society, members of the Council and diplomats from the European High Council of Others, but here she was all the same. She'd gotten all dressed up, put on one of the useless, slinky dresses her grandmother had picked out for her, strapped herself into high heels that promised to be the death of her and schlepped herself across town to the Upper East Side all because Nana had told her tonight's event was an important one. Hell, she'd even put up her hair for it!

She had to face it. She was nana-whipped.

Cassidy slipped her shoes off and padded along the flagstone aisles of the greenhouse, barely seeing the collection of blooms and vines that surrounded her. The slight coolness of the slate beneath her bare feet and the warm humidity of the air against the exposed skin of her arms and shoulders reminded her of one very important fact that she considered obvious, but that her grandmother had never managed to accept. Much to Adele Berry's dismay, Cassidy would never be a diplomat, and she would never be a politician, and she would never be able to keep a pair of shoes on for more than an hour at a time.

She stared into her empty champagne flute for a moment before sighing and setting it down on a table between a spray of fern and a potted hibiscus. She could use another drink—or five—but running downstairs for a nip and a belt didn't top her agenda at the moment. She'd rather stay up here and hide.

Cassidy had a talent for hiding. She'd developed it over a lifetime, first as a toddler playing games with her mother in the yard behind their old farmhouse in Virginia; then later as a confused child in the enormous brownstone her grandmother kept just a few blocks from Central Park. When her mother had been teaching her how to use the talents of a Foxwoman, she'd thought of them as a game, something to do on a whim, the source of a good giggle and a fun round of hide-and-seek. She hadn't realized until later that foxes used their ability to blend into their environment as a defense mechanism. And it wasn't until she moved to Manhattan that she discovered the same talent could be quite useful for a Foxwoman who shared it.

She had moved in with Nana just after her sixth birthday, two days after her parents died, and she had learned very quickly that hiding could be even easier in the city than it had been in the woods back home. There, a girl had trees and rocks and tall, prickly grass to shield her from prying eyes. But in the city, the eyes hardly ever paid attention. Soon she had learned how to hide in plain sight, even when people were looking right at her. If she wanted to, she could make sure they never even registered she was there.

If only she'd been able to make the talent work on her grandmother. The problem with having a talent unique to Foxwomen was that it almost never worked on another Foxwoman.

That being the case, Cassidy figured she had about seven and a half more minutes before someone came up here to find her, instructed where to look by Adele herself. For a woman in her seventies, Cassidy's nana could teach sharp to an ice pick.

Taking a deep breath, Cassidy tilted her head back to look through the glass-paned roof to the night sky above. In Manhattan, no one could really see the stars, but it still made her smile to know they were there. When she was little, she had imagined that the stars were the eyes of the angels watching over the world, and if that were true, she knew two sets belonged to her mother and father. Sarah and David Poe had both had eyes that seemed to always sparkle with warmth and amusement, so it seemed fitting. And it made her miss them a little less to know they still looked out for her in whatever way they could. Even as an adult, she found it comforting to know that even when the world changed, the stars would still look constantly down.

With her head tilted back and the low back of her cocktail dress exposing her skin to the humid air, she missed the silky tickle of hair against her skin. Reaching up, she pulled the elegant silver sticks out of the knot of her hair and let the long, reddish waves tumble down, as a soft growl filled the night air.

A growl?

Cassidy shook her head as if to clear it and heard the low vibrating sound again, coming from somewhere behind her. Spinning on her heels, she found herself facing a strange, towering shadow with the glowing amber eyes of a Lupine.

And he was growling with a low, smoky rumble.

Naturally, Cassidy did what any self-respecting fox would do when confronted with a predator twice her size and three times her level of aggression. She turned tail and ran, leaving the hair sticks, her evening bag, and possibly a few minutes of the end of her life clattering to the floor behind her.

Quinn had the best of intentions. Honestly, he did. He intended to introduce himself. Smile warmly, offer to shake her hand. Maybe compliment her on her dress, which draped enticingly over a ripe set of curves that made his mouth water and his palms itch. He had intended to do all of that, to be a gentleman and a scholar, but every single one of those intentions flew out the glass walls of the greenhouse the moment she turned and ran from him.

That was when instinct took over, and after that, he had no choice. His man lost the battle with his beast, and the chase was on.

He couldn't stifle the flash of disappointment he felt at knowing how short the game would be. He loved to play chase, but there was no way the woman could out-run him. He could double her stride, and her muscles could never outpace his, but it would be fun while it lasted. He took two long, bounding steps (during which he couldn't be sure his tongue wasn't hanging out the corner of his mouth in a wolfish grin) and reached for her, his hands closing easily around her shoulders.

Or rather, that's what they would have closed around if her shoulders had still been there. Instead, they grasped thin air as she ducked, twisted, and darted away, flinging herself in one fluid motion out of his reach and up onto one of the long trestle tables that held the exotic plants surrounding them.

As if the fact that she'd eluded him wasn't enough to pique his interest, while he watched, eyes sparking with pleasure at the unexpected extension of playtime, she shifted. In the liquid second between her launch off the slate-flagged floor and her landing on top of the wooden table, she shimmered and stretched and shifted, melting in his sight from lithe, silk-clad woman to slinky, red-furred fox.

His breath hissed in appreciation. Her were form was gorgeous, small and sleek and lushly furred. Her ears and paws were tipped in black, as if she'd been in-vestigating through a tar patch, her tail a thick brush that waved like an invitation before him. With a glad roar he gathered himself, shifted, and leapt after her.

He heard the sharp crack of pottery hitting the stone

floor as he dove into the space she had recently occupied. Being considerably larger than a red fox—in this form he was a timber wolf of rather formidable proportions—his mass required some accommodations hers had not. Since he had no intention of losing her, the large clay pots on the table had to do the accommodating, and they shattered to the ground.

Her claws scrabbled against the wooden table as she fled from him, sending leaves and fronds rustling madly after her. In comparison to her sleek new form, the potted plants could have been a jungle, but it didn't matter. She could have run over hot flowing lava and he would have caught her.

She leaped off the edge of the table in a russet blur. Crouching to absorb the impact, she didn't pause for breath before she turned and darted through a curtain of ornamental grass into the next aisle of the greenhouse. He followed right on her heels, slipping on the slick floor. He barked in irritation and threw on a burst of speed, nearly catching her beside a well-groomed shrub. His jaws snapped on air and her tail waved tauntingly against his nose as she made a hairpin turn to scoot beneath a potting bench.

He hadn't had this much fun since he wrestled a weretiger in India during a diplomatic assignment a few years back. And his quarry at the moment smelled a hell of a lot better than the tiger had. She also had better legs, from what he'd seen in the split second during her change when her dress had fallen away.

He attempted to dive in after her, banged his skull on a table leg, and sat back on his haunches, shaking his head to clear it. Time to regroup.

Pausing, he cocked his head to the side and listened. The frantic clatter of the chase had subsided, leaving the greenhouse eerily still. Somewhere deeper in the forest of plants he heard the splatter of a water fountain and the low hum of the pump that powered it. He heard the rustle of the leaves and, from outside, the sounds of Manhattan droning on as usual. What he didn't hear was the click of neatly trimmed fox nails on the floor. Swishing his tail restlessly, he tilted his head to the other side and listened harder.

There. To the left, at the other end of the potting bench. He heard the distinctive sound of something small, furry, and delectable trying to catch its breath.

His mouth drew wide in a wolfish grin, and he pushed back to his feet. Shoulders rising, he dropped down into a crouch and began to slink slowly toward the sound of the brisk panting. He kept to the shadows, fur standing on end, skin crawling with excitement. Animal instinct warred with human emotion, both pushing him forward in his chase. The man inside him wanted to meet this woman, to get to know her, to find out her favorite color and whether she liked Thai food.

The wolf wanted to flush her from her cover, chase her down, roll her onto her back, and treat her like prey. Whether that meant killing her or fucking her, the beast didn't care. It would be up to the man within to make the right decision.

It helped that she still smelled so damned good.

He found himself licking his chops and forced himself to stop thinking about how she would taste.

Rich and sweet and spicy—

Forced himself to *stop* thinking how she would taste.

Pulling his tongue back into his mouth, Quinn dropped another inch closer to the floor and eased forward on his belly. He got his nose under a fall of creeping vines and inhaled deeply.

God, she smelled like heaven.

Quinn was the fifteenth male of his family line to be called *guth* of his pack. Too restless to stay in one place as Alphas, his ancestors had always been storytellers, negotiators, and ambassadors, literally the voice of the Black Glen pack. They had roamed the earth and raised their voices, but always, they had returned to the pack, mated within the pack, raised cubs within the pack. It was a point of pride in his family, something his father had woven into the story of their history in the Glen, and the implication had been that Quinn would continue that lineage just as he'd continued the lineage of the eldest Quinn male becoming *guth*. But all thought of that went out the window the minute he drank in her scent. He wanted this woman, pack or not, Lupine or not, and he intended to have her.

Now, if the gods looked on him favorably.

Pressing his muzzle as far under the table as he could, Quinn gave in to one last grin, gathered his breath, and howled right into the ear of a wily female fox.

Three

Cassidy crouched beneath the potting bench and trembled. Not with fear, but with the hot rush of adrenaline pumping through her.

She didn't know who the wolf was. She couldn't remember ever seeing him before—in either form—and he wasn't the sort she would have forgotten. She sure as hell couldn't picture forgetting him now. A girl never forgot a werewolf who attacked her in a deserted greenhouse. Or so she assumed.

To be honest, "attacked" was a pretty strong word. While the Lupine *had* reached for her, she hadn't detected any sort of threat from him, and she usually had pretty reliable instincts about those types of things.

She usually had pretty reliable instincts, period.

The plant whose shadow she hid in had some sort of spiky leaves that tickled her nose, and she raised her forepaw to scratch before she could give in to the urge to sneeze instead. Even though she didn't have the impression that the Lupine meant her any harm, she wasn't feeling up to taking the chance that she might be wrong.

Peeking out from among the foliage, Cassidy sniffed

the air and tried to pinpoint the wolf's location. He'd been right on her heels from the moment she shifted, not missing a beat even when she changed from woman to fox right in front of him. Of course, when one attended a party at the oldest and most exclusive private club for Others in Manhattan, one had to expect to see some things beyond the ordinary.

Like this Lupine.

She sensed something extraordinary about him, something beyond the average and not-so-average pack members she had met through the years. Oh, he smelled like wolf, that dark, earthy, evergreen smell they all had in common. And he certainly looked like one. She'd caught a glimpse of him over her shoulder when she took a corner at top speed, so she'd seen the huge white teeth, the rich charcoal-colored fur, and the deep black pigment of his skin. The eyes she'd noticed the moment she'd turned after hearing his growl. You couldn't miss those eyes—a dark, rich color something like ancient gold that seemed to glow in the dim moonlight.

They had fixed on her with an intensity that set her pulse racing. Along with her feet.

She'd read his intent to touch her in those eyes and instinct had kicked in, sending her darting out of the way a split second before skin made contact with skin.

Skin against skin, flesh against flesh, mouth against mouth—

Down, girl.

She shook her head again. Where had that come from? Clearly, the adrenaline was messing with her head. She pricked her ears forward, listening for the sounds of his movement. He was still out there some-where; she just couldn't pinpoint where.

"Arrrooooooooooooooooooo!"

She bolted, sprung like a pheasant by a spaniel, at the sound of the howl so close behind her. He'd man-aged to sneak up on her somehow, but she sure as hell didn't intend to stand around and ask about his tech-nique. She ran as if the hounds of hell were on her heels. Some might argue they were.

She felt her sides heaving as she ran, air billowing in and out of her lungs, her paws searching for purchase on the slick slate tiling the floor. When she hit a corner, her hind legs skittered out from under her, and she lost a valuable nanosecond righting herself. The slip let him get so close she could feel his breath ruffling her fur. Desperately, she poured on another burst of speed and dove frantically for the greenhouse door.

She never made it.

She managed to get herself airborne only to collide mid-flight with a much larger and more vigorously propelled body. He knocked her off course and sent her hurtling back to the floor before she could so much as wriggle away.

Cassidy lay there, dazed, the wind temporarily ham-mered out of her, while he stood above her, tongue hanging out, one massive forepaw planted against her chest, pinning her in place. She had about as much chance to get away as she did to become the next Mr. Universe. Faced with that harsh wall of reality, she gave one disgruntled yip and shifted.

If she had counted on the element of surprise to give her an opportunity to escape, she needed a recount.

She stretched and shivered, fur replaced with smooth skin, newly broadened palms planting themselves on the slate to help her slither away.

They didn't.

She blinked, and he shifted with her. Though she had spent her entire life moving between forms, between worlds, and watching other shifters do it, too, she'd never been this close to anyone during the transformation. She'd never gotten to watch skin expand to envelop fur, bones shifting from animal to human, features shifting from muzzle to nose, jowls to lips. She'd never felt someone shift against her skin, tickling in ways she would have tickled him. It fascinated her, and put her just far enough off balance that her movements slowed to give him an advantage. Before she could scoot away, he dropped, his weight pinning her to the cold slate, legs between hers, hands darting to capture her wrists and pin them to the floor above her head.

He smiled down at her then, and somehow the expression looked as feral on the human face as it had on the wolf. Her eyes widened, and she became acutely conscious of her nakedness as this man pressed intimately against her. She kept her gaze fastened on him as the grin widened and he dipped his head toward her throat. She braced herself for the pain of teeth in her flesh. or the intimate lash of an exploring tongue, but instead he pressed his face to her skin and inhaled deeply.

"God," he growled, in a low, smoke-and-whiskey voice, "you smell so damned good. It's been driving me crazy all night. I have to know if you taste half as delicious."

She felt his mouth open against her skin and parted her lips to scream.

She opened her mouth. She even drew in breath, clenched her diaphragm and began to pass air through her vocal cords. The sound never made it any farther, though. Instead, Cassidy was taught a valuable lesson about the difficulty involved in screaming when a very determined Lupine had his mouth plastered against her own.

His aggressive, warm, persuasive, delicious—
Whoa-hoa-hoa, Nelly!

Screaming seemed to be out of the question, but that didn't mean Cassidy intended to remain quiet. She gave an indignant squeak instead. Right after she un-curled her toes and managed to convince some of her less independent bits that being pinned to the floor and kissed by a strange, naked man wasn't really in her plans for the evening.

Was it?

"Mmfrmrrrf!" she squeaked again.

Said strange, naked man responded with a rough growl and a sort of full-body shimmy that made her eyes roll back in her head. Then her hips arched in sympathy, and suddenly she remembered why she didn't usually strip naked and make out with unfamiliar men on the roofs of Manhattan brownstones. The re-minder currently pressed against her right thigh, mak-ing itself known to her in a rather pointed introduction.

"Mmfrmm-mmkrfm!"

She finally mustered enough common sense to make a play for freedom, shifting her wrists into paws and sliding free of his grasp before his reflexes could catch on and tighten his grip around her instantly smaller limbs. Trading on the element of surprise, she slithered free and scrambled a few feet away before he could do more than growl and curl his lip in a snarl.

"Back off, Benji!" Her voice sounded husky and dense, as if she should maybe consider a new career in the field of adult telecommunications. But talking still beat kissing.

In a responsible, it's-not-nice-to-have-sex-with-total-strangers sort of way.

"Did you just call me *Benji*?"

She almost couldn't understand the question. At first she thought it might be because he'd rumbled it through clenched teeth, but then she realized it had more to do with the fact that he wasn't speaking English. He was speaking Lupine, and being a Foxwoman listening to Lupine was sort of like being an Italian listening to Spanish—you kinda-sorta got the gist of what was being said, but it sounded pretty darned weird all the same. Even when his words did sink in, they didn't do much to calm her panic.

"You're right. Bad analogy." She scooted a few inches farther away and drew her knees up to her chest, crossing her ankles to cover her pinker and not-for-public-consumption parts. "Benji was the mellow, acid-trip Lassie of the seventies. You're more like a modern-day Cujo on meth."

"That's twice. Twice in one bloody day someone has called me Cujo. Are you all Stephen King freaks in this godforsaken city?" He winced and shifted position, probably trying to make more room for his . . .

um . . . point. "Try reading some Poe, by God, if you really want a fright."

Poe? Was that supposed to be a joke?

He had switched to English, but it took a moment for Cassidy to catch on, because even that language sounded unfamiliar on his tongue. Then she figured it out. He had an accent. A shamrock-and-peat-brick accent that seemed to thicken with every growl. Her Lupine was Irish.

Irish and Lupine.

"Oh, shit."

According to her grandmother, the head of the international delegation honored by tonight's party was Irish and Lupine. Damn it, why hadn't she paid attention when Nana had rattled off the names of the delegates? At least then she'd know who she was showing all her beauty marks to.

Cassidy scrabbled to her feet and began to calculate the distances between her, the door, and her downfall. But before she could finish, the Lupine rose, too, in a ripple of mouthwatering muscle.

He raised an eyebrow. "What? You don't like Poe?"

Honestly, what Cassidy didn't like was the glint of determination in his wily predator's eyes.

"He's . . . ah . . . he's tintinnabul-icious," she said, figuring a Poe fan might get the reference. She'd always loved the work of the mad writer whose name she shared. She edged backward, now too focused on escape to worry about clothes. In a battle between modesty and self-preservation, call her an exhibitionist every time.

"Ah."

She watched a slow grin bloom across his face. She wasn't comforted. In fact, she backed up another step.

"Are you worried, then? Afraid I'm neither beast nor human?"

He took a step closer, his body a symphony of coiled power, amber eyes catching the faint echo of lights from outside and seeming to ignite as they watched her.

She shivered and tried to tell herself it came from being naked on a roof in January. Herself snorted. "You seem to have both those bases covered."

"I do," he all but purred. If she hadn't seen him shift with her own eyes, the deep, rough rumble might have made her wonder if he could be Felix instead of Lupine. It was that close to a purr. "But rest assured, I have much more interesting plans than locking myself up in a steeple with naught but a bellpull for company."

He'd taken her Poe reference and run with it, and she tried not to like the fact that he recognized "The Bells," one of her favorite poems. She felt his gaze rake over her and fought against wishing it were his fingers. Her libido, however, started lighting birthday candles and taking deep breaths. Stupid hormones.

"I can see that," she said, trying quite hard *not* to see. Or at least not to stare. "But, uh . . . you might want to put a leash on ol' King there before he slobbers all over someone."

A fang glinted silver in the moonlight. "Oh, but he's ever so friendly. Wouldn't you like to give him a pet, love?"

Cassidy nearly swallowed her tongue. She also nearly hyperventilated at the images that offer sent racing through her mind. "Um, thanks, but my mother always taught me not to pet wild animals."

He stalked forward, eyes intent and amused. "No need to be afraid. I promise not to bite." He paused, grin widening. "Much."

"Right. In that case, I promise not to scream." She paused. "Too loudly."

The Lupine raised an eyebrow and made a point of looking around them with exaggerated thoroughness. "I'm afraid it looks as if the cavalry might have suffered a puncture, love. A flat tire, as you Yanks so elegantly put it. I don't see anyone coming to your rescue."

"What makes you think I need rescuing?" she bluffed, eyeing the short distance between herself and the door in her peripheral vision. "I'm not the one who has to hunt in a pack and let someone else have the first taste of my prey."

Danger, Will Robinson! Danger!

Cassidy ignored the blaring alarms in her head and the narrowing of the Lupine's eyes. Apparently, the warranty on her common sense had just expired. She couldn't think of any other logical explanation to justify the next words that came out of her mouth. Well, aside from suicidal tendencies, which she'd never exhibited before.

"And the last time I looked, of the two people in this greenhouse, I was not the overgrown, oversexed golden retriever who seems to have missed one too many obedience classes."

She was already running before the growl rumbled any farther north than his sternum. Once again, she had to count on surprise to give her an edge as she bolted for the door. She reached it at a dead run and slammed it open. The tinkling clatter of breaking glass didn't slow her down. She didn't even bother to look, just put her head down, said a swift prayer for strength and launched herself into another change as she charged out of the greenhouse and across the moonlit rooftop.

She wished fervently for an eclipse, a storm cloud, a really big shuttle coming into LaGuardia Airport. Anything that would block out the pale glow of the moon and give her a few shadows to hide in. The Lupine wouldn't have had that much trouble seeing through the darkness, but at this point, Cassidy was ready to take any small advantage she could get.

Gulping for air, she flew across the black-tarred concrete, claws clicking in a frantic rhythm. Around her, she heard the sounds of Manhattan drifting up toward them and the rasping, growling breath of the animal chasing her. She'd seen too many movies to bother looking back. She kept her eyes straight ahead and prayed some more.

She was just beginning to wonder if she should consider converting to another faith—one where the chief deity actually *listened* in an emergency—when she saw the gates of salvation opening before her.

Well, actually, she saw a skylight on the far side of the roof that was propped open just far enough for a very small, very determined, and very willing-to-suck-it-in fox to fit through. Just then, it might as well have been pearly white and guarded by Saint Peter, it looked so good.

Giving a sharp yip, she dove, eyes squeezing shut as she felt and heard the snap of powerful jaws just inches from her hind leg. If she had needed her coat trimmed, he'd have had her. But she made it, by the skin of her everything, flinging herself headfirst through the narrow opening of the skylight and wriggling the rest of the way faster than a chipmunk in a nut-eating contest.

She landed on all fours with a thud, breathless and dizzy with exertion. She'd been braced for impact, but her messages must have finally gotten through to the powers that be, because she landed and bounced on a superfirm mattress in one of the private rooms somewhere on the upper floors of the Vircolac Club. The bed didn't even squeak when she shifted back to human, just dipped and recovered, leaving her crouched in a puddle of down-filled duvet, while above her a howl of pure frustration rose over the city and echoed in the crisp winter air.

Four

"Um, hello?"

Grabbing a corner of the duvet, Cassidy twitched it over her to cover the most vital spots and looked toward the sound of the greeting. A woman stood in the doorway of the bedroom, one hand on the doorframe while the other adjusted the chic wire-rimmed glasses that perched on the end of her nose.

Cassidy tried to pretend her cheeks weren't the color of ripe pomegranates and forced a smile. "Hi."

"Hi." The brunette gave a casual smile, as if she walked into rooms occupied by unknown naked women every day.

"I, ah—I guess you must be wondering what I'm doing here . . ." Cassidy struggled to think of a plausible explanation and turned up a big, fat nada.

"Not really." The brunette smiled and closed the door behind her, not sparing Cassidy another glance as she crossed to the small dresser placed against the bedroom wall. "If I were here with your grandmother, I'd need a few minutes of peace and quiet myself." The woman gave a short chuckle. "No offense."

"None taken." Cassidy shrugged deeper into the

duvet and resigned herself to an unusual evening. As if she often had any other kind. "Um, do you know my grandmother? Or, um, me?"

"Dame Berry? Only by reputation. I've met her a time or two, when the pack and the Council have had reason to meet up, but I doubt she'd remember me. Same with you, which I think proves my point."

Cassidy took a discreet breath and smelled the Lupine on the other woman. Good thing the stranger didn't have an accent, or she might really have freaked.

"Silverback?" she guessed.

The brunette nodded, took a small book from the dresser drawer, then turned back to Cassidy and smiled.

"Yes. I'm sorry. I should have introduced myself. Just because I know you, that doesn't mean you know me." She held out her hand. "Annie Cryer. And there's no reason you should know me. My wandering around the place has more to do with the fact that I'm friends with the Alpha's wife than that I'm someone important. I'm just pack rank-and-file. Your average growl next door."

Cassidy pinned the duvet to her chest with her left arm and shook Annie's hand with the right, smiling at the Lupine's sense of humor. Especially given the circumstances. "Cassidy Poe."

"Oh, I know. In these parts your family is a little like the Kennedys are to humans."

"Don't say that where my grandmother can hear you. She doesn't need the encouragement."

Annie laughed. "She doesn't seem to, does she?" She watched Cassidy adjust the duvet yet again. "You look like you've had an interesting evening. Did you leave your clothes in the bathroom? I could leave you to get changed. Or run in and get them for you, if you want."

"Ah . . . no. They're not in the bathroom." Cassidy grimaced. "It's a long story, but I'm afraid I lost them."

"You lost your clothes."

"Yeah. There was a . . . an . . . incident. I have an emergency change of clothes in my car, but I'm going to have to figure out how to get to it without, you know, getting arrested."

Or being seen by Nana.

"You have a car in Manhattan?"

The question about the car sounded more incredulous than the one about the clothes had. Only in New York.

"Yeah. I like to get away from the city on weekends. Stretch my legs. And my tail."

"I know the feeling. Sometimes Central Park just doesn't cut it, does it?"

"Not so much."

Annie shared a commiserating smile and gestured toward the door. "If you tell me where you're parked—and what patron saint you use to get a parking space in this neighborhood—I'd be happy to run down and get them for you. Or if you don't want to give me your keys, I'm sure I can scrounge up something for you to wear so you can get them yourself."

Cassidy groaned. "Shit. Keys."

"Oops. Are they with your clothes?"

Cassidy shook her head and slumped back onto the bed. "They're on the roof."

"On the roof? Your keys or your clothes?"

"Um, both, I assume. In the greenhouse. Fat lot of

good the clothes will do me now, though. They're probably shredded."

Annie's eyes widened and her voice took on mingled notes of shock and admiration. "Okay. You *have* had an interesting night."

"In the Chinese sense of the word. Yeah."

The other woman paused. "Do you want to talk about it?"

The laugh came out before Cassidy could stop it, even though she wasn't quite sure what she found funny. "Thanks, but honestly, I'm trying not to think about it."

She swung her legs over the side of the bed, tugging the duvet with her. "I think I'm going to have to go back up on the roof and get my keys, if I ever want to get home. Did you mean it when you said you might have some clothes I could borrow? I don't think we're the same size, but I'm not going to look a gift sweatshirt in the mouth."

Annie smiled and headed back to the dresser. "Sure. They're not mine, though. They're emergency stock the Luna of our pack keeps here in the guest room. When she first met our Alpha, she found herself needing to borrow clothes a few times, so she always makes sure to keep a few things available in case someone else ends up in a similar situation. When you lead a pack, someone is always turning up on the doorstep looking the worse for wear."

Cassidy just nodded, absorbing the chatter and gratefully accepting the mismatched garments Annie handed to her.

"I appreciate it."

"No problem. You look like you're about a ten, so I hope those aren't too big."

"Twelve. But I'm sure they'll be fine."

"Good. I'll leave you to it, then." Annie grinned. "You know where the stairs to the roof are, right? Of course you do. How else would you have gotten down here?"

Cassidy paused on her way to the bathroom door Annie had indicated.

"Um . . . actually . . . I've got a pretty lousy sense of direction." She forced a smile and tried to sound sheepish. Which wasn't too difficult, come to think of it. "Could you just refresh my memory before you go?"

"Don't worry. I'll do better than that. I'll show you. This place is riddled with hallways and weird hidden doors." The brunette made shooing motions toward the bathroom. "Go ahead and get dressed. I'll wait here."

It only took Cassidy a minute to tug on the soft navy sweatpants and the lighter blue sweatshirt. She avoided looking in the mirror, sure her hair had to be a rat's nest, and instead glanced down at her bare feet. Rose-polished toes shone up at her, and she gave a rueful smile.

Told you so, Nana.

Rubbing her hands over her face—damn . . . there goes the mascara—she took one deep breath and headed back into the bedroom. Time to get her keys, change into the emergency clothes she kept in her trunk, and get the hell out of Dodge before anything else could go wrong tonight.

She stepped from cool tile onto padded carpet, and Annie looked up at the sound.

"Hey, not bad," she said, closing her book and rising

from where she'd been perched on the edge of the bed. "I was afraid they'd be falling off you. Oh, do you need me to find you a pair of socks or slippers or something?"

Cassidy smiled. "No, thanks. I'm fine. But I think I've officially reached my adventure quotient for the evening. I'd better get my keys and get changed so I can go home. The city will be a safer place for it."

"Don't worry about getting changed. You've just put all that on, so it seems silly to take it off again. Keep it. That's what Missy has it here for. Or if you're determined to give it back, go ahead and stick it in the mail. Or drop it off at the club anytime. No worries."

The chatty brunette led the way out of the room Cassidy had landed in and down a darkly wainscoted residential hall. More residential than any Cassidy had seen at Vircolac before. She frowned.

"You know, I thought that with Nana dragging me around here for so many years, I'd seen all there was to see of the club. But I have to confess, I don't remember this."

"We're not in the club. We're in Graham and Missy's house next door," Annie said and glanced back over her shoulder. "I assumed you knew that. I guess it's a good thing I'm taking you back to the roof then. You really are lost."

She had landed in the private residence of the Alpha werewolf of the Silverback Clan?

"I guess I am," she said, trying to laugh it off. "That will teach me to give Nana the slip, won't it?"

Annie stopped in front of a paneled door and reached for the handle, holding it open so Cassidy could step through. At least she was grinning, though, and not filing a police report for trespassing. "Don't worry about it. If there's anything the Alpha and his mate understand, it's the desire to get away from friends and relatives. Especially the well-meaning ones."

Cassidy laughed and stepped through the door onto the cool tar of the rooftop. "Thanks for the guidance," she said. "I'm just going to run and get my keys and get out of here. The stairs back down into the club, I think I remember."

"Sure thing." Annie smiled, stepping back inside with a little wave. "Have a good night, Ms. Poe. It was nice to meet you."

"Cassidy, please."

"Cassidy. Just give a yell if you need anything else. Anyone you ask will know how to find me."

"Thanks."

Annie waved again and disappeared inside. The door clicked shut behind her, leaving Cassidy alone on the roof.

Which was what had gotten her into trouble in the first place.

After a cautious look around, she moved with quiet steps toward the greenhouse, eyes, ears, and nose open for any sign of her Lupine attacker from earlier. A slight breeze stirred the crisp air and carried the scent of the winter city to her, but no trace of wolf. She blew out a relieved breath, still moving quickly and quietly toward where she'd last had her keys. It didn't pay to let down her guard.

The warm air of the greenhouse felt strange after the chilly night outside and raised goose bumps on her skin. She shivered and glanced around the plant-filled area, her keen night vision scanning the slate for the glint of metal.

Over by the dahlias.

She hurried to the spilled ring and found her small clutch under the table to the left. She took one look at her dress, which was covered in dust and rust-colored fur, and was torn in at least two places by sharp black claws, and abandoned it as hopeless. A quick glance revealed no men's clothing, so maybe the werewolf had gotten dressed and left. Still, she wasn't taking chances.

Grabbing her keys and her purse, she took another wary look around and beat a path to the stairway door. Time to get the hell home and forget this night had ever happened.

She wrenched open the door, took a step forward, and felt her stomach sink into her ankles.

"Good Lord! Cassidy Emilia! What on earth happened to you?"

Five

If luck had been on her side—the good kind rather than the kind she could usually count on having—she would have been on her way to a quiet apartment, a steaming hot bath, and a very, very large glass of white burgundy. But instead, she was frozen solid on the threshold of the rooftop door and trying to muster a calm smile for her outraged grandmother.

"Nana. Are you having a good evening?"

"What in the world is going on here, young lady? I demand an explanation."

Not surprising, considering how good Adele was at making demands. Cassidy scrambled for a plausible cover story. One that didn't involve a naked game of chase with the Lupine leader of the European delegation whose name she still didn't know.

"I'm sorry, Nana," she said, trying to sound repentant. She'd had years of practice. "I developed a searing headache earlier and I just came up here to try and clear the fog. I thought the quiet and fresh air might help."

Adele folded both hands over the top of the cane she didn't quite need and raised one dark, arching eyebrow. "And how do you explain your attire?"

Cassidy looked down at herself and blinked. She'd forgotten about the sweat suit. "My attire. Right. Well . . . you see . . ."

"Cassidy."

Her grandmother spoke her name and Cassidy looked up, feeling like a four-year-old caught with her fingers in the cookie jar. It amazed her that even at the age of twenty-nine, it only took one look from Adele to send her right back to that place.

She shifted uncomfortably in the silence. Even though she recognized the tactic as one of her grandmother's favorites, she was helpless against it. Which explained the whole "favorite" thing.

"Cassidy," Adele finally repeated, using that weary voice that brought guilt slamming down on her granddaughter's head like divine retribution. "I don't know what to say to you. I'm so very disappointed. I thought you knew how important this evening is. I hoped you would realize when I requested your company that it would be critical for you to set aside your rebelliousness for one evening and act as the lady I raised you to be."

Cassidy fought the animal urge to drop her head, curl her body, and show her belly to Adele. She would deal with this in human terms just as Nana was doing. She took a deep breath and squared her shoulders.

"I wasn't rebelling, Nana." She kept her voice low and even, and spoke clearly. "I told you I wasn't feeling well. I decided to come up here to clear my head and I . . . I spilled champagne on my dress." Okay, so that wasn't quite the truth. In this case, it was better. "A friend lent me something to wear so I could run down to my car to get a change of clothes. I was on my way there when you found me."

She felt a little better as she eased back toward almost not lying. It allowed her to muster something akin to a smile.

Adele looked as if she almost believed it. "You spilled champagne on your shoes, as well?"

"You know me. Klutz and a half."

"Mmm."

The sound was low and noncommittal. Adele tilted her head to the side and sniffed the air delicately. Her brow furrowed—something she spent a fortune on face creams trying to prevent—and she sniffed again.

"Why do I smell something odd?"

Oh, shit. Cassidy braced herself, her mind furiously grasping for plausible answers even as she saw her grandmother's lip curl into a snarl. There was no way Dame Berry would react well to the news that her granddaughter had been rolling around on the rooftop with a "common" Lupine. Adele viewed all Lupines as commoners, and she and her kind as aristocracy.

"You smell of wolf!" Adele spat the words and lifted her cane in a white-knuckled grip. "Explain yourself!"

"Nana, it's not a big deal. Honestly." She held up her hands and tried to smile. "The girl who loaned me the clothes is a Silverback. But since I didn't think it would be appropriate to scurry among the guests downstairs in my unmentionables, I could hardly turn down her offer of something to wear, could I?"

Lips pursed and eyes narrowed, Adele remained silent.

"Honestly, Nana, what would have been worse? Having me seen downstairs in a Lupine's borrowed jogging suit, or having me seen downstairs naked and dripping with Cristal?"

Silence.

"Do you need another minute to think about it?"

"Cassidy—"

"Nana, honestly. Let's be sensible here. It's not like I eloped with a werewolf." *Or rolled around on the floor with one. Or kissed one. Or wanted to strip one naked and—* "It's a borrowed sweat suit. If you're so bothered by it, give me fifteen minutes to run down to my car, and I'll change out of it. Will that make you feel better?"

The amused exasperation in her voice was real, and the familiar argument eased enough of her tension that the vaguely nauseated feeling generated by her frayed nerves was starting to fade. She considered that a good thing.

Adele held some old-school attitudes about more than cocktail dresses and Emily Post manners. She also believed that Lupines, and all werefolk who followed the moon cycles in their changes, were somehow inferior to herself and her kind. Because Foxwomen were not technically werefolk—they appeared along an entirely different ramp on the evolutionary highway—some of them believed their magic was stronger than that of the Lupines and the other werekin.

Cassidy had never gotten that. As far as she was concerned, a change was a change, and humans would shoot her with a silver bullet just as fast as someone like Annie. They all experienced pain; they all bled the same color; and they all sprouted fur. Sometimes.

"I would appreciate it if you would refrain from twisting this conversation into that old argument, Cassidy." If Adele pinched her lips together any tighter, Cassidy thought they might go permanently numb. "That is not the point of this discussion."

Cassidy sighed. "Then what was the point, Nana? That I managed to disappoint you again? Unfortunate, but hardly unexpected, is it?"

"Please do not use that tone with me, young lady. I might be an old woman, but I am still your elder and you were raised in my den. I expect better of you."

"Yes, ma'am." Cassidy gritted her teeth.

"Now, come inside." Adele punctuated the order with a thump of her cane and held the door open for Cassidy to follow. "There are still people here I want you to meet, and you need to be wearing something more presentable than that before I admit you're my granddaughter."

Cassidy bit back a groan. How she wished that Nana really would pretend not to know her. But nothing was ever that easy with Adele Billinghurst Spencer Berry. If Nana wanted her to meet the queen, she'd better learn how to curtsy, and if Nana wanted to introduce her to some friends, she'd better get a move on to her car and find that emergency outfit.

Drawing on years of practice, Cassidy morphed her groan into a barely audible sigh of resignation and followed her grandmother into the stairwell. "Who is it I have to meet?"

"Several important people with whom I'd like you to become acquainted." Adele's voice rose clear and crisp over the click of her heels on the stairs. "I've been far too indulgent in allowing you to avoid the social responsibilities that come with being a member of this family. Most of my circle barely knows you, and I'm certain the majority wouldn't recognize you if they passed you in the street. It's high time you started to shoulder some of the duties that your parents and my parents and *their* parents did."

Oh, God, not again. They'd had this argument too many times to count. Cassidy had thought she'd finally won it after the incident last summer, when she had broken the toe of the visiting prince of a very influential family of djinn. She'd warned him she didn't know how to samba, but djinn always thought they could charm anyone into anything.

"Nana," she began cautiously, "maybe it would be better if we wrote off tonight. I mean, even if I change, I'm sure I look a mess. My hair must be—"

"Out of the question," Adele snapped. "I have already let everyone know that the granddaughter I have told them all about is here tonight, and I refuse to make still more excuses to the Council as to why you can't be bothered—"

Cassidy froze just as the door clicked shut behind them, her hand still curled around the knob. She blinked in the dim light of the stairwell. "The Council? You want to introduce me to the members of the Council?"

"Yes. And an exercise suit is hardly suitable apparel for the situation."

"Why in the world would you want to introduce me to the Council?"

Okay, so maybe a note of panic had crept into her voice, but the extent to which this was not a good idea could make anyone panic. Cassidy became tongue-tied in front of authority figures. She'd barely made it out of her dissertation defense alive, and she was supposed to not make an idiot of herself in front of the most powerful Others in the city?

Adele swept her way down the stairs, her spine perfectly straight and unbowed with age.

A tornado couldn't bow Adele Berry's spine.

Cassidy hurried after her. "Nana, you never said I'd have to meet anyone from the Council. That was not part of our deal when I agreed to show up tonight."

"Cassidy, darling, you are a well-educated woman with a normally sensible head. You hold a doctoral degree in anthropology, and you lecture regularly before classes of five hundred students at Columbia University. Do you honestly have stage fright about making the acquaintance of fourteen crusty old buggers like me?"

"Some of those crusty old buggers could tear my throat out with their teeth. And would enjoy it."

"Darling, any and every one of them could do that."

"Wow. Your compassionate response has so comforted me."

"Sarcasm is the wit of a small-minded thinker, Cassidy."

Shaking her head, Cassidy stepped off the last rooftop stair and followed her grandmother down the hall. "Nana, seriously. I'm not trying to be funny. This is ridiculous. There's no reason for me to meet anyone on the Council. I'm never going to take a seat on it. We agreed on that."

"You agreed, dear. I refuse to believe that the Council will be forced to operate for an entire generation without the benefit of a member of this family in its ranks." Adele began to swan her way down another staircase with Cassidy scurrying behind. "Rafael De Santos agrees that the very idea would be tragic."

Cassidy walked straight into the banister. "Who agrees about what?"

"Dear, do watch where you're going." Adele took her granddaughter by the elbow and guided her down the rest of the stairs. "The last thing we need is for you to knock yourself silly and bleed all over your change of clothes, as well."

"Nana!" Cassidy dug her heels into the parquet flooring of the club's entry hall and refused to take another step. "You've gone round the bend. There is no earthly reason for Rafael De Santos, the head of a Council I've never met, to have any idea who I am. I'm a nobody! I'm an anthropologist! An academic! A nerd! And . . . and . . . and . . . and stuff!"

"Very eloquent, dear. It's no wonder you command such respect in your field."

"The slow-minded, Nana. Remember?"

Adele placed her hand between Cassidy's shoulder blades and nudged her toward the front door. "Go run and get changed. I've already wasted enough time looking for you."

"Nana!"

"Cassidy! Go."

Rolling her eyes and repressing the urge to stomp her feet, Cassidy turned to the front door, jingling her keys angrily. "Fine. But I still want an answer when I get back."

"When you get back, we can discuss it."

Cassidy ignored that answer—the one she'd hated since she was a toddler—and headed for her car. She'd taken about five steps toward the exit when a tall, intimidating figure stepped in front of her and blocked her path.

"I'm sorry, miss, but I can't let you leave."

"Okay, where the hell is the camera? Because this has got to be some twisted kind of reality show."

"Young man, what seems to be the trouble?" Adele stepped forward with an imperious scowl, her cane tapping impatiently. "I am afraid I have not the pleasure of understanding why you refuse to allow my granddaughter to fetch a change of clothes."

"I'm sorry, ma'am," the bouncer said, standing firm, his arms crossed over his broad chest. "I have orders that you and your granddaughter are to stay. There's been an emergency meeting of the Council called, and you're both wanted downstairs."

That managed to accomplish something Cassidy had never seen—it left Adele speechless for nearly a full minute.

"An emergency meeting?" the older woman finally parroted when she had drawn herself together. "But tonight was to be only the reception. The meeting is scheduled for tomorrow night. What has happened?"

The man's expression and stance did not change. "I'm not privy to that information, ma'am. It's a closed-door meeting."

Cassidy was more concerned over the previous part of his statement. "Both of us? You mean, I'm supposed to go to the Council meeting? That's impossible. I'm not a member of the Council at large, let alone of the Inner Circle."

The bouncer stared above her head. "I was instructed to be sure you accompanied your grandmother. I wasn't given an explanation."

She decided to try reason, even if it was a long shot. "There must be some sort of mistake. Maybe they just meant I was supposed to stay downstairs, meaning here, and not upstairs, where I was before and shouldn't have been. I think that makes a lot more sense than—"

"Cassidy!" Adele's voice sounded even snappier than it had on the roof, and Cassidy turned to her in surprise.

"This is not an appropriate moment to argue. If the Council wishes to see you, then of course you will be present. And you'll just have to go as you are. There's no time to change clothes now. We'll have to hope the Council will not take offense at your appearance."

This was quite an about-face for the woman who, ten minutes earlier, had made it sound as if the civilized world as she knew it would come to an ignoble end if any of her peers saw her granddaughter in casual clothing. Not to mention that the old woman actually sounded agitated. Adele *never* sounded agitated. It would have implied the entire universe was not firmly under her control.

"Nana, it won't take me more than a minute to grab my things and follow you."

"No. We will not keep the Council waiting. Come along."

Adele didn't wait for another argument. She turned abruptly, rapped her cane once on the floor, and set off down the hall with a gracefully intimidating stride.

Cassidy watched her go, brow wrinkled in a frown. "I wonder if the world is coming to an end."

"I don't know," the man behind her rumbled, his granite mask cracking just enough for Cassidy to catch a glimpse of the curiosity beneath. "But if it's not, it must be nearing intermission, because I've never seen that group of people look so worried in my life. And I'm two hundred and forty-seven next month."

Cassidy caught a glimpse of fang as he spoke and took note of the worried crease in his forehead. Whatever had the Council in an uproar was enough to worry a two-hundred-and-forty-seven-year-old-vampire. Oh, right. Now the evening was looking up.

Six

It might lack the cliché-worthiness of a cold shower, but the news Quinn received the moment he returned to the party downstairs managed to calm his libido just as effectively.

"What did you say?"

He'd heard the report perfectly clearly, but shock made his lips move before he could stop them.

"Ysabel Mirenow is missing," Richard Maccus repeated, his voice offering almost as creditable a growl as any Irish Lupine could have managed. That was saying something, considering the British representative to this summit was a Scot and a Selkie, one of the shapeshifting seafolk who populated the rugged coasts of the British Isles. It must come from having been Quinn's close friend for at least a decade. "We just got word from Moscow. She disappeared sometime last night. Yesterday afternoon in this time zone. While she was out shopping. No one saw the actual incident, but Gregor became suspicious when she didn't return in time to accompany him to the opera."

Quinn swore under his breath. Gregor Kasminikov was probably the most powerful vampire in Eastern

Europe. Rich as Croesus before the fall of the Soviet Union, he'd since become even richer, thanks to his involvement in the black market. He had also amassed greater power in the region than most governments, but then, he'd had almost five centuries in which to do it. He'd only had his human companion, Ysabel, for about sixty years, but that was still long enough for a woman who didn't appear to age to acquire a great deal of information about the Other world. Information some human groups would go to great lengths to have for themselves.

"There's no chance she's just run off?" Quinn asked. "Maybe they had a fight. After all, Gregor is not known for his skill with fidelity."

"No. The shocking part is that he swears he hasn't strayed. It's the longest the man has gone since his change without getting bored with a mistress."

Gregor was not the sort to imagine things, either, which only made Quinn swear again, even more colorfully. Still, he clung to his last shreds of hope.

"He can swear all he likes; that doesn't make it true. Why don't we think she'll call from a friend's house in a day or two?"

Richard shook his head. "Gregor sent his best men out searching for her. He was truly worried. They returned after nearly eight hours, reporting that a shopkeeper in one of the high-rent districts saw her speaking with a priest less than half an hour before she was last seen."

The bottom of Quinn's stomach took a quick dive south. "A priest?"

"So he assumed," Richard said, mouth set in severe lines. "He called the man a priest, but when pressed, he admitted all he could swear to was that the man wore black and had an ornate, silver rosary around his neck."

Well, shite.

"I don't suppose there has been any demand for a ransom?"

"Not a word. Whoever took her seems inclined to keep her. At least for a while."

Quinn clenched his teeth. "You mean until they get the information they want from her."

Gregor had been right to worry. Ysabel had been a human servant for several decades, her aging suspended indefinitely by the occasional ingestion of the blood of her immortal lover. The blood exchange also gave a human servant limited increases in strength and sensory perception, but nothing too far out of the range of ordinary. As a human, she remained vulnerable to attack in a way no Other could be, and she'd been immersed in their world long enough to know almost as much about them as a native. Quinn should have known Gregor wasn't the type to overreact. You didn't live that long as a Russian vampire without the ability to distinguish between an inconvenience and a crisis.

Hell, Quinn hadn't lived thirty-five years as an Irish Lupine without developing that skill. He added up the puzzle pieces in his head: the human mistress of one of Russia's most powerful vampires had gone missing, she had last been seen with a man who looked like a priest and wore an eye-catching rosary, and there had been no demand for ransom, despite the fact that Gregor was one of the richest men in Eastern Europe. That could only mean one thing. The kidnappers didn't want money; they wanted information.

"What are the chances that she's still alive?"

Richard shook his head. He looked about as bleak as Quinn felt. Like the rest of his seal-shifter brethren, he was more prone to isolation than to violence. But in this situation, a saint could feel driven to the edge.

"At the moment, there's a chance," he said, "but no one has much confidence that will last. If it is the Light of Truth who've taken her, she'll be dead before much longer. They'll use whatever means necessary to get the information they want, and then they'll kill her. And probably congratulate themselves on saving her soul."

Quinn knew his friend was right about what would happen to Ysabel and about who had taken her. The fanatic religious sect that called themselves the Light of Truth had been around in one form or another for many years now, but few Others had believed they would ever come this close to achieving their goal: gathering enough proof of the existence of vampires, werewolves, and all nonhumans to inspire a crusade that would wipe those "monsters" from the face of the earth.

It had taken Others like Quinn and Richard and the rest of their delegation the better part of the last two years to convince the European Council to take groups like this seriously. Now, at least they understood that the best way to counter the ever-increasing wave of threats from people like the Light of Truth was to take away their ammunition. By revealing themselves to the human world before the choice was taken entirely out of their hands, they could destroy their enemies' most powerful weapon. The delegation had come to explain that to the Americans, just in time for fate to hand them a big piece of ammunition of its own.

"I'm sure Gregor has someone out looking for her," he said with a touch of desperation.

"Of course. He's still holding out hope. And even if he isn't, he knows he can't allow the Lightheads to go unchecked." Richard sneered when he mentioned the cultists, as if the derogatory nickname hadn't offered a clue to his feelings about them. "But that's not the worst part."

Quinn blanched. "There's a worse part?"

Richard nodded. "Gregor also said that one of the initial trails they followed in trying to find Ysabel didn't lead to her, but it did lead to some other interesting information."

"Like what?"

"Like the original orders for the kidnapping might not have come from the Light of Truth cell in Moscow. It might have come from outside the country."

"How far outside?" Quinn tensed.

"From America."

"ShitepissfuckbollocksChristJesusandHolyMary." The string of curses stopped when Quinn ran out of breath but continued to rain down in his head. "You're telling me they might have already established working cells in the United States?"

The Lightheads had operated in Europe for decades— centuries if one cared to count their antecedents, such as the perpetrators of the Inquisition and the crusades against heresy that had run rampant during the Middle Ages. But until now, the Others had at least known small comfort of believing them confined to that continent. Sure, America had its small groups of troublemaking humans with penchants for conspiracy theory, but they had neither the long history nor the fanatic dedication that made the Light of Truth so dangerous. Knowing the group had spread might add urgency to the European delegation's appeal to the Americans, but Quinn couldn't be happy about it. It meant things were getting worse a lot quicker than anyone had anticipated.

"We came on this trip to tell the Americans we feared we'd be forced to Unveil sooner than any of us had planned, but if we don't do something about the Lightheads now, they could rip away the Veil any second, whether we're ready or not." Richard's voice was as grim as his face.

"Brilliant," Quinn growled. "I'm sure the Americans will be thrilled to hear this."

"I'm sure. So who's going to tell them?"

Quinn reached into his pocket and drew out a one-euro coin. "Heads or tails?"

If Quinn hadn't flipped the damned coin himself, he would have sworn it was weighted. No way could Richard have won best three out of five any other way.

Unless, of course, God simply hated him. Which he'd long since established was a strong possibility.

He knew for certain that the member of the Council whom he'd cornered a few minutes ago hadn't liked him much when he'd insisted that the meeting scheduled for tomorrow night couldn't even wait another hour. The changeling whose name Quinn couldn't remember had argued for a good three minutes before Quinn had threatened to pull his intestines out of where his wings should have been. Changelings, the descendants of humans and Fae left after the Fae had fled the human world a few millennia ago, almost never actually had wings, but this one understood the imagery well enough. It had convinced him that Quinn's message for the head of the Council was urgent, and

Rafael De Santos had agreed. As soon as he finished hearing the changeling out, he'd moved the start time of tomorrow night's Council meeting to tonight. To right now, if you wanted to be technical about it. Quinn didn't; he just wanted it done.

But he'd have been happier not to be the one to do it. So much for that famed Irish luck.

He hadn't felt this much tension in a room since he'd negotiated a peace between his pack back home and the prince of the local Deerskin Clan. That mess had started when the prince's lover had been eaten after she wandered too close to Quinn's clan's hunting grounds in her doe form on a full-moon night. The gentle, distant relatives of an extinct race, the Deerskin used the preserved hides of their magical deer ancestors to shift shapes, but they weren't the brightest stars in the sky.

If Quinn had thought that was a messy situation, he now figured it had only been a warm-up for tonight. He needed to concentrate on the business at hand, not on playing show and tell with the locals or drooling over luscious young foxes with honeysuckle fur—

Well, hell. That's what he got for trying to think of something more pleasant than the missing mistress of a vampire who was likely being tortured to death even as he spoke. Taking a deep breath, he pushed the remembered scent of sweet, female flowers out of his mind and looked around the room instead.

When the club staff had led them down into Vircolac's basement and through a warren of stone tunnels with vaulted ceilings and torchlight, he'd almost thought it was an elaborate practical joke being played on the new wolf in town. Did the Manhattan Council actually meet in this Gothic nightmare, or were they going to have someone dressed like Bela Lugosi jump out at him from a suitably dark corner as a hazing prank?

No, they had been perfectly serious. They'd led him through the bad movie set and into the underground stone chamber filled with firelight, dark old mahogany, and rich Corinthian leather. As he settled into his massive, creaking chair, he heard the voice of Ricardo Montalban in his head and rolled his eyes.

"I almost wish someone would crack a smile. This place is too close to a tomb for my liking." On Quinn's right, Richard leaned in and grumbled through a scowl. "And I doubt we'll find much amusement in the rest of the night's proceedings."

"I'm trying not to think about that."

"Mark my words. These American Others are nearly as narrow-minded as their human countrymen. They wouldn't have liked the news we came here with, let alone tonight's twist in the plot."

Quinn couldn't disagree with his friend, especially since he disliked said twist so much himself, but he had rowed too far up Denial to come right out and agree with him. "Everything I've heard about their Council leader points to his level head and sound judgment. Let's not give up hope too soon."

"Oh, I've no quarrel with Rafael De Santos. He's a fine chap. It's his constituents who scare me down to my soles."

Quinn snorted and shifted in his seat, his attention caught by the new group of delegates entering the room. Rafael De Santos stepped into the melodramatic torchlight accompanied by two other men and two women Quinn hadn't met. They exchanged quiet greetings with those already in the room.

Tall and lean, with an innate and fluid grace to his movements, the Felix werejaguar—a loose equivalent to an Alpha pack leader in the less structured world of the feline shifters—was hard to miss. He entered the room as if he owned it, which some might argue he nearly did, looking dangerous and elegant in a well-tailored suit the color of slate.

The dark-haired, bronze-skinned shifter had taken over the leadership of the Manhattan Council when the former head had stepped down. His greatest coup so far had been the treaty brokered between the Council of Others and the American Witches, with whom they'd been feuding for the better part of four centuries. Quinn had even heard De Santos had sealed the deal by taking a witch as his mate. That made quite a statement of professional dedication. Witches weren't known for being all that easy to live with, but the sharp and watchful glint in the man's eye made Quinn think if anyone could handle a witchy wife, it would be Rafael De Santos.

He tried to place the other newcomers based on the descriptions he'd received while researching the Council before his trip. The two women were easy. One had the delicate, exotic looks of a geisha and the aura of a displeased cobra. That made her Chikako Izumi and an *oni,* one of the Japanese race who had been spawned by the demons before their banishment from the human world. The *oni* delighted in meddling with humans just for fun. Quinn would remember to stay out of her way. The other woman was short, a little solid, and the most remarkable shades of brown he had ever seen. From the top of her short, potting-soil brown hair, to her cocoa skin and the chocolaty brown of her clothing, she lacked any other color but that of the earth. Clearly, he was looking at Emma Higgenbottham, a brownie, to overstate the obvious.

The two men weren't quite so easy. Both were tall, lean, and of indeterminate age. The major difference between them seemed to be the air of arrogance one wore like a bad Dracula cape and the intense blankness of the other. If he had to hazard a guess, Quinn would say the clean slate was most likely Jeffrey Saxon, one of Manhattan's most prominent doppelgängers—those who could assume the shape and face of any human-like individual. The other he couldn't be sure about, but he was leaning toward guessing the man was one of the Council's several vampire members. The arrogance always gave that kind away.

Quinn watched as the group began to take their seats around the massive council tables. De Santos settled into the thronelike chair at the center of the head table, flanked on one side by a short, stocky fellow with a close-cropped goatee and on the other by an elegantly pale and befanged type. An assortment of vampires, werefolk, changelings, and Others occupied the remaining seats, most of whom Quinn had been introduced to at the party earlier. The Americans outnumbered the European delegation fourteen to five, but he supposed that was natural. This was their sandbox, after all. He just gave thanks they were only facing the Inner Circle of the Council, not the full company of them, which was nearly one hundred strong.

Quinn saw De Santos glance down at an elegant gold wristwatch and frown. He barely had time to raise an eyebrow before a soft but deliberate thump drew everyone's attention to the chamber entrance.

Adele Berry stood in the dimly lit archway, draped in burgundy silk and expensive perfume, leaning on her silver-handled cane. "Forgive me, gentlemen," she said in a voice that sounded far feebler than the one she'd used on Quinn a couple of hours earlier. "I don't get around quite as quickly as I did once. I hope I haven't kept everyone waiting."

De Santos shook his head, his mouth betraying a hint of amusement, and waved for an attendant to pull out a chair. "We are honored as always to have you join us, Mrs. Berry. Please take a seat and we can begin."

"Thank you, Rafael, but first allow me to present my granddaughter to the Council." Adele stepped aside to reveal the petite form concealed in the shadows behind her. "Ladies and gentlemen, may I present Cassidy Emilia Berry Poe? Forgive her appearance. She had a mishap upstairs with her cocktail, and I'm afraid we weren't prepared for a Council meeting this evening. I had understood we were to meet tomorrow."

Quinn watched, curious to see what sort of woman could have been born with the grande dame's genes and not ended up in a convent in the mountains of Switzerland out of self-defense. The blushing figure who stepped forward did so with a reluctance with which he could sympathize. Life in Dame Berry's household couldn't be a bowl of pudding. His eyes widened when the girl shifted and the torchlight glinted off her fiery russet hair.

His honeysuckle flower. Dropped right into his lap like a Christmas cracker. His mouth curved into a grin, and he sat forward in his chair. Maybe God didn't hate him after all.

Seven

Cassidy silently cursed her grandmother's flair for the dramatic and edged into the Council chamber. Despite Adele's best efforts to interest her in politics, this was the first time she had gone below Vircolac's inviting main floor or done any mingling with anyone on the Council. So much for her decade-long lucky streak in avoiding it by having "a class to go to/teach that night." It looked like the jig was up, and she was now well and truly stuck in Vircolac's basement. She had to say, it didn't look as if she'd been missing much.

In walking down two flights of stairs, she felt as if she'd traveled back in time seven hundred years. She half expected to look down and see the floor beneath her feet covered with rushes, like a medieval castle hall.

She tugged self-consciously at the sweatshirt she wore. The minute she stepped into view, all eyes turned to her. Of course, everyone else wore their elegant party togs, and here she stood, looking like some white trash cousin from East Bumbleford.

Go, me.

"Ms. Poe, thank you for joining us." The dark, magnetic man at the head of the table flashed her a smile and gestured toward two empty chairs side by side. "Your grandmother has spoken very highly of you. I felt the Council might benefit from your knowledge this evening, as both an educator and a member of a very impressive family."

"Um, thanks." Eloquence had always been Cassidy's strong suit.

She stood awkwardly as an anonymous lackey pulled out her chair, and she slipped into it as quickly as possible. It took a second to get herself settled, mostly because she needed to close her eyes and take a few deep breaths before she felt capable of meeting the gazes of the world's twenty or so most powerful Others filling the room.

A couple of silent "ohm mani padmi ohm"s and a quick prayer later, Cassidy blew out a breath and raised her head to find herself staring straight across the table into the whiskey-brown eyes of a very satisfied-looking Lupine.

What sort of evil god did I piss off recently, and if I make myself a human sacrifice, would my blood soothe his malignant rage?

Cassidy wrestled back the urge to lay her forehead against the table and start pounding, but only barely. She wanted nothing more at that moment than to set her hair on fire with one of the torches. It wasn't as if she could call any more attention to herself than her grandmother already had, so what did she have to lose?

Besides this paralyzing sense of doom, of course.

And the necessity of ever having to look into the eyes of the stranger whom she'd nearly schtupped up on the roof, where anyone could have walked in on them. At the moment, she could feel his gaze on her like a physical touch, and she had to fight not to shiver. The man needed no encouragement.

"Now that we are all together, I would like us to begin." Rafael De Santos rescued her from mortification by rising from his chair and surveying the group before him. He commanded the attention of the Council as surely as he commanded the attention of every female in every room Cassidy had seen him in. She figured his wife must either be a saint or a Playboy bunny. Or maybe both, she considered, remembering a glimpse she'd caught of the curvaceous blonde on her way out of her grandmother's house to one of her "classes."

"First with a welcome to our overseas guests," the Felix continued. He turned to face several people unfamiliar to Cassidy, along with the Lupine Who Would Not Be Named. "Mademoiselle Mireille Chaleur of France. Herr Martin Geist of Germany. Señor Cristos Allavero of Spain."

Each of the delegates nodded to the assemblage while Cassidy tried to put faces to names. It gave her a fabulous excuse to avoid looking at the Lupine across the table.

The Frenchwoman was easy. Tall, brunette, and striking, with pale, porcelain skin and remote, dark eyes, she reminded Cassidy a bit of Cyd Charisse, the dancer in all those 1950s musicals, but about ten times as gorgeous. She was also the only woman who had been named. The men cooperated by being suitably ethnic to distinguish themselves from each other. Geist had the looks of an Aryan poster boy, blond, slim, and faultlessly erect, while Allavero was shorter, darker, and stockier and gave the group a courteous smile along with his nod.

"And of course," De Santos continued, "we have Mr. Richard Maccus representing Great Britain, and Mr. Sullivan Quinn of Ireland."

Damn the Felix for forcing her to look back at her nemesis.

Bracing herself, Cassidy took her time memorizing the man from Britain. His features ran in sharp lines and planes that should have made him look harsh but instead lent a sort of austere beauty to his face. It helped that he looked right back at her out of liquid dark eyes the color of mink, glinting with curiosity and magic. She would never describe him as harmless, but he looked a heck of a lot less predatory than the man seated next to him.

Cassidy whipped out a few Zen techniques—though she'd have chucked every last one of them for a Valium—and forced herself to look once more at the Lupine. At least she knew his name, now. She didn't have to keep thinking of him as the anonymous wolf she'd nearly screwed. Now she could call him Sullivan Quinn, the named wolf she'd nearly screwed. That relieved oh so much of her anxiety.

Cassidy, remember: A lady does not hurl all over the Council chambers.

A few deep breaths kept her hors d'oeuvres in her stomach, but the control felt tenuous. If the Lupine's gaze got any more smoldering, she'd end up wreaking havoc on the polyurethane.

"We are pleased to have you all here with us." De Santos once again came to Cassidy's rescue. She'd have to remember to name her firstborn son after him. "I apologize for the abrupt way in which you have all been summoned to this meeting, but I am told a matter of utmost urgency has prevented us from waiting for tomorrow's scheduled hour."

The Felix turned toward Quinn, one dark eyebrow raised.

It looked almost as if the man sitting next to the Lupine had to elbow him in the side to get him to notice the cue.

"Uh, yes," Quinn said, snapping to attention and clearing his throat. In any other circumstances, Cassidy might have laughed. In these circumstances, she just gave thanks that he'd finally stopped staring.

"I'm afraid we're faced with a matter of some urgency," the Lupine said, his voice growing stronger and more forceful as his attention focused back on the Council. By the time he completed his sentence, he had every eye upon him and looked every inch the diplomat. Yet one more reason why Cassidy should stay far, far away from him. She'd grown up in a family of diplomats. She knew they were trouble.

"When we planned this trip, my compatriots and I intended to come here and regale you with stories of the history of our kind." His voice became compelling as he set the stage for his tale. "We were going to remind this Council of the early days, when humans were the minority among Others. When the Fae ruled their kingdoms in far corners of the globe, and the werekin roamed the plains, fields, and forests. When magic-users held a place of respect among us. And of the days even before then, when those from the world below could walk freely where they held no ill intent."

As he spoke, Cassidy could hear the Lupine's soft Irish brogue grow thicker, like a gathering mist hovering gently over the room. He spun the yarn with skill, drawing everyone's attention and holding it fast, like some old bard or storyteller reciting the history of his people in the light of a village fire. As an anthropologist, Cassidy had a deep respect for the storytellers in any culture. They were the ones who passed that culture on, into the hands of the next generation. Sullivan Quinn was one of the best she'd ever listened to.

"Then man began to spread, growing more numerous and more powerful until they outnumbered us, tens of thousands of them for every one of our kind. The Beautiful People retreated to Faerie. The fur-folk began to walk more in the image of man, and to conceal their differences in the shadows. Magic became something to hide, lest the fear of the humans lead to suspicion and loathing, or worse. Those like us went into hiding, living beside the humans, but never allowing them to gain real knowledge of our society. We became their fairy tales and folk stories, their ghost stories and nightmares."

Cassidy had heard all this before, they all had, but the Lupine had woven a spell around every being in the room.

"Now, the world around us is changing once again. The humans are learning more about their environment, beginning to accept the possibility of things they might before have dismissed as superstition. But that very change presents a new danger to our people." Quinn looked at each of the delegates in turn as he went on. "We have always known that our greatest vulnerability to the desire of humans to destroy us has been the very truth of our natures. For centuries we have lived in peace among them because we concealed our powers and our numbers from them. The key to our downfall always rested in the possibility that one day, a human fanatic would be able to find enough compelling evidence to tear away our veil of secrecy and leave us exposed to a new and deadly wave of persecution."

Cassidy heard the room begin to stir, and frankly, she couldn't blame them. If this speech was leading where she thought, things could get messy. Quick.

"The truth is that change is upon us, whether we choose to prepare ourselves for it or not." Quinn leveled his rich, whiskey gaze at De Santos and spoke firmly. "In fact, we have learned tonight, just a few hours ago, news that tells us change is upon us now, and we have no choice but to face it."

The murmurs from the Council members grew louder until De Santos shifted in his chair and held his hand up for silence.

"While most of us are too strong to fall prey to those who hate us," Quinn continued, "our few and carefully chosen human companions and confidants are not, and many of them possess just as much knowledge and evidence of our existence as we have ourselves. One of them has been taken."

Her breath already caught in her throat, Cassidy would never forget the next words he spoke.

"Ysabel Mirenow, human companion to the vampire Gregor Kasminikov, has been kidnapped by an organization that calls itself the Light of Truth, and if I and my fellow delegates are correct, she will provide them the evidence they need to expose us to the human world in a matter of days. Our delegation is here to propose that we beat them to the punch and reveal ourselves on our own terms, before it's too late."

· · ·

The tension in the room broke in a wave of angry voices. From all sides of the room, Others made their disbelief and their upset plain. Surprise filled them, along with a good dose of unease, not that Quinn could blame them. He wanted them uneasy. Hell, based on what he and Richard had learned less than half an hour ago, he wanted them shaking in their ruddy boots.

"Quiet, please," De Santos ordered. After another short burst of whispers and muttering, the gathering complied, and the Felix turned his attention back on Quinn. "This is quite a revelation. How long has the woman been missing?"

"About twenty-seven hours. Too long for us to hope we could reach her before the Light of Truth gets what it wants. We have to take action. We need to come up with a plan for revealing ourselves to the humans before the Lightheads do it for us."

"And there is no chance of a misunderstanding? No chance that she and Gregor have argued, and she's gone to visit her mother?"

"Her mother has been dead at least fifty years."

De Santos ignored the sarcasm. "What have our friends in Russia already done about this?"

"Kasminikov has his best men out looking for her, of course," Richard supplied, finally sharing some of the bloody responsibility for this fiasco. "Not only is he upset that his mistress was taken, but he also comprehends the gravity of the situation. Even if it's too late to do anything for Ms. Mirenow, he understands something has to be done to contain the fallout generated by the kidnapping. We're not talking about rushing into the Unveiling for kicks. We no longer have a choice."

The Unveiling was what Others called the eventual revelation of their kind to the humans. It had always been a theoretical term, a reference to something that would happen in a far distant future, but not something anyone needed to worry about today. Quinn had started worrying.

"Well," De Santos said, after an eternity of stillness. "This does put events in a whole new light, doesn't it?"

"I don't see how," a new voice broke in. "She's just one human. Hardly anything over which to excite ourselves."

Quinn glanced down the length of the Council table to identify the speaker as one of the three vamps in the Inner Circle, but he couldn't be sure which one. Like all vampires, this one sat like a king giving an audience to the peasants, simultaneously bored, arrogant, condescending, and vigilant against his own overthrow. Quinn didn't need to know the man's name to dislike him. He just had to look into the eyes as flat and empty as a snake's and watch the expressions of anger and contempt on his aristocratic face. The two-thousand-dollar suit and diamond-studded tie tack didn't hurt, either.

"One woman, easily dismissed and easily replaced," the vampire continued. "There is no reason for us to concern ourselves with her unfortunate predicament. If the Europeans think it's such a problem, let them deal with it. It's no reason for us to take action, let alone to Unveil."

Oh, yeah. Quinn hated him on spec.

"This is not only a European problem," he said, his teeth gritted against a snarl. "The Atlantic Ocean doesn't insulate you from this threat."

"There is a lot more than an ocean between us, Mr. Quinn."

"But there's nothing between you and the Light of Truth. We also have reason to believe that the orders for her kidnapping might have come from a newer cell within their organization. One operating right here in America."

Eight

The news dropped on the room like a mortar blast, echoing off the stone walls and even stonier faces. Quinn braced himself for the nuclear fallout that was undoubtedly on its way behind the shock. He wondered if they'd stocked a room down here with canned goods and blood bags. Though the current residents were more likely to eat each other than a mixed fruit cocktail.

That truth sat up and waved as chaos exploded in the Council chamber. Several of the American Council members jumped to their feet in protest, which made a couple of the Europeans leap up, as well. At least seven languages contributed to the din, and fur flew as strong emotion prompted partial shifts in at least one of the werefolk present. An exchange of blows seemed imminent when De Santos proved why he held his seat by leaping up onto the table and roaring.

"SILENCE!"

The room quieted to a subdued buzz, then after a quick look at the Felix's face, to the requested silence. Quinn didn't need that second look. He knew a powerful animal when he saw one, and he kept his mouth shut.

"We are *not* here to start a war," De Santos growled, glaring the delegates down one by one. "This is a discussion, and we will conduct it civilly. The only bloodshed to occur in this chamber is what *I* will cause if anyone cannot contain himself."

His audience judged the Felix meant business and began retaking their seats, the grumbling remaining at a minimum. When all this was over, Quinn might have to hit De Santos up for some tips, diplomat to diplomat. Cat or no, the guy had game.

De Santos gave another snarl and stepped down onto his chair and then onto the floor. He still looked coiled to spring, though, radiating alertness and tension.

"Now, everyone shut up and stay seated until I tell you to move." Almost everyone shut up and stayed seated. Quinn was definitely making an appointment.

"There's no reason to have us sit when we'll be leaving so soon. This 'emergency' meeting is clearly a waste of our time."

"I said sit, Francis." The Felix barely spoke above a whisper and there was no heat in his voice, but there was a definite threat. The vampire sat.

Hearing De Santos say the name jogged Quinn's memory. Francis Leonard. His mention in the Council briefing memos placed him at no more than four centuries old, but apparently his morals had proved even more corrosive than the average vampire's. That was the danger with being immortal. The longer you lived, the more you witnessed, the further removed from humanity you became, and the more flexibility began to creep into your ethics. It was usually only the very old or very insane vampires who became dangerous. Quinn guessed Leonard might have decided to get a jump on things.

"What does it matter if they have taken the wench?" Leonard snapped. Hostility for the head of the Council rolled off him in waves. "And what does it matter if they're operating out of the White House? It makes no difference. They've captured a human, not an illustrated edition of the history of our kind."

"I think you fail to see the implications of the situation," Quinn said, trying to keep calm when all he wanted was to knock sense into some hard, American heads. "The woman is human, which is the reason the fanatics were able to get their hands on her in the first place. Had she truly been one of us, she would've been able to evade capture or destroy the ones who attacked her. But she's also thoroughly enmeshed in our culture. She's been the companion to a vampire for more than half a century. In that time she's heard and witnessed a thousand things humans should never see, any one of which would condemn us in unfriendly eyes."

"Seeing is very different from being, Mr. Quinn," De Santos said.

"I am well aware of that, but these people aren't only interested in what Ysabel Mirenow has seen. They're interested in what she's become. She's been with Kasminikov since the end of the humans' Second World War, and she was twenty-five when they met. Yet at eighty-five years old, she appears to be barely out of university. That's only possible because of the blood she's shared with her lover. That blood changed the chemistry of her body, the way her cells multiply and divide, the way they keep from dying off. It's evident on every surface of her body, but it will be even more evident under a laboratory microscope."

The murmurs and grumbles began anew, filling the room with a distinctly hostile buzz. De Santos silenced them again with a look. "Even humans are aware that some very mundane things can change the structure of a cell. Disease. Toxins.

"But outside of superhero comics, those things don't allow a human to see in the dark like a cat, or hear a stocking footfall from a dozen yards away. They don't allow a small, delicate woman to wrestle with a human man twice her size and almost win. Even if she can't clean and jerk a Peugeot, she's still obviously much stronger than a human woman of her build ought to be."

"Pure speculation," Leonard said.

De Santos raised an eyebrow. "Are you dismissing the concerns of our guests, Francis?"

"Of course I'm dismissing them. They're nonsense. If they have the woman, they have her. If they decide to examine her blood or anything else, then they do it. Their findings would never be taken seriously by a human public obsessed with science. And in the chaos that still pervades Russia, even if they have access to a laboratory, do the necessary tests, and broadcast the results on satellite television, it's doubtful anyone will pay attention, let alone raise an army to defeat us. To Unveil now would be preposterous."

"And if you're wrong?" Quinn demanded. "Wouldn't it be better to reveal ourselves to the humans on our own terms and learn to coexist with them, rather than be dragged out into the open by panicked mobs bent on our destruction?"

"A move such as this would be utterly foolish," Leonard spat out, his features tight and eyes narrowed in rage. "If we expose ourselves to the humans, it would be like painting bull's-eyes on our chests and handing them the stakes."

"Not all of us get nervous when we see someone holding a pencil the wrong way, Francis," Emma Higgenbottham said in a warm, soothing, matronly voice that sounded utterly out of place amid the rancor filling the room. If she was like most brownies, the small, industrious woman usually wore a smile and offered a quick, merry wit. Right now, she was glaring daggers at Leonard.

"I think you give the humans too little credit," the brownie continued. "I think most of you always have. They're not so bad, really, once you get to know them. A bit thick, maybe, but that's no reason to—"

"And what would you know about it?" Leonard sniped back. "Just because your people have been cleaning their houses for a few centuries without having the decency to kill them in their sleep is no reason to assume you're experts on their behavior."

Breath hissed between his teeth as Quinn mentally lowered his assessment of Leonard's intelligence. Brownies might be looked on by most as jolly, industrious elf types, but he wouldn't have pissed one off on a bet. There were reasons why humans used to leave them offerings of milk and brandy on their doorsteps. To keep them from torching their houses at night.

"We don't live in the Dark Ages anymore," Emma bit out.

Quinn seized the opportunity. "Exactly. And given the present circumstances, perhaps it's time to give

humans the benefit of a doubt that they might be ready
to accept a few unusual truths."

"Bullshit."

The word shot from Cassidy's mouth before she had a
hope of stopping it. Judging by the look on her grandmother's face, Cassidy supposed that Adele wished she
could shove it back in, but her hands were tied by the
large audience of her peers. So at that point, all Cassidy could really do was to go with it.

The Felix looked her way and quirked an eyebrow.
"I take it you disagree with Mr. Quinn's assessment,
Ms. Poe?"

Cassidy shifted in her chair. "You could say that.
But I'm sorry. I'm a visitor here, and it's not my place
to comment."

De Santos smiled. "On the contrary, Ms. Poe. While
the revelation of Ms. Mirenow's kidnapping and the involvement of the Light of Truth may have come as a
surprise, I had a sneaking suspicion regarding the intentions of our visiting delegates."

Ooooohkay. That cleared up precisely nothing.

"I'm afraid I'm not sure what you mean, sir."

"Your grandmother is very proud of you, Ms. Poe.
She shared with me the impressive reputation you have
earned in the study of human culture and intercultural
relations."

Cassidy blinked. They wanted her here because she
was an anthropologist?

"I believe the expertise of a person who has dedi-
cated her life and her very keen intellect to the study of
how cultures interact, evolve, and react to change could
prove extremely valuable to us, Ms. Poe. Especially an

Other with such an extensive knowledge of human cultures." Rafael smiled. "I also have a great deal of respect for your family. I have never met a Berry or a Poe who did not possess a sharp political mind. We can never have enough of those, can we?"

"With all due respect, sir, it doesn't matter how much I know about human culture, or how great my family is at politics. It won't change the fact that you already know the humans are never going to accept us. If we Unveil, we'll need to be prepared for a war."

"We may not be human, but we aren't that dissimilar from them in many ways," the Irish Lupine broke in. That damned accent of his only added to the difficulty Cassidy was having in processing data and, oh, remembering her name. "If we handle this properly, reveal ourselves in the right way at the right time, the European High Council believes we have a good chance to live with them in peace and harmony. And if we ever plan to do so, we have to begin pursuit of that goal immediately."

"Such an assertion is nothing but nonsense, and you know it." Adele replied for Cassidy, seeing as how her granddaughter was too busy trying to will a hole to open up below her chair and swallow her. "The humans have had hundreds of years to get over the fear that drove us into hiding in the first place, and yet they remain convinced that we are abominations cursed by God. Do you not go to the cinema?"

"With all due respect, ma'am, I don't think movies or novels are any way to judge the capacity of the entire human race," Quinn said. "They also write novels in which our kind are accepted members of society."

Cassidy gave up on the restraint thing and screwed

up her courage. She looked straight at the luscious Lupine. "Mr. Quinn, to use human speculative fiction as a basis for a decision of this magnitude is ridiculous. By and large, humans believe themselves to have very delineated boundaries between fact and fiction. They might enjoy the entertainment value of the latter, but they don't allow it into their daily lives. They wouldn't allow *us* into their daily lives."

"You have the right to whatever opinion you wish, Miss Poe, however, I do not think it wise to discount—"

"I can say it with certainty, because this is what I do." Drawing herself up in her chair, she felt her nerves taking a back seat, forced there by the confidence she felt in her professionalism. "I'm a cultural anthropologist. I study groups of humans for a living, what makes them tick, what unites them and what divides them. And I can tell you authoritatively that there is a lot more that divides us from humans than unites us."

"I believe you may overstate the problem, mademoiselle." Mireille Chaleur regarded her from behind those fathomless dark eyes, her face static and remote. "We have lived side by side with the humans since they crawled from their caves. They have dominated the earth for more centuries than I care to count. It has led to the unfortunate consequence of our kind coming to mimic their society. We have become like them in many ways."

"Until they start turning fuzzy and biting into food that can bite back, I think I'll stick by my statement."

Mireille's eyes narrowed and her mouth opened, but De Santos got there first. "Your expertise in this area is why your grandmother was asked to bring you to this meeting, Ms. Poe. I'm interested to hear why you think the idea of the Unveiling is so unwise."

"We don't need her to tell us her reasons, De Santos. We have enough of our own," Leonard said.

Cassidy struggled not to make a face. She wasn't terribly fond of Francis Leonard, but then, neither was the head of the Council. From the gossip Cassidy had heard, the vampire still carried a grudge over losing the leadership role to De Santos. It warmed her heart that someone so old could be so childish.

Leonard shoved to his feet. "I've had enough of this. These arguments are ridiculous and will get us nowhere. I am personally insulted that our brethren from Europe would even think to subject us to this ludicrous exercise. If it's true that there is a threat from this human group, then let us take care of it and be done."

"Take care of it?" Quinn asked much too quietly. Cassidy could almost see his hackles rising. "What exactly does that mean?"

"Kill them."

A couple of voices murmured agreement, but most of the room looked uneasy at the thought, and Quinn's lip curled in an incredibly wolfish snarl.

"It's no worse than what they've done to us," Leonard insisted coldly. "Or have you forgotten your history, wolf?"

"My people remember very well the witch hunts and the werewolf trials. We remember the burnings and the hangings and the burials where stakes were driven through the hearts of our people to bind them forever to their graves. Rest assured, the memories of all Others are long and vivid."

"Very vivid," Richard grumbled. "My great-grandfather was skinned alive by the human fisherman of a nearby village. They'd heard some legends and intended to use the power of a Selkie's skin to control the weather. Don't be telling us we don't remember, vampire. We simply choose not to live in the past. And we choose not to sink to the level of murderers."

"Before we devolve into name-calling," De Santos growled meaningfully, eyes narrowing into glowing yellow slits as a hint of fang glinted between his lips, "kindly remember a few things. One, we are all civilized adults here. Two, this chamber is a place of diplomacy, not chaos. And three, I will quite happily knock together the skulls of anyone here who cannot keep a civil tongue in their heads. Do we all understand each other?"

There was a lot of nodding on either side of the table, but only the bravest of the assembly managed to vocalize anything like an assent. No one offered an objection.

"Good." The Felix settled back in his seat, but no one was fooled into thinking he had relaxed. "Let me understand you, Leonard. You propose that we hunt down the people responsible for Ms. Mirenow's kidnapping and simply kill the lot of them?"

"There's no other way to be assured of their silence."

"Are you daft, man?" Quinn surged to his feet and slammed his palms down onto the table. "There is *no* way to silence them. None. We are going to be revealed. Our only choice is to manage how it happens. Even if we slaughtered every fanatic in Moscow, even if we traced the order for the kidnapping to a cell in America and slaughtered *them*, another group will rise up to take their place. We have no more choices. *We will be Unveiled.*"

"What's to manage?" Cassidy demanded, when her teeth had bitten all the way through her tongue and snapped her restraint. "The consequences are going to manage us, not the other way around. Unveiling won't make the fanatics go away. It will provide a recruitment poster for new ones. There's going to be a revival of *Salem! The Musical!* Right here on Broadway."

"Enough of this," De Santos grumbled, rolling his eyes. "You are turning my headache into a fully blown migraine with a side of annoyance. We're finished here for the night."

The room buzzed again, but Cassidy's grandmother was the only one willing to stick her neck out in front of the Felix.

Adele scowled and thumped her cane heavily against the stone floor. "I hardly think we can adjourn and leave matters as serious as these unaddressed, Rafael."

"I am not proposing that we leave anything unaddressed."

"Good," Leonard said. He wore a smug smile that didn't just make Cassidy's skin crawl, it made it dance a tarantella. "Then the only thing left to do is arrange for the Russians to take care of their cell. I'm sure they can extract the information we need to find the accomplices on our shores. If they're anywhere in the tristate area, I might be willing to do the job myself."

Rafael sent him a frigid look. "I'm not ready to order an execution, Francis. There's no reason to look so excited."

Cassidy frowned and her tongue ran away with her

again. "You can't actually be thinking of planning an Unveiling?"

"I take it you remain convinced this would be foolish."

She ignored the hostile gazes of the Lupine, the Selkie, and most of the rest of the Council, and sighed. "I don't think the Unveiling itself is unwise, sir. I think it's inevitable. I just don't think that now is the time. In the past decade, human society has been growing more insular, more intolerant and protectionist, not less. Hardly the hallmarks of an enlightened society."

"In Western Europe, the values of tolerance and acceptance are finding a wider audience, not a smaller one. The EU has strict policies on individual rights and freedoms."

Quinn practically spat the words at her, and she shook her head. Only she could manage to make a man crazy with desire and maddened with anger all in one banner evening.

"Mr. Quinn, I'm not saying there aren't some humans who could learn to accept us. But by and large, do you really think the majority of them are going to be overcome with warm fuzzy feelings for things that grow big, long fangs and eat raw meat, preferably while it's still twitching?"

The Lupine said nothing, but she saw the muscles in his jaw twitch. He shot a glare at Leonard, then appeared to take a deep, calming breath before he answered her. It wasn't she who had him so angry, she realized. It was the vampire and his bloodthirsty solution to the night's problem.

"I think we're going to find out, Miss Poe, whether we want to or not."

"And I think that before we jump to any conclusions,

we need a great deal more information," De Santos broke in. "We need to know exactly what information the Russians have that leads them to conclude there is a Light of Truth cell here in the United States. We need to know whether this group was involved in the Mirenow kidnapping, as well as what their immediate plans for our demise consist of. And I know exactly how we're going to accomplish it."

The Lupine frowned and Cassidy got the uneasy feeling something unpleasant for her was about to happen.

It was confirmed when the Felix fixed her with his gaze. "Ms. Poe, from what your grandmother has told me over the years, I gather that the study of fringe cultural movements and their relationship to larger society has been something of an area of expertise for you."

Uh-oh. Cassidy did not like where this was headed.

"I don't know if I would say that," she began, but he didn't give her time to finish.

"That's why I called the dean of your department at Columbia to ask his opinion. He confirmed that you are one of the foremost authorities on the matter." He aimed his blasted, charming smile at her. "I would like you to do something for the Council, Miss Poe. I would like you to learn everything you can about this group that calls itself the Light of Truth, and then I would like you to discover what, if any, truth there is to the rumors that the group is currently active in the United States. You will, of course, need to work very closely with Mr. Quinn on this, but I don't foresee that being a problem."

Cassidy just sat there, stunned, and tried to ignore the sudden glint in the Lupine's eyes.

"And you, Mr. Quinn, will keep in constant contact with Russia. If there is a trail leading here, I want you to find it. And if there is an organized cell of the Light of Truth operating in this country, I want you to find that." He nodded to Quinn and then to Cassidy. "The two of you will be working together very closely until this is resolved."

Before Cassidy could say a word, De Santos nodded to the assembly, stood, and sauntered out of the Council chambers.

Had she thought unpleasant? Try nightmarish. Slowly, she turned her head and met the gaze of the Lupine across the table, and goddammit if he didn't lick his freaking lips.

Bastard.

Nine

She bolted faster than a thoroughbred from a starting gate, and Quinn was still grinning over it the next morning when he, Richard, and Cristos trekked the distance from their hotel back to Vircolac. Didn't she realize by now that running only made him that much more eager to chase her?

He wasn't sure if it was anticipation, adrenaline, or just a night full of very satisfying dreams, but he found himself in a rare mood this morning. He had enough energy for ten men and was glad they'd be starting work early and getting something done. As they'd been leaving the club last night, a member of the staff had delivered a message from the head of the Council requesting that he, Richard, and Cristos return at ten the next morning for a conference call with Gregor Kasminikov. The Felix was anxious to move forward.

"Not quite what we'd hoped for, was it?" Richard grumped without real rancor about last night's meeting. "Bloody Yanks."

"I do not think it was so horrible." Cristos grinned, hands buried in the pockets of his khaki trousers. "I had half expected them to laugh us out of the room.

You might agree that things went a small bit better than that, at least."

"Actually, I do agree," Quinn said with a smile he hoped didn't appear too smug. "I think this plan the Council leader has for us to work closely with local experts will be a very important opportunity."

Richard snorted. "I'm talking about the welfare of an entire continent of Others, Quinn, and you're thinking only of getting into the lass's pants. It's not like you."

Quinn frowned.

"Don't try to play innocent. Did you think no one would notice that you couldn't keep your eyes off the dragon's granddaughter last night? I nearly handed you my handkerchief at one point and told you to wipe your chin."

"I was prepared to ignore it and simply avoid stepping in the puddles when I left the table," Cristos said, eyes twinkling.

Quinn flicked them each a two-fingered salute. "You can both feck off. I behaved with a great deal of civility and restraint."

"Sure, if you want me to give you credit for not stripping her bare and leaning her arse up over the end of the table."

Quinn ignored Richard's sarcasm and kept walking. "Thank God, the grandmother didn't notice. As it was, she gave me a tongue-lashing for having the temerity to state an opinion contrary to her own."

"Did she? I must have missed that."

"She cornered me just before we left the Council chambers. Accused me of holding a sword over the neck of the Council leader. Can you imagine anyone holding a sword on that one?"

Cristos laughed. "Did she try to tell you we could take ourselves to the Devil, but the Americans wouldn't follow?"

"Exactly."

"Mad old hen," Richard snorted. "As if the Yanks would have any choice once we Unveil. Does she think humans are so stupid they'd believe Others had never discovered the New World?"

Cristos shrugged. "She is not insane, Richard, merely frightened."

"And her fear gives her the right to ignore good judgment? That's idiotic." They reached the impressive historic edifice of the club, and Richard stalked up the steps to ring the bell. "That's like someone who can't swim jumping into a lake to avoid a bee."

"Perhaps she is allergic to bees?"

Quinn rolled his eyes. "Why, in all the years I've known you, have I not killed either of you?"

Cristos gave an incredibly Latin shrug. "Because you are . . . ah, what's the word . . . a chicken-shit?"

"Listen here, Paddington—"

"Children." Richard stepped between snarling Lupine and grinning Ursa and held them apart. "We might want to consider scrapping about this a bit later on. That is, if the two of you will kindly get your heads out of your asses and stop behaving like idiots."

"But we have the act down so smoothly now, don't you think?"

"Cris, bugger off with that smart mouth of yours before I decide to let Quinn have at you."

"The two of you have entirely lost your sense of fun, you know."

The three men handed their coats to the butler who admitted them, and accepted check slips in return.

"On the contrary," Quinn said. "We'd have a lot of fun kicking your ass, boyo."

"No ass-kicking in the hallway, please."

Quinn looked over his shoulder and saw the American Council leader propped negligently against the wall.

De Santos gave them one of his lazy grins. "I hope I haven't inconvenienced you by asking you to return this morning, gentlemen, but we have a lot of work to do and can't afford to waste time. If you'll follow me?"

"You won't need to apologize if you can manage to produce a very large pot of tea."

De Santos laughed and pushed away from the wall. "I'll see what we can do, Mr. Maccus."

The Felix led the way into a moderately sized and inviting room, lined from floor to ceiling with books. The walls were a deep brick-red where they weren't covered by woodwork, and a faded but elegant carpet covered shining chestnut floors. Two large, multipaned windows shone light onto a massive and decidedly masculine desk without a single bit of clutter on the surface. It made a lovely library, Quinn thought, but it didn't look like anyone's personal study.

De Santos closed the door behind them and gestured for the men to sit. "I've reserved this room for the rest of the morning. The kitchen will send up tea and coffee. Have you gentlemen eaten? We can easily arrange breakfast as well."

Quinn grinned. They had, in fact, eaten before they left the hotel, but Quinn never passed up an offer of food. His Lupine metabolism easily burned seven or eight thousand calories a day, and that was if he did nothing but sit on his arse.

"I wouldn't mind."

"That would be most appreciated," Cristos echoed, his Ursa metabolism much the same. Unlike his animal counterpart, a werebear never hibernated.

Richard shook his head. "The tea will do for me. Leave the food to these gluttons."

After a quick call on a discreet house phone, De Santos crossed in front of the desk and opened the large doors of a built-in cabinet. They tucked neatly away to expose a large, flat-panel monitor, some impressive speakers, and what looked like a state-of-the-art teleconferencing system, including a small video camera. Taking a conference phone from the shelf, the Felix stretched out the cord until he could set the device on the low coffee table in the center of the room.

"I hope you don't mind if we start before the food arrives," he said, settling onto the opposite end of the sofa from Quinn. "Gregor asked that we call as soon as we could. It's just past sunset Moscow time."

"No. The sooner, the better."

While De Santos dialed, a nearly silent waiter entered the room with a tray bearing the tea and coffee. He deposited it on the desk and disappeared as Cristos rose from the closest chair and started to pour. By the time the phone had given its third ring, the cream and sugar were on the coffee table beside the phone and the four men were sipping gratefully.

A click and a brief silence signaled someone had answered. *"Kasminikov mestozhitel'stvo."*

"Rafael De Santos for Gregor. He's expecting the call."

The voice switched to English. "One moment, please."

Quinn heard another click, and a new voice echoed over the line. This one was heavy and deep and decidedly unhappy.

"About time you call, you son of a rabid Himalayan."

"It's a pleasure to speak with you as well, Gregor." De Santos spoke in a mild voice, eyes sparking with humor. "And I have with me the sons of a rabid teddy, walrus, and Pekingese."

Cristos smothered a laugh, but Richard did not look amused. Quinn just rolled his eyes and leaned closer to the conference phone receiver. "Hello, Gregor. How are you holding up?"

"How do you think, Quinn?" the Russian snapped. "I have not slept in two days, and I still cannot work this . . . this camera contraption."

There was a quiet murmur in the background and De Santos picked up a small remote control, aiming it at the monitor in the cabinet. "Let Vasili take care of it. I've just turned ours on. You should have an image as soon as you're up and running."

There was more muttering, several curses Quinn was happy not to be able to translate, and a series of muffled thumps before the video flickered to life. He winced at the image that appeared. Compared to the last time he'd seen Gregor Kasminikov, the huge Cossack of a vampire looked like shite. He was disheveled and glowering, his heavy, sandy-brown brows were pulled low over dark eyes, and his normally ruddy cheeks looked pale and drawn.

Richard spoke first. "Damn it, Gregor, you haven't been eating."

"I have had no appetite," he bit back, "and we have been a bit preoccupied over here."

De Santos played peacemaker once again. "Why don't you give us an update, Gregor? Then we can decide on our next move."

"I have very little to tell." And he didn't sound happy about that. "Ysabel is still missing. My men found one witness who said he thought he saw someone shove her into a big, black car, but he remembered no identification numbers."

"Still no demands from the fanatics?"

"That is not how they operate. These humans do not want anything from us but our deaths. It is a philosophy passed down from their leaders in Germany. Each cell might operate independently, but they all share the same hatred. And the more they learn of us, the more they hate."

De Santos looked into the camera. "I confess I don't know much about them, but how much could they know about us? We have become great keepers of secrets over the years."

Gregor snarled. "They know too much and too little. Most of their 'facts' are little more than the same legends that have been passed among peasants for centuries, but they are always striving to find the proof that will support their insane jihad against us. I fear Ysabel may unwittingly give them that proof."

Quinn frowned. "Has anyone from the local pack tried to scent out her trail?"

"We are not idiots! Of course we tried. The wolf found nothing past a few feet from where she entered the car."

Quinn was disappointed, but not surprised. As keen as a Lupine nose might be, it had been designed to track living prey, not hunks of metal. Unless a car had a distinctive mechanical problem, a werewolf wouldn't be able to tell the path of one from another. And if the car's windows were kept closed, Ysabel couldn't produce an airborne trail to follow, either.

"Okay, so a direct trail isn't going to work. What's been done to trace her down the back end? Do you have any idea where the local Lighthead cell likes to operate?"

The vampire snarled into the video camera in Moscow, and even in Manhattan, they could see the glint of fang he exposed.

"My men raided what was supposed to be a photography shop this morning. I wanted to do it myself, but we did not dare wait for sunset for fear they would already have moved."

"Had they?" Richard asked.

"Not quick enough. Ysabel was gone, but we took two of the bastards and brought them here. One was not very cooperative."

"What did he do?"

Gregor's mouth compressed into a tight line. "He killed himself. Poison."

"And the other?" Quinn held his breath.

"Gave me a mobile phone number. He said it is the one he and his co-conspirators used to contact the mastermind of the kidnapping plot. We traced it, of course."

"To who?"

"To what, actually. It is registered to a corporation. V.R.A. Lumos Enterprises. An American company."

Quinn felt a surge of excitement. "I don't suppose you came up with an address?"

Gregor shook his head. "No. But I was able to . . . persuade the representative of the telephone service provider to tell me where the last calls made on the mobile were placed from."

"And?"

"New York, New York."

De Santos sat forward on the edge of the sofa, his air of lazy relaxation gone for the first time since he'd greeted the European delegation's arrival. "You're saying the American cell of the Light of Truth may be operating out of *my* city?"

"So it would seem."

The Felix uttered something succinct, accurate, and obscene. Quinn heartily agreed.

"You need to go back to that bastard and find out the name of their contact," he bit out. "I don't care what it takes, Gregor, but we need something more to go on."

The vampire's face went blank, his eyes black and shuttered. "I'm afraid that will not be possible."

"Shit. Don't tell me—"

"He's dead."

"More poison?" Richard asked.

"No. I killed him."

Quinn opened his mouth to roar his outrage. What could Gregor have been thinking? Didn't he realize how important an inside source could be for them? Did he not understand how little they had to go on and how quickly time was ticking away? Then he looked back at the image on the monitor, and his jaw snapped shut. The frozen, remote expression and harsh lines at the corner of the vampire's mouth spoke volumes. He thought Ysabel might already be dead.

Instead of railing at the Russian, Quinn took a deep breath. "All right. Did you get anything else before he died?"

"Not from him," Gregor said stiffly, as if he knew what Quinn had wanted to say. "But my men seized a carton full of documents from the shop they raided. They said much of it is financial records and correspondence."

"And that's the kind of trail I know how to follow." De Santos sounded as if he relished the chance. "Gregor, you'll need to get me copies. Fax them, scan and e-mail them, overnight-mail them. Send them by bloody carrier pigeon, but get them here as soon as possible."

"I will." The vampire paused and Quinn saw the muscles in his jaw jumping. "I appreciate all the help you can give me. I would very much like to see Ysabel returned, if it is possible."

The four men on the other end of the video conference looked at each other, their expressions grim. No one had to say out loud that the chances of that were slim and diminishing rapidly.

"We'll do what we can, Gregor."

He squared his shoulders. "Thank you. And no matter what happens, I want to find the ones responsible. They will not be allowed to get away with touching what is mine."

De Santos looked as if he knew exactly what the Russian was feeling, but he only nodded and terminated the connection. "I think we have our work cut out for us, gentlemen. I'll begin sorting the documents Gregor sends as soon as they arrive, but it would be best if we didn't concentrate all our efforts on one lead."

Richard gave a harsh laugh. "Do we have any others?"

"We know the American cell is here in the city," Cristos offered. He had been silent during the call, but Quinn knew his sharp mind had worked overtime. "If that is true, there must be a way to find them."

"There are—what?—eight million people in New York City? Shall we start knocking on doors?"

"I don't think we'll need to employ measures so drastic," De Santos said, some of his amusement returning. "A bit of old-fashioned detective work might be required, but I have every confidence Quinn will prove up to the challenge."

Quinn started. "I will?"

"Of course. With a bit of assistance from Cassidy Poe."

Now that didn't sound so bad.

"Why the girl?" Richard asked, his eyes full of mischief. "I don't see why Quinn should have to work with her. She's not a private investigator or a police officer. How would she be able to find these lunatics?"

Quinn shot his friend a quelling glare, but the Selkie only smiled back.

"As we discussed last night, Ms. Poe is an expert on fringe groups and their operation," De Santos explained, his own face reflecting suppressed mirth. "She should be able to assist with insights on how they will be operating, where they might choose to establish themselves, how they will go about recruiting members. I have great confidence in the pair of you."

"Which is more credit than most of that lot last night were willing to give."

De Santos heard Richard's sotto voce grumble and quirked an eyebrow. "Do you refer to anyone in particular, Mr. Maccus?"

"Richard, for Christ's sake. And aye, a name or two springs to mind. Along with a sharp tongue and airs I've not seen since the summer I passed through Balmoral during the queen's visit."

"Ah, yes. The inimitable Dame Berry." De Santos's mouth curved in a rueful smile. "She's been a force on this council for at least fifty years. While that may not be impressive to some of our less mortal members, the force of her personality does impress them, as does the reputation of her family."

Cristos looked intrigued. "The Berry family has been around for very long, then?"

"Not the Berrys specifically. Adele's mother's name was Spencer, I believe. And the mother before that was . . . Chancellor? No, Chalmers."

Quinn noticed he didn't mention any men. "Are they some sort of matrilineal clan? That's unusual among werekin. At least among the predatory races."

"Ah, but Dame Adele is not werekin at all."

Frown deepening, Quinn searched his recollection. He'd skimmed through files on all the members of the Council's Inner Circle before coming to the States, but it had been the kind of bare-bones information that distilled the species of each member down to "shifter," "magic-user," "changeling," "vampire," or "other." He distinctly remembered Adele Berry being listed as a shifter. "Isn't Cassidy Poe the dragon's granddaughter?"

"She is."

"Then she's werekin," Quinn insisted. "I saw the granddaughter shift into a red fox."

"I won't ask how you managed that," De Santos said, though curiosity underlined his lazy air. "Not this minute, anyway. But the fact that you saw the girl shift does not make her werekin."

"Bloody hell," Richard breathed, realization dawning. "D'you mean she and the dragon are Foxwomen?"

De Santos nodded. "Not the only ones I've ever met, but among the few. The very few."

Quinn racked his brain for the information he knew was in there somewhere. It didn't take him long to find it. "I remember hearing some sort of Native American story, female shifters who used magic to transform instead of DNA. And I think there was something about it being maternally inherited—always women, no men. I thought they were a myth."

"Does Dame Adele look like a myth to you?"

"But I saw her change." Quinn shook his head. "There was no chanting or hand waving or . . . glittery dust in the air. How was that magic?"

De Santos winced. "Keep your voice down if you're going to mention glittery dust and magic in the same breath. My wife is wandering about the club somewhere, and that's not the type of terminology I want her to overhear. She's a bit sensitive about those magic stereotypes."

The door opened to reveal a laden catering cart and an exceedingly feminine blonde with tousled gold curls, big blue eyes, and a wicked smile. "As long as it isn't coming from your mouth, kitten, you're perfectly safe."

Quinn saw the Felix close his eyes for a split second before he smiled and held his hand out to the intruder. "Sweetheart. Come in and meet my guests."

She stepped inside and closed the door behind her. She wore a pair of hip-hugging jeans and a snug, V-neck sweater the color of ripe berries. All four occupants of the room raked their gazes over her in the habit of men, and then did it again, for which they could hardly be blamed. Her clothes happened to cling quite enticingly to an impressive little body. The curvy kind with hips that swayed as she stepped farther into the room. She had a sort of Marilyn Monroe look to her. Not in her features, but in the air of bone-deep sexiness about her. The smiling red lips and curly blond hair didn't hurt, either. Combine that with the look of keen intelligence in her baby-blues, and a man couldn't help but appreciate her.

Until he heard her husband snarl. Then he would find the meal the waiter laid out on the desk visually fascinating, just as Quinn, Richard, and Cristos did.

"Down, Simba," the woman said, taking her husband's hand and catching a hip against the edge of the end table beside him. "Give these guys a break. I am pretty darn adorable, you know."

She gave a cheeky grin that suited her a little too well, and De Santos answered with a rumbling purr. "I know."

She laughed. "Now, now. You'll embarrass your friends."

Cristos grinned wickedly and reached out for the woman's free hand, raising her knuckles to his mouth for a gallant kiss. "Not at all, señora. Please, go on."

"Nope, you can't distract me." She shook her head

and turned her killer blue eyes on Quinn. "I want to talk about what Mr. Peat-Smoke and Shamrocks had to say."

The Felix's mouth quirked. "Gentlemen, allow me to present my wife, Tess De Santos. Sweetheart, this is Richard Maccus and Cristos Allavero. And Mr. Peat-Smoke and Shamrocks is going by Sullivan Quinn these days."

"Right." Tess shifted to perch on the arm of the sofa beside her husband and leaned with casual intimacy against his shoulder. "So, Sullivan, what's this about witches and glitter dust?"

Somehow Quinn got the impression that her raised eyebrow was not a good sign. He cleared his throat. "It was honestly just a . . . a figure of speech, Tess."

"Mrs. De Santos. And that's not what it sounded like." The Felix let loose something that suspiciously resembled a chuckle. Tess ignored him. "It sounded like you think magic is all about chanting and incense and sparkly little wands."

"I don't recall using those terms . . ."

"You didn't have to. I know what you were thinking."

She did? Quinn froze, remembering Tess was a witch.

De Santos burst out laughing so hard he nearly launched himself off the sofa. His wife plucked his coffee mug from his hand before it could shatter on the floor.

"I didn't mean it literally," she said. " 'Cause, ew! I know what goes on inside the average male mind, thanks, and I'm so not going there. What I *meant* was that you clearly share the same misconception about magic as the rest of the world. Magic is nothing but the concentrated application of will on the material world. To be blunt, it's like thinking really, really hard."

The Felix smiled up at her indulgently and rested his hand against the small of her back.

"The only time you see a physical manifestation of magical energy is when the intensity of the focus is enough to generate massive quantities of heat." Tess crossed her legs and seemed to lean back into her husband's touch. "That's the whole 'beams of blue light shot from her fingertips' thing you might have heard about."

"Right, but wouldn't shifting from one physical shape to another require enough focus to at least . . . I don't know . . . make her glow or something?"

She gave him a pitying look.

"Magic is something that requires less focus the more often you use it toward the same goal. I mean, if I scrub the kitchen counter every day, it takes me a lot less time and effort than if I only do it once a year, right? So someone who, say, has been shifting between human and fox forms for twenty-odd years probably sees it as second nature by now. I mean, she wouldn't even have to sweat. Just picture the new form and there it is."

Quinn rubbed the bridge of his nose and wondered if he could get the concierge at his hotel to locate some aspirin for him when he got back. And then he'd wash it down with every tiny minibar bottle of whiskey he could get his hands on. "Right. So I'm an idiot, and she's a wizard with a bushy tail."

"Yes and no. You may very well be an idiot, but she's nothing like a wizard. Foxwomen are reputed to have very specific powers, so I doubt she could just pick up a spellbook and start casting, or use any magical power she wanted. I'm betting she's limited to shifting."

"And how many Foxwomen have you met in person?"

"Two."

"Thanks, I'm reassured."

"Good." De Santos broke in, his voice a clear indication that he'd finished with the discussion. He reached into his pocket and withdrew a square of folded paper. "This is Cassidy's contact information. I suggest the two of you get started as soon as possible. She's only slightly easier to convince of something than her grandmother."

Quinn took the paper with a sigh, looked at it, then looked back at De Santos. "I haven't known you long enough for you to hate me this much, boyo."

De Santos threw back his head and laughed, which Quinn found oh so reassuring. "I don't hate you, Quinn. In fact, I think you're going to find your time with Cassidy Poe to be very rewarding."

Ten

Cassidy knocked on her cousin's door just as her cell phone started beeping "Ride of the Valkyries." Sighing, she flipped the thing open and lifted it to her ear. "Good morning, Nana."

The door swung inward and Miranda—who answered almost exclusively to Randy—waved her into the apartment with much rolling of the eyes. She must have heard Cassidy say "Nana." Adele and Randy shared a mutually satisfying love-dislike relationship. Calling it hate would go too far, but the less time they spent in each other's company, the happier the entire family was. That's what came of Adele playing favorites with her grandchildren. She made it no secret that she felt the human one was a bit of a disappointment, and Randy reacted with a very mature, if unspoken, "Oh, yeah?"

Cassidy let Randy take the bakery bag she offered and shut the door behind her. She followed her cousin through the disheveled living room and over to the island separating it from the kitchen, all the while listening to the third lecture her grandmother had chosen to deliver in the last twelve hours.

"I know, Nana," she said, pulling out a stool and sliding onto it while Randy set a cup of coffee in front of her. She mouthed a heartfelt "thank you" and gulped gratefully. A full-fledged caffeine addict, Cassidy could barely manage to face a shower without coffee, let alone one of Adele's lectures. "Again, I'm sorry, but the Council was very understanding and no one even mentioned my clothes. I think things went fairly well."

She looked up and met Randy's expression of amusement with a grimace. Sometimes she envied her cousin for *not* being Nana's "favorite." All being the favorite seemed to get her were biting lectures and much too much attention to her personal life.

"I realize that, Nana, and I promise I'm going to take this very seriously." She paused to sip her coffee and listen to more ranting. "Of course not. You know I disagree with the entire concept of Unveiling at this time. I'll find out whatever I can for the Council, but that's the end of it."

Randy snickered, set down her mug and dug through a drawer, coming out with a bread knife that she used to dissect two of the bagels Cassidy had brought. She popped one into the toaster oven and bent to rummage in the refrigerator. She held up a tub of cream cheese and mouthed a question. Cassidy shook her head and pointed to the butter dish.

"Nana." Cassidy rubbed her forehead and flipped Randy the finger when her cousin delivered the butter, a small plate, and a quiet "nyah-nyah-nyah-nyah-nyah" in the background. "Yes, Nana. I understand." Pause. "Yes, I promise. Yes." More eye-rolling. "Fine. You, too. Bye."

"And how is the Queen of the Universe this fine Saturday morning?" Randy plunked the golden-brown bagel down on Cassidy's plate and stuck the second in the toaster.

"Fine. She said to tell you hello."

"Liar."

"Okay, maybe not. But she should have."

"Put down the crop and step away from the deceased equine, cuz. I'm not crying into my city roast." Randy grabbed a jar of strawberry jam to doctor her bagel. "But I am curious what bee got into her bonnet today. She usually waits until after brunch to harangue you on the weekends."

"Ugh. You don't want to know. It's political crap."

"Hey, just because I'm not the one in the family with a tendency to get furry doesn't mean I don't care about the politics. If I need to chain myself to an iron fence to protest for Other suffrage, I'm all for it. Just let me make sure the leg irons won't chafe. I hate chafing."

"Randy—"

"No, really. It drives me crazy. I won't even use chafing dishes on Thanksgiving . . ."

Cassidy swallowed a bite of bagel. "Ha-ha. I see your career in standup is really beginning to take off."

"I'm in negotiations with the networks."

Grabbing the carafe a split second before her cousin, Cassidy refilled her coffee cup, then relented and topped off Randy's, as well. "Well, I suppose it's silly not to tell you, since if I screw this up, it's likely to be all over the news."

"What is?"

"Last night at the Council meeting—"

"The Council of Others? Since when do you sit in on that kaffeeklatsch?"

"Since I got an imperial summons from Nana."

"Okay, so what happened last night?"

Cassidy sighed and leaned her chin on her palm. "The Others in Europe think we need to Unveil within the next few days."

Randy's brows shot up over the rim of her mug. "That's a hell of a revelation."

"Tell me about it. And that wasn't the half of it." She summarized the news about the vampire's kidnapped mistress, the religious wackos, and their spread to closer environs. When she was done, Randy gave a long, low whistle.

"Wow. I'm sure the Council was thrilled by that bulletin."

"Right. Just as thrilled as the Faerie Queen when she threatened to toast us for insulting her nephew two years ago."

Cassidy remembered the mess that had been. The Fae weren't supposed to enter the human world without the Queen's permission, but somehow the Council of Others had ended up the fall guy in that one. Of course, no one had ever accused the Fae of being logical.

Randy dusted off her fingers and pushed away her plate to lean her elbows on the counter. "So how did a nice girl like you get mixed up in the hoopla?"

"A freak genetic accident. Don't think I'm not bitter that you aren't hip deep in this with me."

Randy grinned like a Cheshire cat. "That is why I'm glad to be my daddy's little girl, cuz. His sister was nice and all, but I wouldn't take her genes on a bet."

"Thanks for rubbing it in." Cassidy scowled. Randy's father and her mother had been siblings, though Adele viewed her human son with a sort of bemused apathy. When she'd been younger, Cassidy had instinctively tried to make up for it by loving her uncle fiercely, as if she could somehow replace Adele's missing affection. Uncle Matthew had just smiled and told her she had a heart as big as her mother's, but that he'd made peace with it years ago.

Cassidy thought she'd gotten over her teenage resentment of the differences between herself and her cousin, but every once in a while she harbored a secret wish that the DNA that made a Foxwoman could pass along the paternal as well as maternal lines. Then even if she had to be in this mess, Randy would have to join her. Instead, since Randy was the daughter of Adele's human son, the jerk was excluded from the family legacy.

"So, once again, all this involves you how?"

Cassidy sighed. "Apparently, I've become an expert on cultural relations and the growth and impact of fringe cultural groups."

"Didn't that happen when you got your Ph.D. from NYU?"

"You're not helping."

"Why should I start now?" Randy slapped her hand over the top of Cassidy's coffee cup and slid it out of her reach. "Spill, fuzzbutt."

Cassidy grumbled. "Nana's years of uncontrolled bragging have convinced the Council that they should consult me for my 'expert opinion' on whether these Light of Truth people really are over here, and if so, what sort of threat we're looking at. And I got the impression they might ask about the possible consequences for the American Other community if the Europeans do actually come out of the closet."

"You mean out of the crypt and the kennel, unless the

bogeyman is real, since he's the only thing I remember hearing lives in closets. And if he is real, by the way, please don't tell me." Randy pursed her lips. "So in your expert opinion, what are the possible consequences?"

"Do the Salem witch trials ring any bells?"

Randy looked serious for the first time since she'd opened her front door. "Do you really think it would be that bad?"

"What do you think?" Cassidy shook her head and smiled without humor. "People who claim to be Wiccan are still fighting custody battles over their kids when an ex claims they're unfit to parent. How do you think a human judge would react to a parent who actually *could* cast a hex if she tried? And do you think a human parent wouldn't protest to a school board if he found out his daughter's biology teacher was a werewolf? When the only thing most humans know about lycanthropy is what they get from midnight re-showings of *The Howling*? Humans would be bringing torches and pitchforks back into style before the week was out."

Randy sat for a moment in silence, then pursed her lips and shrugged. "Well, in Manhattan, they wouldn't. I mean, where's the sense of style in that? Pitchforks are so not trendy. But I think I do have a Maglite and a fondue fork in the junk drawer."

"You grew up knowing about the Others, Randy. You're *related* to some of them. You've seen that we're not homicidal freaks of nature. But you're not the average human."

"True. No one's ever accused me of being average. And of course your freakishness has nothing to do with homicide. Occasional bunnycide, but I prefer not to think about that."

Cassidy ignored the smart-assed remark. "Humans like you are so far in the minority, I don't think your existence is even statistically significant. Ninety-nine point nine percent of the human population in this country is going to be running through the streets screaming that the sky is falling. And even if this starts with a bunch of religious fundamentalists, I'm pretty confident the nonfundamentalists won't be in a hurry to disagree. How will you feel when they start rounding up me and Nana?"

"Can I have time to think about the Nana half of that question?"

"And even if by some miracle the zealots don't come after us, I'm pretty certain the scientists will," she continued, on a roll now. "We'll be the next great lab rats. When they discover we heal hundreds of times faster than them, they'll vivisect us just to see what happens. They'll try to decode our DNA and use it to make a profit. We'll be rounded up for scientific studies and have about as much right to protest it as the average chimpanzee."

"Cassidy—"

"And the military will be all over us when they find out Others can do things ordinary soldiers can't. We're stealthier than humans, so we'd make great scouts and spies. We can take more damage, so we're the perfect cannon fodder. And we're stronger and do more damage in hand-to-hand combat, so we'll become the soldier of the future. But we won't need to enlist. We'll be drafted, and because we're not human, the laws that protect them from that kind of treatment won't apply to us."

"Well," Randy finally said. "Aren't you just a bright little ray of sunshine?"

"What about when they come for you?" Cassidy wasn't in a joking mood anymore. "No one is gonna believe that being related to a monster doesn't make you one, too."

Randy shifted on her stool. Apparently, this was something she'd never thought about before. To her, Others were normal, and she'd never considered what it meant that most humans didn't agree. "All they need to do is watch me for a while, and they'll see that I don't sprout a tail on the full moon."

"Ever try to prove you're *not* something? It's like trying to sled uphill. Just doesn't happen."

"So what are you going to do, then?"

"What can I do? I'm going to try to find out what the Council wants to know. And I'm going to have to start by dealing with that Neanderthal furball again."

"Ooh, ouch. I guess the famously suave Don Rafael really got your goat with this request, huh?"

Cassidy frowned. "What do you mean?"

"You just called the head of the Council a 'Neanderthal furball.' I thought you might be a bit miffed with him."

Cassidy felt her skin begin to heat. "No. I mean . . . I wasn't talking about Rafael De Santos."

Randy looked intrigued. "Then who's the Neanderthal furball you were talking about?"

Her blush deepened. "No one."

Randy grabbed her cousin's mug again and grinned like a loon. "Ah-ah. I sense a story here, cuz, and I think this one is a hell of a lot more interesting than the politics of the preternatural. Spill."

Why, oh why hadn't Nana waited to call her until after brunch? Then Cassidy would have already been gone from Randy's apartment and her cousin never would have heard this story.

"I've got nothing to spill," she said, hunching her shoulders and squirming in her seat. "I wasn't talking about anyone. It was, you know, metaphorical. I . . . I have . . . a lot of conservative people to work with on this. That's all."

"Uh-uh. Not buying it." Randy lifted the coffee over her head where her shorter cousin couldn't reach it and pressed. "You distinctly mentioned a figure of the male persuasion. So who is he?"

"No one."

" 'No one' has never made a woman blush like that. Tell me. Now."

"No!"

"Cassidy, spill your guts this very moment, or I swear to God, I am dumping this Dominican blend right down the sink and making you drink instant decaf every weekend for a year."

Cassidy twitched, watching her mug tilt to a precarious angle over the kitchen sink, and crumbled. "He's just a man. One of the Europeans who came to meet with the Council. It's no big deal."

" 'No big deal' doesn't have you wriggling around like a cheerleader on prom night." Randy righted the mug, but she didn't move it away from the sink. "What's his name?"

"I don't remember." Cassidy saw the coffee start to trickle from the cup and shouted, "Quinn! It's Sullivan Quinn. Damn it, give me my coffee."

"Not yet. So he's European, and his name is Quinn. Irish?"

Cassidy nodded.

"Hm. And he both got you riled up over the cause and did something that made you blush at the very mention of him. This is interesting news, coming from my dear nunlike cousin who hasn't gotten laid since the Carter administration."

"Randy, I was four during the Carter administration."

"You know what I mean." Randy's expression turned thoughtful. "Cousin who lives like a prioress. Adorable Irish Furby. Hmm . . ." Randy tapped her chin, her brow furrowed and eyes twinkling. "Hey, did you see him naked?"

Cassidy's blush went from a slow burn to a five-alarm blaze and Randy's laugh choked off in disbelief.

"You did! You saw him naked!"

Dropping her head, Cassidy pounded her skull against the counter and wished for a great, gaping hole in the floor to swallow her up.

Randy jumped to her feet, plunked the coffee mug on the counter, and did a dance like her linoleum was an end zone and she'd just made the winning touchdown.

"Cassidy Emilia, I am so proud of you!" She squealed and dashed around the counter to hug her cousin, who sat stiff as stone on her bar stool. "I suppose it's too much to hope that he saw you naked, too?"

By now, Cassidy was certain the color of her face roughly matched the color of her cranberry sweater. And Randy had no trouble telling what that meant.

"He did! Rock ON! Score one for the Cassidy! The last virgin in New York has bitten the dust! Woo-hoo!"

"Oh, for God's sake, Randy," Cassidy snapped, grabbing her coffee and cradling it to her chest with a scowl. "I did *not* have sex with him. I only met the man last night."

The touchdown dance came to an abrupt halt, and Randy frowned. "So? Why didn't you have sex?"

"Because I was too busy running away so that he couldn't take a friggin' chunk out of me for dinner, okay?"

Randy crossed her arms over her chest. "You ran away from an adorable Irishman who wanted to see you naked?"

"How do you know he's adorable?"

"Weren't you listening before? He's an Irishman, and he made you blush."

Cassidy rolled her eyes and lied through her teeth. "He is not adorable. And anyway, he didn't exactly seem to want to whisper sweet nothings in my ear."

"To hell with sweet nothings. Dirty little somethings are my choice any day of the week."

"Then you go ahead and ask him to say them to you."

"I'm not the one he wants, now am I?"

"I'm sure it wasn't me he wanted, either. I just happened to be there when testosterone poisoning killed that last brain cell."

Randy snorted. "You just happened to be there and naked."

"Oh, for God's sake. It's another long story, okay?"

Randy darted back into the kitchen, grabbed the coffeepot and topped off her cousin's mug. "Good. I'll start a new pot while you tell me all about it."

After barely doing justice to his second breakfast, Quinn slid his key card into the lock and let himself back into his hotel suite, fully intending to brood over the events of the last fifteen or so hours.

Ireland was full of curses, or at least the stories of

them, and he could think of no other logical explanation for the fact that he'd discovered the female he wanted above all others three thousand miles and two species away from his home. And not only was the object of his obsession not Irish and not Lupine, but after last night, he was lucky she was *not* pressing charges.

Feck.

He tossed his key onto the entry table and stalked over to the phone. He needed a distraction from himself just now, and he knew for certain the one thing that would provide it.

Ten seconds later, he listened to the double ring at the other end of the line and waited for an answer.

"And what the hell do you want?"

The greeting startled a laugh out of him. "Is that how your mother taught you to answer a telephone, Michael Patrick Sheehan?"

"No, it's how you did," his cousin shot back. "I thought you were in America and safely out of our fur for days yet."

"I am. But does that mean a man can't call home to talk to his sainted mum?"

Michael snorted into the receiver. "Don't let her hear you talking about her that way, boyo, or you'll find your arse tossed clear across Dublin center."

"Is she around, then?"

"Aunt Molly? Sure, she's around somewhere, but she'll be far too busy to waste time on the likes of you. There's dinner to manage. Ow!"

Quinn heard the sharp smack of his mother's palm on his cousin's head and grinned. A moment later, Michael was grumbling something in the background and Molly Quinn's sweet, delicate voice came clearly over the phone line. And she'd have smacked him, too, if she ever heard him describe her that way.

"Sullivan, darling, I was hoping you might ring us. How do you find New York?"

"Noisy," he said. "And crowded. Lord, I thought Dublin was getting bad, then I came here. I'll never speak a harsh word of her again."

Molly laughed. "Of course you will. The very next time you're stuck in traffic down by the university. Now, tell me everything. Is it true what they say about the movie stars on every corner?"

"Not so far." He heard his mother's little sigh of disappointment and hurried to reassure her. "But I'm nearly certain I saw Robert De Niro walking into a restaurant the other day."

"Oh, how lovely. And does he look as he does in his films?"

Quinn heard a brief rustling sound, then his father's voice in the background, demanding, "How much time have you been spending watching Robert De Niro, Molly Margaret Sheehan?"

"I haven't been a Sheehan since 1967, and you know it, Declan."

"Just want to make certain you remember, mate."

Quinn laughed at the familiar exchange. God, it was good to talk to his family. "Does Da have a minute, Mum? I'd like to fill him in on the first meeting."

"He does, love, but don't keep him too long. We'll be eating in a few minutes."

"I won't."

He waited for the receiver to be exchanged and Declan Quinn's deep, familiar greeting. "Well, then, son, how are they taking it?"

"About like we expected," Quinn said. "They're not thrilled about the idea, but they might not have too much choice."

He summarized the news of the Light of Truth situation for his father and got the reaction he expected, which would have earned a good, swift smack from Molly, had she overheard.

"Shortsighted idiots! Do they think we're doing this for laughs? It's not as if the members of our Council got together and said, 'You know, mate, I've decided I'm bored. Let's feck up the world and scare all the humans into killing us! Whaddaya say?'" He swore again.

"You and I know that, Da, but I'm afraid a few of the Yanks still need convincing."

"If anyone can do that, the *guth* of the Black Glen can." The pride Declan felt in his son and his pack was obvious. It was something he'd inherited from his father and passed on to his son, just as he had the title and the job. "You just need to find the right way to tell the story."

"I'm working on that." He paused, weighed his next words, then spoke cautiously. "I have a feeling there's one mind I need to convince first. If I manage that, it might be the key to the others."

"The head of the Council, d'you mean? I hear he's not bad. For a cat."

"Actually, no. It's not a Council member at all, though other members of the family have apparently been on for generations. It's a sort of outside consultant they've brought in to deal with the situation."

Declan knew his son well, and it didn't take him more than a second to understand why Quinn was beating around the bush. When he spoke again, his amusement was plain. "Pretty, is she?"

Quinn blew out a long breath. "She's gorgeous."

His father laughed, the rumbling sound echoing over the line. "Tell me about her."

"She's a tiny little thing," he began, recalling her features to his mind and trying not to be surprised by how fast and clearly they came. "No more than a couple of inches over five feet, but you'd be surprised at how strong she is, how resilient."

"I don't think I would, son. Remember, I've been mated to your mother for nearly forty years."

"She's an anthropologist. A university professor, and her mind is an intimidating thing," he continued. "Sharp as tacks. Just like her tongue."

"Used the edge of it on your hide, did she?"

"More than once. She drives me crazy, but I can't seem to mind. I'm too busy trying to sniff her." He raked a hand through his hair and began to pace restlessly in front of the wide hotel window. "God, her scent drives me crazy. It's like I've lost my bloody mind. That's never happened to me before."

Quinn frowned. He couldn't remember getting this worked up over a woman since puberty. He had taken one look at Cassidy Poe and twenty-two years of experience had bolted, leaving him with all the finesse of a thirteen-year-old at a school dance. It made no sense.

Not that sense had anything to do with attraction. Quinn was man—and wolf—enough to know that.

"Well, now, that's a fine thing to hear." Declan's brogue thickened, and Quinn could almost hear the crack of his father's grin splitting his face in two. "When will you be bringing her to visit? Molly will want time to make everything just so."

Quinn stopped and scowled into the phone. "Who

said anything about bringing her to meet you? Christ, Da, I only just set eyes on the woman last night. You're being a bit premature with the welcome to the family, don't you think?"

"No, I don't. This is an important moment for your pack and for your family. A man only takes a mate once in his life, Sullivan."

A mate. Sweet Christ.

Cassidy Poe was his mate.

That thump he heard was the floor dropping out from under him. He was Lupine, a werewolf, and like the animals they were named for, werewolves mated for life. His people knew that at some point in every Lupine's life, fate would take him by the nose and lead him straight toward the sweetest scent he'd ever encountered, and that would be it. It was a day most of them looked forward to—but did it have to be now?

Last night he'd been too distracted by his hormones to realize the significance of his reaction to the elusive Foxwoman. His brain had been too obsessed with following her scent to recognize why that particular scent had grabbed him by the balls and led him straight into his honeysuckled destiny.

What was he supposed to do now?

Panic.

"Ah, I'm sorry, Da," he rushed to say, throwing frantic glances around the room as if a savior might appear out of thin air. Instead, his gaze fell on his cell phone, and he did something he'd been raised never to do. He lied to his father. "I've got a call coming in on the mobile. It's probably about the Lightheads. I'd better take it. Give my love to Mum. I'll call again when I can."

He hung up before his father could say another word

and headed straight for the bathroom. A cold shower would have done him a world of good just then, but he settled for running the coldest water he could manage into the marble sink and splashing it over his face. Here he'd finally found himself a mate, and his own father had realized it before he had. Perfectly humiliating.

He had to admit the first meeting with his mate hadn't quite gone as he'd always envisioned. He'd behaved like a total savage. A barbaric cretin. A horny dog, for Christ's sake. It didn't matter that he was one. What mattered was that he might very well have blown his chances with her before they'd even been properly introduced.

How could this be happening? Not that Quinn hadn't wanted it to happen. He'd expected it to happen sooner rather than later. He had recently turned thirty-five and wanted to have cubs while he was still young enough to play with them, but this wasn't how it was supposed to go. In fact, if someone had put the question to him, he supposed he would have said his mate would be a lot like him. Irish, probably, and Lupine, certainly. That was to be expected. And even if he hadn't mated with another Black Glen, there were other packs in Ireland to choose from. Then he would have had cute, little purebred pups that would have made his pack and his father proud.

He didn't want to paint his father as a racist. It was more that the elder Quinn had a deep sense of the traditions of his family line. Declan Quinn had held the title of *guth* of his pack just like all his fathers before him as far back as the stories he handed down could tell. He had handed that title down to Quinn, and he expected

Quinn to hand it down to *his* son. And nowhere in that lineage could Quinn recall ever hearing about a Fox-woman. Quinn's father just assumed, as Quinn had up until a few minutes ago, that his son would mate with a Lupine as Quinn men always did and have a Lupine son to carry on the name of the next Black Glen *guth*.

Nothing in Lupine society held a more important place than pups. Pups represented the future of their race, another generation that humans had not suc-ceeded in destroying, another lifetime of the fall of broad, furry paws on the floor of the earth's dwindling forests. It meant another chance to save what was left of those forests from the encroachment of man, and another generation who would raise their voices to the moon to sing the glorious songs of their race.

Pups meant life, and to get pups, a man required a mate. And in one of the least amusing cosmic jokes he'd ever heard, it seemed that fate had chosen Cassidy Poe as his mate.

Quinn stalked back into the sitting room and paced from the entry to the windows and back again, hands deep in his pockets and a frown heavy on his face.

How much did it matter to him that Cassidy wasn't pack? Not all that much, when he thought about it. He had to admit it would be simpler to mate with a Lupine. There would be no doubts or questions or explanations required. He would live a quiet, orderly life and never have to worry about how the combination of Lupine and Vulpine DNA would battle it out to leave him with pups or kits or some new blend of the two. If Quinn were to mate with a Lupine, no one would question his choice.

But if it meant having Cassidy Poe, Quinn wouldn't mind answering a few questions. It seemed a small enough price to pay.

He stopped in front of the window and looked out at the city below him. The revelation of the source of his attraction to Cassidy flummoxed him and reassured him and excited him. It meant the beginning of a whole new stage of his life, one he wasn't shy about admitting he hoped included an awful lot of naked time with his foxy mate.

And that brought him back full circle to the root of his current problem. How in the world was he supposed to get within twenty feet of said foxy mate when the last time he'd seen her, he'd forced her out of her clothes, chased her around a rooftop, and practically fucked her on the cold, hard floor of another man's greenhouse?

When he thought about it that way, Quinn winced. It sounded so much worse laid out in black and white. He wouldn't let himself within five city blocks of Cassidy, if he were in her shoes, and that was bad on several levels. First of all, it made it a little tough to have all that sex he was looking forward to, and on top of that, it put a crimp in the plans of the head of the American Council. It was a bit of a challenge to complete an important political assignment when your partner had a tendency to run away and call the police when you got near her.

Bloody hell. He'd bollixed things up royally, hadn't he? It was completely unlike him. Quinn had spent most of his life either acting as an ambassador or being groomed for it. He'd learned early on that the key to being *guth* was to keep cool, keep quiet, and keep control, but he'd lost all three as soon as he'd smelled that honeysuckle.

Well, he decided, squaring his shoulders and grabbing his key card and his coat, it was time to regain the legendary composure of the Quinn men. And he could think of no better way to do that than to take the bull by the horns and beard the Foxwoman in her den.

Eleven

A buildup of frustrated aggression sent Cassidy into her bathroom to wreak vengeance on the unsuspecting grout of her bathroom tiles. Three and a half hours after leaving Randy's apartment, she stood in her bathtub, barefoot, wearing her oldest, bleach-stained yoga pants and tank top, wielding a scrub brush with the fury of an avenging angel.

She had started off thinking that if she kept busy doing chores around the apartment, she might be able to keep her mind off Sullivan Quinn for at least a few seconds. When doing the laundry hadn't worked, she'd moved on to vacuuming. Then to cleaning out the refrigerator. Then laying siege to the soap scum in her shower. None of it had helped.

Groaning in frustration, she let her scrubbing arm drop to her side. This wasn't getting her anywhere in dealing with aggressive, Irish Lupines, overbearing relatives, or the end of the world as she knew it.

She stepped out of the tub and cranked on the shower with unnecessary force. The hard spray of water sluiced the suds from the tiles and sent a wave of foam swirling toward the drain. She wished she could wash away the last twenty-four hours so easily.

"And that's what makes you a big fat liar, Cassidy Emilia," she muttered to herself, cutting off the water and packing her cleaning supplies back under the sink.

She scowled as the cabinet door snapped shut. Her subconscious was getting to be a real pain in the ass. Next thing you knew it would be trying to force her to admit she'd enjoyed those few minutes pinned under Sullivan Quinn's gorgeous body more than she'd ever enjoyed anything in her life. And she was *not* ready to take that step.

Her overstuffed living room sofa gave a soft whoosh of protest as she threw herself down onto it to brood.

Cassidy considered herself a pretty average woman. Sure, there were a few days a month when even hot wax and an industrial-strength pair of tweezers couldn't make a dent in her excess body hair, but even that seemed normal. She'd never known anything different.

She'd grown up in a world where everyone shifted . . . or so it had seemed. Her parents and her grandparents had been prominent members of Other society, so she'd been constantly surrounded by were-folk and witches, vampires and changelings. Adele had, of course, always held court over the nonhuman population of Manhattan, and before they had died, her parents had made a significant place for themselves in the social realm of Washington, D.C. Sometimes Cassidy speculated that if her parents had survived their last diplomatic trip, Adele would have urged her to relocate to Atlanta, just to be sure the family had the entire Eastern Seaboard covered.

But she would never know, because her parents had finally found a conflict they couldn't negotiate themselves out of. They had been killed during the vampire clan wars that raged in the Mid-Atlantic States in the early eighties, and Cassidy had been whisked back up north to Adele's elegant brownstone. When she'd been in elementary school, her favorite playmates had been Randy and the little boy down the street who had to be reminded not to catch the Frisbee with his teeth. In high school, she'd passed notes during study hall with a girl who took advantage of the 1980s fad for hats and big hair to cover the small buds of horns that tended to peep out from beneath her brown curls. Cassidy had never met Allison's father, but it didn't take a genius to spot satyr blood in someone's family tree.

Suffice it to say, Cassidy had met just about every form of Other there was to meet, from shifters to sorcerers. She'd gone to her senior prom with a changeling, and in college she'd had a mad crush on the great-grandson of a stone giant. He'd been a great linebacker and a lousy conversationalist and had moved on from their breakup to a lucrative contract with the NFL.

The thing was, all that was just . . . normal. It was totally average for an Other in today's world. In a lot of ways, Cassidy wasn't that different from your run-of-the-mill human Manhattanite. She worked, she paid taxes, she cursed the city traffic, and she scoffed at the idea of getting good pizza anywhere outside the five boroughs.

So how had she ended up tangled in the biggest crisis to confront her people since the last of the witchcraft trials?

Cassidy propped her feet up on the coffee table and

contemplated her rose-polished toenails. Personally, she was inclined to blame it all on Sullivan Quinn.

Irrational? Sure. But satisfying all the same.

That's not exactly fair, her conscience niggled, and her head flopped back onto the sofa cushion behind her. She let out a heartfelt groan, blinking up at her blank, white ceiling.

She knew perfectly well that her entire reaction to Sullivan Quinn bordered on obsessive. She couldn't explain it, and she sure as hell didn't seem to be able to help it. Part of her didn't really want to.

And there lay the root of all her problems. She had enjoyed those moments on the roof. A lot. She'd enjoyed them more than she could remember enjoying anything in a long, long time.

Damn it. It was as if her body were trying to get revenge for all the sex she'd lost out on in the last six months. Okay, nine months. Definitely no more than twelve. But she hadn't been committing social suicide on purpose. She'd had good reasons for turning down the men who had asked her out. Most of them had been nice guys, but none of them really interested her. It hadn't seemed like a big deal to offer a polite "no, thanks" when none of them had made her skin tingle.

Sullivan Quinn made her tingle. Hell, he practically made her burst into flames. The man had a direct line straight to her sex drive, and that had never happened with anyone before. It made Cassidy more than a little uneasy.

Despite the shameless begging of her hormones, she had no intention of getting involved with a diplomat with wolfish tendencies and an Irish brogue. She'd grown up with diplomats. She knew the dangers involved in trying to keep the peace in the world of the Others, and she wasn't willing to put herself through that again. Even when someone in that line of work did manage to live to a ripe old age, matters of business always took precedence over matters of the heart, and Cassidy had spent enough of her life playing second fiddle.

Her parents, as doting and devoted as they had been, had viewed their jobs as more of a calling than a duty, and even their daughter couldn't compete with a higher purpose. Diplomacy had been their lives' work, and they were dead because of it. They had been killed during an assignment playing negotiator between two powerful vampire clans who hadn't particularly cared if they reached a peaceful settlement to their dispute. But if it hadn't been that mission, it would have been another. Sticking a nose into the business of creatures who didn't want it there and had the power to rip it off your face was hazardous to your health.

Once Cassidy had come to live with Adele, her grandmother had spent more time in meetings with Other politicians than at parent-teacher nights. It was like a family curse. There were days—especially yesterday when she'd found herself playing a reluctant negotiator—when Cassidy could feel the grasping tentacles of diplomacy twining around her own ankles. She wasn't going down without a fight, though, and Sullivan Quinn looked like a slippery slope if she'd ever seen one.

She groaned again and pushed herself up, contemplating a dust-bunny massacre in her bedroom and maybe color-coding her wardrobe. She only made it about halfway across the room when her front door buzzer rang. Figuring it had to be either Randy or her grandmother, she considered not answering it. Then again, she wouldn't put it past them to start buzzing other apartments to find out if she was in. She winced, remembering the last time that had happened. The satyr down the hall, who was the only Other she knew of in the building, had offered to forget about reporting her to the super if she'd come in to look at his etchings.

Turning on her heel, she stalked over to her door and pressed the button for the intercom. "Yes?"

"Sullivan Quinn, Miss Poe. Are you ready to get to work?"

A long moment of stunned silence was followed by her oh so articulate, "Uh . . ."

"Not to be rude, Miss Poe, but I'm not wearing my fur coat this afternoon and it's a tad chilly out here at the moment. Do you think you might let me up so we can talk?"

What she thought was, *Can I have some time to put on my little red riding hood?* What she said was, "Certainly, Mr. Quinn. I'm in five-seventeen."

"I know."

She unlocked the front door, then looked down at her ratty old clean-the-apartment clothes and bolted for her closet.

The doorbell to her apartment rang three and a half minutes later, about the time Cassidy was sprinting back toward it, tugging a cotton sweater over her head. Lucky for her, she knew her floor plan well enough that she didn't need to see to make it from one room to the other. She skidded to a stop in front of the door, smoothed the hem of the sweater into place, and checked to be sure she'd zipped up the jeans she'd shimmied into in five seconds flat. She took a deep breath, said a fervent prayer against self-humiliation, and tugged open her door.

She should have worn a blindfold. Maybe that would have helped keep her pupils from dilating and her salivary glands from kicking into overdrive. Sullivan Quinn looked even better than she remembered, and she remembered damned good. His coat was open to the cold, which she figured was because of the infamously revved-up Lupine metabolism, and beneath it he wore a thin cashmere sweater the color of good burgundy. His jeans were just tight enough to be interesting, and his hair looked mussed and rumpled from the wind. She swallowed hard against the drool.

Then she got a whiff of his scent, dark and musky and evergreen, and she decided only complete unconsciousness would have spared her from the magnetism of his presence.

"Good afternoon, Miss Poe."

The rough, liquid gravel of his voice washed over her and did unspeakable things to her nerve endings. She exerted great force of will to keep her eyelids from drifting shut. "Mr. Quinn. I wasn't expecting to see you so soon."

"I could hardly stay away." He flashed her a charming grin and pushed his way inside. He didn't actually have to push all that hard. As soon as he took a step toward her, she took a reflexive step back until he was inside her apartment. She realized she looked like an idiot standing there holding on to the doorknob like the end of a rope in a game of tug-of-war.

She snapped her mouth closed, the door shut simultaneously, and she turned to face her visitor, her arms crossed over her chest. "So what can I do for you, Mr. Quinn?"

His expression of friendly relaxation shifted almost imperceptibly at her words. She thought she saw a flash of something darker there, more Lupine. Something almost like hunger. But even if the fleeting glimpse made her belly tumble and her heart flutter like a teenaged girl's, it was over so quickly, she couldn't have said whether it had even happened outside of her very vivid imagination.

Vivid when it came to this particular Lupine, anyway.

"Actually, there is something," he said, in a voice so mild and so utterly nonthreatening she almost looked over his shoulder to see if it were coming from someone else. "You can accept my apology. I behaved inexcusably last night, and if there is anything I could do or say to make it up to you, you have only to name it."

To call her stunned would have been doing Cassidy's reaction to his words a disservice. She was speechless.

Unfortunately, her hormones chose that moment to pipe up with a truckload of ideas about things he could do to make it up to her—some of them involving positions she wasn't even sure were anatomically possible—and the heat rushed to her face like a volcanic eruption.

God, she was doomed.

Quinn watched her, seeing her skin bloom poppy-red and her eyes glint yellow-gold. Add a nice green bow and he'd look forward to opening her on Christmas morning.

Right now, though, she didn't look as if she'd appreciate the sentiment. He was going to have to be very careful in wooing this mate of his.

Cassidy cleared her throat in the quiet of her apartment and fussed for a moment as she engaged the locks on her front door. When she finally turned around, her face looked flushed but otherwise expressionless, and her sharp little chin jutted into the air at an even higher angle than usual. She had also wrapped her arms around herself, which he was sure she wouldn't have done if she'd been able to see how it pushed her breasts together and lifted them up to him like offerings.

"I think it would probably be best if we simply forgot about it, Mr. Quinn," she said, her voice cool and calm and very at odds with the sharp tang of nervous tension he could smell on her skin. "I expect that from now on we can keep our interaction strictly on a business level."

For a moment, that tone of voice made her sound so much like her grandmother that she almost won the war then and there. He couldn't in his wildest fantasies imagine snuggling up to Dame Adele.

"Well, I'm not so certain about that," he said. "In my experience, I've always found cooperation to be a lot easier among people who get to know each other than among those who try to keep themselves distanced from their partners."

"I wouldn't go so far as to call us partners. We've been assigned to work on a project together, but that's it."

He aimed for an ingenuous smile and knew he'd be lucky if it didn't come out feral. "But it doesn't have to be that way, does it?"

He saw her eyes narrow and thought she could teach suspicion to a customs agent.

"Oh, I don't know. I find I have a hard time making friends with men who attack me before we've been properly introduced."

He wrestled down his inner beast and reflected on how much easier things were in his pack. If Cassidy had been Black Glen, she would have been his as soon as he managed to pin her on the roof last night. The lines of dominance and submission were clearly drawn among Lupines, but he was beginning to think Fox-women might be as stubbornly independent as their vulpine namesakes. It made him contemplate the consequences of flipping fate an obscene gesture.

"Am I to take it you're not going to be accepting my apology, then?"

"What do you think?"

Her tone was sulky, even downright hostile, but Quinn couldn't smell any real anger on her. The only things marring the sweet musk of honeysuckle and woman were a whiff of embarrassment and the hint of something subtler.

"I think you've every right to be angry with me." He aimed his most charming smile at her, then toned it down when her frown deepened. She required something other than the irresistible-rake tactic. "I behaved like a beast, and I know my own mother would be ashamed to call me her son. I pray you'll have a bit of mercy on me and not mention this to her."

Cassidy stiffened. "I'm not likely to ever meet your mother, Mr. Quinn, but you're an adult. I don't blame the behavior of a grown man on someone who I'm sure taught him better."

"I'm relieved." He made a show of glancing around her apartment, taking in the warm, earthy colors and comfortable furnishings. "You have a lovely home, Cassidy. D'you think you might invite me into it?"

He stood still and tried to project nonthreatening patience while she stared at him for a long moment. He knew very well that she was trying to figure out a way to refuse without sounding rude, and almost sympathized with her when she realized there wasn't one.

"You seem to have invited yourself, *Mr. Quinn*."

Her emphasis on the formality of the address didn't faze him. He had no intention of calling the future mother of his pups by her family name.

"In that case, I'll just invite myself to a seat, shall I?"

She gave in, but wasn't particularly gracious about it. "Fine. Come in and have a seat."

She stepped around him, giving him a wide berth, and led the way farther into her apartment, trailing her enticing scent behind her. He doubted she'd have done that, either, if she'd known how much he enjoyed seeing the feminine sway of her hips beneath snug blue jeans, or the way the smell of her tightened the fit of his own jeans.

She stalked into the living room but chose a chair opposite the sofa where he sat. She kept the low coffee table between them, as if she thought she might need to use the piece of furniture like a lion tamer to fend him off when he got out of line.

Clever girl.

"So why don't you tell me why you're here," she said, her voice tight and laced with impatience. "I have a hard time believing you tracked me down just to apologize."

"You'd be right," he admitted, "though I'm glad enough to offer an apology when it's warranted. Unfortunately, I came on business."

"What sort of business?"

Lord, but she was a hard one. "The sort we discussed last night. The sort with which the leader of your Council asked for our help."

She didn't appear to relax, but she did uncross her arms, and her glare shifted into something more like a concerned frown. "Has something new happened?"

"Earlier today, we had a phone call with Gregor Kasminikov."

Cassidy bolted up in her chair and leaned forward in excitement. "Did he find his mistress? Is she alive?"

"We don't know. They haven't been able to locate her yet," Quinn said, holding her gaze with his own. "But they were able to unearth some information leading to the American cell that they believe gave the original order for Ysabel's kidnapping."

"Where is it?"

"New York."

Cassidy felt as if she'd been poleaxed. She wasn't sure what a poleaxe was, but it sounded like something that could turn her world on its end as easily as that terse answer had.

God, was he serious?

"How did Kasminikov's people figure that out?" she demanded when she could finally speak. Her voice still sounded strangled and hoarse, but she got the words out. "What makes them think the Light of Truth has an operation in New York? I thought that group was based in Germany, or someplace like that."

"They are. And the Mormons are based in Utah, but that doesn't mean you never find them in Des Moines," Quinn retorted. "Gregor's people didn't decide anything. They followed the evidence, which led them to New York."

"What kind of evidence?"

"The kind supplied by a captured member of their organization and the cell phone records he handed over." Sighing as if no one had ever given him this kind of trouble before, Quinn summarized the call he'd been on that morning.

Cassidy took a moment to digest it. "And they're certain it was the group here that ordered the kidnapping? Not one of the European cells?"

"Dead certain. There was a trail of communications and messengers. It all leads right back to New York."

"Shit. So if the orders came from here, do they think that she was brought here?"

Quinn shook his head. "No. Where they took her is an entirely different trail, and one they were much more careful to cover up. Gregor and his men are still searching, but the more time that passes, the more difficult it will be. I don't think the Lightheads were worried about anyone finding out they've been expanding. I think they want us to know."

"Why?"

"So we'll get nervous. The more nervous we get, the more chance there is that some Other somewhere will take it upon himself to do something about them."

"As in . . . kill them?"

He nodded. "And if someone were to strike out, the Lightheads could use it as evidence we're a threat to society at large. Not to mention we would have just given them evidence of our existence that they could broadcast to the world."

Cassidy sighed. "Enough with the pointed looks. You've made a good argument. I'm just not sure that the situation is as black and white as you make it out to be. I understand that we're in a very precarious position at the moment, made more so by Ysabel Mirenow's disappearance. But I'm not certain the Council wouldn't rather explore the possibility of dealing with the source. Why not do something about the Light of Truth, instead of exposing a few millennia worth of secrets?"

"Do something? As in kill them?" Quinn mocked.

She glared. "No. As in, discredit them. Or force them to disband somehow. There must be something."

"I'm afraid it's too late for that. The organization is too large and too diffuse," Quinn said. "The only question now is what you and the Council plan to do about it."

"Do I have to answer that now?" Cassidy groaned.

"That's why you get paid the big bucks, as they say."

She peered at him through her fingers. "You do know I'm a college professor in an unglamorous field, right?"

He shrugged and leaned back into the plump sofa cushions. "I do. Now why don't you use that expertise of yours to tell us where we should be starting this investigation?"

Cassidy shook her head. "Most of the groups I deal with and do research on don't try to hide from me. They figure talking to an academic is almost like advertising. It's not like I'm an archeologist. I don't have to dig things up. I just interview members of cultures and social groups that are still around, and usually, they're not hard to find. They speak out, they have churches or Bible studies, they recruit. Hell, I've found a few good informants by just talking to the people handing out religious tracts on Times Square."

"I don't think that will work with this bunch. At least not until they gain more of a foothold. Gregor may have traced them to New York, but that doesn't mean they're well established as yet. They've made a name in Europe because there are so many of them, but here, I doubt anyone has even heard of them."

Cassidy nodded thoughtfully. "You're right. Which means their big focus at the moment should be recruiting. And as determined as people are in handing out tracts on Times Square, most of them realize there are much better places to reel in people curious about alternate life philosophies."

"Where would you go if you were trying to recruit an army of the gullible and turn them into the zealot warriors of tomorrow?"

"That's easy." Cassidy smiled grimly and pushed to her feet. "I'd go to work."

Twelve

Cassidy tugged open the door to Lerner Hall and stepped out of the chilly winter air. At nine o'clock on a Saturday night, most of the student population of Columbia University had something a lot more exciting to do than hang out in the Student Center, but there were still a few milling around, talking on cell phones or sipping lattes with their friends. Even fewer sat hunched over piles of books, cramming for exams or quizzes or the weeks' worth of reading they should already have done by this stage in the semester. Cassidy made it a point not to check to see if any of those specimens were in her classes.

Quinn walked quietly beside her, sharp eyes taking in their surroundings, including several young coeds who ought to have known better than to wear outfits that skimpy in this weather. Cassidy had to give him credit, though. His gaze skimmed over them with about as much attention as he gave to the new building's comfortably modern architecture.

They paused in front of the elevators, waiting for a car, and Quinn turned back to her with a small smile.

"I admit I hadn't thought that a university in such an

enormous and bustling city would sport something so very collegiate as a student union," he said, "or that it would be a place where sophisticated metropolitan teenagers would care to spend their free time."

Cassidy shrugged and stepped into the elevator when the doors slid open. "A lot of them don't, but they need a place to hold student meetings and events. Clubs need places where they can organize and have access to phones and computers and printing services. After all, what's a good student protest without a few thousand flyers to hand out?"

Quinn laughed and followed her out onto the third floor. "You have a point. Is that what we're looking for? Flyers?"

"Yup."

"Then wouldn't we be better off waiting for a time when there are more students about? Surely no one will be handing out flyers here at this time on a week-end night."

Cassidy led the way through the mostly deserted third floor and pointed out a vast expanse of tiny, metal-doored mailboxes covering the walls. The sea of cubbies was saved from depressing monotony by bulletin boards covered on every square inch with colorful papers, brochures, and flyers.

"They don't have to hang out here, but sooner or later, they all have to pick up their mail," she said, walking over to the closest board and scanning the jumble of folded and torn papers. "If I were trying to recruit students into a cult, this is one of the places I'd start."

He stepped up next to her and smiled. "Clever girl."

For several minutes they remained quiet, each reading through the hundreds of posted bulletins and looking for anything that might offer a clue to the presence of the Lightheads in the city.

Cassidy was skimming over her seventh amateur punk band announcement when she heard Quinn chuckling.

"What's funny?"

He pointed to a shocking pink sheet of paper with a grainy photo of something that might have been more than vaguely pornographic. "The idea of the average broke college student paying a professional escort service, rather than just crashing a party and hoping for the best. At least, that's the way it was when I was at university."

"This is Columbia. You'd be surprised how many young millionaires, children of old billionaires, and child stars are enrolled here. Plus the daughter of the governor, the sons of two Middle Eastern sheiks, and at least three members of titled European aristocracy. Not all of the student population is hurting for beer money."

Cassidy turned back to her own half of the board and tried to wipe the image of what she now knew to be an entirely pornographic photo from her mind. They were here for a reason, and her fantasizing about doing to Quinn what was being done in that picture did not fit the bill.

"Hold on."

Quinn tore a sheet of plain, white copier paper off the board, scanned it quickly and then handed it to Cassidy without speaking. She glanced down at the black typeface and swore.

" 'Free lecture. The Bible and Tomorrow. Come hear renowned lecturer D. Y. Young speak about a new interpretation of history and the impact it will have on our future. Sponsored by Students for Greater Truth.' " Cassidy read the text aloud and swore again.

"Have we found something?"

"Maybe. Read the next line."

Quinn glanced down at the paper and frowned. " 'Refreshments will be served'?"

Still scowling, Cassidy nodded. "First two rules of college students: One, never register for a class before ten A.M. and two, always attend any lecture, event, meeting, or function that offers free food. If a student plans it right, he may never have to see the inside of a dining hall. It's a guarantee there will be butts in the seats."

"Do you suppose they'll be checking student ID cards at the door?"

"Probably not. I don't imagine they care if they're recruiting students or civilians, so long as they're malleable and don't ask too many questions. But even if they do, I have a faculty ID, and faculty get admittance to all university events. I can even bring a guest."

"Ah, lovely. And can I ask what plans you might have for"—he glanced down at the flyer—"Tuesday evening at seven?"

"Why, I think I might just be free," Cassidy said with exaggerated innocence, smiling coyly and batting her eyelashes at him. "I don't suppose you'd like to attend a lecture with me, would you?"

She saw a spark of hunger ignite in Quinn's eyes.

"I can tell you for a fact that I'm free that night," he all but purred. "And I could hardly refuse when such a lovely woman asks me for a date."

"It's not a date. It's business." Cassidy took great care in pulling her calendar out of her purse and making a note on the page for Tuesday night. It kept her from having to look at the werewolf. "We'll meet there on Tuesday before the lecture and make sure we get good seats. It shouldn't be hard to figure out who the organizers are, and once we have that information, we can do a little digging to confirm if they're affiliated with the Light of Truth."

"I'm certain we will, but first we'll go out for a civilized dinner. I've heard of a lovely little restaurant not far from Vircolac that I want to try." He slipped the flyer into his pocket, then placed a hand on the small of her back and guided her back toward the elevators. "I'll pick you up at five. We'll eat, and then we'll go to this lecture. I don't know about you, but I always think better on a full stomach."

Just as Cassidy was about to put an elbow in his ribs, the elevator doors opened and let out three female students. The girls' chatter stopped abruptly when they saw Quinn. Two of them let their jaws drop open as they stared. Quinn only smiled politely and held the door open for them to step out. They barely made it without tripping over themselves, and by the time Cassidy had boarded and the doors closed behind them, she was pretty sure the brunette would have to see a chiropractor. It couldn't be healthy to crane your head around a full one hundred and eighty degrees like that.

"Will that give you enough time to get ready?"

Cassidy stopped staring holes through the doors and glanced back at Quinn. "What are you talking about?"

"Five o'clock on Tuesday. Will that give you enough time after work to get ready?"

"My classes end at three on Tuesdays and Thursdays," she said, then frowned. "Wait. What are we talking about?"

He had the gall to chuckle. "About our date on Tuesday, Cassie love. I'll pick you up at five, we'll have dinner, and then we'll catch the lecture. I thought it a sound enough plan."

"Well, sure, if you forget about the fact that I haven't agreed to go on a date with you."

The elevators deposited them on the first floor and Cassidy made a beeline for the exit, colliding with a student who smelled suspiciously like a gargoyle. He had that particular stony smell they all shared, and bumping into him felt a lot like bumping into a brick wall. Polite as all of his kind, he set her back on her feet and smiled before continuing on with his friends. Quinn caught up a moment later, his long stride eating up the ground she had hurried to cover.

"Think of it as a sacrifice for the greater good."

She pushed open the doors and stepped into the brisk night air. "I'm not sure the good is quite great enough for that kind of sacrifice."

"Tsk, tsk. Shame on you for thinking so ill of your fellow folk, Cassidy." He sounded way too amused for her taste, speaking in that teasing lilt that made her stomach do little flip-flops under her wool coat.

"I'm not thinking ill of anyone. I just think it's better if we keep this relationship strictly professional. After all, we barely know each other."

The excuse sounded lame, even to her. It wasn't like he was her boss, or she his. This wasn't lust in the lunchroom, for Pete's sake. They were two healthy, unattached people, who happened to find each other mouthwatering, going for a nice dinner. How else did people get to know each other if they didn't date?

Lame or not, the excuse was reflexive. Sullivan Quinn

scared her. Not in the sense that she thought he might hurt her. Even last night on the roof when he'd been chasing her down like a gazelle, she hadn't really felt her life was threatened. Her virtue, maybe, but not her life.

No, Quinn scared her in a much more insidious way. He made her want to break her own rules. He made her wonder what would be so bad about getting involved with a man who lived the way her parents had died, enmeshed in the dangerous world of Other politics. Losing her parents had been a blow to Cassidy, had changed the course of her life, and while she had learned to live without them, she never stopped missing them. If she got involved with Sullivan Quinn, would she lose him, too? After all, the last twenty-four hours had shown her with perfect clarity that the role of an Other diplomat hadn't gotten any safer since her parents had died. Would she be able to get over that kind of pain again?

She stepped up to the corner and hailed a cab, which ignored her. She was all too aware of him standing close behind her. So close that she could feel the warmth radiating off him like a furnace. It made her shiver, and even she couldn't think of a way to blame that on the cold.

Raising her arm, she flagged another cab. This one slowed and headed toward the curb. She dropped her arm back to her side and took a deep breath. Quinn drove it right back out of her when he wrapped one strong arm around her from behind and leaned close to let his breath tickle the hair beside her ear.

"I intend to change all that, Cassie love," he growled, low and intimate, and she felt the scrape of his teeth against the delicate shell of her ear. "I'm going to get to know you very well indeed."

Thirteen

Quinn feared he might have pushed Cassidy just a little too hard. She sat silently beside him on the cab ride back to her apartment, staring out the window as the city blocks rolled by.

Normally, he was a man comfortable with silence. He'd learned over the years that sometimes the best way to get information wasn't to ask for it, but to sit patiently and wait for it to present itself. The sort of people who couldn't seem to stand the quiet, who felt compelled to fill it with chatter even when they had nothing to say, those were the sort of people he couldn't understand.

Cassidy, it seemed, was not one of those people.

He was starting to think maybe he should apologize, tell her he hadn't meant to be so bold, but he felt uncomfortable with the lie. He'd meant every syllable of that quiet promise, and the moment he sensed another opportunity, you could lay odds he'd seize that one, as well. But he didn't want his mate upset, and he certainly didn't want her freezing him out.

He shifted in the back seat of the cab and brooded. Again, he thought of how much easier it would be to have a Lupine for a mate, a woman who recognized his intensity and returned it in kind. Someone who instinctively understood how the whole process worked, how there was no escaping the hand of fate in this kind of situation. He realized Cassidy probably knew how things worked for werewolves on an intellectual level, but there was a big difference between knowing that a male Lupine claimed his woman by force and bound her to him with the act of mating, and experiencing it in person. Since he was damned sure Cassidy wasn't mated to one of his kind, her knowledge could be dismissed as purely theoretical.

He was guessing here, since he knew next to nothing about Foxwomen—though given what he'd observed of Cassidy so far, he didn't think he was too far off the mark—but it seemed to him that they must have almost as much in common with foxes as Lupines had with wolves. Lupines operated in packs and had the same system of hierarchy and rank, of dominance and submission. If he remembered his *Wild Kingdom* right, he was pretty sure foxes tended to live in groups no larger than a family unit, so they didn't need the same formalized rules and rituals used by a wolf pack. Maybe they also lacked the same ideas of fate and destiny that Lupines had. Since Cassidy and her grandmother were the only Foxwomen he'd ever met—or even heard of outside of legends—it was hard to be sure.

Either way, his Foxwoman seemed to lack a Lupine's basic understanding of the futility of fighting against destiny. Not that it surprised him. During the short time he'd known her, he'd come to realize that Cassidy Poe would fight city hall, the law, and the battle of the sexes all at the same time and never ask for reinforcements. It both fascinated and exasperated him.

He was on the brink of an apology when the cab pulled to a stop outside her apartment building. Cassidy had the fare in her hand before he had a chance to reach for his wallet, and the fear that she would leave without so much as a word began to fill him. He opened his mouth to speak, but she got there first.

"Do you like Chinese?"

Not quite what he had expected. He blinked. "The food?"

"Yeah. The only thing I've eaten today is a bagel, and if I don't get some protein soon, I'm going to do something drastic."

"We certainly can't have that," he said, cautiously. This woman made him feel very cautious.

"There's a little restaurant down the street. It's tiny and a total dive, but the food is good. And they deliver."

Quinn froze, terrified he'd misheard her. "You want to order Chinese for dinner?"

"Yeah. You've got to be hungry by now, too." She shifted awkwardly from foot to foot. "Plus, it will give us a chance to talk some more."

Quinn had less interest in eating than in finding out what this woman was up to and how her next move always managed to be the one he hadn't expected. But at least she hadn't told him to go home. She hadn't invited him into her bed, either, but he could be patient a little while longer.

"Lead the way," he said, and followed her into her building.

They walked to the elevator in silence and rode it up

to her floor the same way. In fact, she was quiet long enough that when she spoke, her question took him by surprise.

"Do you think she's already dead?"

Quinn looked down at her, but she had her gaze fastened on her doorknob as she struggled with the locks, and her expression was pensive. He didn't need to ask to know she was referring to Ysabel. "It's likely."

"But why would they do that? I mean, if all they wanted from her was the evidence to prove we exist, they could have gotten it without killing her, right?"

He followed her inside, shed his coat, and joined her on the sofa. "They could, but why would they want to? They hate us, and they'd consider Ysabel tainted by association. Plus, if her death prompted Gregor or someone else from the community to retaliate, it would only give them more rope to hang us with."

"Do they really need more rope?"

Her face wore an expression of sadness that tugged at his heart, and he wanted nothing more than to erase it. He never wanted to see his mate look like that. Unable to resist, he lifted one hand and pushed a strand of hair back behind her ear, his knuckles brushing tenderly against the curve of her cheek.

"Why is it that you're so determined to get involved with me, Quinn?" she asked after a silent moment, her dark eyes wide and watchful. "I mean, somehow I doubt you're lacking for female companionship. So why me? Is it just the situation? Am I a way to blow off steam? A distraction from thinking about an unpleasant situation? Or am I a novelty because I'm American? Because I'm a Foxwoman?"

He blinked and fought the urge to ask her to repeat herself. He had excellent hearing; he just couldn't believe she felt it necessary to ask that question.

"This isn't about novelty," he assured her. "I'm not the sort of man who feels he's more of one the more women he has."

"Then what is it about?"

"It's about you." He knew he probably sounded incredulous, but he couldn't help it. He was. "You can't tell me you don't know you're a beautiful woman, Cassidy. You've mirrors in this place. I see one right over there. Surely you look into them from time to time."

"I know I'm a long way from ugly, but I'm not America's next top model, either."

"What use have I for a model? Skinny, pale little things with bones I'd be afraid to touch for breaking. I'm not interested in models. I'm interested in you."

"Why?"

He ran a hand through his hair in frustration. If this had been any other woman, he'd have accused her of fishing for compliments, but Cassidy Poe looked genuinely perplexed.

"You call to me," he finally ground out. "Before I ever saw you up on that rooftop, I smelled you. Downstairs, at the party. There was this trace of . . . something in the air. Like full-bloom honeysuckle flowers. It drove me mad and led me right to you. Then all I had to do was look at you to know I wanted you."

"Does that happen to you a lot? You just see a woman and decide right there you have to have her?"

"No, damn it, it doesn't. I won't deny I'm a man, Cassidy, and I won't deny I've had my share of women, but I'm not the sort who's ever had trouble taking no as an answer. Before, there have always been other women if one I fancied refused me."

She watched him. "And now?"

"Now if there are others, I don't see them. It's you I want, Cassie love. No one else."

"But you don't know me."

"And whose fault is that?" He growled, pushing up from the sofa to pace across the floor. "I've been trying to get to know you from the moment I set eyes on you. Before that. From the moment I scented you. You're the one who keeps pushing me away."

"Can you blame me? The manner of our meeting was a bit disconcerting, and as of now we've known each other for a total of "—she glanced at her watch— "about twenty hours. I think I have a right to be wary."

"Damn it, I know you do." He shoved a hand through his hair and bit back another curse. Maybe this was a bad idea. He shouldn't have agreed to come upstairs. His nerves were too frayed to try and have an intelligent conversation when all he wanted to do was strip her naked and make her admit she belonged to him, which wouldn't do much to reassure her.

"I know you do," he repeated, struggling for a calmer tone. "I'm in unfamiliar territory here, Cassie love. I'm used to a woman being pack. I'm not accustomed to one I have to treat . . . delicately."

"You sound like you're blaming me for that."

"I'm not," he said, sinking back to the edge of the sofa and taking her hand carefully between his. "I don't want you to think that I am, Cassie love. But I need you to understand what you do to me. You go to my head like whiskey, and I'm asking you nicely to please let me have another sip."

• • •

Cassidy stared into those warm amber eyes and felt her stomach do a slow somersault. Gods, this man got to her, on every one of her levels. And after the night and day she'd had, she wasn't sure she had any strength left to fight her response to him. If ever in her life she'd needed a distraction, it was now. She needed to take her mind from the thoughts of kidnapping and death. She needed to shut her mind off altogether and just glory in the feeling of being alive. Her mind might still be enumerating the reasons why it would be the height of self-destruction to get involved with this man, but her body had stopped listening. If she wasn't careful, she was very much afraid that her heart might follow suit.

Run! Run away! her brain screamed. *The man is emotional Häagen-Dazs. You'll enjoy it for a few minutes, but you'll pay for it in the end!*

Oh, let her live a little, her hormones countered. *No one is talking love here. This doesn't have to be about happily ever after and a white picket fence. What's the harm in two healthy adults spending some quality time together?*

Cassidy shivered at the thought of that kind of quality. The argument presented by her hormones was making a lot of sense to her right now. And the heat radiating from the gorgeous and very intense Lupine beside her was not helping.

"You've naught to fear from me, Cassie love," he murmured, raising her hand to his lips and brushing whisper-soft kisses against her palm. She could see the mingled sincerity and hunger in his eyes and her resistance crumbled. "I swear it."

"All right." She surprised herself with her words,

but just then she couldn't care. She felt overwhelmed by the situation and by her reaction to this man, and her fear was easily outweighed by desire. By need.

He jerked a little in surprise, his eyes narrowing with suspicion. "All right what?"

"If you want to get to know me better, go ahead. Ask me something. I promise I'll answer. But if this is going anywhere, I need to get to know you better, too. For every question I answer, I get to ask one in return."

She thought for a minute she might have really thrown him for a loop—she'd certainly thrown herself for one—but in the end, he just nodded. "Fine."

"You're the one with all the curiosity." She tucked the hand that still tingled from his kisses between her knees and nodded to him. "You go first."

Quinn was silent for a moment, as if wondering where to start. "Tell me about Foxwomen. I thought they were a myth until Rafael De Santos introduced me to your grandmother. I'd never met anyone like her."

"There isn't anyone like her. My grandmother is a force unto herself." She smiled wryly. "But I'm not surprised you've never met any others. We're the only ones in the city. The next closest den I know of is in Montreal, or maybe the one in northern Michigan. There just aren't very many of us."

He shook his head. "It's hard for me to fathom. My pack is nearly three hundred strong, and the Stone Circle Clan's territory borders ours outside Dublin. Here in Manhattan, it seems you can't throw a stone on a full moon without hitting someone furry, but maybe that's the company I've been keeping."

"Yeah, it's a bit different for us. Nana says there used to be more, but not in a long time. Most of us are descended from the Native American population, if you go far enough back. And we all know how well they fared in American history."

"True enough."

"If my grandmother were here, I'm sure she'd go into a really long explanation about what makes Fox-women unique and how important our legacy is and why it's my responsibility to carry on our family heritage in a way that would make my ancestors proud. But since she's not, I'll tell you I don't think we're all that different from you guys."

"From Lupines?"

She nodded. "We shift, just like you do. I mean, you guys don't only do it when there's a full moon, and neither do we."

"I'm not so sure about that. If you were just like werewolves, for one thing, there'd be a damned sight more of you." He grinned. "We've none of us ever been hesitant to be fruitful and multiply."

Cassidy snorted a half-laugh. "Yeah, I had noticed that. But it's not that Foxwomen don't multiply, it's just that since the trait is only passed from mother to daughter, only the female part of that equation can really be called Foxwomen."

"So it really is only Fox*women*. You don't have any Foxmen hidden away in a closet somewhere?"

"Not a one. Something about that pesky Y chromosome seems to throw a wrench into the DNA. Only double Xs have the option to get furry."

"But if your father wasn't a fox-shifter, what was he?"

She smiled, remembering, and it was her father's smile. "He was human."

Quinn looked genuinely surprised. "Human? You mean you're . . ."

"A half-breed. Yes. We all are." She snuggled deeper into the corner of the sofa and shrugged. "Foxwomen have only ever mated with humans, as far as I know. It's just what we do. I'm not even sure what would happen if one of us mated with a werekin or a Fae or something, which set of DNA would win out. Who knows? I'm sure Nana would say we'd spontaneously combust."

Quinn didn't seem to find that amusing. He scowled. "I'm sure nothing so drastic would happen. I'll bet it would be perfectly safe for both of u—for both parties."

"I know. That was a joke. Nana's a bit of a snob about the whole heritage thing, which is kind of ironic when you think that half of that heritage is nothing more than the human next door. But the stories seem to indicate that even before Europeans came to America, there was some sort of taboo against Foxwomen mating with anything other than a human because it might weaken their spiritual powers." She shrugged. "I guess there just haven't been enough of us to really test the theory. Since there are so many more humans in the world than there are Others, there's not much incentive for anyone to go bucking tradition."

An expression Cassidy couldn't quite define passed across his face at that, but he kept quiet.

"I think this means it's my turn," she said after a moment. "So now you get to tell me about your family."

"They're fairly average, really. Mum and Da have moved to a small town just outside Dublin, but the pack has been in the city since before the city was, so I'm still there."

"Do you have any brothers or sisters?"

"No. I'm a singleton. Plenty of cousins, though. It's that fruitful thing again. Though I have to say, large families don't draw attention in Ireland quite the way I imagine they would in Manhattan."

She smiled wryly. "True. So I guess no one thinks twice about pack members all living in such close proximity? You just seem like the average extended family."

"We are. The average extended furry family, in any case." He settled farther back into the sofa cushions but kept his body canted so he could continue to watch her face as they talked. "I've met your grandmother, and you mentioned you had a cousin, but you never said anything about other family. Where are your parents?"

Cassidy hesitated, her gaze skipping away from his. The question tugged at her heart, the way memories of her mom and dad always did. "They're dead."

Quinn winced. "I'm sorry, Cassie love. That was insensitive of me. I apologize. Were they ill?"

She shook her head, her mouth curving in a sad smile. She couldn't remember either of them ever so much as sneezing. They'd seemed invulnerable and immortal to her back then. "Not a day in their lives. And it's okay. You didn't know. Besides, they've been gone a long time. I was only six when they died."

"And you've lived since with your grandmother?"

"Yup."

"They must have been quite young themselves. How did they die? Was there an accident?"

"Not at all. It was very much on purpose." She took a

deep breath and raised her hand to push a fall of hair behind her ear. She didn't enjoy reliving it, but time had allowed her to at least retell it without faltering. "They were diplomats, just like Nana. And you, for that matter. They were helping with the negotiations between two of the important vampire houses in Washington, D.C., when the treaty broke. They were killed along with at least two dozen vamps and nearly a hundred humans. It was a mess, in more ways than one. The local council burned down three city blocks trying to cover it up."

Quinn swore under his breath. "I'm sorry, love. That's horrible."

"Like I said, it was a long time ago. And that was two questions in a row for you. Don't think I'm not keeping track. Now I get another one." She forced a smile onto her lips and hoped he'd let her get away with it.

"Have at it."

"What made you decide to be a politician?"

He raised an eyebrow. "Well, I don't consider myself to be one. I'm *guth* of my pack. The *guth* of Black Glen has always been a Quinn. It's a tradition in my family, a bit like diplomacy is in yours, I imagine."

She ignored that last statement. "*Guth*. That's like an ambassador, right? I don't think any of the packs in this area have kept up with the custom. In fact, I can't think of a single pack I know that does."

"It's something a lot of Lupines have forgotten. A *guth* is an ambassador of a sort, but he's also a herald and a storyteller. Like a Norwegian skald, I suppose. I'm not surprised a lot of packs have forgotten the custom, since the *guth* of a pack is the one charged with passing on the customs to each new generation. It's a bit of an irony."

"I guess so. Okay, so I get another question to even things up—"

Quinn shook his head. "Oh, no. It's my turn again."

"But I only asked one question."

"You asked two. You asked about why I do what I do, then you asked me to explain what I do, remember?"

Cassidy frowned. "That second one wasn't a real question."

"Now, now," he said, grinning. "No cheating, Cassie love. It isn't ladylike."

She rolled her eyes, but gave in. "Fine. Go ahead."

"Good. Then I want to know if you're romantically involved with anyone right now." She hesitated until Quinn raised an eyebrow at the pause. "It's a simple question, Cassie love. I asked if you were involved with a man. Or a woman, for that matter. If you've an understanding with anyone, I want to know what it is and with whom."

"Isn't that something you're supposed to find out *before* you jump a woman in a public place?"

"I've already apologized for last night."

He inched forward and inhaled deeply. She knew he was smelling her and she hoped her scent wasn't giving her away. If she wanted him to believe she was still undecided about whether to accept his advances, she really shouldn't smell aroused.

"I intend to make your romantic entanglements very much my business, Cassie love. You see"—he paused, breathing her in—"I intend to make certain that the only one you're entangled with in the future is me."

She forced out a laugh, but even to her ears, it sounded more nervous than amused.

"Down, boy," she said, leaning slightly away from

him. "I think you're getting ahead of yourself here. I said I was willing for us to get to know each other better, but I haven't decided yet whether or not I'm willing to get involved with you."

Somehow she got the impression that Quinn wasn't paying attention. He shifted even closer until the narrow width of space between them ceased to serve as any barrier at all.

"I mean it," she said, trying to lean away when there was really nowhere for her to go. "I'm not going to be rushed into anything, Quinn. This is not something I take lightly."

He inhaled deeply, his grin turning feral as he scented the rush of desire that pooled between her thighs. "Let's just see about that, shall we?"

Growling soft and low, he leaned across the distance that separated them and brushed his lips against hers.

Fourteen

Cassidy held her breath and sat frozen as he leaned in for the kiss. Her mind whirled and her heart raced and her stomach Jazzercised, but she held herself motionless in anticipation. As stupid as it might be, she wanted this kiss more than she wanted her next breath. Which was a good thing, since she'd stopped breathing the moment he began to ease forward.

A whimper escaped her when he finally made contact, a sharp, breathy little squeaking sound she couldn't hold back. The soft, beguiling pressure of his lips on hers sent heat coursing through her body; not the fiery conflagration set off by their wrestling match of last night, but the slow, invasive warmth like that brought on by a heavy shot of pure, single-malt whisky. This kind of heat started where his mouth touched hers and eased its way on liquid tendrils up into her cheeks and her head, clouding her thinking further. Then it slid down her throat to her stomach and between her legs, drawing an echo of moisture from another source.

God, he tasted good. She'd tried not to notice last night, but he reminded her now. She caught a faint tang of something citrus buried beneath layers of spice, clove, and cinnamon and freshly candied ginger. It all mingled with the earthy palate of a Lupine and that intoxicating, underlying flavor that was all his own. Essence of Sullivan Quinn. She sipped him thirstily.

She parted her lips further, unconsciously urging a deeper tasting, but he frustrated her by pulling back and hovering a hairsbreadth away, so that his breath tickled her oversensitive skin and made her shiver. She forced open her heavy eyelids.

"What's wrong?"

He watched her mouth as he spoke, eyes shining with hunger and humor and devilment. "I didn't want to push myself on you, sweet Cassie." His murmur was dark and rough, another sort of caress. "You seemed . . . displeased by my earlier attentions. I wouldn't want to trespass where I'm not invited."

Cassidy knew he was right. She knew she'd spent quite a bit of energy keeping him at arm's length, and she knew she ought to continue to do so. But he tasted so good and he smelled so amazing and his mouth felt like heaven on hers and what harm could one more little kiss do?

She whimpered and leaned toward him, like a flower to the sun.

Quinn chuckled and eased a fraction closer, his tongue tracing the parted seam of her lips. The teasing touch made her breath catch in her throat. How did he do this to her? Why wasn't he doing entirely different things to her? Things that involved nudity and sweat and unlikely feats of gymnastics?

Impatient and incautious, she scooted closer to him until she nearly climbed into his lap. Poised there on all fours, she pressed into the kiss. Her insistence won her about three seconds of actual mouth-on-mouth, full-fledged kissing before he pulled away again.

It wasn't enough.

She opened her eyes and her frustration rushed forth. "What? What's wrong? I thought you were attracted to me. Last night you could barely keep your paws off me even while I was running away, and now you're pulling back from a kiss? I didn't even get any tongue!"

"You noticed that, did you?" He settled his hands on her hips and grinned back at her. "I'm afraid that last night did make an impression on me, love, no matter what you might think. What if you change your mind on me after a bit?"

Cassidy made a strangled sound and tried to drag his mouth back down to hers. She knew this was a bad idea, knew Sullivan Quinn was the wrong man for her, knew the last thing she wanted was to get involved with a politician, but her body didn't care. His kiss had hit her like a drug. Now that she had tasted him again, she wanted more. "I won't change my mind."

"So you say." The moment her lips brushed the surface of his, he pulled away. She groaned. "But I'm afraid I find it hard to trust you at this point, Cassie love. I need a bit more in the way of reassurance."

Cassidy froze, and her lashes parted to eye him with suspicion. "What kind of reassurance?"

The grin that stole over his face screamed of wicked satisfaction. "Nothing painful, I assure you . . ."

Cassidy weighed his potential price against the magic of his kiss and shivered. Damned if he wasn't worth at least hearing the bargain. "Go on."

"Accept my invitation to have dinner before the lecture."

Okay, she'd been expecting him to demand a kinky sexual favor, at the very least. Whips and chains. Liquid latex. Perhaps a really big bowl of Jell-O. Or maybe something a bit tamer, like a full-body massage or a strip show. Something that put her in the role of catering to his desires. But a date? That was almost enough to snap her out of her haze.

"Why?"

"Because." He reached out and caught a lock of her hair, curling it around his fingers while he watched her. "I've decided that what I wanted from you last night is not what I want from you now."

"You don't want sex?"

She sounded so horrified that he laughed. Personally, she didn't see the humor in the situation.

"Of course I want sex. Lots of it, Lord willing. The kind that makes it difficult to walk afterward. But I want more than that." He used the gentle grip on her hair to urge her closer. "I want you to agree to see me again. I'll not lay another paw on you, Cassie love, until I know you won't run from me before I'm good and finished with you."

Cassidy tensed her muscles to keep herself from melting into a puddle all over her sofa. "Finished with me? Like a bowl of cornflakes?"

"Oh, no," he said, and she could have sworn he purred it. "Nothing so boring. Though I do intend to gobble you right up." He tugged her even closer until she wound up straddling his lap.

"So I really am Little Red Riding Hood, huh?"

She saw a flash of teeth and the spark of whiskey-gold eyes. "Did you ever wonder what the big, bad wolf really wanted from little Red?"

He released her hair and slid his hands over her shoulders, down her goosefleshed arms, to close around her hips. She felt his fingers flex against them, as if testing her softness. Ruthlessly, she suppressed a whimper and went for the smart-aleck retort.

"A really good recipe for zucchini bread?"

He shook his head slowly, close enough that she could feel his breath against her mouth. Her tongue broke free of her control and came out to wet her lips. His gaze fixed on the flash of pink, and Cassidy heard the beginnings of a rumble in his chest. She felt it, too, with the force of an earthquake.

Still hovering with his lips nanometers from hers, he reached one hand up to cup the side of her face. "He wanted what I want, Cassie love. Complete. And total. Surrender."

The punctuation to each demand came from sharp, intensely erotic nips to her trembling lips. He moved too fast for her to catch him in the real kiss she longed for. In a second she was going to commit a felony just for one more taste. She strained closer.

"Just agree to have dinner with me," he breathed, nuzzling her lips, taunting her, "and you can have that kiss you've been begging me for."

"I don't beg," she managed, fighting for breath.

She lost when his eyes glinted and his lips curved in a textbook illustration of wickedness.

"Want to see if I can make you?"

As much as she would have loved to wipe the smug smile off his face, she had other plans for his lips.

"All right," she whispered, straining to get closer, willing to give up a lot more than dinner to feel his mouth on hers once more. "Fine. Dinner. Please."

He shifted her a fraction closer, let her feel the tickle of his mouth on hers, let her taste the sweet spice of his breath, then gave a deep chuckle. "There now. Was that so hard?"

Cassidy didn't answer. Driven to the breaking point by his ruthless teasing, she did the only thing she could think of. She grabbed him by the back of the head, hauled his mouth down to hers, and kissed him with the full force of her passion.

Fifteen

Quinn's chuckle quickly disappeared into the stark hunger of Cassidy's kiss. Apparently, once his little vixen decided on something, she got right to it. Enthusiastically. He didn't plan to complain.

Grunting in satisfaction, he met her eager kiss with demands of his own, slipping his hands from her hips, one wrapping more securely around her waist to press her close, the other sliding up the long trail of her spine to cup the back of her neck. Her skin felt hot and soft and inviting. Surprisingly silky strands of fiery russet hair tickled his palm as he stroked her. He couldn't wait to have those soft tresses wrapped around him while he stroked into her.

That brought out a growl, which she swallowed eagerly and offered back in the form of a quiet moan. She began to squirm, and he resisted her movements at first. Right up until her agile shifting brought her knees around his hips, her ankles behind his back and the seam between her legs into perfect alignment with the increasingly uncomfortable zipper of his jeans.

God, she tasted sweet! The soft, flowering essence of honeysuckle flooded his senses just as it had the night before. It danced across his tongue, filled his nostrils and seeped into his skin. He wished he had her bare again, to increase the rate of absorption, but he refused to sacrifice the kiss for that. He *needed* the kiss.

He needed all sorts of things from this woman, and now that he'd won the argument, he had no intention of waiting to collect. He had her promise that this would not be the end of them, and he trusted her to keep her word. Especially since he knew where she lived.

Quinn deepened the kiss again, hands dropping to her hips to settle her more firmly against his erection. She felt amazing and mind-bending as she kneeled over him, but he was willing to bet she'd feel even better stretched out beneath him. Executing a lightning-fast roll, he flipped her to her back on the soft cushions of the sofa. He felt her surprised gasp and the subtle melting of her body under his. Her arms clung to him, and her hips cradled his, her knees still bracketed around him. It felt like heaven.

It felt even better when her hands slid over his shoulders and up the back of his neck to thread through his hair. Her nails rasped across his scalp and sent electricity racing down his spine. He shuddered and dove more deeply into her. One hand stroked up her hip and under the hem of her sweater to explore the pale, silken skin of her torso. The touch of his fingers against bare flesh made her whimper, but a shy, delicate miss she was not. She let go of his hair and began to slide his sweater up over his stomach to his chest.

The Hallelujah chorus began to play on infinite loop inside his head.

He lifted his hands high and let her strip the garment off him, not even waiting for her to toss it aside before he reached for her again. He hadn't liked the break in their kiss necessitated by the removal of his sweater, and he hurried back for more as soon as his head came free. He dipped toward her mouth, but an eddy of scent rose from the heated skin of her throat and distracted him. He changed course at the last minute and went after it.

She mewed a protest as his lips slid past hers and kept going, but he couldn't stop now. Not when the flushed, satin warmth of her skin was so close. Roughly, he shoved the collar of her sweater aside and buried his face in the crook of her neck. He inhaled deeply and felt the same swirling head rush as if he'd just slammed back a liter of whiskey. A growl rumbled up from his chest, and he opened his mouth to taste her.

Glorious. Fresh and sweet as April sunshine, but a thousand times more delicious. His tongue swirled over the tendon on the side of her neck, and he felt her shiver beneath him. He loved that. It made him feel ten feet tall and bulletproof, even without his were form. It stirred the hunger inside him to new levels and let loose his beast.

That beast wanted to devour her, bit by juicy bit, consume her until his senses were so full of her, he couldn't take any more. He had to rein in the urge to bite into her delicate flesh. He had no idea if she could take the sort of damage a Lupine female could. Instead, he closed his teeth over her shoulder with infinite care, biting down just hard enough to leave a faint impression of his teeth in her skin. His breath caught in his throat as he waited for her reaction. It came in a flood of heat and a low, shuddering moan that echoed in his ear.

Thank God. Now he could slip his leash with a clear conscience.

He tugged roughly at her sweater, yanking it over her head and throwing it somewhere in the vicinity of his. The sight of all that creamy woman had him wiping his mouth to counteract the drool. He couldn't remember a sight so beautiful. Her gorgeous, feminine curves stretched out beneath him, encased in burgundy lace that dipped low over her breasts and lifted them to his hands and mouth. And—praise God!—the bra fastened with an invitingly simple clasp nestled against her chest.

She beat him to it, her fingers already on the little tab of plastic. She flipped it open and began to peel the cups away from her skin, but he stopped her. This was his present, and he wanted to do the unwrapping.

He held his breath as he took over. His eyes met hers for a moment and read an equal heat before falling again to the treasure under his hands. He revealed her breasts with reverent attention, the sight a marvel of pale mounds crowned by tightly beaded nipples of dark, sandy rose. Again, his mouth watered and he leaned down to her as if drawn by an irresistible magnetism.

A taste. Just a taste.

So he lowered his head and tasted.

Cassidy went into meltdown the moment his lips closed over her breast. She felt her entire universe distill down to the liquid burn of this man's mouth drawing at her sensitized nipple. She could all but trace the spread of the fire from one nerve ending to the other, from her breast to her belly to the very heart of her, already melting and liquid with arousal. No man had ever been able to do this to her, and she wasn't sure how she felt about this one's ability to render her into a pile of trembling goo with little more than a touch.

The fiend had timing, though; she had to give him that. Just as the flicker of unease crossed her mind, his tongue curled around her nipple and tugged, sending her mind winging off to parts unknown. Her senses took over control of her body and threw an under-new-management party. She wrapped her arms around Quinn and arched her back to encourage the warm, rough suction at her breast. With her palms pressed against his back, she could feel the rumbling of a growl too low for her to hear and the twitch of heavy muscles pulled taut by arousal.

She knew how that felt. Her own body shook with tension as his mouth skimmed across her chest to latch onto her neglected breast. The hands that had clenched tight around her rib cage to hold her in place began to skim across the surface of her torso. Fingers explored the dip of her waist, the soft, slight rise of her belly, and the stiff metal button at the waist of her jeans.

He flicked it open with one hand in a move so quick and graceful she might not have noticed it if he hadn't slid the same hand into the new opening to tickle the small mat of curls at the top of her mound. She definitely noticed that. Her hips arched into the touch to encourage further exploration. He looked up as his fingers slid down, and their eyes met again, amber burning into gold. She saw her own needs mirrored there with stark clarity. He wanted her, intensely, desperately, consumingly. Which was about half as badly as she wanted him.

Cassidy reached up to cup his face in her hands and draw him back to her. She reveled in the way he settled over her, letting her take just enough of his weight to feel covered but not pinned. His broad shoulders blocked out the light, and his hips nestled in the cradle of hers as she parted her thighs in welcome. She could feel her heartbeat speed up and tugged him closer to her.

Her lips brushed over his, soft and teasing, and her tongue traced the seam of his mouth.

"This isn't a surrender," she whispered, her voice low and breathless in her own ears. "It's a demand."

She released him so that her hands could slide down between them and go to work on the button fly of his jeans.

"I'm demanding that you make love to me. Here. Now. Until I say you can stop. Will that do in place of surrender?"

He shuddered, and a surge of feminine pride curved her lips. She raised her hips to help him ease her jeans down, kicking them off one foot and letting them fall to the floor. The power she had discovered she had over him was like a drug, heady and addictive, and she rode the high with abandon. Every tremor in his hard body, every spark of arousal in his eyes, every hitch of his breath in his throat made her want to laugh out loud and shout her triumph. She had taken a situation composed of a dominating man and an unexpected sexual spark, and she had seized control of it. She, Cassidy Poe, had unleashed her feminine power and triumphed on the field of sexual battle. This was a feeling she could definitely get used to.

That was the last thought to flicker through her addled mind before Quinn knotted his hand in the lace of her burgundy panties and tore them off her with the ease of a feather duster tearing through cobwebs. Holding the ruined lingerie up where she could see it, Quinn stared down at her with an expression of feral amusement and purred.

"It's a start. We can negotiate from there."

Another day on another sofa with another woman, Quinn might have prolonged their little battle of wills just for the thrill of combat, but not today. Today, he had to have this woman in the next thirty seconds or his head was going to explode. Since he hated to see a sound mind go to waste, he knew he had twenty-seven more seconds to get inside Cassidy's luscious little body before disaster struck. He intended to waste not a single one.

He relished the look of shock and arousal on her face when he tore her panties out of his way and made his taunting little challenge, but not nearly as much as he relished the way her body went all soft and inviting beneath his. He intended to go on relishing that for as long as he could possibly manage, and with any luck, on numerous occasions in the future.

But first things first.

Her scent wafted up to him, intensified by her arousal, and he nearly came right then and there just from the mind-numbing power of her honeysuckle heat. It took some serious willpower to maintain his control. He only managed it by burying his nose against her throat and breathing her in while he struggled with the sudden cardboard-stiffness of his jeans. His tongue flicked out to taste her skin again—God, he could live on the taste of her—and a renewed flood of urgency made him settle for pushing the recalcitrant denim down onto his hips and abandoning it.

Cassidy wasn't lodging any protests. In fact, her hands stroked frantically over him, caressing any patch of bare Lupine she could reach. The touch of delicate, feminine fingers sent his testosterone into overdrive, and he grabbed her wrists, pinning them beside her head before she destroyed his control.

"No," he snarled, holding her in place against her confused struggles. "No touching. Next time. Maybe next time. Can't take it now."

He didn't give her the chance to launch a protest, just covered her mouth with his and kissed her as if he could consume her. Quickly and a little roughly, he tugged her hands higher and took both in one hand. He needed that free hand for something a lot more important. It snaked down over her arm and her chest, pausing to cup and squeeze a breast, then trailing over her belly to the dark, sweetly scented valley between her legs.

Their groans echoed together as his fingers dipped between her trembling thighs and slid through the gathered moisture at her core. Her flesh felt hot and swollen and oh-so-inviting as he stroked deliberately over it. The bare whisper of one callused fingertip against her brought a breathless cry to her lips and made her arch against his hand. His caress firmed, as her wetness eased his way and drew him irresistibly to her center. Testing her carefully, he felt how ready she was for him, and the knowledge made it impossible to wait.

His fingers slid reluctantly from her warmth and closed about her hip, holding her in place as he set himself against the snug barrier of her entrance and began to push carefully inside.

She froze at the first contact of flesh against flesh. Her breath caught in her throat, and her muscles clenched in tense anticipation. He kept his eyes on her face, searching for any sign of fear or discomfort. He saw none. She gave no evidence of nerves or of being intimidated by the thick length pressing her for entrance. Her head was tilted back, her neck a pale, graceful arch. She looked like a statue, like Bernini's *Andromeda,* spread naked and waiting on the rocks, but she felt a thousand times warmer than stone.

He could hear the ragged pant of her breathing, feel the faint trembling of her muscles, but her body remained pliant beneath his. He could feel her hips twitch up toward his as he forged deeper. Teeth clenched, Quinn threw his head back and tried not to come at the feel of her tight passage closing over the head of his cock. He felt as if he were drowning, waves of sensation overcoming him. He'd never felt anything like it, but he knew in that instant he would never have enough.

"Quinn!"

The sound of his name on her lips nearly ended him. She choked it out, all breathless and frantic, and he had to picture his primary schoolmistress, Sister Mary Augustine, to keep from exploding. Even that almost wasn't enough.

"Please," she gasped, her hips lifting up off the sofa in an attempt to lure him deeper. "More!"

Far be it from him to deny a lady. Especially one so eager to have exactly what he wanted to give to her. He bowed his head, feeling the light sheen of sweat building on his body from the exertion of self-control, and eased deeper. He was trying to be careful, trying not to hurt her, knowing some women found him difficult to take the first time, and preferring to tear out his own intestines than cause this woman any undue pain. He would rather wrestle Hydra. Walk from here to Tasmania. Become a vegetarian. Give up strong drink—

Small, sharp teeth bit hard into his forearm and jerked him back to reality.

"Ow!"

"For God's sake," she panted, glaring up at him with fury in those clear, yellow-green eyes, "would you stop screwing around and *fuck me already!!!*"

Quinn's mind indulged in a single moment of shock before springing into action, but his body didn't wait half that long. Before the last vowel sound had finished echoing through the living room, he was thrusting full force inside of her and reveling in the brand-new shout that filled the apartment and probably made more than one neighbor very curious.

"Yes!" she screamed. Bent like a bow beneath him, she took every inch of him eagerly and wrapped her legs around his hips to keep him from leaving.

Quinn had no intention of going anywhere. He'd just found Shangri-la, after all. Did he look stupid?

But it didn't take long for his instincts to outweigh his common sense, and a few seconds later he was battling against her powerful hold so he could muster the leverage for a hard thrust. Once he managed it, she stopped fighting to keep him close.

In fact, she began to lever her hips up and down beneath him, as if trying to force him away just so she could take him back again. He obliged her with pleasure.

One hand was still clenched at her hip, the other wrapped hard around her wrists. Not because he feared her trying to get away, or even because he couldn't stand for her to touch him—at this point he was so hot he doubted he'd even notice—but because his fingers had locked into place and he didn't think he could let go if he tried. It felt as if all nonessential bodily functions, the ones not involved in claiming her, had shut down, leaving him with nothing to do but to thrust in and out of the amazing, delicious woman underneath him.

As if there were anything else in this world or the next that he would rather be doing.

He heard her cries reaching a fever pitch and sped up his thrusts. His hips moved in a fury of motion now, so fast the human eye would have detected little more than a blur, but this woman took everything he had to give and demanded more. She met him stroke for stroke, taking him deep, deep, deeper than he would have thought possible. He could feel the tingle of impending climax building in the base of his spine, preparing to overwhelm him, and he gritted his teeth against it.

"No!" he growled, the tendons on his neck bulging with strain. "Not . . . before . . . you . . . !"

He needn't have worried. As if on cue, he felt Cassidy begin to tighten and shake. Her body clenched around him, trapping him deep inside her as her orgasm hit, buffeting him with waves of pleasure. Her inner muscles squeezed and released around his cock, massaging him until he couldn't hold off any more. His control snapped with a dull roar, and he spilled himself inside her, howling his pleasure to the far ends of the universe.

They may very well have heard him there.

Sixteen

"Fabulous," Cassidy said, just as soon as she was capable of speech, oh . . . fifty-eight millennia later. "Listen for sirens, would you? I'm pretty sure my neighbors have called the police by now."

The huge Lupine pinning her to her sofa cushions never budged. He didn't even grunt.

"Actually, I wouldn't be surprised if people all the way in Queens heard us."

"Screw them. And screw the cops," Quinn finally muttered, though the sound got half-buried in Cassidy's hair.

She shifted, looking for a position under her two-hundred-pound heating pad that would allow her to, you know, breathe. "I'm not that kind of girl."

Quinn raised his head and glared at her. "You won't be screwing anybody. Ever."

Considering he was still half-buried inside her as he said that, Cassidy decided to let the ultimatum go. For now. She could always bring it up later. When he least expected it. And it could be best used to her advantage.

For now, she joked it off. "That's too bad. I thought

this was pretty fun, all things considered. But if you really think we shouldn't do it again . . ."

"Anybody but me," he corrected hastily, a note of panic creeping into his voice. "You won't be screwing anybody but me."

She snorted. "Right. That's different, then."

He gave her a suspicious glare, which she countered with a look of wide-eyed innocence, then grunted and dropped his face back into her hair. He relaxed again above her, and his weight made her feel as if someone had rested a grand piano on her chest. Shifting as much as she could, she unlocked her ankles from around Quinn's back and let her legs drop to her sides. No good. She still couldn't breathe. Maybe this required a more direct approach. Before her skin turned blue.

"Um, Quinn?" she questioned quietly and oh-so politely.

He grunted again, and his hands began to stroke lazily over her hips and thighs. Her stomach flipped, and her breath might even have quickened, if she'd had any left.

"Not that I don't enjoy a good snuggle, 'cause, hello? I am a woman and all, but maybe we can try snuggling with me on top? Because I think about thirty more seconds of this and I'm going to pass out from the lack of oxygen to my brain."

That earned her another unintelligible man noise, but this one was followed quickly by a sigh and the feel of his body slipping free of hers. Before she could even register the twinge of regret, he had flipped off her, landed on his feet, and scooped her up into his arms. He was halfway across the living room when her mouth caught up with them.

"Um, where are we going?"

He didn't bother to look down at her, just shouldered open the door to her bedroom and kept walking. "I got you all sweaty. I thought the least I could do would be to clean you up. And I thought you'd prefer a shower to a quick hosedown with the spray nozzle on the kitchen sink."

She rolled her eyes. "I love a man with that kind of intuition."

"I try."

When he set her down, her feet made contact with the cold ceramic tile of her bathroom floor, and she shivered. While he slid open the shower curtain and began fiddling with the faucets, she reached into a cabinet and pulled out two fluffy towels that she set on the counter. Then she watched as he tested the water temperature, set the showerhead to full-spray massage, and turned back to her.

"After you," he said.

He meant it, too, because he scooped her up and set her down under the hissing shower before she could move.

She blinked water out of her eyes and glared up at him as he climbed in after her. She probably now resembled nothing so much as a drowned rat, but she was getting used to this man seeing her at less than her best.

"Do you think you might let me make use of these things I call legs from time to time?" she grumped. "Just a suggestion, but I find if I don't practice walking now and again, I start to lose the knack."

He grinned down at her and reached for her bottle of shampoo. "I was being gallant, Cassie love. Thought you lasses liked that sort of thing."

He sniffed the shampoo, shrugged, poured a dollop into his hands, and began scrubbing it through his thick hair.

"We also like not to be treated like invalids." She understood him not taking her griping all that seriously, since she wasn't, either. But she felt she had to make some sort of protest before he got used to doing everything his own way.

"I'll mind that the next time." He rinsed the soap away and shook his head like a sheepdog coming out of the rain.

Cassidy flinched away from the spray and ducked back under the shower, grabbing the shampoo herself and wishing she went in for some sort of girly, floral thing instead of an unscented brand. It would serve him right to walk around smelling like a petunia for the rest of the day. "Yeah, I'm sure you will. You'll be an absolute cheerleader for women's liberation."

"That's my girl. Always have faith in your man."

"Who said you were mine?" But she let him take the shampoo without a struggle, even tilting her head back for him to massage it into her scalp. "And what's the return policy?"

He chuckled. "All sales are final."

"Oh, well," she hummed, leaning back against his slick chest, enjoying the feel of his hands tangled in her hair.

He turned her into the spray to rinse the suds out of her hair, carefully sluicing the water away from her face so the soap couldn't run into her eyes.

She opened her mouth to make another wisecrack, but all that came out was a yawn. The late night and the strenuous activity seemed to be catching up with her. She leaned against Quinn's chest while he soaped and rinsed the rest of her body, too sleepy to even quibble over the places where he decided to pay extra close attention.

When he had them both scrubbed and rinsed, he turned off the water, lifted her out and dried her off. The yawns came fast and furious by the time he had her hair toweled and picked her up to carry her back into the bedroom. She felt as though one more would crack her jaw clear in half.

Her eyelids were drooping when he pulled back her sheets and laid her gently on her pillowy mattress. She snuggled under the blankets, barely noticing when he crawled in next to her, making the bed dip and shift with his weight. But she did notice when he wrapped his arms around her waist and pulled her back up against his chest. She shifted more comfortably in his embrace and sighed, feeling sleep overtaking her. Her last thought before she slid into total unconsciousness was that it felt good to have someone lean over like that and kiss her good night.

Given that it was Sunday morning, the lack of an alarm clock jangling her awake didn't surprise Cassidy. What surprised her was that something else felt compelled to do the honors. Reaching blindly from under the covers, she groped on and around her nightstand, throwing two books, a flashlight, a bottle of vitamins, and a shoe across the room before she woke enough to realize the horrible wailing buzz was coming from a telephone. Fumbling it off the cradle, she dragged it under the blankets with her and held it somewhere in the vicinity of her ear.

"H'lo?"

Silence. From the phone, anyway. Unfortunately, a new and equally infernal buzzing began almost immediately.

Something stirred beside her, an infinitely more interesting and warmer thing than her telephone. Then a low, husky rumble asked, "Where the hell did I leave my pants?"

Her eyes flew open and focused on the rumpled, sleepy, and incredibly naked Lupine beside her. She squeaked.

Quinn pushed himself up on the mattress and looked around blearily. "Come to think of it, where did I leave your pants?"

Cassidy shook her head and tried to look casual as she clutched the sheet to her chest. She knew it made little sense at this point, but there was a big difference between being seen naked in the heat of the moment and being seen naked the morning after with bedhead and morning breath.

"I distinctly recall both of us having pants. Damned things kept getting in the way." He grinned at her and flopped back onto the bed. "Luckily, I'm a man who believes in never leaving things half done."

"Uh . . ."

That was about the best she could manage in the way of conversation. Mostly because it didn't involve opening her mouth very far and exposing him to the harsh reality of life before toothpaste.

"Cassie love," he said gently, still grinning. "I believe that buzzing sound you hear is a cell phone. Your cell phone, I hazard to guess."

"Oh, shit!"

Cassidy jumped as if she'd been electrocuted, tucked the sheet under her arms, and leaped from the bed to sprint into the living room, which was the last place she remembered seeing her cell phone. The sneaky bastard had other plans for the sheet, though. His hand darted out and grabbed the corner of it as it slipped away, leaving Cassidy streaking buck naked through her apartment before she even knew she'd lost a round of tug-of-war.

She froze stock-still in the middle of her living room, shivering at the chill, and looked around for her cell phone, only to realize the buzzing had stopped. She cursed again—this time with much greater fervor and imagination—and scooped up Quinn's jeans and her cell phone, which she found half-buried in the sofa cushions. Along with the remains of her panties.

Torn between wanting to bury her head in a sandbox and wanting to grin and high-five the universe, Cassidy grabbed the rest of their scattered clothes and turned back to her bedroom and to the only man who'd ever managed to confuse, arouse, exasperate, and melt her all at the exact same time.

She'd gotten two steps past the sofa when she heard the chime of her doorbell, followed by the scrape of a key in the lock and a voice shouting from the hallway.

"I'm coming in! If you're naked, you'd better put some clothes on! Stat!"

Randy!

Cassidy bolted for the bedroom.

"Cassidy? I know you're home. I heard your bedroom door close. Why didn't you answer your phone?"

Pressed flat against the back of her bedroom door, Cassidy looked around in wide-eyed panic before the sound of the water running in her bathroom managed to register. Quinn was taking a shower. Bless his cleanly Irish soul. She tossed his jeans onto the end of the bed and yanked the first thing she touched out of her dresser drawer, which turned out to be a pair of pink and blue pajamas emblazoned with the phrase "GIRLIE GIRL." She could have cared less. She whipped them on in two point seven seconds flat and hurried out of her room before her cousin could take it into her head to walk in there uninvited, too.

"I've got a date tomorrow night," her cousin yelled, and Cassidy heard the apartment door close behind her. "Any chance of me conning you into lending me those brown dress boots of yours? The ones with the kick-ass sexy heels?"

"Damn it, Randy, did you ever hear of giving a person notice before you barge right into their home?" she called out, tugging on the hem of her pajama top and hurrying out to the living room. "I really was naked."

Randy dumped her purse, coat, scarf, gloves, hat, and keys on the chair-and-a-half and carried a large, white bakery bag into her cousin's small kitchen. "If you didn't want me barging in, you never should have given me a key."

"Yeah, trust me, I'll remember that for next time."

"So, since I do have a key, why should I wait for you to answer the door?" Making herself at home, Randy popped the two miniquiches she'd brought into the microwave and grabbed plates and utensils to carry into the dining alcove.

Cassidy looked from her cousin to the door of her bedroom and back again. "The thing is, this really isn't a good time."

"Besides," Randy continued as if she hadn't heard, "it's not like my cousin the nun was likely to be doing the nasty with some stud on the middle of the living room floor."

Cassidy choked on her tongue and began coughing uncontrollably, causing Randy to jerk around in surprise, her big brown eyes open as wide as garage doors.

"Oh. My. God!" Randy shrieked. "You mean it. You really were naked when I knocked. You got *laid*!"

The squeal nearly punctured Cassidy's eardrum, and the tackling hug shoved her back into the refrigerator with a grunt.

"Geez, Ran! Lay off. You're acting like I just told you I won the lottery."

"Ha! Lottery, schmottery. You needed sex a hell of a lot more than you needed money, missy." She looked Cassidy over from head to toe and raised an eyebrow. "Well, you can still walk, so I'm a little disappointed. Was it any good at all?"

"It wouldn't be any of your business if it was." Cassidy watched her cousin making herself thoroughly at home and prayed Quinn wouldn't run out of hot water before she could get rid of their uninvited visitor. *If* she could get rid of their visitor. "Like I said, Randy, this isn't a good—"

"Damn it! I had hopes for this guy. I thought you said he was Irish."

"He is."

Okay. Casual. She had to play this casual. If she tried to hustle Randy out of the apartment on one of their regular Sunday brunches, the other woman would definitely get suspicious. Damn it, how could Cassidy have forgotten it was Sunday?

"And he was a lousy lay? What happened? Was his little leprechaun just a bit too wee for your taste?"

Good God! Cassidy could testify firsthand that there was nothing wee about Sullivan Quinn. In fact, the idea of him being any less wee made her thighs clench together in protest.

Clearing her throat, she put one hand to her temple as if trying to press away a headache. "Don't you have better things to do than harass me on a Sunday morning? I think I'm getting a sinus thing, and I didn't get much sleep last night, so—"

"Well, I hope the hell not! So what was it like? What did you do? What did *he* do? Tell, tell, tell!"

Cassidy's look of wide-eyed horror probably didn't add much weight to her headache story. "For God's sake, Randy, I'm not giving you a blow-by-blow account of my sexual experiences."

"Oooooh! So there was blowing?"

"RANDY!"

Her cousin gave Cassidy a look of wide-eyed confusion. "What?"

"Get your mind out of the gutter. If you want that much detail about sex, go rent an adult DVD."

"You won't even give me a little bitty hint about it? Say, if your toes curled or something? Prude!"

"Slut."

The familiar and meaningless exchange brought them back to their traditional Mexican standoff.

"All right," Randy said to break the silence. "I can accept that you want to keep some things private. I don't understand it, but I can accept it. But you have to give me something."

"No. And I'd really appreciate it if you let me get—"

"Come on," her cousin wheedled. "I won't ask what it was like anymore, or even what sort of 'its' it entailed. Just answer one question. Would you do it again?"

Cassidy pursed her lips to hide her Cheshire cat grin. "Standing on my head in Grand Central Station."

Randy cheered and raised her hand for a high five. "So then where is he now? Did he turn tail and run, or did you kick him out of bed when you'd finished using him for your own lewd purposes?"

Cassidy shifted awkwardly. "Well, uh . . . I, um . . ."

"Or are you still hiding him in the bedroom?"

Choked silence.

"You are? No way! You're shitting me." Randy rocked back on her heels as if she'd just been told the earth was flat. "You're shitting me, aren't you?"

Cassidy stood mortified in her kitchen doorway, shifting her weight from one foot to the other until an amused, male brogue cut through the tension like a chain saw.

"Why, Cassie love, if you had wanted to go dancing you should have said something. I'd take you and be glad of it."

Cassidy squeezed her eyes closed, but she swore she could hear the wind caused by her cousin's head whipping around so fast. Randy would be wearing a neck brace by the end of the day. She also didn't need to be watching to guess that right about now, Sullivan Quinn would be flashing Randy one of his boyishly charming grins and shaking her hand, while politely ignoring the fact that her cousin was drooling over his bare, muscled chest. Why the hell hadn't he put on something more than his jeans before he decided to go prancing around her apartment?

"Sullivan Quinn," he drawled. "I'm happy to meet you."

"Thanks. I'm Randy Berry, and trust me, I'm absolutely delighted to meet you."

"Wonderful." Gritting her teeth, Cassidy forced her eyes open and pasted a huge, fake smile on her lips as she grabbed her cousin by the arm and began dragging her toward the door. "Now that the introductions are made, I'm sorry to hear you have to be on your way, Randy. Thanks so much for stopping by!"

"But—"

"It was great to see you, too." Cassidy yanked open the door and all but shoved her cousin out into the hall. "No, it's fine. I understand how busy you are. I couldn't possibly ask you to stay, what with your schedule. You go ahead and don't worry about me. I can take care of myself."

"Hey! Wait—"

"I love you, too, sweetie." She threw Randy's things out after her. "Come back and see me another time. Smooches! Bye!"

Then she slammed the door right in her favorite cousin's face and slumped against it, exhausted. She indulged in one drawn-out moan before she looked up to find Quinn watching her, chuckling his damned-fool head off.

"What's so funny?"

"Oh, Cassie love," he managed, pausing for air, "I don't think I've seen anything so rude or so amusing as that in all my born days. Lord, but you're a riot, darling."

"I'm glad you find my predicament so damned amusing," she snapped. "How would you like it if one of your relatives walked into your apartment without so much as a by-your-leave and then proceeded to drool all over the man you had just slept with?"

Quinn only laughed harder, stepping forward until he could pull her snugly into his arms. "First of all, no one in my family would ever enter my personal territory like that without permission. And second of all, I imagine that if they did and they found me with a man I'd just slept with, we'd all die of shock right then and there."

She swatted at his shoulder. "You know what I meant."

"I do, love, though I've not decided quite yet whether or not that frightens me."

"Har-har."

Still chuckling softly, he leaned down to nuzzle the tousled hair at her temple. She was almost prepared to let him make things up to her when her phone rang again. Lips poised halfway to his, Cassidy groaned and dropped back onto her heels.

"Damn it," she growled. "It's Sunday morning! What the heck did I do to become so damned popular all of a sudden?"

Quinn just shook his head and followed her over to the end table where she kept the cordless phone, nibbling the side of her neck while she picked up the receiver.

"Hello?"

"Miss Cassidy, how lovely it is to hear your voice,

dear." Patricia Phillips sounded as warm and affectionate over the phone as Cassidy knew the woman to be in person. "How are you?"

Trish had been Adele Berry's housekeeper since before Cassidy had come to live with her. The daughter of two minor witches, she had inherited a kind of magic that wouldn't thrill many spectators but that enabled her to keep the tidiest, most orderly house in Manhattan. Compared to her spells, the kitchen scene in *Fantasia* looked like an inefficient debacle. She was a medium sort of woman—medium height, medium build, medium brown hair—but she had a heart the size of any ten people and a smile that could light up at least three out of the Five Boroughs. Cassidy had loved her since the moment she'd set eyes on her.

"I'm fine, Trish, thanks." Actually, Cassidy felt a lot more than fine with Quinn scraping his teeth along the delicate skin of her neck, but she wasn't about to discuss that with her grandmother's housekeeper. "Is there something I can do for you? Does Nana need me for something?"

Quinn's teeth closed around the plump, tender lobe of her ear and began tugging. Cassidy's knees turned to Jell-O.

"Oh, no, it's nothing like that. Mrs. Berry is perfectly fine. I was just passing on a message. It sounded important, so I didn't want to wait until you arrived for Sunday dinner."

Quinn smirked as Cassidy's knees buckled beneath her and left her a sagging lump of hormones. For all of the five seconds it took for Trish's words to really register.

"Sunday dinner!" Damn. She'd forgotten all about

it. "Oh, Trish, I'm so sorry. I meant to call and tell you I'm not going to be able to make it tonight. Something's . . . come up."

As he laughed softly against her neck, Quinn's hips gave a slow, deliberate roll against her backside that nearly had her swallowing her tongue.

Lord! That was something, all right!

"I'll do my best to stop by for a drink afterward," she added hastily, trying to keep her voice from quivering, "but it probably won't be till after nine."

"Oh, that's a shame. I'm making roast lamb. Your favorite."

It was her favorite, but tonight Cassidy was focused on an entirely different appetite. "That sounds delicious, Trish. I'm sorry to miss it. Will you apologize to Nana for me? Let her know I'll be by next week if I don't make it later."

"Of course I will." Trish was probably the only person Cassidy had ever met who wasn't afraid to tell Adele Berry bad news to her face. With great respect, of course.

"Thanks. You're a sweetheart."

"Wait!" Trish stopped her before she could hang up. "There's still the reason I called, Miss Cassidy. Your phone message."

Cassidy frowned. "Someone tried to call me at Nana's?"

She hadn't lived with Adele since she started college.

"I thought it was a bit odd at first," Trish said, "but when he mentioned the Council, it made a bit more sense."

Not really, but Cassidy shrugged. "Okay. What was the message?"

"It was a gentleman, but he didn't leave his name. He said he was calling on Council business, and the voice sounded familiar, though I couldn't place it. He left a number and asked you to call as soon as possible."

Cassidy pinched the telephone receiver against her shoulder and reached for a pen. Quinn grumbled and switched to the other side of her neck. "All right. Go ahead and give me the number."

Trish rattled it off. "I hope I wasn't wrong to call you and let you know immediately . . ."

"No, don't worry about it. I'm sure it's fine. I'll give him a call and see what's going on. Give Nana my love."

"I will, dear. Good-bye."

Cassidy murmured a response and dropped the phone back into the cradle, before rounding on Quinn with fire in her eyes.

"You're going to have to pay for that," she said, trying to muster a glare when her mouth kept trying to grin.

"Oh, am I?" He smiled right back and snaked his arms around her waist, tugging until her hips bumped hard against his.

"Yes, you are," she purred, wrapping her arms around his neck and plunging her fingers into his hair. "In fact, I think you'd better put down a deposit right this very minute."

He chuckled, his mouth lowering slowly to hers. "Whatever you say, darling. Whatever you say."

She didn't *say* anything for a good solid hour at least.

Seventeen

Quinn lay in the darkness of Cassidy's bedroom and watched the rise and fall of her breathing. The clock on the nightstand read just after five P.M. He could see the rosy-gray light of sunset filter in around the edges of the window shades, but since she hadn't stirred in the last hour at least, he doubted the subtle glow now was going to disturb her.

A wave of russet hair lay across her cheek, and he brushed it away with a careful finger. Her skin felt smooth and warm, urging him to linger and trace the silky texture. She murmured in her sleep and shifted, a soft sigh passing her lips, her head turning into his touch. He loved that, loved her responsiveness. Even when she had been half-afraid he planned to snack on her liver, she still hadn't been able to stop herself from reacting to his touch. Now, in her sleep, she couldn't stop from turning to him. It made him feel like a god.

He laughed softly at his own thoughts and settled back into the mattress, tugging her against his chest. She nestled close beside him like a puzzle piece designed to fit. One of his arms curled under their shared pillow, and the other draped over her waist, his hand cupped around the soft curve of her belly. He loved the feminine feel of it, all warm and yielding. His hand stroked, and he imagined it taut and swollen with his seed.

The vision overwhelmed him, fierce and violent, and he buried his face in the tangle of her hair to wait out the trembling that overtook him. He'd gone through his whole life and never really understood what it would feel like when he found his mate. All of a sudden, the theoretical had become real enough to drive him to his knees, and his head spun with the impact.

In his family, in his world, matings had happened all around him. It was instinctive and natural and a cause of celebration among the pack, but no one spent too much time *thinking* about it. A wolf met a bitch, he smelled something tasty, he tasted it. And if it tasted good enough, he kept it around. Quinn had never waxed philosophical on the issue, because where he came from, mating wasn't a philosophy. It was an action. Quinn had known it would act on him one day, but he hadn't thought it would happen now, here, with this woman.

He wasn't sure whether he felt terrified or exhilarated. There in the dark, feeling Cassidy's bare skin against his, the sweetness of her scent filling his senses, he leaned toward exhilaration.

His hand swept down the curve of her belly until the tips of his fingers tangled in the soft curls at the apex of her legs. He couldn't help it. He loved the textures of her, soft skin, silky hair, sweet liquid secrets.

He loved *her.*

The knowledge stole over him, slipping into his thoughts so naturally that it almost didn't register. It tickled the edges of his mind until his hand froze and his breathing stilled and his heart expanded, threatening to burst from his chest. For the first time, he understood the part of mating no one had ever explained to him, the part that kept his parents curling together every night after almost forty years. Quinn had been so focused on the heat and drive of the mating instinct, he'd never stopped to wonder what it signified.

He'd been so busy concentrating on possessing Cassidy, he hadn't noticed when she took possession of his heart.

Overwhelmed, breathless, he buried his face in the curve of her neck and pulled her tighter. He could never get her close enough, never get his fill of her. He needed her in a hundred ways he couldn't define, wanted her in a thousand more.

Cassidy stirred and shifted back against him. Her legs slid open until she lay half-draped across him like a blanket. Could any man resist the temptation? Would any man want to try?

He eased his hand lower until it cupped the slick warmth between her legs. God, she amazed him. They should both be unconscious, considering the amount of energy they had expended trying to devour each other for most of the afternoon. They'd finally drifted to sleep with no more than a drowsy kiss between them, but now all he had to do was touch her and her body reacted without hesitation. Instinct had her softening and melting for him, and he matched the anticipation with the watering in his mouth and the deep hunger at his core.

The hunger took on a life of its own, stirring and stretching inside him. He felt it flex its claws into his gut, taking hold and sending potent images of his woman spread and writhing beneath him. He saw sweat sheening their skin, bodies twisting together. He felt her body wrapped around him, his fingers biting into her hips. His temperature spiked, and he was just about ready to toss her onto her back and have at it when he saw the flutter of dark brown lashes against her pale cheeks.

He took a deep breath and fought for self-control, a battle he won the instant her golden eyes opened and smiled sleepily up into his.

"Mm. G'morning."

Her voice was rough and husky with sleep, and Quinn cleared his throat as his heart pounded in his chest. "Evening, really."

"It is? What time is it?" She craned her head to read the clock on the nightstand. "Yikes. I can't believe I slept so long. Why didn't you wake me?"

Quinn shrugged and leaned down to kiss her shoulder. It looked so pale and soft and warm he couldn't resist. "You were tired. You needed the rest."

She laughed. "I got enough rest for a three-toed tree sloth." She turned to face him and snuggled into his chest. "Did you get any sleep?"

"Plenty." *Damn. Is her neck always this luscious?* He leaned down to nibble, his body tightening as she murmured in sleepy contentment. Her fingers sifted into his hair, cradling him against her. As if he wanted to be anywhere else.

"You do seem to have a bit of energy."

"What can I say? I'm inspired."

She chuckled, a sleepy sound that tightened parts of

him that didn't need tightening. "I'll take that as a compliment."

He growled and slid down to trail kisses along her neck, over the hollow of her throat to the space between her breasts. "It's a bloody benediction."

"Well, hallelujah."

Quinn heard the laughter in her voice, but he was too focused on lapping the sweet, salty Cassidy taste off her chest to notice the hand she slipped between them to curl around his erection. Well, he didn't notice until the moment of the actual curl. Then he noticed plenty.

As his breath hissed between clenched teeth, his head fell backward and his body arched into her touch like a bowstring. "Sweet, merciful Christ!"

"Uh-uh. Just me. And I'm not feeling even remotely merciful." Her voice purred against his ear a moment before she shimmied her way under the covers to close her mouth over the head of his cock.

"Shit!"

He hadn't intended to speak—hadn't actually known he was capable of it—and as soon as the word was out of his mouth, he regretted it. Only because Cassidy seemed to find it deeply amusing, and her muffled chuckle sent vibrations strumming against nerve endings that already felt liable to implode.

"Wwwwwitch!"

Tensed like a racehorse, Quinn gave himself up to the torture and sank his fingers into her hair while she tried to kill him with swirling motions of her tongue. And deep, heavy suction. And—Mary, mother of God!—were those her fingernails scraping up the insides of his thighs?

How much of this was a man supposed to endure? Does she think I'm made of iron, for the love of—

Auuggghhhhh!

Later, he wouldn't be able to recall much of the next few minutes. He blacked out like a drunk after happy hour and heard, saw, felt nothing but the roaring in his ears and the painful tightening in his groin. He didn't remember pulling her off him or flipping her to the mattress beneath him. He didn't remember yanking her thighs up over his shoulders, or bracing his hands on the bed, or the claws sprouting out of the tips of his fingers and shredding her sheets to confetti. The only things that managed to penetrate the fog of his lust were the sensation of sinking balls-deep in her lush warmth and the long, high-pitched scream of pleasure she gave when he did.

He came to awareness somewhere in mid-thrust, his head thrown back, his lips curled in a ferocious snarl. His first, frantic thought was whether he'd scared her with his animalistic attack, but judging by the way her hands were knotted in the sheets and her body twisted and writhed beneath his, she looked like she'd overcome any sense of trauma.

Her breath came in ragged gasps and moans, ringing like music in his ears. It spurred him to ride her harder, thrust deeper, take more of what she offered so freely. He wanted to climb inside her and wear her like a wrapping until she could never get away from him. He wanted to drown in her, get lost in her, spend the rest of his life buried in her so that she forgot what it felt like not to be stretched full of him.

But he was only Lupine.

While his mind made plans for fucking her into the

next century, his body focused on fucking her into the next minute. He thrust faster, slamming into her with bruising force, and she welcomed him with breathless cries and arching hips. He lasted a Herculean forty-two seconds before she clenched around him and threw him headlong off the cliff into climax.

He hit bottom and bounced a couple of times before collapsing on top of her and sucking in air like a drowning man brought to the surface.

"Jesus wept," he gasped, when he could. "I think all my bones have melted into my skin."

She laughed harder than she should have had the energy for, and it was like lying on a waterbed in an earthquake. "Not quite, honey. I think one of those 'bones' melted into me."

She'd called him "honey." God, he loved his woman. This mate of his. He grinned into the sheet beneath them—heaven only knew what had happened to the pillow—then blew little scraps of cotton out of his mouth.

Mental note: Buy her new linens.

"And whose fault is that?" he demanded. He even managed it without gasping this time. "You're a wicked little temptress to drain a man's strength in such an illicit and perverse manner."

"Are you sure you aren't a vampire? 'Cause I haven't heard a sentence or a sentiment that archaic since sometime in the seventeenth century."

Quinn laughed and mustered up just enough strength to wrap his arms around her and roll onto his back with her draped cozily over his chest. She snuggled in with a kittenish yawn and rubbed her cheek against his slowly receding fur.

"I was a bit of an animal there, wasn't I?" he mused, lifting his hand up and watching as it shifted sluggishly from monstrous claw to simple, human appendage. Apparently, the force of his orgasm had left his shapeshifting talents as drained as the rest of him.

"Don't get carried away. You only had a couple of animal bits."

"Well, that's for the best, isn't it? You're a little bit of a thing as it is, Cassie love. If I'd shifted in the middle of all the excitement, I could have hurt you."

"I'm a Foxwoman." She lifted her head, her eyes narrowing in challenge. "I can take whatever you dish out, big boy."

His grin flashed, bright and wicked, as he flipped her easily onto her back. "Let's just test that theory, shall we?"

Eighteen

Quinn strolled back to his hotel late that evening, torn between infinite satisfaction and considerable worry. His time with Cassidy had done him a world of good, not only getting him one significant step closer to claiming his mate, but also leaving him with a renewed sense of energy sufficient to take on armies. He figured he'd need the lot of it to deal with the situation hanging over their heads.

The information they'd collected at Columbia would come in handy, but beyond that, there hadn't been much more they could do until they heard from De Santos again. Cassidy had placed a call to the student activities office at the university during one of the moments when he hadn't had her pinned against some flat surface, but they showed no record of a recognized group called "Students for Greater Truth." That left them with a dead end until the night of the lecture. Unless something turned up in the documents Gregor had sent from Moscow, they existed in limbo. He had checked his mobile phone before leaving her apartment, but somehow he couldn't convince himself that the fact that he'd missed no calls was a good sign.

"Quinn!"

He turned at the sound of the familiar voice and watched Richard unfold his frame from a low easy chair near the concierge's desk. The Selkie picked up a bulging manila folder and strode toward him.

"Where the devil have you been?" the Scot demanded. "I've been buzzing your room every five minutes for the last hour!"

Quinn felt a cold rush of fear. "What is it? Have you heard from Gregor? Is it Ysabel?"

"It's not Ysabel, though I've been back and forth so much on the phone to Russia, I swear to God I'll be pissing borscht till Thursday."

Quinn nodded toward the elevators. "Come upstairs for a drink. You can fill me in while I change my clothes."

"It'll need to be a big bloody drink," Richard muttered, but he followed his friend into the elevator. "And trust me when I tell you that your sophisticated fashion sense is going to be the last thing on your mind when you hear—"

Richard's mouth snapped shut just as the elevator dinged their arrival on the tenth floor. Quinn fished his key card out of his pocket and headed straight for his suite, not noticing that Richard had frozen in place, staring silently at his back.

"Bloody buggering bollocks!" Richard jogged up to Quinn's side just as the Lupine stepped through his door and flipped on the light switches. "You did it, you rat bastard. You spent the night with that foxy little redhead of yours, didn't you?"

If someone had given Quinn a million dollars and a swift kick in the arse, he couldn't have contained the smile that grew in response to that question.

Richard shook his head and threw himself down into a well-padded chair. "You did. I can't believe it, you shite. Here I've been slaving away trying to do a bloody job, and you've been locked up in some love nest somewhere trying to spawn a new generation of fwolfs. Or wolxes, or something."

Quinn sent his friend a warning look. "Whatever your gutter mind might be thinking, the truth is that Cassidy and I spent quite a bit of time on the clock ourselves. We found some interesting information that might tie in to the local cell of the Light of Truth."

Briefly, Quinn told Richard about their theory on the sect's recruiting practices and about the upcoming lecture he and Cassidy planned to attend.

"I think it's a good lead," he concluded. "We should at least be able to identify some of the key players in this cell, and hopefully exchange a few words with them. We might get somewhere with this."

"And I'm sure you're not even thinking about the chance it will give you to get the fox horizontal again, eh?"

"It's not about sex," Quinn growled as he crossed the room to the small bar where he had stored a fifth of Black Bush whiskey. Cassidy was his mate, and he didn't like having her thought of as nothing more than a pleasurable diversion.

Then again, he couldn't deny that he *did* want to get her horizontal again. At the first available opportunity.

He poured two glasses of the liquor and turned back to Richard. "All right. It's not *just* about the sex."

"There you are." Richard accepted his dram and raised it in toast. "Now, does that mean the sex wasn't all that good?"

That idiotic smile returned full force. "Sweet Mary, I thought I'd died and gone to heaven."

"That's what I thought. When is this lecture again?"

"Tuesday. And we'll be having dinner beforehand." Quinn swirled the golden liquor in his glass and watched it coat the heavy crystal. "I've a plan in mind."

"I find it's always best to keep things simple. Trousers off first, then knickers."

That brought a scowl to Quinn's face. He wasn't sure he liked the idea of Richard talking about Cassidy's knickers. Or thinking about Cassidy's knickers. Or really even being aware of the existence of Cassidy's knickers.

"What do you say you keep your mind on business, eh?" Quinn snapped. "Leave Cassidy out of this."

Richard's eyebrows shot up in surprise. "Well, well. That certainly explains a lot."

"What do you mean?"

"Cristos and I have been wondering what the bee in your bonnet has been the last couple of days. You've been acting too strangely for it to just be the job. Cristos is the one who pegged it. You're taking the little fox to mate, aren't you?"

Quinn's head jerked in a nod, and Richard raised his glass in a toast. "Congratulations, then, man. Though considering the family you're mating into, maybe I should offer good luck instead."

Wincing, Quinn decided Cassidy's family was the last thing he wanted to think about just then. "Fill me in on what you came here to tell me. You made it sound important."

Richard raised his glass and downed a healthy measure without blinking. "It is. I won't bore you with all the details of the hours Cristos and I spent as De Santos's clerical slaves, sorting through reams of paper, cross-referencing names and numbers. The man made us use color-coded highlighters!"

"You said you wouldn't bore me."

"Right. Then you'd better take a look at this." Expression now serious, Richard picked up the manila folder he'd brought with him and handed it to his friend.

Quinn took the sheaf of paperwork, brow wrinkled in curiosity, and opened it. He noticed there were indeed about five shades of highlighting marker decorating the pages. But the interesting part was what the colors revealed.

For several minutes, the only sound in the room came from the papers Quinn flipped through at a faster and faster pace. The amount of information here staggered him, but the volume didn't even begin to compare with the content. He skimmed through the first few pages in their entirety, trying to absorb information that didn't immediately make much sense. There were photocopies of banking receipts and account statements, as well as invoices from several firms for everything from courier services to plumbing repair. Quickly, his attention focused on the recurring flag of the green highlighting.

It appeared first on several financial transactions from a numbered foreign account to an account owned by someone named Daniil Yukov. The name meant nothing to Quinn, but the trail that led from it did.

He swore and looked up. "Who is this Yukov character?"

"According to Gregor's sources, he's a Ukrainian

national and a deacon in the Light of Truth organization. One of their prelate's—Heinrich Berger's—right hands."

"These records indicate that Yukov relocated from Kiev to Moscow eighteen months ago."

Richard nodded.

"And that a year after that, he withdrew a substantial amount of money from his Russian accounts and used them to open a new one at Manhattan United Banking Company on East Fifty-seventh Street."

"Two new accounts. One in his own name, one in the name of the Lumos Corporation."

Quinn's curses got more creative. He looked back down at the papers, and his eye caught something else. "The records of his New York account, which I won't ask how we obtained, say that among the first transactions made in the Lumos Corporation's name was a check written to Kaplan Long Realty."

"For a lease on a commercial property located on East Eleventh Street. A basement storefront, apparently."

"What did you find when you went by it?"

Richard gave his friend a slow smile and pushed to his feet. "Now, Quinn, old chum, did you think we'd leave you out of all the fun? Cristos is going to meet us at a coffee shop near the location at two A.M."

Feeling his own, predatory smile forming, Quinn set aside the folder and stood. "Then, as the Americans say, let's get ready to roll."

Even at two o'clock on a Monday morning, the streets of the East Village weren't quite deserted, but they were about as close as they could get. Far fewer people wandered about to witness the bit of judicious breaking and entering that Quinn and his merry men had planned. Quinn gave thanks for the small favor as he and Richard tried to look nonchalant. Behind them, Cristos fiddled and swore at a stubborn lock.

"Will you hurry it up, man?" Richard hissed. "Or were you hoping more than one of the bloody neighbors would be calling the police?"

The impatient Scot stood up on the sidewalk, carrying a backpack and leaning casually against the iron railing that blocked the basement entrance to the Lumos property. A couple of feet away in his wolf form, Quinn tried to look as much like an ordinary dog as was possible for a two-hundred-pound timber wolf. Fortunately, no one was out walking a real dog at this hour. The only other animal he'd seen hadn't been an animal at all, but a wererat who had given him a curious look before darting away into an alley. Hopefully, said Racine wasn't also an off-duty police officer gone for backup.

Cristos ignored Richard's comment, gave one last sharp twist to the slender metal pick in his hand, and grunted in satisfaction. "After you, my cantankerous friend. Unless you'd like to invite the neighbors to join us?"

Richard let his glare answer for him.

Silent as wraiths, the three slipped through the unlocked door, shutting it tightly behind them. All of the shifters saw almost as well in the dark as in daylight, so the dim interior didn't faze them. Cristos glanced around the room, while Quinn shifted back to his two-legged form and pulled out the clothes Richard had stashed in the backpack.

"I think our friends may be overpaying on their

lease," Cristos said, surveying the dingy, nearly empty room.

Quinn finished zipping his jeans and pulled a black T-shirt over his head. "We're not here to analyze their investments, Cris. We're looking for information."

The space Yukov had rented might be listed as a commercial storefront, but Quinn saw no evidence the zealot planned to use it that way. Instead of goods lining the walls, someone had taken to decorating with religious icons and artwork that consisted mainly of saints and sinners in various stages of violent deaths. Lord, how could a man get any work done when a dozen martyrs watched him day and night?

Other than the artwork, there didn't appear to be much in the small room. Quinn saw two stacks of battered-looking chairs, the kind usually found in church basements and at AA meetings, and a small but new-looking photocopier. In one corner, there was also a narrow, three-drawer filing cabinet and a dented metal desk topped with a shiny new computer.

Richard had already made himself comfortable and was booting up the system. "You lads take a better look around. I'll see what I can dig out of their files here."

Confident that the Scot knew more about electronic information than he ever would, Quinn looked at Cristos and jerked his chin toward the door in the rear corner of the storefront. If this had been a commercial space at some point, there had to be a back room for storage and inventory.

The Ursa nodded and led the way, easing the door open and peering into another dark room. Confident no one lurked in the shadows, he pushed open the door and both men stepped through.

Clearly, the space had been used for storage at some point, because a set of tall metal shelving units had been pushed into one corner and sat empty out of the way. In their place, someone had set up a small living area, complete with a narrow, foldaway bed with rumpled blankets, a crucifix hanging above it. Beside it was a small nightstand topped with a rickety lamp, and another old filing cabinet had been drafted into service as a dresser. A sock hung over the lip of a half-open drawer. Against the back wall, Quinn spotted a deep old utility sink and, next to it, a card table covered with clutter and a small hot plate.

"All the comforts of home," he muttered, and Cristos grimaced. "Shall we?"

They worked quietly and efficiently, rifling through drawers, checking under the mattress, and even sorting through a couple of piles of junk that looked as if it had been left by the previous tenants. They found nothing.

Disgruntled, they made their way back into the storefront where Richard still sat before the glowing monitor, tabbing through a series of windows.

"There's nothing back there," Quinn said, leaning against the edge of the desk and trying not to think about where he'd rather be at three in the morning.

"Unless you count what is likely the illegal residential use of a commercial property," Cristos added.

"Doesn't matter." Richard never took his eyes off the computer screen. "What I've got here is more than enough to make this little criminal escapade of ours worthwhile."

"What is it?"

"The idiots apparently think password protection is

the log-in window the operating system makes you use to start up." Richard had made a fortune in the technology stock boom several years ago, partly because he invested wisely and got out early, and partly because he was a computer genius. His tone indicated the Lightheads weren't. "They've got way more incriminating documents on here than is remotely wise. Or even remotely not stupid as shite."

"What kind of documents?" Cristos asked.

"The kind that give us a much better idea of how their organization works and tell us we're in even more trouble than we thought," he said, finally looking up at his friends. "According to what's on this system, the Lighthead cells all seem to be independent operations, each led by a deacon trained in Germany under the Prelate before hiving off to 'shepherd his own flock.' Brother Daniil Yukov is the Shepherd of Manhattan."

Quinn scowled. "We already knew about Yukov, and could probably have guessed the rest. That's not news."

"No, but the fact that the cell in Manhattan is being fed information about the Others by someone in the know, is."

Quinn froze. "I take it you're not referring to Ysabel."

Richard shook his head. "No, I'm talking about an Other."

"What do you mean?" Cristos growled, his light-hearted manner giving way to the angry bear beneath. "Who among us would even think of giving aid to an enemy who wishes to destroy us?"

"That it doesn't say, but it *is* happening. They've recorded it all in black-and-white."

"If it doesn't say who it is, then how do you know it's one of us?" Quinn didn't doubt Richard, but he had just as hard a time as Cristos imagining anyone in their community who would do such a thing.

"'Received another call today from the Damned Soul,'" Richard read. "'DS claims to have been at recent meeting of monsters. They seem to have a sort of unholy governing body of their own. Told us of decision by this council to destroy an innocent who witnessed one of their many crimes. If allying ourselves to one of the monsters allows us to bring them to everlasting judgment, the Lord will forgive us. These demons must be stopped.' End quote."

"I'd like to see their faces if they ever ran into a real demon," Cristos bit out, stepping away from the desk to prowl restlessly around the room.

"But who would do it?" Quinn shoved a hand through his hair and wished he'd been able to concentrate more on the Council at their meeting the other night and less on the woman seated across from him. "Most of them were against the idea of coming out at all, and I guarantee none of them would have lifted a finger to speed it along, let alone gone to the trouble of aiding a group of human fanatics."

Richard pulled up another document and gestured toward the screen. "Well, it's at least someone with enough resources to donate generously. Whoever this 'Damned Soul' is, he's been giving tidy little sums to the cell for at least the last couple of months."

Cristos swore vividly in Spanish. "I wonder what else they have done to betray us?"

"Right now, 'what' matters less than 'who.' Richard, can you get copies of the documents that we can take with us? I think De Santos is a lot more likely to be able to identify this character than we are."

Richard tapped a finger on the tiny USB drive that stuck out from the front of the CPU. "Already got it. I'm taking most of their correspondence and a few other interesting files."

Cristos flashed his teeth. It couldn't be called a smile. "Take everything. The better to hang them with. When we get—"

"Quiet!" Quinn hissed as a whisper of sound caught his attention. It had come from the back of the store.

Surprised, Cristos took one look at the Lupine's face and stiffened. He followed his friend's fixed gaze to the door to the back room and inhaled deeply. Behind them, Richard was already speeding through the computer files and preparing to power down the system the second he got what he needed.

Quinn stretched and shifted, shimmying out of his clothes. He ghosted through the door they had left slightly ajar. Cristos accompanied him on two human feet, keeping close to the walls to take advantage of the deep shadows. Nothing in the back room looked out of place, but Quinn's senses told him something was. The scent of the human who lived here was getting stronger, and again he heard the quiet clinking sound that had caught his attention. He butted his head against his friend's knee and hunkered down to slink soundlessly toward the back door. That noise had been the jingling of a key ring. Someone had decided to come home before morning.

The Ursa moved in a blur, covering the distance between the shop door and the back door in two great leaps. He flattened himself against the wall, while Quinn crouched in the shadows under the bed and waited.

It didn't take long.

A few seconds after they'd gotten in place, Quinn

heard a human mumbling something on the other side of the rear door and caught a quick, pungent whiff of incense. Their Lightheaded friend had come home. Quinn was betting they could have him down before he drew breath to scream.

That's pretty much how it happened.

In a flurry of time and motion, a key turned in the lock, the door began to creak open, and Cristos darted forward, grabbing the figure and hauling him inside before he knew what had happened. The momentum of the Ursa's tug threw the human to the floor where Quinn took over. He sprang from under the bed and landed on top of the young man. He smelled the rush of panic from his victim, and his sharp, white teeth clamped menacingly around a slim throat.

The human drew breath for a scream, and Quinn's jaws tightened in warning.

"I suggest you keep quiet." In the dark, Cristos's deep voice and threatening posture were enough to make the human go instantly still. Well, except for the trembling muscles, which Quinn supposed he really couldn't have helped. "If you manage that, I can promise you are unlikely to come to any harm."

If Cristos was surprised by who their zealot turned out to be, he didn't show it. Quinn didn't know what they'd been expecting, but a skinny kid barely out of high school and two sizes too small for the rough black monk's robe he wore hadn't been it.

"Who . . ." The human tested the freedom he was likely to be given, which allowed speech at nothing above a whisper. "Who are you?"

"Given the circumstances, don't you believe we're the ones who'll be asking the questions, laddie?"

Richard asked as he appeared in the other doorway. He stepped forward until he stood over the young man's wolf-pinned form and glared down at him. "What's your name?"

A slight tightening of Quinn's jaws elicited a stuttered response. "D-David."

"Well, David, my friends and I are wanting your help with something. You will help us, won't you?"

David trembled, and the sharp stink of fear filled Quinn's nostrils. He snorted and concentrated on blocking it out.

"W-what do you want?"

"Just some information, laddie. For instance, who is this person you call 'the Damned Soul'?"

Quinn felt the kid's surprise at the question and smelled the suspicion that followed. "Where did you hear that name?"

A growl rumbled in Quinn's chest, and Richard made a soft tsking sound. "Remember, laddie. We ask, you answer. Who is he?"

"I don't know what you're talking about."

"My friend doesn't like liars, you know."

Quinn emphasized Richard's point with a subtle flexing of his jaws, as if testing how difficult it would be to tear out David's throat.

It would be very, very easy.

The kid gulped in fear. "I don't know."

"David . . ."

Richard's voice wasn't half the warning that Quinn's teeth were, or Cristos's menacing step forward, but it didn't hurt.

"I swear!" David squeaked. "I don't know who he is. He's never told us his name."

"What does he look like?"

"I don't know that, either. Brother Daniil put us in touch. We talk on the phone, and I only handle some of the calls. It's always a different time, so whoever is in the office answers. We don't meet him in person. You can't trust a monster that close."

None of the Others liked the answer, but the rush of words and fear from the young man made it difficult to disbelieve.

"I'll let that comment slide just now," Richard said in a low, unhappy voice. "Tell me what he sounds like."

David frowned. "Like a kidnapper in the movies. Like he's using one of those machines to disguise his voice. He probably knows what we'd do to him if we knew how to find him."

Considering the human's current position, the threat lacked force. Quinn snorted, and the kid nearly jumped out of his skin.

"Can you tell us anything that could identify him?"

"No. Like I said, it's not a normal voice. It's all mechanical and distorted. I don't even really know if it's a man or a woman."

Richard muttered something under his breath. "All right, then let's try something different. Where is Daniil Yukov?"

"I don't kno—"

"Spare us. You can deny whatever you like, but the money for your rent comes from an account whose only signatory is Daniil Yukov. Is he Brother Daniil?"

The kid squirmed, and Quinn added a broad, furry paw to his chest to keep him in place.

"Brother Daniil is a holy man. I won't—"

In his shadowed corner, Cristos pressed his right fist

into the opposite palm and cracked his knuckles one by one. "If he won't give you a straight answer, let me try. He can scream once for yes and twice for no."

Quinn wrinkled his nose and hoped Cristos would leave the threat at that. He wanted the kid to cooperate as much as anyone, but he didn't want to be this close if young David lost control of his bowels out of sheer terror.

"I don't think that will be necessary," Richard said, his voice as quiet as his footfall when he took one deliberate step forward. "Will it, David?"

"No, but you're too late," the human whispered, trembling. "Brother Daniil is gone. He left Wednesday to do God's work."

Quinn stiffened and his teeth sank deeper into the boy's throat, drawing a strangled scream. He hadn't intended to hurt the human, but a very unpleasant thought had occurred to him.

It occurred to Richard as well. "And what kind of work is that?"

"A mission of salvation." David's words were defiant, but his tone had weakened with fear. "He returned to a stronghold of evil to gather evidence against the monsters among us, so that the world can know they must be destroyed."

Ysabel.

It couldn't be coincidence. Daniil Yukov had flown back to Europe on Wednesday so he could assist in Ysabel's kidnapping in Moscow on Thursday. Quinn wanted to howl in frustration.

"I would not speak so eagerly of destruction, if I were you," Richard bit out. "You might find yourself reaping what you sow."

He gestured to Quinn to release the young man. Quinn complied reluctantly, but more because David's polluted mind left a bitter taste in his mouth than because he didn't want to tear the human's throat out. Such blind hatred enraged him. He lifted his head, but kept a paw firmly planted on the kid's chest to keep him from going anywhere.

"This has been useless!" Cristos snapped. "Yukov is gone and whoever this 'Damned Soul' is, he's covered his tracks too well for us to find him."

"Not useless. We still have more information than we had before we got here." Richard patted the pocket containing the USB drive. "It would be convenient if the lad could tell us more, but the files will help."

David jerked under Quinn's paw. "You stole our computer files? You can't do that! You—"

"Oh, shut up." The impatient order came with another foot on David's chest, but this one landed on his solar plexus with more force than absolutely necessary. Quinn grinned a wolfish grin. "You can't tell us anything else, so the least you can do is keep silent. Quinn, let him up. We need to get back to the club and give these records a more thorough going-over. And we need to let Gregor know about Yukov. Maybe if he can find this maniac, he will also find his Ysabel."

Cristos frowned. "Do you think it's wise to just leave the human here, my friend? The minute we are out the door, the imbecile is likely to try and follow us, or to call the police. Or call some of his less lawful and more violent friends to seek us out."

"No he won't. You're going to stay with him while Quinn and I start back. I'll call De Santos and ask if his wife or one of her other witchy friends can meet you here in a few minutes and do a little something about young David's memory."

The human started to launch a protest, but Quinn hadn't shifted just yet. He pressed his muzzle into the kid's face and drew his lips back into a snarl. David went quiet.

"Come on, Quinn. De Santos needs to hear all this."

With one last grumble, Quinn lifted his paws off the human's chest and took a step away. Then he arched his back, lifted his head, and shifted back into his human form.

David passed out in the middle of a girlish scream.

Chuckling, Cristos went to the front of the store to retrieve Quinn's clothes, his good humor beginning to recover. "Leave the intrepid monster slayer to me," he said, handing over the rumpled garments, "but not for too long. I haven't eaten in hours, and even if he is skinny, he's better than nothing."

Quinn dressed quickly. The threat was meaningless, but he knew Cristos's talents would be better used dealing with the crisis at hand than babysitting a zealot-in-training. "Try the peanuts over on the table. They're more likely to fill you up."

Beside him, Richard flipped his cell phone closed and nodded to the door. "Come on. De Santos is going to meet us back at the club, and he's sending someone here right away, Cris. He said it won't be more than thirty minutes."

"Damn it, Richard, why didn't you let me talk to him?" Cristos grumbled. "I could have asked him to make the witch stop and pick me up a pizza."

Nineteen

Cassidy never did make it to her grandmother's house for cocktails that night. She had intended to, had even pushed Quinn out the door around seven-thirty so she would have time for a hot bath. She needed to soak away the soreness inspired by the overuse of long-neglected muscles, but first she sat down on the edge of her rumpled bed just so she could catch her breath.

When she woke, the dim green numbers on her alarm clock told her it was coming up on twelve. Judging by the look of her windows, she was guessing midnight. It felt decadent, having slept so much, but she didn't regret a minute of it. After all, when was the last time she'd gotten so much vigorous exercise?

Way too long ago, she mused. She couldn't deny she felt a little bruised and more than a little raw, but she didn't regret that, either. In fact, it put an exceedingly goofy grin on her face that she wore while she shrugged into her favorite cotton robe and shuffled out to the kitchen for a midnight snack. She seemed to have worked up a bad case of what her mother had always laughingly called "the munchies."

She stood in front of the fridge snacking on cheddar

and contemplating something more substantial when her phone rang.

She swallowed the last of her cheese and moved to the living room to grab the cordless. "Hello?"

"Miss Poe."

"Speaking." She wasn't all that fazed by a call this late. After all, Others kept some crazy hours, but she was trying to decide if it would be too much trouble to whip up a batch of buttermilk biscuits, so she might have sounded distracted.

"Miss Poe, we have been trying to reach you for most of the day. Do you have a moment to speak?"

Cassidy hitched her hip against the end table and frowned. The voice sounded familiar, but for some reason she couldn't quite place it. "It's kind of late. Who did you say you were?"

The man on the other end of the line ignored her question. "It is important. A matter of great concern to the Council."

The light bulb over her head went on, and she stood up straighter. "Oh. You're the one who left me a message at my grandmother's house. I'm sorry, I was going to call earlier, but . . . er, I got tied up most of the day."

"We did say it was important."

"Well, these things happen," Cassidy said, frowning at the caller's rudeness. It wasn't a quality she was used to finding in a Council member. "I'm not quite sure what I can help you with, but of course I'll do whatever I can for the—"

The caller cut her off. "Then we'll send a car for you. It will pick you up outside your building in fifteen minutes. Don't make the driver wait."

The hackles on the back of Cassidy's neck rose. The

call had just cruised past rude and made a left turn into creepy. Her instincts did *not* want her getting into any vehicle sent by this caller. Maybe it was the time of night, or maybe she was just losing her mind, but a feeling was a feeling.

"Did you say you were calling on behalf of the Council?"

There was a pause. "No. But the Council would do well to listen to what we have to say."

Okay, now Cassidy really wasn't going anywhere. And she was also feeling a lot less inclined to play whatever game the caller had in mind. The Council had earned her respect, but people who called her in the middle of the night just to freak her out were another story.

"Unfortunately, you've caught me at a bad time. As I said, it's been a busy day and I was just about to get some sleep. If you want to leave me your name and number again, I can call back tomorrow. I'll be a lot more useful once I've gotten some rest."

There was a short pause, and the speaker on the other end of the line somehow managed to make it sound displeased. "This is a matter of some importance, Miss Poe."

"I'm sure it is, but I can barely keep my eyes open." She inserted a yawn for effect. "I would be totally useless to you at the moment."

"Miss Poe." The voice began to sound testy. "I'm afraid you don't fully grasp the situation that my colleagues and I would like to discuss with you."

Cassidy's temper hit its limit. She scowled into the receiver. "Forgive me if this sounds rude, but since you didn't say what you wanted to talk about in the message you left with my grandmother's housekeeper, and since you still haven't felt compelled to share it with me during this conversation, you're right about that. I don't know what it is you want to discuss."

"And that is why we should meet right away—"

"Look," she snapped, as did her control, "since you seem to have trouble hearing, let me make this clear. I'm *not* available tonight. End of story. If you want to talk to me about important business, small business, big business, or monkey business, you can call back in the morning."

She pushed the phone's off button and thumped it down onto the cradle. She couldn't remember a conversation so unsettling since college. And that one had likely involved the use of an intoxicating agent. This time, she'd been stone-cold sober.

Shaking her head, Cassidy decided to put it out of her mind and pulled a dozen free-range eggs out of her refrigerator. She had better things to do than speculate about political whack jobs who called her in the middle of the night to insist the world was about to come to an end if she didn't cater to their little fantasies. The only fantasies she planned to cater to for the foreseeable future were the very reason she was standing half-naked in her kitchen in the middle of the night prepared to administer massive doses of protein to herself.

After all, a girl had to keep up her strength.

Quinn felt as if someone had lined the insides of his eyelids with sandpaper, and perhaps whacked him sharply over the head with a lead pipe for good measure. It left him somewhat cranky. Given that the time was now closing in on four in the morning and he could think of at least a hundred other places he'd rather be—most of them involving a certain redhead and a horizontal surface—he thought himself very restrained for pacing the library at Vircolac rather than resorting to violence.

But oh, how the violence tempted him.

Hands fisted in his pockets, he reached a wall, spun on his heel and stalked back in the other direction. Richard had taken the opportunity to stretch out on the sofa and close his eyes, and De Santos successfully ignored Quinn by immersing himself in the documents seized from the Lightheads' computer. Within five minutes of their arrival at the club, the Felix had printed out the contents of the USB drive and settled himself behind that massive, immaculate desk with a cup of coffee and five colors of highlighter. He'd been making notes and keeping silent for the past forty minutes, and Quinn gave himself ten more of his own before a complete mental breakdown.

A minute and a half later, he revised his estimate.

"For the love of all that's good and right in this world, De Santos, a blind ninety-seven-year-old with gout wouldn't take so long to read a few pages! Are you translating them into Sanskrit, or do you plan to tell us what the hell you think?"

De Santos looked up from his pages, his expression no more than mildly irritated. "Has anyone ever mentioned that you can be a real pain in the ass, wolf boy?"

"Only every day," Richard called out from the sofa.

Quinn couldn't make up his mind over which of them to throttle, so he just glared and brooded while the head of the Council shuffled through the documents. Then the Felix pulled out six sheets and laid them out in a neat row on the desk.

"This is no small matter, Quinn. I wanted to be very careful not to jump to conclusions."

"Just so long as there's a conclusion in there somewhere."

"You tell me." De Santos tapped the first of the printouts he'd laid out and leaned back in his chair. "I suggest you pay particular attention to the passages marked in yellow."

Reining his impatience in hard, Quinn braced his palms on the desk and bent his head to read. He felt Richard's presence when the Selkie rose and moved to stand behind him, but he didn't look up. He didn't even snap about someone reading over his shoulder. He was too busy following the trail of dots that De Santos had connected with his damned yellow highlighter. With each new sentence, he felt the knot in his throat tighten until he almost choked on it. Richard had to be the one to speak.

"Buggering hell. The dragon! Adele Berry is the Lightheads' informant?"

Quinn waged war against the compulsion to howl his outrage to the skies. His tightly clenched jaw told him he managed it, but the close watch De Santos kept on his face said it was a near thing.

"Most of the entries are signed with the initial *D,* for David, I assume. The boy has been helpful, but nothing here can be called conclusive," the Felix warned. "It amounts to more of a collection of implications and innuendos than anything resembling fact. Whoever has been aiding these radicals has done an impeccable job covering his, or her, tracks. The evidence pointing to Adele is limited and subtle, but very definitely present."

Speech failed him. Quinn held on to his control with a tenuous grip. Emotion drove the urge to shift until it threatened to overwhelm him. *Cassidy.* What would she do? How would she cope? Instinct demanded that he protect her, but how could he defend her against the betrayal of her grandmother? He was reduced to impotence, and the helplessness only fueled his rage. His skin began to tingle in the first sign of his change, and he tensed, fighting against it. He couldn't afford to relax his control, not when his animal impulses whispered at him to tear apart anyone who dared to hurt his mate.

Sheer force of will beat the beast back into its cage, but when he raised his head to meet De Santos's eyes, he knew his own would still be glowing a bright, golden amber. The Felix watched him for a long minute before nodding.

"Good. Now, if you will allow me to continue, I will show you something else." Picking up the six sheets he had originally laid out, De Santos replaced them with five more. "The papers I just showed you contain some circumstantial but worrying evidence against Adele. They tell us the one referred to as the 'Damned Soul' is one of our most respected and influential members, that he or she possesses frightening powers, and that he or she also possesses great wealth, evidenced by several substantial monetary donations to the cell's cause. These things could refer to any member of the Council. Then, the diaries of the contact between the cell, someone referred to as 'R,' and this Damned Soul say the Other is privy to the most secret workings of our governance, which narrows the field and leaves us with only the members of the Inner Circle. There are fifteen in that group, but again more than one of us match the diary's description. Adele is mainly implicated by one statement."

The Felix picked up one of the three papers and read, " 'This monster with whom we cooperate for the higher cause, neither harnesses the powers of evil for works of dark magic'—and I take it to mean they believe all works of magic to be dark—'nor is forced by the light of the moon to take hideous shape, but believes itself above the lunar pull, unique and superior among all the accursed.' "

Richard raised his brows and spoke over Quinn's low growl. "That sounds like more than an implication to me."

De Santos nodded. "At first glance I would agree, and that troubles me. For someone so careful not to give the humans any hint of his true identity, why reveal so much detail as to allow any first-time reader familiar with the Council to guess it?"

"She would have had to tell the Lightheads something, otherwise why would they agree to work with her?"

"I'm sure the informant did have to reveal something, but such an important and unique detail? It doesn't make sense." He set down the page of diary entries and pointed to the other documents spread before him. "The passage strikes me as nothing more than a clumsy attempt at misinformation, so I looked more closely at some of the financial documents. They're difficult to trace because they were routed through offshore accounts, but if you will follow the blue lines, I think you'll notice an unusual commonality."

Quinn just glared at De Santos and curled his lip. He

was barely managing to keep his shape. No way could he see through his haze of anger well enough to read anything yet.

"Well, if you did read the sections I marked, you would notice that the transfer request origins are recorded based on whether the orders were placed electronically or by phone. In each case, the location of the originating computer or telephone is indicated by a numeric area code. Most of them come from Manhattan, which again fails to narrow anything down, but several of the orders were placed in Connecticut."

His snarl gradually turning to a scowl, Quinn squinted at the papers. "And what is that supposed to mean to us?"

"Adele Berry was born and raised in Manhattan, as were her mother and grandmother at the very least. This is a woman who finds the Hamptons wild and uncivilized. I doubt she'd set foot in Brooklyn unless threatened with bodily harm. This woman does *not* make regular jaunts into Connecticut."

Quinn's haze cleared in a rush of hope. "Then it means someone else must be the informant."

"I can't call it proof, but I'm inclined to say yes."

"But why point to her if she wasn't involved?"

De Santos looked grim. "That is what has me concerned. The most recent entries in the diary mention that the informant's aid has allowed them to plan a strike against us that would either give them the final proof they need to expose us, or force us to take action against them, thus exposing ourselves."

He pulled one final sheet of paper out of the stack and handed this one directly to Quinn. The Lupine scanned the contents and felt his muscles tense all over again.

"What is it, man?" Richard demanded.

"It's a bill from a private investigator." Quinn's fingers tightened until the paper crumpled in his hand.

"For what?"

"For surveillance on the person and the home of Adele Berry."

Twenty

On Monday afternoon, Cassidy followed the last of her Cultural Anthro 102 students out of the small lecture hall and switched off the lights in relief. Normally, she loved her job, but today she'd rather go home and crawl back into bed next to a certain Lupine who hadn't let her get much sleep over the past day and a half. There were just two problems with that. One, he wasn't actually in her bed at the moment, because she'd kicked him out of it yesterday evening; and two, she had a hundred and fifty new papers to grade.

This called for coffee.

Decision made, she hefted her pack higher on her shoulder and left the campus building for her favorite coffee shop three blocks over. It was owned by a gnome whom most humans mistook for a particularly grumpy midget. Cassidy knew the key to not getting kicked out of his shop was to come often and praise lavishly. Gnomes melted at the slightest compliment.

The café was typically quiet when she stepped inside, a rush of warm, coffee-scented air greeting her. She nodded and waved to the hostess and wove her way between the tightly packed tables to her favorite booth near the back window. It didn't overlook much, just a small patio that served as extra seating in the summer, but Cassidy was a creature of habit. And besides, she liked watching the squirrels. They ran away like speed demons every time they saw her coming.

She settled in and, armed with a self-serve pot of café au lait and a red felt-tip pen, dove into her freshman classes' impressions on the meaning and boundaries of culture. Thank goodness freshmen eventually turned into seniors and their papers started to make sense.

Her pen flew over the pages, and within an hour, she'd made a reasonable, if unimpressive, dent in the stack. The dent she'd made in the coffee was considerably larger. In fact, it necessitated flagging down a waiter for a new pot.

She stretched the kinks out of her back and looked around for a server. Instead a tall, pale blond woman slipped into the other side of her booth and stared at her with ice-blue eyes.

Cassidy pursed her lips. "What can I do for you, Grendl?"

"Gretel."

"Whatever."

The other woman didn't blink at Cassidy's old dig. Either she'd never read *Beowulf,* or she'd gotten used to being called a monster.

The Nordic ice queen and professional gofer to the Other stars had never been one of Cassidy's favorite people. She had the looks of a supermodel—all painfully slender limbs, sharp cheekbones, and oversized lips—and the morals of pond scum. Cassidy didn't know all that much about her personally beyond that she had been the lover/distraction technique for a series of the city's more wealthy and less ethical Other men. Frankly, she really didn't care to learn more. There was just something about the lack of a soul in a human being that set her teeth on edge. Go figure, but she had always thought if vampires, shifters, sorcerers, witches, and Fae could have souls, a human being ought to be able to manage one.

"What do you want?" Cassidy asked after a brief, mutual dislike-filled silence.

"A meeting."

"It seems like half the city is just foaming at the bit to have an audience with me these days." She couldn't quite manage to contain the sarcasm.

Gretel shrugged, sending the curtain of her long, nearly white blond hair shifting like water. "I can't see why, but I suppose it's none of my business."

Cassidy folded her arms over her chest and slouched back in the booth. "So what is your business? Still whoring for that sorcerer on the Upper West Side?"

"I have a new employer," the blonde said mildly, refusing to take the bait. "Someone who has been very anxious to meet with you. In fact, he's already attempted to contact you twice. And he's rather unhappy at having been put off."

Cassidy lifted an eyebrow. The person who had called her at home and at Adele's house was Gretel's boss? "And who are you working for now, Grendl? Could it be . . . *Satan*?"

Gretel looked blank. Maybe she'd never watched Dana Carvey on *Saturday Night Live*. Yet another reason not to trust her.

"I work for Mr. Leonard now."

Cassidy swore silently. She wasn't sure she was comfortable with Francis Leonard seeking her out for anything. She wasn't terribly fond of the old bloodsucker. Plus, she didn't trust him any further than she could kill him.

As amoral as his employee, Leonard held a seat on the Council's Inner Circle, but Cassidy had never been quite certain why. From what her grandmother said of him, the vampire lacked just about everything the position required, from insight to diplomacy, but he did have money. A lot of it. And even though he wasn't a particularly old vampire, a few decades over three hundred by the best estimates, he'd spent nearly all that time in New York. If Francis Leonard possessed any talent, it was for making beneficial alliances and weaseling out of them at the most opportune moments.

"My, my," she finally said, keeping her voice bland. "Isn't that an interesting career move?"

"He offered me a most advantageous position."

Cassidy could guess what sort of position the megalomaniac vampire had offered, and she figured it was the kind that aired in a thousand adult movie booths across the nation every day. Only, you know, with more bloodsucking. "Let me guess. You provide the meals and he provides the . . . wait. What does Leonard provide his human servants, other than chronic anemia?"

"I am very satisfied with the arrangement."

Cassidy knew enough about the relationship between a vampire and his or her human servant. Usually it was based on trust, mutual benefit, and even a certain amount of friendship. She'd known lots of vamps over the years who used humans as their eyes and ears during the day and to provide blood in emergencies. In exchange, those vamps usually offered protection and increased longevity, with a bit of extra power and some financial aid thrown in. But that was the average vampire. Francis Leonard wasn't average. He was, in fact, an extraordinarily nasty being who never did anyone a favor if he could get the same result through manipulation, intimidation, or brute force. Cassidy liked him even less than Gretel.

Still, the blonde was right. It wasn't any of her business.

"Fine," she said, smiling at the waiter who dropped off a fresh pot of coffee. The expression faded fast once she turned back to her visitor. "So then why don't we cut to the chase, and you can tell me why Leonard is so anxious to get to know me after all these years. I didn't know he cared."

Gretel ignored the sarcasm. "About you? He doesn't. But he is keenly interested in the affairs of the Council."

"Don't tell me he's still pouting about De Santos being appointed head instead of him? I mean, talk about sore losers."

Something shifted behind the other woman's hollow eyes. "We, of course, respect the head of the Council. However, we do not feel that such respect requires our withdrawal from important matters of debate. The voices of all Council members are valued and should be heard."

Cassidy was betting Gretel had spent hours rehearsing that little response. "No doubt. But that still doesn't shed a whole lot of light on the reason why your boss has been stalking me for the last two days."

The blonde's hands remained folded neatly on the

table in front of her. " 'Stalking' is a bit harsh, don't you think?"

"Not really. He's attempted to contact me at my home, at my grandmother's home, and now at a public café I'm known to frequent. He's left numerous messages, and he's sent a human servant to harass me when I didn't respond quickly enough to his demands for a meeting. In my book, that's stalking. The only thing he hasn't done is left a dead cat in my mailbox."

"That could be arranged."

"No, thanks."

She shrugged. "None of the methods to which you protest so strongly would have been necessary had you simply agreed to a meeting as Mr. Leonard requested."

Cassidy's eyebrow shot up. "I never disagreed to the meeting. I just told him that the times he wanted to meet were inconvenient for me. It's not my fault he's a spoiled little vamp who refuses to wait for a mutually agreeable time."

"You haven't offered any alternative meeting arrangements."

"Well, he hasn't given me the chance. I said I'd call him today, and I will. I haven't exactly had a ton of spare time on my hands."

Gretel made a point of looking around the café and down at the cell phone that rested on the table beside Cassidy's coffee cup. "I do not see any restraints on you at the moment. And you clearly have access to modern methods of communication."

Okay, that snotty tone of voice was not winning the vamp's lackey any points. "I happen to be working right now. I'm a professor. I teach classes, then I mark papers. When I finish my job, then I have time for extraneous nonsense like playing phone tag with self-important bloodsuckers. Besides," she said, scowling, "shouldn't your boss be asleep right about now?"

"Yes. He is."

"Well, then get off my case!" Cassidy thought her tone made her exasperation clear, but if there was any confusion, she was prepared to take action. Like tearing out someone's stupid blond hair. "If the guy can't even form a sentence till sundown, why the hell are you harassing me?"

"Aside from the entertainment value?" Gretel smiled. "I have my orders. I am authorized to book all of Mr. Leonard's appointments. Since you were unable to schedule a time with him, we thought it might be more convenient to set the time with me."

The blonde reached into an inner pocket of her blazer and pulled out a slim PDA. She turned it on and slid out a stylus, tapping the screen a few times before raising expectant eyes to Cassidy. "How does this evening look for you? Around nine?"

Twenty-one

The universe hated her. Cassidy knew it.

Her apartment was empty of werewolves when she walked in the door, her answering machine held four new messages from friends whom she'd stood up in the last couple of days while chasing down lunatics, and her phone started ringing again the moment she threw the locks behind her. Picking up the cordless unit, she glanced down at the caller ID and saw her grandmother's number in the little window of doom. Groaning, she girded her mental loins and pressed the talk button.

"Hello?"

"So you're not lying dead in a ditch somewhere being devoured by insects. I was beginning to wonder."

Oh, for gods' sake. "No, Nana, I'm fine. How are—"

Adele didn't give her time to finish. "Especially given what's just happened."

Cassidy frowned. "What do you mean? What's happened?"

"Governor Thurgood's daughter has been in a car accident."

Cassidy was aware her grandmother knew the governor, but she didn't know why this was big news. She searched for an appropriate comment. "I hope she's not seriously injured."

"Unfortunately, she was. It seems her car was struck by a drunk driver on her way home from a party in Connecticut. She was taken to a local hospital and admitted to the ER before anyone could be notified."

She started to murmur something else polite when the implications of Adele's news struck her. "The governor of New York is Other. He's Racine."

"A wererat," Adele confirmed with a sniff. "As is his daughter."

"But no one is supposed to know that."

"No, but if the doctors in Connecticut performed a thorough exam on Alexandra, now somebody does."

"Are we too late? I mean, haven't they already run tests? Don't they already know whatever they're going to find out?"

"No one is sure," her grandmother admitted. "The Council only found out about this a few minutes ago. Her father was in Beijing meeting with members of their Olympic committee in hopes of improving the chances of one of the state's major cities in the next bid for the games, so it will be a day at least before he can get there himself. Rafael De Santos is sending two representatives to Connecticut right now. One is posing as the girl's fiancé, the other as a member of her father's staff. Naturally, they will be very concerned about her injuries and the tests and treatments that have been administered. We hope their questions will give us a good sense of what the doctors know."

"Does the Council need my help?" Cassidy asked warily, thinking of the last things the Council had asked her to do.

"I thought Rafael might already have contacted you."

Was it her imagination, or did her grandmother sound as if she were fishing for something?

"No, this is the first I've heard about it. I haven't spoken to Mr. De Santos since the meeting the other night."

Cassidy imagined her grandmother's spine stiffening.

"When he asked you to work with that Irish dog."

"Irish dog? Nana, the man has a name, you know."

"I'm not concerned with his name, Cassidy. I'm concerned with yours. With the good name of this entire family. What could you be thinking to get involved with such a . . . creature?"

"Nana, the head of the Council asked me to cooperate with Mr. Quinn on a serious matter. I could hardly refuse. You know. You were there."

The temperature of Adele's voice dropped from its usual chill to something akin to permafrost. "I don't see how a Council-ordered collaboration requires the beast to be seen entering your apartment at eleven at night and not leaving until seven the following evening."

Oh, shit.

"Did you have someone *spy* on me?" she demanded.

"Honestly, Cassidy, don't be insulting. Why would I need to have someone spy on my own granddaughter?"

"Then what makes you say Sullivan Quinn spent the night at my apartment?"

"It's all over the community, Cassidy, thanks to your cousin. Everyone knows. And I don't think I need to tell you how unhappy that makes me."

Not so much. Cassidy could hear her grandmother's disapproval loud and clear.

"I hesitate to tell you how to live your life," Adele continued, and Cassidy had to work to suppress a snort. "You are, after all, a grown woman. However, I must say, this . . . fling of yours shows a remarkable lack of good judgment. In the first place, the two of you are co-workers—"

"We're digging up some information together, Nana. It's not as if he's my department chair at the university."

"It doesn't matter. I raised you to know better than to get involved with a common animal like that," Adele continued. "The man is a werewolf. He's not our kind, Cassidy."

"Not our kind?" Even to herself, her voice sounded incredulous. "Nana, we're Foxwomen. Almost no one is our kind. You make it sound like Quinn is from another planet. He's Lupine. So what? He's a shifter; I'm a shifter. What other kind are you talking about?"

"You know very well what I mean," the older woman snapped. "A werewolf is a very different thing from a Foxwoman. How can you compare their crude, childish attempts at shifting to what we do? A kit could do better than one of their elders."

Okay, now Cassidy was sure she had a migraine. "Nana, we shift from human to fox. They shift from human to wolf. It's really not that big a difference."

"I'm not talking about end results, Cassidy Emilia. I'm talking about methods and about finesse. We shift because the magic of the transformation flows in our blood. We choose our time, our place. We are women, or we are foxes. We do not become stuck in some monstrous half-form. We do not feel a compulsion from the moon. They are like grotesque shadows of us. They are not magic; they do not use magic. They are used by it. They have no will to battle the force of the moon on their change. How can you compare them to us?"

"How can't I?" Cassidy's voice was quiet after Adele's vitriolic diatribe. "Yeah, they're different, but that doesn't make them monsters, Nana."

"It makes them unlike us, Cassidy. Our family has preserved our heritage through more generations than we can remember. The women of our family are Fox-women, and we pass on that heritage by taking human mates. What do you think will happen to your daughters if they have an animal for a father?"

Unbidden, an image of little girls with whiskey-dark eyes and smiles that could charm the bark off a tree sprang to her mind and promptly melted Cassidy's heart. Quinn's daughters.

She yanked herself right out of that fantasy. What on earth was she thinking? She'd slept with the man once. Okay, half a dozen times, but it was only one night. And a day. She had no reason to believe he had any intention of sticking around long enough to make Valentine's Day plans with her, let alone babies.

But the idea of his babies made her stomach flip and her ovaries sing the Ode to Joy.

"Nana, I won't deny I'm interested in Sullivan Quinn, but I don't have a relationship with him. Calm down. Don't you think it's more important to focus on Alexandra Thurgood? I imagine her accident has sped up the time line the Council has to take action on the Unveiling."

"Don't try to use that as a distraction. The Council is

taking care of it. I already explained that. What you should be concentrating on is thinking about whether you're willing to sacrifice the dignity of your family to mate with an animal."

The next sound Cassidy heard was the dial tone droning in her ear. That and her heart thumping along in her chest at about three times the speed and thirty times the volume of normal.

Mate?

Why had her grandmother had to go and do that? Why did she have to bring up the m-word?

She replaced the phone in its cradle and sank down onto her sofa with a pitiful groan. Her stomach was twisting and clenching behind her navel, and the instinctive tightening in her throat didn't do a lot to help her calm down. Once the word "mate" had come up, calm stopped being an option.

This wasn't supposed to be about mating. This was just supposed to be two single adults, who happened to get each other really hot, having a mutually satisfying and indeterminately temporary relationship. It was supposed to be fun and sexy and casual, not scary and life-changing and permanent.

Cassidy might not know the details of how Lupines formed mate bonds, but she could guess that it was all speed and intensity, just like them. It had to involve dominance and submission and the male staking a claim on the female in that brutally basic way they had. It would be emotionally and physically messy, and it would definitely not come with an escape clause. After all, werewolves were ruled by their instincts, and she had no reason to think their love lives would prove an exception to that.

God, she almost wished she had asked the Lupines she knew some really personal questions through the years, just so she would have something more than speculation to go on. Her own instincts, though, told her she couldn't be far off the mark.

The whole idea stood in stark contrast to the mating traditions of Foxwomen. For her people, the process closely resembled that of humans. A Foxwoman met a human man she liked, they dated, got to know each other, and if he didn't freak out and run when she told him what she was, they'd mate and make babies. Some of whom would be Foxwomen and some of whom would be normal human males. It was all very calm and civilized—honestly, would Adele Berry have stood for anything else?—and built on a foundation of mutual respect and affection for one's mate.

Cassidy had figured she could handle that. One of these days. She wasn't ready for a mate anytime soon, but if nothing else, she could appreciate her responsibility to preserve a dwindling race. Still, in her mind the day she would mate had been lifetimes away, something that would happen when she had gotten her life in order, settled down and met a nice, nonthreatening human man she wouldn't mind seeing across her breakfast table for a few decades. She never planned for it to be anything other than a matter of companionship and children. She wanted calm and civilized, because the alternative was intense and frightening and involved things like lust and passion and need. And love.

The word sent her stomach flipping again.

Cassidy wasn't sure she wanted to fall in love. The idea terrified her. She'd loved her parents, and they'd been taken away from her. Her father had loved her mother so much that he'd uprooted his entire life for her. He'd given up a perfectly normal, human existence to become the mate of a woman who wasn't even the same species. He'd had to learn how to live with the burden of hiding the truth about his wife from strangers. He'd even had to learn how to raise a daughter who kept losing her clothes in the forest because she'd gone out to play and had shifted and come back home in her fox form, forgetting all about the clothes she'd been wearing when she left. He'd done it gladly, and neither he nor his wife nor their daughter had ever thought it should be any different. His love for Cassidy's mother had been so strong that he'd given up his own career to help with hers, learning how to negotiate regarding things he couldn't possibly understand with people who could tear him into pieces without breaking a sweat. Finally, they had.

And Sarah Poe had loved her husband so much that she had died trying to protect him.

In Cassidy's mind, love equaled loss.

When she thought about it, Cassidy admitted the emotion made her feel slightly panicked. She wasn't sure she was even capable of being that selfless. What would she have done if she'd been her mother? If she'd been given a choice between dying with love and living without it?

She honestly didn't know. And if she didn't know, how could she consider taking a mate?

She grew very, very still.

Was she considering taking a mate?

Shoving down a surge of childhood fears, Cassidy searched for an answer to that question. Did she want Sullivan Quinn for her mate? Regardless of his species and his profession, did she want *him,* the man she knew him to be? The exasperating, sneaky, adorable, trustworthy, persistent, caring man she knew he was?

Oh, shit. Yeah. She kinda did.

Cassidy groaned and buried her face in her hands. Damn, but she had some lousy timing. Here she was, in the middle of an international political nightmare, and she picked this as the perfect time to consider mating with a man from another species who made his home on another continent and who probably wouldn't be interested in her in another two weeks?

Good work, Cass. Now that's what's called picking a winner.

Twenty-two

A few hours later, Cassidy was still brooding as she stepped out of the shower and quickly dried her hair. She braided it into two simple plaits and padded into the bedroom to dress, all the while studiously avoiding the thoughts that had been plaguing her ever since her grandmother's phone call. She had plenty of other things to worry about without obsessing over the word that would not be named.

What was the appropriate attire for a forced meeting with a vampire, anyway? Was she supposed to go the Anne Rice route and try to find something frilly and Victorian? Or maybe go all Gothic, with lots of black eyeliner and a pair of combat boots?

In the end, she pulled out her favorite pair of blue jeans, the ones that were worn white at the seams, along with a scooped-neck pullover in faded, sweat-shirt gray. Leonard could live with the disappointment of not seeing her all gussied up. Besides, her daddy had always said costumes only made it harder to concentrate on what was important.

She left her apartment at eight-forty and ignored the elevator, jogging down to the lobby with the directions

Gretel had given her in one hand. She used the other to flag down a cab and spent the next few minutes battling the desire to tell the driver to forget the address she'd given him, just drop her off someplace with bad lighting and Guinness on tap.

The idea tempted her mercilessly, but the cab jerked to a stop before she worked up the nerve to be quite that rude.

"This is it, lady."

Cassidy paid the cabbie and slid out onto the deserted sidewalk, looking up at the old garment warehouse while the taxi peeled off behind her. The building hulked in the middle of the block, surrounded by the kind of narrow streets that marked one of the city's older neighborhoods. The structure looked pretty old itself, all chipped brick and decaying concrete. Looked as if Leonard really knew how to live it up.

She made a face and stepped up to the door, a graffiti-covered, black steel thing with a speakeasy-style peephole in the door. Good God. Talk about your vampire melodrama. These guys couldn't seem to get past the whole "Legend of the Wampyre" thing to save themselves.

Her knock brought several seconds of silence, followed by the faint rustling of footsteps and a slow creak as the door swung open. Grendl stood on the other side looking about as friendly as her namesake, if a little better dressed. She wore a severely tailored suit in dark blue with a silver watch fob dangling from the coat pocket. Judging from the plunge of the neckline, the suit looked to be all she was wearing.

The blonde gave Cassidy's casual clothes an unhurried once-over, but her expression never changed.

It didn't have to; it had been disapproving from the start.

"I'm here to answer the royal summons," Cassidy said. "D'you think the queen will grant me an audience if I promise to curtsy low enough?"

"King."

The vampire's servant stepped back from the threshold, making room for Cassidy to pass through, frowning. "What?"

"King."

The door shut with an ominous thump, but Cassidy absolutely refused to twitch. She met the other woman's icy gaze with a level one of her own.

Gretel smiled unpleasantly. "In your little metaphor there, Mr. Leonard would be the king, not the queen. As I'm sure you're well aware."

The woman so knew how to take the fun out of a snide insult. Cassidy followed her down a dimly lit and graffiti-decorated corridor to a steel-gated service elevator. "I'm aware of the fact that he isn't a monarch at all, actually. But that's where my knowledge of him ends. And my interest in him."

"Oh, I would be surprised if you don't find meeting with Mr. Leonard this evening to be very interesting, indeed."

Any rolling of Cassidy's eyes then was done with absolute discretion. Honest. "Right. He's off to a great start with that. Because I just adore it when I'm threatened and harassed into having a few words with someone. I find that really puts me in a receptive frame of mind."

Her guide stepped forward as the elevator ground to a halt, sliding open the gate without so much as a pause. "And me without my thumb screws. How positively tragic."

Cassidy made a face at the woman's back and fell silent as they moved through another corridor, this one looking much less likely to fall down around their heads. The hall ended at a reinforced steel door with yet another Capone-style viewing hole. She almost expected a Chicago accent to demand the password before letting them in. Instead, the cover over the viewing window slid open without so much as a knock from Gretel. There was a brief pause, then the snapping of locks, and the entrance made room for them to walk inside.

Oh, goodie.

After the melodrama that had greeted her so far, she had half expected to step through the doorway into a replica of Dracula's castle, complete with cobwebs in the corners, smoky torches on the walls, and the howls of wolves echoing in the distance. Perhaps even three scantily clad, bloodthirsty women writhing around in the faint, silvery glow of the moonlight. She wouldn't have been surprised.

Instead, the door closed behind her on what looked more like a very exclusive gentlemen's club. Not the kind of gentlemen's club they had on the sides of highways, advertised with pink billboards and the words LIVE NUDE GIRLS! She was thinking more along the lines of the gentlemen's clubs you read about in Victorian novels. The ones where disgustingly wealthy and probably aristocratic men went to read newspapers, smoke cigars, drink brandy, and play card games no one without at least a "Sir" before their name had ever heard of.

The room was dimly lit by subdued chandeliers and small table lamps with leather or Tiffany-style shades.

Cassidy could see two fireplaces, both blazing cheerfully and managing to keep the somewhat expansive space of the former warehouse comfortably cozy. The air smelled faintly of fine cigars, pipe tobacco, and old leather. A dark, polished bar stretched along the left wall, and the room that opened up in front of it was filled with clusters of comfortable club chairs, card tables and leather sofas. The bare spaces on the wall had been covered with a dark flocked paper in a mellow shade of mossy green.

If someone had shouted "Tallyho!" just then, Cassidy would not have been at all surprised.

"Miss Poe. So glad you could join us."

The voice lacked the cultured, British accent Cassidy had been half expecting, and she turned to see its source. A grouping of furniture stood in front of the closer of the two fires, curiously ill-lit for its positioning. A shadow stirred in one of the black club chairs and unfolded into the tall, narrow shape of a man. Francis Leonard.

He stepped toward her until the light caught in his pale, blond hair and illuminated his fine, sharp features.

Cassidy forced herself not to grimace. "I try never to ignore a summons to a command performance, Councilman. Especially when I'm given the impression it could lead to more rude phone calls."

Leonard laughed, though he managed not to sound amused, and held out his hand. Cassidy shook it as briefly as possible and reminded herself it would be impolite to then wipe it on her jeans. Something about her host didn't sit right with her. It never had. It had very little to do with him being a vampire. Mostly it had to do with him being a supercilious, smarmy, altogether repulsive individual. She felt pretty sure he'd still been all those things before he became a vampire.

"Ah, yes. I apologize if you felt our efforts to arrange this meeting were ... heavy-handed." His smile reflected about as much regret as his laugh had amusement. "But my associates and I felt our business together necessitated moving quickly." He gestured with the brandy snifter he cupped in one elegantly soft hand. "Can I offer you a drink?"

Cassidy resisted the urge to point out how she was so not there to hang. She shook her head. "Thanks, but no."

"Well, then. Come and take a seat. We've all been looking forward to talking with you."

She stepped closer to the fire, watching as the shadows on the furniture distilled into distinct shapes. Two figures sat at either end of an old-fashioned, camelback sofa upholstered in claret velvet. On one side, the firelight reached just far enough into the darkness to gild the edges of a woman's smooth, honey-colored complexion. Marie-Claudette Touleine, priestess, voudun, and altogether terrifying woman of power.

Cassidy felt a surge of awareness in her gut, and reluctantly looked to the other side of the sofa. In the second seat, the light held even less sway, but she could still make out the scarified visage of an ebony-skinned man of indeterminate age. Thabo Ngala. Animus.

Neither witch nor sorcerer, animi figured sparsely in the history of Others of the Western world. They appeared chiefly in the aboriginal cultures of Africa, Australia, and South America. They possessed the ability to take animal shapes, but unlike werefolk, they could assume more than one; and unlike a Foxwoman, their change was not merely a shift in form.

An animus took the shape of an animal through sympathetic magic. He needed to drape himself in the skin of the animal, or wear a bracelet made of its teeth, or a necklace of its claws. He had to use the power inherent in the animal in order to mirror not only its form, but its spirit. When the animus took the shape of a leopard, he didn't become a man in a leopard's body. He *became* the leopard, his mind thinking the thoughts of the leopard and his soul raging as the soul of the leopard.

They were powerful and dangerous magicians who could be consumed with the predatory instincts of their animal forms, whereas a were or other shifter retained the morality of a human mind. Maybe it was a good thing they were so rare.

She fought off a wave of uneasiness and took the seat Leonard indicated for her.

"Madame," she said, nodding respectfully. "And Mr. Ngala. I'm honored to meet you both in person."

"Miss Poe." Madame Touleine didn't have one of those fake Jamaican/Creole accents. She spoke in a quiet voice touched with the lilt of the bayou. "I have heard much about you."

Somehow, that didn't make Cassidy feel any better. Madame's was not the sort of radar she'd ever wanted to be on. In fact, the longer she sat there, the less she wanted any of this to be happening.

"I'm flattered," was all she said.

"I know more of your family than of you, Miss Poe," Ngala said, drawing her attention. His voice was deep and smooth and exotically accented. And it sent cold shivers down Cassidy's spine. "Of your grandmother in particular. She is a woman to be respected greatly. Wise and powerful. If you share even a bit of her mind or her talents, I am sure you must be a force to be reckoned with in your own right."

She didn't like the light in his dark eyes, or the way the elaborately patterned scars on his face seemed to writhe and dance in the firelight. Struggling for a casual air, she pushed her long hair back over her shoulder and reclined into the cool, button-trimmed leather. "Call me Cassidy. All of you. I'm not much into formality."

"Cassidy, then." Leonard smiled, keeping his fangs to himself, probably in an effort to be charming. "I suppose you must be curious why we insisted on setting up this meeting."

"You might say that."

"Let me first assure you that this is all informal, and we are pleased to count you as a sort of ally of ours."

Ooooookay. "Well, that's good to know."

"Indeed, Cassidy," Madame added. "From what Francis has told us of your recently expressed sentiments, we feel very fortunate to know you share with us a certain way of thinking."

Not something Cassidy had expected. "Really? I'm sorry, but I'm not quite sure I understand what you're talking about."

Leonard settled back in his chair, cradling the bowl of his snifter in his hands. "What Madame Touleine means to say, Cassidy, is that I told them about your speech before the Council the other night. I was quite impressed with the points you made to De Santos and the rest of those cretins on the sure folly of allowing our secrets to be revealed to the humans. I simply had to share the tale with my friends."

"You see, Cassidy," Ngala murmured, "we feel very much the same way. We do not believe the humans are ready to have their eyes opened quite so wide as the Europeans have suggested."

Cassidy's uneasy feelings intensified. "Well, Mr. Leonard must also have told you that circumstances might have already taken that choice out of our hands."

"We know the story of the missing Russian woman. It is of little consequence." Madame waved a long, thin hand heavily decked in silver and gold. "Much more depends on the Council's ultimate decision on what action they will take in response."

Cassidy raised her eyebrows. "If that's what this is about, you might have been better off harassing, you know, an actual member of the Council. I'm not exactly the first person they run to tell when they make a big decision." She looked at Leonard. "In fact, as a member of the Inner Circle, Mr. Leonard, you're a much better source of information about the Council's actions than I am."

The vampire's lips tightened. "Unfortunately, De Santos and I are not on the best of terms. But we all know your grandmother holds considerable sway over the Council and has for quite some time. And, of course, she has spoken of you often as someone she envisions following in her footsteps. Upholding the family tradition, as it were."

"My grandmother envisions a lot of things, Mr. Leonard," she said cautiously. What the hell were they fishing for? "But you know how it is. When you get older, your sight gets blurry."

Madame fixed her with a stare so sharp, she wanted to make some sort of sign to ward it off. "Does that mean you do not see the same future for yourself, Cassidy?"

"No matter what the family tradition might be, I'm an anthropologist, not a politician, Madame."

"Ah, but a woman changes when she finds herself in love, *n'est-ce pas?*"

"I think what Madame meant to say, in her very polite and feminine way," Ngala put in, "is that a woman's mind can often be swayed by the opinions of her lover. It is the nature of the female to meld her wishes with those of her mate, after all."

"In what century?" Cassidy shook her head and gave a quick, uncomfortable laugh. "My wishes are my own, thanks very much."

Leonard smiled and shrugged with particular snobbery. "It does seem awfully rude to pose these sorts of questions to such a new acquaintance. But surely you can understand our concern."

"Not really, but that's probably because I still don't get what you all want from me. Grend, er . . . Gretel made it sound like this meeting was a high priority for you guys, but I'm still not sure why."

"Then let us be clear," Leonard said, his ingratiating smile still in place. "We represent a rather large contingent of the Other community who feel it would be imprudent to move toward Unveiling at this stage."

"Not really a surprise, and not something you needed to drag me out here to tell me."

"Perhaps not, but we hoped the four of us could have a frank discussion, away from outside influence. Not that we believe you to be a woman who is easily influenced, of course."

All the "of course"s felt a little like being deferred to by a pit of vipers.

"I'm being frank. How about you?"

"Absolutely." Leonard's smile turned haughty. "As I said, we represent a larger contingent of our peers, some of whom have a great deal to lose should they find themselves the subject of unfriendly human speculation."

Cassidy took a moment to chew on that. She knew very well that Others had made their way into all facets of the human world by this point, from the entertainment industry to the business world to politics. It didn't take much of a leap to conclude the "associates" Leonard had mentioned belonged to those spheres. They were the type of folk who had the most to lose if their identities came out.

"Then you should be glad the Council is looking into the people behind Ysabel Mirenow's disappearance," she said after a beat. "The faster we find out who's responsible, the better chance we have to contain the repercussions of the incident."

She didn't mention the governor's daughter. Somehow she didn't want to be the bearer of those particular bad tidings.

"We believe there are ways the Council might not consider to achieve that containment, *chère*," Madame said, her dark eyes seeming even blacker. "That is where we need your help."

The only way Cassidy felt inclined to help these three was over the edge of a cliff, but she thought it might be imprudent to say so. Instead she leaned forward, covering up a wince when a few strands of hair caught in the chair's buttons behind her. No way did she want to show even that small a sign of weakness in front of this crowd.

"I'm not quite sure I know what you mean."

Ngala smiled at her. "We ask only a small favor,

young lady. Mr. Leonard has told us that De Santos requested you discover if the religious sect responsible for Ms. Mirenow's disappearance is operating here in America. All we need for you to do is share that information with us before you share it with the Council at large. Tell us if the Light of Truth is in this country and who their leaders are. You see? It is a tiny thing."

He sat back in his seat, looking like a smug and benevolent tiger shark, the kind who struck for no reason. Cassidy kept her expression neutral, but her mind was racing. She wasn't an idiot. Between Madame Touleine's talk of "other ways" of dealing with the Lightheads and Ngala's request for their names, she knew very well the Terrible Trio here intended to cover up all the problems the sect was causing with a little bit of murder. And quite likely torture. With maybe a side of mayhem thrown in.

The question was, did Cassidy want to stop them?

She was shocked to find herself hesitating over that. On the one hand, things would be so easy if the whole problem just disappeared, the way these Others seemed to imply it would if she helped them. But on the other hand, could she live with the responsibility for all those deaths? After all, the Lightheads seemed to have no compunctions about murder, but would the Terrible Trio stop at the Lightheads? What about innocent people who might get caught up in their web? Like witnesses to Mirenow's disappearance. And what would happen if these three found out about the governor's daughter? Would they kill the doctors at the hospital just because they might know too much? What about the EMTs? The police? The secretary who'd processed the girl's admittance?

Then on the third hand, saying no to Thabo Ngala, Madame Touleine, and Francis Leonard probably wasn't the world's healthiest decision, either.

"That doesn't seem like all that big a deal," she hedged, trying to sound as positive as possible without actually committing herself to anything. "I don't see why I couldn't."

"Excellent!" Leonard clapped his hands, and this time he smiled widely enough that Cassidy caught a glimpse of fang. She'd been around enough vampires in her life that it shouldn't have bothered her, but she had come to realize that Francis Leonard wasn't just a vampire, he was a heartless bloodsucker. Sort of like being a bastard. Some people were born that way, and some had to work at it.

"We appreciate your assistance," Madame said, her own smile soft and contained and no less chilling. "Perhaps the three of us are getting old, but we have not the desire to rock the boat, as it were, and to Unveil our existence at this late date, especially to do so hastily, seems to us unwise."

"Our ancestors have been doing quite well with the present system," Ngala added. "We should not assume it must change now."

Cassidy offered him a false smile. "Everything changes, Mr. Ngala. It's only a matter of how and when."

The animus chuckled. "Beware of your words, Miss Poe. Someone might think you're going to change your mind after all."

"Oh, I don't think so," she said, forcing a laugh. "I'm pretty set in my ways."

They watched each other for a few moments, and

Cassidy thought she saw something unpleasant flicker in Ngala's gaze. Before she could pin it down, Leonard stood and neatly cut through the tension.

"Well, we do thank you for indulging our request for a meeting, Cassidy," he said. "Would you care to join us for dinner before you leave?"

Cassidy looked around her at the vampire, the voudun, and the animus, and any hint of an appetite fled screaming.

"Thanks, but uh . . . I think I'll have to pass."

Twenty-three

By the time the cab left Cassidy back at the corner near her building, she was wishing she'd waited to bathe until after her meeting with the terrible trio.

She felt as if a ton of sticky, tarry grime were weighing her down as she trudged up the block to the entrance of the apartment building. How had her parents been able to stand night after night of meetings like the one she'd just had?

She huddled deeper into her coat and entertained visions of a steamy hot shower, crisp cotton sheets, and a full night of sleep. Her attention became so focused on the pictures in her head that she nearly didn't notice the figure leaning against the wall beside the front door. With the way her day had been going, she was about to assume it was either a mugger or a messenger from some newly cranky faction of Others, but the light showed a much more welcome image.

Quinn smiled and pushed himself out of his casual slouch. "Good evening, Cassie love. I've been wondering if you'd decided to go and sneak off without leaving me a forwarding address."

The gentle teasing made Cassidy smile, and the smile

made her realize how utterly exhausted she felt. She was physically and emotionally drained, and her instincts guided her straight to him. She never said a word, just crossed the last few steps, wrapped her arms around his waist and laid her head against his shoulder, burrowing into the soft, dark cashmere of his coat.

"Ah, what's this, love?" he murmured, slipping a hand under her chin and lifting her face to his. "What's the matter?"

Cassidy just shook her head and tucked her cheek back against his chest. "Long day. Long, annoying, surreal day."

"I know it, sweetheart. I've had one of those myself. Did De Santos tell you about Alexandra Thurgood?"

She nodded but didn't bother to open her eyes.

"Richard and I have been working on that all evening. Not to mention a whole mess of finance stuff De Santos dragged out of the Russians." He paused and she rubbed her cheek against his coat. "We've started to make some sense of everything. Enough so that you and I should probably talk."

"Tomorrow."

Quinn opened his mouth to protest, but Cassidy just hid her face against his chest and pressed her fingers to his lips.

"I can't right now," she said. "I really can't. I promise we can talk about it first thing tomorrow, but just . . . not now."

His arms tightened around her, and she couldn't help but think about how fabulous it felt. A portion of her tension began to drain away, and she gave a contented sigh.

"All right, Cassie love, we'll wait till morning. But perhaps you'd be warmer waiting inside?"

"Probably." Her words came out muffled by cashmere.

"Right, then. Up with you, *mavourneen*. I'll tuck you in and let you get a good bit of rest. That's what you need just now." He didn't give her a chance to weigh in, just hooked one arm behind her back, one under her knees, and swung her up in his embrace. "Get your keys, love. You'll have to let us in."

She fumbled in her pocket and drew out the ring. It took a couple of tries to get the lock opened, but she finally managed it. The elevator and the halls were empty as he carried her to her apartment, waited for her to open that door as well, and then brought her directly to her bed. As he leaned down to deposit her on top of the duvet, Cassidy locked her arms around his neck and refused to let go. He resisted briefly before letting her tug him down beside her. Immediately, she curled up on her side with her head pillowed on his chest and her arm draped over him.

"Comfy?" he asked, his voice smiling.

"Mmm."

She heard the chuckle rumble deep inside his chest before he made any actual noise. It comforted her. Just having him there comforted her. She wasn't quite sure she wanted to analyze why, but she knew that the minute she'd seen him standing outside her building, the nastiness weighing her down had begun to ease. Now, lying beside him, listening to his heart beat in steady rhythm, feeling his chest rise and fall with his breath, she felt a peace she hadn't expected after the day she'd had.

He made such a comfortable pillow that she felt herself begin drifting into sleep. It made no sense to her cloudy mind to struggle, so she turned to burrow in closer and let the exhaustion take her.

"Let go, sweetheart," she heard just before unconsciousness claimed her. "I'll take care of you. Just sleep."

Remarkably, she did.

Cassidy had no concept of the time when she woke, but the apartment was pitch-black. She lay still for a moment, blinking as her eyes attempted to focus in the minimal light seeping from behind the window shades. She felt warm and drowsy, but something bothered her. It niggled at the back of her head until she couldn't stand it. She hadn't woken enough to remember the reason for it, but she knew she wanted a shower. Badly.

Doing her best to move silently, she slipped out from under the arm that pinned her in place and padded toward the bathroom.

She didn't bother to turn on the lights, her eyes finding the shower in the darkness. She opened the taps and let the water heat while she stripped. She couldn't remember why she was still dressed, and didn't really want to. All she wanted was to get undressed, get under the hot spray, and get clean.

The first needle-sharp spray scalded her, but she didn't care. Let it boil the uncomfortable feeling of contamination off her skin. She raised her face to the water and let it pour over her, sluicing her discomfort down the drain.

Traces of sleep still clung to her, making her drowsy and slow-moving, barely aware of anything outside the beating cone of water. Her eyes stayed closed and the patter of water on porcelain drowned out all other sounds. It felt like standing in a cocoon, warm and private and safe from the world beyond the shower curtain. Her mind shied away from thinking of why that was so important, and she didn't force the issue. The foggy semiconsciousness she currently floated in was just fine with her. She could stay here for a while.

She heard the scrape of the curtain rings against the rod in the back of her mind, but she didn't react. It set off no alarms, so she continued to stand under the spray, still and silent. A set of muscular arms curled around her from behind and tugged her gently back against a warm, solid body. Her mouth curved in an instinctive smile and she leaned into the embrace, letting her head fall to rest on Quinn's broad shoulder.

He said nothing, just cuddled her closer and bent his head to kiss the curve of her neck. His tongue came out to taste the water beaded on her skin, and Cassidy sighed as her body stretched itself awake under his touch. Her nipples tightened despite the heat of the water, and she felt the muscles low in her belly tense in anticipation.

A deep rumble shook against the curve of her shoulder, tickling her with gentle vibrations. She felt it against her back, too, through the thick veil of wet hair that separated them. She frowned. She didn't like the idea of anything coming between them. Shifting, she leaned her upper body forward, which nestled her bottom more snugly against the hardness of his growing erection. She reached back to pull her hair from between them, draping it in a wet, silky rope over her shoulder. Quinn murmured his approval and pressed closer, letting her feel the solid presence of him down the length of her back.

They fit together beautifully. Her head tucked neatly against his chest, and her soft curves yielded to his hard planes. Like yin and yang, they completed each other in a way Cassidy had never experienced before. He loomed behind her, so much larger that she felt surrounded by him, but the difference in their mass didn't threaten her. It comforted her. He made her feel protected and secure and relaxed. It was as if her subconscious knew it didn't have to keep alert with him nearby. She could drain away years of tension just by feeling a few minutes of the rise and fall of his chest.

He pulled her out of her reverie with the slick glide of his hands against her skin. They slid over rivulets of water, one heading up her torso, between her breasts to rest possessively at the base of her throat. She felt the weight of it, the warmth of it seeping into her skin, and she relaxed more completely against him. His other hand traced a languid path over her ribs and belly, down to the vee of her thighs and cupped the tender curve of her mound.

Hmm. Maybe she could be persuaded to wake up after all.

She lifted one arm behind her to loop around his neck and pressed the other hand against his flank. Her hips arched under his hand, encouraging more. She heard a soft chuckle in her ear and then his fingers slid deeper, sifting through her curls to part her slick folds before halting abruptly.

She made a small, frustrated noise and spread her thighs a little farther. Quinn's mouth curved against her shoulder just before his lips parted and his teeth scraped over her suddenly hyper-aware skin. A shiver rocked through her, making her tremble in his arms. They flexed around her, and his exploring hand ventured farther, bypassing her clit to tease over her center. He found her entrance with a light touch and circled it, sliding through the moisture there and drawing even more from her body. She wept for him, and he seemed pleased with the discovery. She felt his head turn and the gentle-sharp press of his teeth as they closed over her earlobe.

Cassidy's hips shifted again, an involuntary action, winding small circles in an attempt to capture a more intimate touch. But Quinn would have none of it. He offered another chuckle instead and withdrew his hand completely.

"Quinn . . ."

His name tumbled from her lips, half a plea, half a protest. The arm around his neck tightened, and her fingers tangled in his hair to try and tug him to her.

"Ah, ah. Be good, Cassie love." His voice sounded husky with sleep and arousal, and his beguiling brogue held a trace of amusement. "If you abandoned a bed for a shower, you must have a desire to be clean, so let's take care of that first."

The hand she wanted to have touch her again stretched out to grab the bar of unscented soap from the little rack in the corner. He pressed it between his two palms, rubbing to create a rich, white lather, and Cassidy's anticipation suddenly edged out her disappointment. She could have sworn he moved in slow motion while he set aside the soap in preparation for putting his hands back on her.

She gasped when they settled at her waist and began to stroke the slick foam over her skin. She felt the path of each finger creeping inch by sensitive inch up her torso. By the time they closed around her breasts, she had stopped breathing. When the first touch came, she whimpered and leaned into it, pressing herself into his hands. He responded by flicking his thumbs over her ruched nipples. Her body tensed as if it had been hit with a bolt of lightning, and she felt just as electrified. A moan broke from her lips. She tried to turn to face him, wanting his mouth, but he tightened his grip to hold her in place.

"Not yet," he murmured, teeth nipping again at her ear. "I've not finished with you yet, love."

The idea of more of this torture brought a groan of mingled pleasure and dismay, but Quinn exhibited no intention of stopping his play anytime soon. He left her breasts with a fond squeeze and slid his soapy hands down over her chest, her stomach, and the silky length of her thighs. She kept waiting for them to slip between, where she most wanted them, but the Lupine was exhibiting a perverse desire to torture her.

He ignored the parting of her legs, the pleading tilt of her hips, and clasped her behind the knee, raising one thigh and urging her to brace her foot against the cool, tiled wall.

"Stay there." His voice coasted over her water-slicked skin and sent a chill through her. "I'll hold you, love. But keep still for me. There's a girl."

She balanced herself on her other foot, leaning back against his chest for added support. Both of his hands closed around her leg, coating it with the last of the soapy suds. He worked the dwindling lather into her skin, down her calf to her foot, seeing that every inch of her was squeaky clean. All except the inches she really wanted him to pay attention to.

He repeated the process and the orders on her other leg. Once he'd positioned her as he wanted her, though, he had to reach around her for more soap. She took advantage of the greater closeness to shift her hips with subtle precision, rocking her soft bottom against his erection. That earned her a strangled groan and the pleasure of feeling every inch of him tensing against her before he chuckled and swatted her flank.

"Enough of that, saucy minx." His hands clamped around her hips to still them, and he leaned down to press a kiss against her shoulder. "We'll get there soon enough, but I've not finished with you yet."

She growled in protest, but held still while he tortured her with even more prolonged attention. She was about ready to hang by his neck, hook her other leg behind his knee, and beat him to the floor when his soapy hands slid up her calf and thigh and kept going. They insinuated themselves high between her thighs and parted her to the warm, steamy air.

Cassidy trembled, her muscles tensing as she waited for his next move. She felt as if her very existence depended on how and when he touched her next. The seconds slowed to a crawl. She could have sworn that an hour passed before he settled one hand against the inside of her raised thigh and pressed to open it just a little more.

She tried to say something, to give thanks, to shout encouragement, to moan, to do anything, but her breath froze in her throat and not even a whimper came out. It didn't seem to matter to Quinn. He didn't need the encouragement.

He propped his chin on her shoulder and gazed down at her body. His hand slid through her swollen folds, coating them with thick lather. Her muscles tightened, if that were possible, and her body pulsed with desperation. Her mind focused only on the slow journey his fingers took over her most intimate terrain.

He took his time exploring every ridge and valley, learning her like Braille, reading her desire and her need and her passion.

Cassidy opened her eyes and turned her head to press her lips against his temple. Her chin dropped until she shared his view. She saw the dripping shape of her own body, her skin pale as always and drawn into gooseflesh, her nipples peaked so tightly they ached. His arm cut across her, darker in the darkness of the shower. Her night vision allowed her to clearly see where his hand disappeared between her thighs, and the sight sent her into another round of shivers.

Quinn just pressed more firmly against her raised thigh to keep it from closing. She turned her head until she could see his face beside hers. He looked fascinated. His expression was intense and focused and utterly enthralled. She could read his excitement in the glint of his eyes and the subtle tightening of his facial muscles. Clearly he enjoyed touching her as much as she enjoyed being touched.

Then his fingers shifted and "enjoy" ceased to apply.

She felt his fingertips brush over her clit and watched the wicked grin that spread across his features as her hips jerked in instinctive response. Whimpering, she set her cheek against his and watched as he twisted his wrist and slid two long, slick fingers inside her.

Oh, God!

She heard a deep chuckle against her ear. "Nothing so lofty, sweet. But I appreciate the compliment."

She hadn't realized she'd said that out loud. She felt heat climbing up her throat and into her cheeks, but it was nothing compared to the heat building against his exploring hand.

"I take it that means you like when I do this." He made some sort of arcane magic with his hand and the tips of his buried fingers scraped against her inner walls in a way that made her cry out—not a whimper, not even a moan. A real, genuine, "God I hope the neighbors can't hear me" cry.

"Quinn!" She choked out his name, her body bowed and trembling against him. "You're killing me . . ."

"And why should I do any such thing, Cassie love? I like you very much alive."

He allowed her sensitized internal flesh one last, teasing massage and slipped his fingers free. Cassidy moaned in protest and grabbed to keep his hand where it gave her so much pleasure.

"Ah-ah," he scolded, pressing her hands to her sides with gentle compulsion. "Be a good girl for me, love. You need to finish your bathing before we move on to play time."

The fog of arousal kept his meaning from reaching her. She stood there, wet and confused and desperately aroused while he played his little games with her. If she hadn't been able to feel the evidence of his arousal pressing hard and hot against her bottom, she would have started to wonder if this wasn't some kind of sick torture. As it was, it was still torture, but she was reserving judgment on the sick part until he finished with her.

She refused to stoop to begging, and he'd reduced her to too much of a quivering mass for her to do anything else, so she just stood there and waited for his next move. Unfortunately for her, she'd allowed her eyes to drift shut while he had been busy between her legs, so she never saw it coming. He moved so fast that she had no warning between the time the hot shower spray stopped pounding down over them and the first pulsing jet of water hit her swollen clit.

Cassidy nearly jumped over the curtain rod. Her eyes flew open, her head flew forward, and her heart flew into her throat. Her fingers clenched in Quinn's hair, tugging hard, but he didn't seem to care. In fact, he laughed softly and pressed her raised thigh farther open as he held the shower massage and directed the spray at her core.

She tried to close her legs. The sensation was just too strong, but Quinn held her mercilessly in place.

"You . . . you . . . you're . . . a . . . demon. God!" She squirmed her hips, trying to avoid the mind-numbing pressure of the spray, but he followed her every move. "Stop torturing me and . . . ah!"

He had her where she couldn't even complete a sentence. Damn it, she was going to get him for this.

"Now, now, none of that, Cassie love." The hand that had been resting on her throat slid down and pressed against her belly to still her frantic movements against his erection. She could feel him twitching and got a grim satisfaction from knowing at least she wasn't alone in the unbearable-arousal department. "Had to get you all clean and rinsed. No one likes the chafing of dried soap in these tender spots."

He angled the force of the spray just behind her clit and Cassidy screamed. She could *not* take this anymore.

Slipping her free hand over his hip and insinuating it between their bodies, she searched blindly for his erection. Her fingers curled possessively around the shaft and squeezed. The spray between her legs bobbled off course and a rough groan tore from his chest, echoing in her ear. She turned her head to glare at him and saw his head thrown back and his face pulled taut in a battle for self-control. She meant to see he lost it.

She shifted just enough to the side to press her lips to his ear. "I'm washed, I'm rinsed, and I'm ready, so unless you get inside me within the next ten seconds, I'm going to spend the rest of my life making you wish you had."

Quinn blew out a harsh chuckle and shifted his hold around her waist. "Heaven forbid."

With a quick upward heave, he lifted her clean off her feet, raised her above his waist, and urged her hips back into a receptive angle. It took her all of seven nanoseconds to decipher and approve his plan. She shifted her grip on his cock and guided him to her entrance, not letting go until he gave a warning growl and thrust forward with heavy force.

He filled her in a single stroke. Cassidy heard his muffled roar and answered with a strangled scream of her own. The water still pounded relentlessly between her legs, but she couldn't have cared less. He was too distracted to keep his aim, and she was too enthralled with the opening and stretching sensation of having him inside her to notice. Her need had built to a fever pitch, and she could no longer wait for him to make the next move. She needed more. Now.

Jackknifing forward, Cassidy thrust her hips back hard and slapped her palms against the tile wall in front of her for leverage. The force of her movement slid Quinn so deep she swore she could feel him in the back of her throat. The head of his cock nudged her cervix and sent shock waves coursing through her. The sensations overwhelmed her and intensified her cravings.

She used the leverage of her hands against the wall

to work herself back and forth on his erection. She heard high, sharp whimpering sounds as if from a great distance and realized vaguely that she was the one making them. Not that she cared. All she cared about were the feelings of need and hunger and sublime joy that filled her as they moved together in the steamy heat of the shower.

Behind her, Quinn howled his need and dropped the shower massage to grab her by the hips and drag her harder into his thrusts. The metal and plastic shower-head slammed against the tile with a loud thud and sprayed water aimlessly at the back wall of the tub, but neither of them paid any attention. Cassidy concentrated on the shift inside her as Quinn repositioned his feet on the rubber mat to gain more solid ground. Better footing allowed him to siphon even greater power into his thrusts. She met them eagerly, hating the loss she felt with each withdrawal, but glorying in every return.

Her arousal built with a kind of sneaky pressure. Each time she thought she couldn't possibly be any hotter, he would move somehow to enhance the friction of his body inside hers, and the fire would rage even higher. She burned with it until she wasn't sure if it would consume her.

Quinn's fingers bit into her hips with bruising force, yanking her back in time with his thrusts. She felt his urgency and understood the frustration in his growl as he tried to get closer. It felt like he wanted to climb inside her skin, and she couldn't argue. She felt the same need to join so completely neither would be able to tell self from partner.

She let out a shuddering moan as he leaned forward, his hands leaving her hips to slide forward and cup her breasts. The position draped him across her back like a wolf covering his mate, and something primitive inside her rejoiced. His chest pressed against her back as his hips slapped rhythmically against her. His hands kneaded the softness of her breasts and plucked the tight nipples. The added stimulation was either a blessing or a burden, but there was no way she could think clearly enough to decide which.

Behind her, Quinn uttered a low, rough sound, halfway between a grunt and a growl, and shoved forward with ferocious strength. Cassidy gloried in the consuming pleasure of being claimed by her mate. She answered the stroke with a feral cry and clamped down around him as the first wave of spasms took over, shaking her like prey in the jaws of a hungry beast.

Dimly, through the torrent of her climax, she heard him shatter around her. She felt the wind driven out of her by the force of his final thrust. He tensed and shook like a too tightly coiled spring. His hands trembled, as if struggling not to crush her tender breasts in their grip even as he lost another battle. She felt his head turn and his teeth sink into the pale skin of her shoulder, deep enough to leave his mark on her. He rumbled as he did it, a sound of intense satisfaction and possession. Cassidy could almost sense the earth shifting beneath her feet as he marked her as his. His woman. His mate.

The knowledge sent another wave of orgasm rushing toward her, but this time the force of it swept her away. She let the undertow pull her down and drowned in the glory of their joining.

Twenty-four

Quinn woke the next morning, tickled into consciousness by the rich, earthy smell of brewing coffee and the utter lack of a soft, naked Foxwoman by his side. It would have been enough to make him cranky if he hadn't been able to hear her moving about in the other room. That was a good sign. For a while last night, he'd thought he'd killed them both.

Their mating had been raw and furious, and afterward he'd lain curled around her like a blanket. He'd slept better than he had in ages, and he remembered thinking just before he nodded off that he couldn't wait until Valentine's Day. He'd promised his mother he would bring her to Ireland by then.

God bless his mother. During one of the least pleasant phone conversations of his life, she'd been the one to raise her hackles and lower her foot and tell Declan Brendan Quinn what he could do with his prejudice. A mate was a mate, she'd yelled—because, as she'd said, there was no other way to penetrate his thick skull—and she didn't care if the one her son had chosen was a Foxwoman, a human, a mermaid, or a Martian. That was the mother of her grandbabies her mate was talking about, so he could shut his mouth until something civil came out of it.

Quinn didn't really blame his father for what he knew to be an instinctive reaction. Especially since his own reaction to the knowledge of his mating hadn't been unadulterated joy. It had taken him a few minutes to get used to it, too. But by the end of the call, his father had grudgingly offered them his congratulations, though he'd be reserving final approval until he met the lass. Quinn knew then that everything would be fine. His mate would have his father wrapped around her little finger five minutes after she got in the door. Yet another instance of "like father, like son."

With unpleasant conversations in mind now, he heaved himself off her bed, paid a quick visit to the bathroom, and tugged on his jeans. No point in putting this off any longer.

Cassidy looked up when she heard him approaching and grabbed something off the counter beside her. "Here. I got you a present."

Quinn caught the object easily and felt his yawn melt into an entirely idiotic grin. She'd bought him tea. Real tea. Loose leaf Bewley's in the lovely yellow canister.

Bending down, he kissed her cheek. "Thank you, love. That was incredibly sweet of you. I don't suppose you've a kettle I might borrow?"

"Boil is t minus two minutes and counting."

"Bless your sainted heart."

He didn't bother to take offense when she rolled her eyes. He just grabbed a mug from her cabinet, followed her pointed finger to a much neglected tea ball, and set about to rescue himself from the painful injustice of

American hot beverages. It gave him a moment to hone his strategy.

Cassidy leaned back against the counter, cradling her own mug of heavily creamed coffee, and watched him. "I fell asleep last night before I got a chance to thank you."

Startled, he looked up from drowning the tea ball in water and scowled. "Thank me? What for?"

"For taking such good care of me. I'm not convinced I could have dragged myself up here if you hadn't been downstairs waiting for me."

He snorted and dunked the tea ball in the water.

"Daft girl," he muttered, talking more to himself than to her. "As if I'd have done anything else. And she thanks me."

"Well, I still appreciate it. It was a nice surprise. I wasn't expecting to see you last night."

"I wasn't sure I'd make it." He dumped the tea ball, took his mug in one hand and her elbow in the other, and led them into the living room, tugging her down onto the sofa beside him. "I had a bit of an interesting day myself."

Cassidy laughed. "Let's have it. I want to hear how it compares to mine."

"Unfavorably, if there's any justice in the world. I spent most of it with Richard Maccus and Rafael De Santos, who are not nearly such good company as you."

He knew he'd have to ease himself into this. He just couldn't rush into anything he knew would upset his mate.

"You're only saying that because you didn't have sex with them."

Quinn nearly spewed his mouthful of tea all over

her cocktail table. "Jaysus, wench! Don't say things like that. Not even in fun." He shuddered. "Most of the time we were piled arse-deep in bank statements, transactions records, and photocopied deposit slips."

She nodded. "Did you find anything interesting?"

"A bit." He set down his mug and leaned forward, his gaze serious and intent. "Cassie love, I need to ask you something, and I need you to answer honestly."

She looked at him uneasily. "What is it?"

He took her hand between his and chose his words carefully. "Cassie love, did you ever hear your grandmother mention someone by the name of Daniel Young?"

"No. But what does my grandmother have to do with this?"

"How about Daniil Yukov?"

"No! What are you leading up to with this?" Cassidy tried to tug her hand free, but Quinn held on tight.

He braced himself. "The name appeared in several of the documents we reviewed. As did your grandmother's."

Cassidy jerked as if she'd been struck. "What the hell does that mean? Are you trying to say that my grandmother is involved in the American cell of the Light of Truth? That's the dumbest thing I've ever heard!"

"Cassie love—"

"Don't you 'Cassie love' me!" She snarled and jumped away from him to pace to the other side of the room. "My grandmother is not in league with the type of people who would kidnap and kill and torture innocent people. The very idea is preposterous. Not to mention the fact that you said the goal of the Light of Truth

is to expose the Others to the world so they can exterminate us. My grandmother is one of the most vocal members of the community *against* Unveiling. It doesn't
make any sense!"

"Cassidy!" Quinn stopped trying to soothe her and
now just needed her to shut up for two minutes so he
could finish a thought. "I didn't say your grandmother
was in league with the Lightheads. You ought to be
careful jumping to conclusions like that before you
land wrong and break something. Like your stubborn
little head."

She glared at him.

"What I was trying to get out before you ran off on a
whim entirely your own," he growled, "was that the information we went through yesterday gave us more
than names. It pointed us toward the cell's headquarters, where we found a lot more. And some of that gave
us a small glimpse of their strategy."

"How small?"

"Small enough that we didn't wake up to find our
problems a thing of the past. But we did find out who
masterminded Ysabel's kidnapping."

Her eyes widened. "Who?"

"A Ukrainian national named Daniil Yukov. He relocated here from Europe several months ago to set up
the cell and begin recruiting new members. That lecture we were planning to attend is one of the ways he
and the few followers he's already collected have gone
about getting them interested."

Cassidy frowned. "I'm not quite following where
you got that from."

"Daniil Yukov didn't mean much to me, but Daniel
Young sounded familiar. I followed an instinct and

asked De Santos for a favor. He had a Silverback who also happens to be an FBI agent run the names through their databases. It turns out Daniil Yukov and Daniel Young are one and the same."

He reached into the pocket of his jeans and handed her a crinkled piece of paper. She unfolded it and scanned the familiar text.

"Oh, my God. 'Renowned lecturer D. Y. Young.' Daniel Young." She looked up at him. "Are you certain?"

Quinn nodded. "The FBI agent confirmed it, but I wouldn't worry about the lecture. It's been canceled."

"Why?"

"Because Yukov flew to Moscow on Wednesday for the kidnapping."

"Does Gregor know?"

"We told him as soon as we realized. His men are out looking for Yukov now."

She hesitated. "What about Ysabel?"

Quinn's jaw clenched. "We were too late. Her body was delivered to Gregor last night with her tongue cut out. A nasty little message from the Lightheads, but one that means she didn't give them the information they wanted." He had no doubts about what would happen when Gregor tracked down the kidnappers, and once she saw his face, he doubted Cassidy did, either.

She swallowed hard. "So what happens now?"

"De Santos and I talked about it yesterday. We think the important thing right now is to stop the actions the Lightheads here have already taken. We need to find Alexandra Thurgood."

"Wait, wait, wait." Cassidy shook her head and held up a hand, clearly confused. "What do the Lightheads have to do with the governor's daughter's car accident?"

"It wasn't an accident. De Santos heard from a member of the White Paw Clan, the pack that controls the territory around the accident. According to the White Paw, there were two vehicles involved in the accident, but Alexandra was the only person found at the scene. The other car was severely damaged, but the driver was missing."

Cassidy crossed back to the sofa and sank down beside Quinn, shaking her head. "This is too much. The Lightheads were responsible for the accident? But why didn't they take Alexandra the way they took Ysabel? Why didn't they want to torture her for information?"

He shrugged. "We can only speculate, but if they believed the truth about her would come out because of her hospital treatment, they might have thought that would be a simpler way of revealing us. And it wouldn't leave them looking like they had orchestrated anything, which boosts their credibility with the billions of humans who need to find ways to deal with learning their next-door neighbors might be monsters."

"Shit." Cassidy glanced back down at the flyer in her hand and frowned. "Okay, I get how the lecture ties in with the Lightheads, ties in with Alexandra Thurgood, ties in with Ysabel Mirenow. But I'm not seeing how any of it ties in with my grandmother. Or the Terrible Trio."

Quinn frowned and tried not to admit he was stalling about answering the grandmother question. "Terrible Trio? What are you talking about?"

She gave a weak laugh and slumped back onto the sofa, drawing her legs up beneath her. "Sorry, I forgot I never got around to telling you last night. That's what I was coming back from when you caught me outside. And the reason why I needed to wake up in the middle of the night for a shower. I got a summons from three of the members of the Council to join them for a private meeting last night."

"Who?"

"My three least favorite Council members, as a matter of fact." She paused. "Actually, I think they qualify as my three least favorite beings ever. Francis Leonard, Madame Touleine, and Thabo Ngala."

Quinn searched his recollection and came up short. "I recall Leonard from the Council meeting the other night, but the others don't sound familiar."

"You haven't met them. They're on the Council, but not in the Inner Circle, which was the only group present for the emergency meeting," Cassidy explained. "Madame Touleine is voudun. Very powerful and very scary. And Thabo Ngala is an animus. I'm just going to assume he's very powerful, because he scares me even more than Madame."

Quinn stiffened. "What did they want?"

"That's what was so weird. They said they wanted the Light of Truth. Leonard had told them we were digging up information on the sect, and they asked me to give them any names I found before I gave them to the Council. They didn't tell me why, and the only thing I can think of is that they're planning to launch a preemptive strike. But since I don't plan to tell them anything, I don't know what they'll do now."

"I've no idea," he said, "and I'm afraid you aren't going to like my explanation of how the Light of Truth ties in to your grandmother."

"What do you mean?"

He took a deep breath and decided to do this fast, like pulling off a bandage. Or shooting himself in the foot.

"The reason your grandmother's name came up during our investigation is because it appeared on several invoices we collected from the Lightheads' headquarters. They were from a private investigation firm, for surveillance performed on an address on the Upper West Side of Manhattan." He paused, gentled his voice. "On your grandmother's house, Cassie love."

He watched as her blank look slowly gave way to confusion, then disbelief, and then fear.

"Nana? They were watching Nana?" She shook her head, her eyes unfocused as she tried to make sense of the revelation. "Why would they do that? What could she tell them that they didn't already know?"

Quinn took her hand again and squeezed gently. "We're not sure, but I don't want you to worry about it. You had a right to know, but I don't want this making you crazy, love."

"Not make me crazy? To know a bunch of pathological lunatics with a taste for torture have been stalking my grandmother? Why on earth would that make me crazy?"

She jumped to her feet and headed for the door, oblivious to the facts that she was dressed in nothing more than a faded green robe and that Quinn still had a firm grip on her hand.

"I have to tell her to be careful. I should be with her. Someone needs to keep an eye on her!"

"Cassie. Cassie love." He tugged on her hand, trying to get her to look at him. When she just pulled harder, he swore and yanked her right down onto his lap. "Cassidy, listen to me!"

He waited until she really looked at him, then smiled in reassurance. "We won't let anything happen to Adele. De Santos has had a car watching her home since we made the connection yesterday. She's being looked out for. I promise."

"I need to call her," she insisted. "I need to talk to her."

"I understand that, sweetheart. Of course you want to talk to her. But Cassidy"—he took her chin in his hand and brought her gaze to his—"you can't tell her. She isn't to know about this."

"Why not? She deserves to know if someone might be planning to kidnap her!"

"Cassidy, I've known your grandmother for a total of five days, and even I know that if you told her, she would not sit by and let us take care of it. She'd want to handle it herself."

"Well, can you blame her?"

Quinn struggled against impatience and kept his tone firm and reasonable. "No, I don't blame her, but this is too important to take chances with, Cassie love. The Light of Truth is responsible for Ysabel Mirenow's kidnapping and murder, and for Alexandra Thurgood's car accident. We are this close to finding out who they are and where they're based. If your grandmother goes off after them half-cocked, they could scatter to the four winds before we have a chance to connect the last dots. We can't jeopardize that because your grandmother feels the need to demonstrate her power."

Cassidy threw up her hands. "Fine. I won't tell her. But I still need to call and make sure she's okay. And then I'm going over there to keep an eye on her myself. If you and Rafael and Richard made so much progress yesterday, I'm sure you can take care of the rest of this without my help."

She leaned across his body and grabbed the cordless

phone from its cradle, quickly punching in her grand-mother's number.

Quinn sat back against the sofa cushions with his arms curled around her and kept silent. He understood this was important to her, and he wanted her to be reassured that everything was all right and her grand-mother was safe. He wanted to hear that, too, and his sense of hearing was acute enough that he could listen to both sides of the conversation just fine where he was. He heard the phone ring three times before the other end picked up and a man's voice answered.

"Berry residence."

Cassidy frowned. "Who is this?"

"This is the Berry residence. Can I help you?"

"Yes, you can," Cassidy snapped. "You can tell me who the hell you are and why you're answering my grandmother's phone, and then you can put her on the line before I call the police."

The voice on the other end of the phone sighed. "That won't be necessary, Cassidy. This is Rafael De Santos and the police are already here. I'm afraid your grandmother is missing."

Twenty-five

"What the hell are you talking about?"

Cassidy felt her heart stop beating. She knew exactly what Rafael meant, but the words leapt out of her mouth of their own volition, as if by making him repeat himself, she could force him to take it back.

"I'm very sorry, Cassidy. We thought we would be able to prevent this, but whoever orchestrated it clearly knew what they were doing."

"What happened?"

"Two of my men were stationed right outside the house, but they never saw it coming. The only explanation is that the kidnappers used magic to take my men by surprise. They used a spell to give them the element of surprise, then cracked the guards' heads open and bound them with silver cuffs."

"I don't give a shit how they did it," she roared. "My nana is gone, and you were supposed to make sure that didn't happen! I want you to go and get her back *right now*!"

Her scream still echoed through her living room when Quinn tackled her to the sofa, grabbed the phone from her hand, and sat on top of her to keep her in place. "Shit! What the fuck happened? How did Adele disappear out from under your fucking nose?"

Cassidy cursed loudly and brutally and lay into Quinn with a vengeance, trying to get free of his restraint. She punched and beat and scratched and clawed and made a few good attempts to bite until he pressed the heel of his hand against the middle of her forehead and pinned that to the sofa cushions as well.

"Yeah, how did you think she'd be taking it, ya gob-shite? She's a bloody wreck! How long ago did you realize she was missing?"

His anger and distress came through loud and clear, but it was the question about her grandmother that managed to bore through Cassidy's red fog of panic and rage. She wanted to know everything Rafael De Santos knew. And then she wanted to find whoever had taken her nana and kill them. And then she might have to get nasty.

She stopped struggling and lay beneath Quinn, panting and concentrating on Rafael's end of the conversation.

"Only an hour ago," the Felix was saying, "but we think she must have been taken during the night, so they've got a good head start on us."

Cassidy quickly calculated the time between sunrise and now. They could be hours away. She yipped in frustration and tested Quinn's hold with a desperate squirm.

He just rode it out and glared down at her. "And your men didn't see anything?"

"No. They didn't have to. I've been trying to tell at least one of you that the kidnappers got sloppy. They brought silver cuffs because they knew the guards at Adele's house were shifters and wouldn't be able to break out of them, but they didn't count on shifter healing rates. One of the guards had healed enough to regain consciousness in time to see the car leaving. He got a make and model and a partial plate."

Quinn lifted his hand from Cassidy's forehead, but it hovered just a few inches away until she gave a terse nod, acknowledging that she wouldn't try to bite him again. It wasn't because she didn't mind being pinned down by a macho idiot. It was because she needed to save her strength to tear out the throats of the stupid bastards who had taken her grandmother.

"Did you run a trace?"

"Of course."

"And?"

"Our friend at the FBI says the car is leased out of a dealership in Fairfield, Connecticut. The name on the leasing agreement is D. Yvan Young."

Quinn swore. "Then it is the Light of Truth."

"We think so."

That time, Cassidy took her turn swearing.

"Do you have any idea where they might have taken her?"

Cassidy sat up as much as she could with a two-hundred-pound werewolf on her chest and listened intently.

Rafael hesitated. "We aren't positive. The car makes us think Connecticut, especially given the Thurgood situation, but that's still an awfully big search area."

Cassidy snarled. "Then get an awfully big search party together. We need to find her."

"Easy, Cassidy, you're not the only one around this conversation with good hearing," Rafael said. "I understand your sense of urgency—"

"Do you? Is it your grandmother who's been kidnapped?"

The Felix's voice remained low and calm, but an unmistakable cord of steel entered it. "No, it isn't. But I've a family of my own, Miss Poe, and I know how I would feel if someone were to try and take one of them from me. The streets would run with blood."

She wanted to howl her approval of the imagery.

"But I also know that I would want those with cooler heads around to keep me from doing anything stupid. If we go rushing out, beating every bush in Connecticut, the Light of Truth will hear us coming from three counties away. They'll either move her or kill her before we get anywhere close to finding her."

Quinn rubbed his hand over Cassidy's shoulder and felt her flinch at the words. "So what do you suggest? We can't afford to wait around and hope they have a change of heart."

"I don't propose we do. I've already spoken to the two men I sent to Greenwich to look into Alexandra Thurgood's situation. They think they might have found a contact at the hospital who would be willing to provide us with some information we can use to track the Lightheads. If it leads us to them, it can lead us to Adele."

"Well, what the fuck is he waiting for?" Cassidy demanded. "What's the information?"

"He refuses to talk over the phone. He wants to meet with someone in person."

Her frustration was reaching a boiling point. "Then have your men talk to him in person. How is this a tough call?"

"I never said it was." There was that steel again.

"Unfortunately, Miss Poe, your grandmother is not the only missing person we have on our hands. Miss Thurgood is no longer at the hospital. My men are a bit preoccupied trying to find her at the moment."

Part of Cassidy wanted to shout at him to screw the damned governor's daughter and tell his men to drop everything and find her nana. But another, admittedly smaller, part of her wondered how she would feel if she were the girl's mother or sister, and she bit her tongue.

"Fine. Then I'll go. Give me the guy's name and I'll talk to him myself. I can be in Greenwich in an hour."

"Make it two," Quinn growled, showing her his teeth when she tried to protest. "We both need to get dressed before we go anywhere."

"I can go myself."

"Over your dead body. I'm driving, and we're leaving as soon as we're dressed."

"I'll let you fight that out among yourselves," Rafael said. "The contact is named Ryan. He's an orderly at the hospital, and he's Other."

"Vamp? Lupine? What?"

"Not sure. The men thought changeling, but they didn't have time to ask a lot of questions."

"All right, then. I'll have my cell phone if anything happens. If it does, I expect a call. We'll be on the road in twenty minutes."

They were on the road within ten and across the state line in thirty. Cassidy sat in the passenger seat of Quinn's rented sedan (he'd vetoed the idea of folding his huge frame into her Mini and refused to let her drive in her condition anyway) and watched the miles crawl by on the road between Westchester and Fairfield

Counties. She knew from slightly less than subtle glances at the speedometer that Quinn was already pushing the boundaries of felony speeding, but to her, they couldn't possibly go fast enough. Her heart had stopped beating the moment she'd heard Rafael's news, and she didn't think it had started again yet.

"Are you all right, love?"

Quinn's voice rumbled more smoothly than the engine and pulled her attention away from the passing scenery.

"If they've hurt her, I'm going to kill them."

She said it quietly, without any flash or exaggeration, and she meant every word. It frightened her a little. She'd never been a violent person, but she knew that if anything had happened to Nana, she was about to become one. She'd felt dislike, but she'd never hated anyone before this. Maybe this was how those misguided humans felt about her and her kind.

The sunlight spilling through the windshield bathed Quinn's profile with yellow light. It seemed to illuminate him from the inside, as if revealing the wolf beneath the skin of the man.

He kept his eyes on the road and his hands steady on the wheel, but he spoke with utter conviction. "If they've hurt her, I'll hold your coat before I take a turn of my own."

And that's when it happened.

Cassidy stared across the car at this man, watching the light play over his hardened expression, and felt the earth shift under her feet.

She loved him.

The intellectual part of her mind gave a mild "huh" of surprise to note that the shifting hadn't happened

during one of their bouts of mind-numbing sex—
which she would happily have rated in terms of the
Richter scale—or in the sweet, tender times after. It
hadn't happened the way she thought it would, with a
dramatic flash and roar. It hadn't even happened in the
sweet, quiet moments when he took such good care of
her or treated her so tenderly.

No, it had happened when she had really looked at
this man and seen the truth. The truth that this Y-chro-
mosome-driven whirlwind who had entered her life in
a rush and a tumble clearly intended to stay in it just
the same way. He would kill for her or die for her,
would kill or die for the ones she loved. And that was
it. Game, set, and match. He had won, and she had
been thoroughly routed.

Her mind just clicked off and that was it. Just like
that, all her fears ceased to matter. Not that they went
away, but they became utterly powerless over her. It
didn't matter anymore that she had sworn never to become involved with a diplomat. It didn't matter that
this man would always have a higher calling to which
he had to answer. It didn't matter that she might spend
the rest of her life being dragged from assignment to
assignment along with him and a passel of pups. It
didn't even matter that they might end up like her parents, killed by the very people they were trying to help.
If she died, she didn't think she would mind so much
as long as this man was by her side.

Shit. Her heart wasn't kidding around about this.

She was on her way to find out whether her grandmother, the woman who had raised her since childhood
and one of the only constants in her life, was alive or
dead. This was not the time to fall in love with a large,

pushy, furry, sexy, exasperating man from half a world and about three species away. There shouldn't be room in her heart or mind for anything but Nana, but the heart, she could see, was an incredibly elastic organ.

It, she discovered in that long, silent moment as she stared across at him, had already made him room. It had stretched and shifted and cleared away old baggage and cobwebs and laid out a welcome mat for its newest resident.

God, how was she supposed to break that to her grandmother?

Quinn steered the car along the exit ramp, his gaze darting between her face and the road ahead. "Cassie love, are you still with me? Cassidy?"

She tore her attention from his face and looked back out the car windows. She needed a second to get a grip on this. On anything that still made sense. She couldn't afford to be picky just then.

"Yeah," she said. "I'm fine. Just worried."

Quinn slowed the car nearly to a stop and made the turn onto a narrow, tree-lined road. "I know you are. But I promise we'll find her, sweetheart. It will be okay."

"You didn't say that about Ysabel Mirenow."

He was silent for a couple of minutes, which didn't do much to reassure Cassidy. She needed reassuring right about then.

"No," he finally said. "I didn't. But I knew why they had taken Ysabel. She was a pawn. That was all she could be for them. She wasn't Other, just connected to one. There was only so much they could accomplish by taking her, and none of it depended on whether or not they kept her alive. That's not true with Adele."

She turned to look at him, almost afraid to let what

he was saying make sense. "Why else would they have taken her?"

"For the reasons I was going to tell you about before we got sidetracked. Adele is an incredibly important figure in the Other community. She's too valuable to discard so easily."

"How do you figure that?"

"Your grandmother isn't just any Other. She's nearly the community in and of herself. I know that much even on such short acquaintance. If I were them, I'd be looking for a way to use her that had nothing to do with killing her."

"Like?"

He hesitated, glancing over at her cautiously. "Like magical control, maybe. Or possession."

Cassidy went still and swallowed against a raw wave of fear. "Great. Well, thanks for making me feel better."

"So my distraction technique might need work," he said, pulling the car to a stop and shifting into park. "But I got us here with no injuries and no full-blown panic attacks. I think it was damned well done of me."

He climbed out of the car and walked around to open the passenger door for her. She was still off balance enough that she let him do it without protest. She finally got her feet back underneath her as they trudged up the path from the parking lot to the front doors of the huge brick building.

Inside, Quinn bypassed the information desk and led the way to one of the waiting areas inside the lobby. He stopped beside a low coffee table and picked up the heavy ivory hospital phone. Digging a scrap of paper from his pocket, he punched in a number and waited for an answer.

"Yes?"

"We're here and we'd like to talk to you," Quinn said. "Can you get us up?"

"I think so. I got a couple of guest badges out of the research director's desk. She's in a budget meeting all day."

"We won't be here long. We just want to ask you a few questions, then we'll get out of your hair. We're in the lobby."

"I'll come down for you. Give me five minutes."

Twenty-six

The lab tech who greeted them in the lobby and escorted them out from under the watchful eyes of Genghis Receptionist looked about eighteen, tops. He stood eye to eye with Cassidy, which made him about five-three (five-six in heels), and he had the smooth, baby-fine skin of a preteen. He also had an unruly mop of straight black hair and the most gorgeous, faintly almond-shaped eyes Cassidy had ever seen, and a shy, flirtatious smile.

Quinn greeted the poor kid with a snarl and they followed him to the elevator. The young man didn't look all that happy about being in an enclosed space with a sulky, possessive Lupine, because he stared at the floor numbers as if they were his last link to sanity all the way up to level six.

By the time the chime dinged and the doors slid open, the clouds of testosterone had grown toxic.

"Thanks for agreeing to help us," Cassidy said, stepping out of the car and following the young man down an antiseptic white corridor. De Santos had called him Ryan, and the name badge that hung from a cotton cord around his neck read R. MARKS. "We don't have a lot of time to waste."

"It's not like I could refuse with the New York Council and the whole White Paw Clan breathing down my neck," he said, turning a corner and picking up speed. "The old break room is this way. No one uses it anymore since the microwave died."

Maybe Rafael had been right about the informant not being Lupine. That comment about the White Paws didn't quite sound charitable. Curious, Cassidy sniffed the air around the young man and detected . . . something she couldn't quite put her finger on. Not Lupine. Not vampire. Not Racine. Not Felix. Not even Fae. In fact, she went through the catalog of every Other she'd ever met and couldn't manage to come up with anything that this guy smelled quite like. One more good whiff, though, and she could swear he didn't smell human.

"I know the Council claims authority over parts of the tristate area," she said, fishing, "but I didn't know the White Paw Clan normally walked around telling non-Lupines what to do."

Ryan shot her a wide-eyed look without slowing his pace. "They're the Council's representative for the whole state. And since the new Alpha came, the ties to the city are even closer."

"But—"

"The break room is through here," the orderly said, pausing to push through a set of wide, swinging doors. "Like I said, most of the staff uses the new one in the middle of the wing, so it's pretty quiet back here."

He stopped in front of a wooden door with a small, reinforced-glass window in the top. The room was dark and the hall was quiet except for the jingling of metal as the kid searched for the right key.

"This isn't the sort of conversation I want anyone to overhear. People can get touchy about stuff they consider weird, and you do not want to see our psych ward."

His voice became muffled as he stepped farther into the room and fumbled along the wall as if searching for a light switch. Cassidy moved to follow him. She had only taken a step or two when she felt Quinn grab her shoulder and yank backward.

"Cassie! Wait!"

Startled, she half turned back to see what his problem was, but she never got to ask. All she saw was the look of horror and rage on his face in the instant before his features distorted and stretched and a huge, angry timber wolf launched himself off the linoleum behind her. She saw the streak of charcoal fur, heard the echoing roar of a furious snarl, and felt the rush of wind pass her as Quinn shifted into his Lupine form and threw himself at the threat he detected in front of her.

Cassidy froze and peered deeper into the darkness. Before her eyes could focus, something slammed into her back and sent her flying into the room.

It felt like she'd been hit by a Mack truck.

Her hands shot out to brace for impact. She hit the floor with a smack and a grunt, wincing at the pain that radiated from the heels of her hands up her arms and into her elbows. The force of the push that sent her sprawling would probably have been enough to shatter a bone in a human, but whoever had decided to push her around wasn't dealing with a human.

Quicker than thought, she tucked and rolled across

the slick, polished floor and into a heavy piece of metal furniture. The breath rushed out of her in a whoosh, and she shook herself briskly to clear away the fog of surprise. Her back against what she guessed to be some kind of cabinet, she scanned the room for any sign of her attacker.

Her eyes adjusted quickly to the dimness, her pupils stretching into wide slits to allow in any stray shards of light. The din of her crashing into metal had covered up the sound of the struggle at the other side of the room. Now that she held still, she could hear the rustle and snarl and grunt of two adversaries locked in a tense battle a few yards away. The problem was that the crowded room they had been led to contained so much equipment and furniture that Cassidy had no clear view of what was happening.

She craned her neck to try and get a better view of the room, but no luck. Whatever Quinn had aimed for was on the other side of a long, high work station with cabinets below and, on top, all sorts of equipment that resembled something out of Dr. Frankenstein's laboratory. She'd need X-ray vision to get a glimpse of them.

The only light in the room came from the small transom window high above the door, and that didn't seem to be traveling far. It was enough for Cassidy to see by, but it left her in a room full of shadows with a disturbingly large number of places to hide. One of which concealed whoever had ambushed her.

She didn't like where this all seemed to be headed.

Pulling herself into as small a space as she could, Cassidy took a deep breath and shifted, her body condensing into the fur-clad form of her ancestors. Dark russet fur would be less visible than her pale, human skin, and besides, the smaller she was, the more places she could get in and out of. The creep who had sucker punched her wasn't the only one who knew how to hide.

Belly low to the ground, she began to creep across the floor, keeping to the shadows close by the bases of the objects around her. Her leathery pads skidded a few times on the slick tiles, but she kept her progress slow to prevent herself from going flying in an unexpected direction.

Inch by inch, she made her way across the room, letting her sensitive ears guide her toward the sound of Quinn's snarls. Then her nose caught the tangy, metallic whiff of blood, and inches became feet as she surged forward in panic.

A split second after she bolted from her hiding place in the shadows, a huge hand clamped around her tail and lifted her to swing nearly eight feet off the ground.

From her new vantage point, she could see Quinn looking a little worse for wear as he circled around a hulking shape. He appeared to be breathing hard, and she thought she detected a limp in his gait. Then her gaze landed on his opponent and even in the dim light she could make out a mountain of flesh the color of rich clay, with a sigil—a sorcerer's sign—carved into the back of one meaty fist.

Cassidy hated golems. Something didn't sit right with her around the molded hunks of blood and clay that only moved and acted because some sorcerer with power to spare had breathed magic into them. Golems had been designed as cannon fodder, just lumps of clay without feelings or personalities that were given only enough life force to walk, talk, and follow commands, and she didn't like anything that couldn't think for itself.

Suspended helplessly above the floor, she was reduced to writhing and snapping at the hand imprisoning her, but it didn't seem to be making any difference. The grip didn't loosen at all. She twisted enough to get a look at the creature holding her, but what she saw didn't make sense to her overloaded mind.

He looked like a man, only he stood well over nine feet tall and radiated the sort of unearthly magnetism that only the Fae had ever possessed. But this man would never be mistaken for Fae. He had the appearance of something very different.

His skin looked as if it were made of the shadows that surrounded him, an inky blue-black that should never have taken on the elastic sheen of flesh. But it had. It stretched over muscles roped thick around his frame. From her vantage point, Cassidy could hazard a pretty good guess that he wasn't wearing any clothes, but judging by the warmth of the hand wrapped around her tail, he didn't seem to need them. He generated his own heat that surrounded him like an aura. He was also generating some kind of power that kept her from shifting.

Now that took some seriously bad juju.

Cassidy squirmed again and managed to get a good look at his face. He should have been handsome. She remembered thinking that. His features were firm and regular and pleasingly sculpted, but he was saved from attractiveness by the glow of malevolence that shone in his eyes. Little pools of flame burned where the irises should have been.

"Well, well," he rumbled in a voice that made it

sound as if breaking glass coated his throat, "I think this hunt has turned up a fox *and* a hound, hasn't it, Ryan?"

Cassidy watched as the X-ray technician stepped out of the shadows and bowed before the figure who held her captive.

"Yes, master," the young man said, his voice somehow both fawning and devoid of life all at once. His name badge had flipped around and Cassidy could see a rosary that looked a lot like the ones Quinn said the Lightheads wore, only this one had been broken and reassembled with the cross hanging upside down. It would have been trite if the situation hadn't been so creepy. "I have brought them to you. How else may I serve?"

The string of invective Cassidy tried to fling at the kid's head came out as an unsatisfying series of high-pitched yips.

"Help the golem with the wolf. We want both of them."

Cassidy had no idea what the creature meant, but she didn't want to hang around and find out. Drawing on every last scrap of energy, she swung back toward her captor and sank her sharp little teeth into the nearest bit of flesh she could reach.

She heard a sound between a roar and a laugh, tasted something like acid on her lips, and saw the wall flying toward her head.

That was the last thing she saw before the blackness took her.

Twenty-seven

When she came to, the first thing Cassidy noticed was the lingering ache in her lower back.

The second thing she noticed was that whatever she was lying on felt rough and cool against her cheek. She was back in human form and completely devoid of fur. Someone had forced her to shift back while she slept.

That shouldn't have happened. That shouldn't have been *able* to happen. Shifting was a physiological function. It wasn't like a spell that someone could break if they knew the right words. Forcing a shifter to change was nearly a form of possession. It required taking total control of mind and body. And someone had done that while she slept.

"Oh, no. This is bad."

It got even worse when the echo of her own soft words sent an ice pick gouging into her temple until her brains leaked out.

Groaning, she lifted a hand to her head and tried to hold everything in. She heard a rustle to her left, followed by a grunt, and then a big, rough hand lay across her forehead.

"Are you hurt?"

She forced her eyes open and squinted against the pain of the dim light in her sensitive eyes. It took approximately six and a half centuries to turn her head, but it was worth it when she saw Quinn. He leaned over her, an intense look of concern on his face. She couldn't have stopped her weak smile if she'd tried.

"No," she said, and started to shake her head, but that didn't last long. The jackhammer in the base of her skull served as a heck of a deterrent. "Not seriously, anyway. A few aches. You were the one who was limping."

"Broken toe. Toes, really. Three of them. But they healed up when I shifted back. I'm fine."

"Right. So why do I get the feeling we're not back in my apartment getting ready to call out for Italian?"

Quinn chuckled and reached for her, gently helping her to sit up and brace her back against the wall beside him. "Quite likely that would be because we're not. We're in what looks like a storage room in what smells like a wine cellar. They threw us in here about an hour ago."

"They?"

"The golem and the . . . other one. They must have felt like a drive, because they loaded us up in a truck and brought us here."

The room finally stopped spinning around Cassidy, and she sighed in relief. "Here? Somewhere in Connecticut?"

"Not sure. We might be, but the ride took a little while. We could be back in New York, too. There's no way to tell."

She groaned and let herself slump against his shoulder. "So long as we know where we stand."

He chuckled and wrapped his arm around her, settling her snugly against his side. "Exactly. Count your blessings, as my Aunt Rosemary would always tell me. Usually when I was being punished for something."

His hand stroked over her hair, which probably looked as though a nest of gophers had taken up residence, and somehow his touch almost made her headache go away.

Almost. She was smitten, not brain-dead.

"So what do we do now?" she asked. "What do you think is going to happen?"

"Nothing either of us would like, I'm certain. Generally, kidnappers don't abduct someone with the intention of granting them the key to the city."

"Good. I'm not dressed for a black-tie affair."

He grinned, but the expression didn't last. "Neither of us is." He paused. "Cassie love . . ."

His voice trailed off hesitantly, which was enough to make her look up at him. Quinn and the word "hesitant" didn't quite belong together. "What is it?"

"Have you thought about the fact that we seem to have walked straight into some sort of trap? Someone obviously knew we were coming."

She frowned. "I suppose so. I mean, it would be a hell of a random coincidence."

"Exactly. And who knew we were coming?"

His questions were leading her somewhere, but she couldn't quite see the trail ahead. "Well, the Council, obviously. And the orderly, who I'm now more than a little miffed with. I should have let you thump him when he came down to meet us."

"You should always let me thump men who smile at you like that. But that's beside the point. Cassidy . . .

do you know what it was you sensed that was odd about that boy?"

She shook her head. "Actually, no. I never managed to put my finger on it. Right before the passing-out portion of the program, I thought I saw him wearing a Lighthead rosary, but even if I wasn't hallucinating, that doesn't explain anything. He smelled . . . different. Not human, but not *not* human, you know?"

"I do know." He paused again, almost as if he were bracing himself against something. "Cassidy, the boy was human, and he could have been a Lighthead before, but he'd been demon-touched."

Say huh?

"Demon-touched?" She gave a weak laugh. "Quinn, there aren't any demons. There haven't been for centuries. Millennia, even. The Fae banished them eons ago."

"There was no banishing involved," he said, shifting so he could look at her more directly. "My pack is one of the few to maintain the position of *guth*. Most of the others have phased it out, and with it, they've phased out the tradition of storytelling. Which means a lot of them get the stories wrong."

Cassidy shook her head and made a confused sound. "What are you talking about?"

"I'm talking about the fact that the story of the Fae and the demons that you've heard isn't what we might call 'true.'"

"Then what's the real story?"

"In a nutshell?" He sighed. "First off, you have to understand that the ideas we have about demons are a lot like the ideas the humans have about us."

"That they're monsters?"

"Right. You'd think that we, of all people, would know there's no such thing as a monster. In modern culture, the words 'demon' and 'devil' have become nearly synonymous. They're both words for evil entities that exist only to wreak havoc on the mundane world."

Cassidy folded her arms over her chest. "If being touched by a demon turns a human into someone like that Ryan kid, I'm failing to see the fallacy there."

"The fallacy is in the assumption that they're all the same," he explained. "It's like saying all Fae are good-tempered, ethereal, merrymaking sprites who live to sing and dance all day long, forgetting about the Unseelie Court entirely. One only exists because of the other."

"You mean there's such a thing as a good demon?"

"There are all kinds of demons. Good, bad, and indifferent. Just like there are all kinds of Others, and all kinds of Fae and all kinds of people. Demons originally existed as messengers. They were the ones who could most easily cross between the worlds. They served a purpose and they did a job, but they never did get along with the Fae. The old stories say that in the beginning, the humans looked at the Fae as gods, and the demons were the ones who told the humans otherwise. I think it led to some bad feelings. So when the Fae decided to leave the human world permanently, they forbade the demons from carrying their messages into Faerie. The demons refused to give up their traditional duties, so they declared war with the Fae."

Cassidy stared at him. "You're telling me that a war that changed the course of Others history started over a fit of pique?"

"Is it really so hard to believe?"

Okay, so maybe he had a point. "Still, I'm not quite getting what that has to do with our current situation."

He raised an eyebrow. "Haven't you stopped to wonder what it was that caught you so easily and managed to keep both of us from shifting no matter how hard we tried?"

She felt her eyes widening. "You mean the big blue guy. That was a demon?"

"You were thinking maybe pixie?"

"Watch it, buster. There's only room for one sarcastic malcontent in this relationship."

He saw her sour expression and laughed, lifting her hand to his lips and kissing her knuckles. "I'm sorry, love. I'll try to remember that. Especially since it means you're admitting we're in a relationship."

Her smile faded, and she sighed. "So, we know what we're up against, but have you managed to figure out why?"

"That's what I'm still having trouble with," he admitted. "The conclusions I've been able to reach don't make that much sense to me, but then, when do the plans of a demented villain usually make sense?"

"Is that who we're dealing with? A demented villain?"

"Is there another sort of villain?"

She wasn't so beat up she couldn't manage to smack him one. "I'm being serious. Who are we dealing with?"

He sobered. "I've been trying to put the pieces together since I came to, but they just don't seem to fit. We have the Light of Truth, the Council, Ysabel, Alexandra Thurgood's accident and subsequent disappearance, your grandmother's kidnapping, a demon neither of us have ever seen before, and a barely voting-age former zealot who's been enslaved by it. I can fit some of the pieces together, but not all of them."

Cassidy's heart clutched at the mention of Adele. "God, Quinn. I hope she's okay."

"I know, sweetheart. I know." He folded her up in his arms and brushed a tender kiss over her hair. "But she's a tough old fox. And we'll find her. As soon as we get out of here. I promise."

The creak of the opening door made both of them look up. Light flooded in from the hallway before being quickly blocked by a huge, bulky form.

"You know," Quinn said, his voice calm and conversational, "I'm developing quite a distaste for golems. How about you, love?"

"Absolutely. I think I'm all golemed out."

Too bad the golem didn't seem to be taking suggestions. He lumbered silently into the room and pointed a stubby piece of wood at them. Cassidy took one look at it and the glowing set of runic symbols carved into the surface and swore.

Or she tried to, but the words never got out. The golem muttered something unintelligible and the wand flashed with brilliant orange light just before she felt her shoulder blades make impact with the concrete wall behind her. She heard Quinn roar and then thump back beside her before her entire body went limp and numb.

She was right.

She hated golems.

Twenty-eight

The next time anyone asked Cassidy to do something for the good of her community, she was going to laugh in their face and go catch a movie. A double feature. After this past week, she figured she'd fulfilled her civic duty for a couple of lifetimes or more. She felt justified in tacking on an extra incarnation for the part where she was bound tightly and dumped on a hard wooden floor from a six-foot height.

If she'd been able to shift, she would have landed on her feet, but the rope binding her made that impossible. If it hadn't been for the burning sensation the cords caused where they touched her skin, she would have assumed it was Faerie rope. That stuff was stronger than steel and lighter than silk and bound power as securely as it bound limbs, but it definitely didn't irritate the skin. The demons must have come up with an equivalent of their own. These guys were resourceful.

She landed on the floor shoulders first and twisted with a grunt to her stomach. From there she managed to push herself up to her knees and look around.

Quinn lay motionless beside her. The golem must

have remembered their last match at the hospital, because he'd given the Lupine an extra blast from the wand before tying him up and then carrying them both up from the cellar. He had dumped them in this room and gone to stand against the wall.

It looked almost like a ballroom to Cassidy, with a huge expanse of polished wood floor surrounded by intricately carved walls painted a creamy white and broken every few feet on one side by tall, floor-to-ceiling windows. At one end was a set of carved double doors, and at the other a small dais, like a band might play on while couples danced below. Atop the dais sat several chairs filled with several people—or at least people-shaped things—whom Cassidy instantly recognized.

She almost wished she hadn't.

On one end of the abbreviated row lounged the blue-black demon to whom she owed her aching back. Now that she had a clear and right-side-up view of him, she saw the tail he whipped restlessly by his side and heard the muffled rustling of wings when he moved. He stared right back at her, his eyes pools of flame, his mouth a cruel echo of a smile. At his feet she saw the crumpled form of a body clad in a dark robe and wearing a rosary just like Ryan's. The demon nudged the body and grinned.

Swallowing a rush of nausea, Cassidy made a point of meeting the creature's gaze for the space of three heartbeats before she allowed herself to move on to the next figure.

The next chair held Francis Leonard, sitting calmly and comfortably between the demon and two other people Cassidy had really hoped never to have to see again. The remaining members of the Terrible Trio.

"I think we've managed to surprise you, Miss Poe," Leonard said, his tone almost teasing as he rose to his feet. He looked for all the world as if he were greeting her at the entrance to a swanky party, rather than, you know, planning to kill her and feed her to a demon in little bloody pieces. "I'm sorry about all this, but I have to say, we could have avoided this whole mess if you had just agreed to be a little more cooperative."

She snorted. "I think that ship has pretty much sailed. I tend not to feel all that magnanimous after I've been knocked unconscious, kidnapped, imprisoned, paralyzed, tied up, and dumped on a floor like a sack of dirty laundry."

"Cassidy, dear—you did say I could call you Cassidy." His grin was ingratiating and vaguely nauseating at the same time. She kept looking for his expressions to be mirrored in his eyes, but they never were. There didn't seem to be anything in those eyes, just an absence of morals behind the glassy blue surface. "Cassidy, I want you to know I never wanted to hurt you. None of us did."

Leonard rose from his chair and stepped down from the dais, approaching her with a big smile and open arms.

She jolted to her feet and took an instinctive step backward. "Yeah, well, you'll understand that I have a hard time believing that when I'm tied up with some kind of demon braid and held against my will in a place I don't recognize by someone I thought was on my side."

"I'm afraid we had little choice. We gave you every opportunity of doing things our way, Cassidy, but you seem to be cursed with the same sort of conceited independence that is your grandmother's burden to bear."

Cassidy froze, her breath stalling in her throat. "If you so much as mussed my nana's dress, I swear by all that's holy—"

Leonard cut her off with a mocking laugh. "Really, Cassidy, you're hardly in a position to make threats, but I understand the effect stress can have on some people."

She bit back another snide comment and glared at him instead. His smarmy "we're all friends here" attitude both disgusted her and made her really uneasy.

"I regret the necessity of bringing you here," he continued, "but neither of you have been willing to listen to reason. You and I both know how foolish this talk of Unveiling is. We should be ruling the humans, not trying to determine ways in which to persuade them to accept us." His lips curled in a sneer, exposing a length of fang. "The Europeans, like this dog you're consorting with, would have us begging their pardon and pleading with them not to hurt us. I have not lived hundreds of years to be reduced to such a pitiful state."

Leonard's contempt for Quinn was obvious, but then, Leonard seemed to feel contempt for just about everyone. His expression never altered and his smile never wavered when he drew back a crisply polished wingtip and planted it hard in the middle of Quinn's rib cage. He was out of his bloodsucking little mind.

She clenched her jaw against the urge to cry out when she heard Quinn groan and saw him shift position on the hard floor. She almost wished he'd stay unconscious. At least then she wouldn't have to worry about him getting into any more trouble.

"The only thing I can imagine right now," she said, drawing the vampire's attention away from the prostrate

Lupine, "is that if I've taken to consorting with this dog, you might want to consider that I'd probably feel more cooperative if you refrained from kicking him right under my nose."

Leonard's smile widened. "Oh, but you come from a long line of politicians, Cassidy. And in politics, I believe this is what they call leverage."

She watched helplessly as he reached down and grabbed Quinn by the hair, lifting his head clear up off the floor and shaking him like a puppy.

"Of course, if you require more persuasion, Cassidy, it could be arranged." Madame Touleine's bayou drawl echoed from her place on the dais. Cassidy followed her gesture toward a small door at that end of the room, which opened to admit the golem, once again carrying a burden. This one looked small and fragile and was covered in purple silk.

Nana.

Ignoring her bindings, her captors, and the distance between them, Cassidy surged forward, intent only on getting to her grandmother, on protecting her from these monsters.

She didn't get three steps before she felt some invisible force tighten around her throat and push her to her knees.

"Tsk, tsk," Madame scolded, holding aloft by the throat a small doll with yellow-green beads for the eyes and rust-colored yarn for most of the hair. Cassidy saw a few strands of much finer, glossier hair stitched carefully to the doll's head and felt her stomach clench. The buttons on that chair in Leonard's parlor. Looking back, she remembered the tug of a few strands of caught hair pulling out, but she'd been too worked up at the time to think clearly and gather them before she left. How monumentally stupid!

Madame smiled and loosed her grip around the doll's neck, allowing Cassidy to breathe. "Do try not to do anything rash, Cassidy. I would hate to see you disappoint me when I have so far thought very highly of you."

Great. Just what Cassidy had always wanted. To be a mad old voudun's pet.

She straightened her spine and backed up a couple of steps. "Fine, I'll stay where I am. But if you want me to do anything for you, you're going to have to give me my grandmother."

"Just hear us out," Leonard urged, still smiling. God, she wanted to wipe that expression from his face. "We think you'll understand our point of view. What we want isn't unreasonable."

"If you want to rule the world and enslave the humans, I think there might be one or two folks around who would argue."

The smile didn't go anywhere, but it did turn brittle. "Our dominion over the humans is inevitable. They are a dead end on the evolutionary trail, and we will triumph in the final act. But we aren't saying it must be today, or even tomorrow. We aren't like the humans. We can afford to be patient."

"You possess something that has become very important to us, Cassidy," Ngala inserted smoothly. He shifted in his chair, scars writhing in the light, and this time Cassidy could see it wasn't an optical illusion. His scars didn't *look* like they were moving. They really were. "Something, it seems, that your family has always had. Influence."

"Influence?" If she sounded half as incredulous as she felt, it would be saying something. "What kind of influence do you think I have? I'm an untenured assistant college professor in an underfunded and unglamorous university department. You've got to be kidding if you think I can do anything for you that you can't do for yourselves."

Leonard shook his head, his smile stretching from politic to beatific in an oily, disturbing shift. "Dear, dear Cassidy. You suffer from the blindness that plagues so many of our folk. You take for granted the resources at your disposal because your access to them has been so easy. You don't see the power lurking at your fingertips."

Okay, the dude was seriously beginning to creep her out. She wanted Quinn to wake up and take over. She wanted herself to wake up and realize this was not actually happening and she'd just gotten hold of some bad couscous or something.

Yeah, well, you've always wanted to be five-seven, too. How's that working out for you?

She forced down the fear and the unease and met the lunatic's gaze. "So what exactly do you think I can do for you, Mr. Leonard? Administer a pop quiz on the characteristics of cultures that use matrilineal lines of descent? Grade some papers? Supervise a dissertation? What?"

"It's really quite simple, Cassidy, and the truly beautiful part of all this is that you won't have to do anything opposed to your own conscience." He smiled again. "All we want you to do is to tell the truth. Tell the Council that you have assessed the situation involving the Light of Truth, and you can confirm that they are indeed active

in the New York area. Then you recommend the only responsible course of action. That the Council should
move immediately to exterminate them."

Whoa. Reality check.

"You want me to do what?"

"I believe you heard me," he said smoothly. "You
must see that it is the only sensible thing to do. And it
is a step we have already begun to take." The vampire
gestured to the body at the foot of the demon. "This
David was a sheep, a minor follower as easily recruited
as the Ryan boy was corrupted. His kind don't worry
us. We need more than them, Cassidy. We need to dig
this cancer out at the root. And you have the power to
help us."

Cassidy's heart clenched in sorrow for the young
man and whatever family would miss him, but she had
her own to worry about, both old and new. Her gaze
flickered from Adele to Quinn. His body remained
limp, his jaw slack, but she thought she saw a glimmer
of old gold beneath the veil of inky eyelashes.

Yanking her gaze from his prone form, she shifted
her position, taking a couple of steps forward under the
guise of listening to the vampire speak. In reality, she
was doing what she could to put herself between the figures on the stage and the werewolf on the floor. Plus, it
was two steps closer to Adele, who still lay limp in the
arms of the silent golem.

"Discuss away," she said, hoping she hadn't halluci-
nated that Quinn was regaining consciousness. "I think
I can give you a few minutes before my next pressing
engagement."

Leonard settled back in his chair atop the dais like a

pretender taking the throne. He leaned back and crossed his legs, smiling indulgently down at Cassidy.

"You may not believe this, Cassidy," he said, tapping his fingers against the arm of his chair. "But I admire your family a great deal. Or most of it. I never could understand that nasty little tradition of taking human mates. The only thing that made sense to me was that at least they would be easy to control."

She struggled to keep her distaste for him and his opinions from reflecting in her face. "We do what we have to."

"As we all do." He sighed and shook his head with false gravity. "Surely you can see that this is the only way. These human fanatics must be destroyed, Cassidy. If they are permitted to live, they will only spread. They are becoming too bold, kidnapping Kasminikov's mistress, stalking your grandmother."

Cassidy must have looked startled, because Leonard paused and smiled.

"Oh, yes, we know about that," Madame interjected, not waiting for Leonard to speak himself. "It's what gave us our little idea, after all."

"Yes," Leonard hastened to continue, "but the important point here is that the humans are growing too bold. They are too close to gathering solid evidence of our existence that they can bring to the masses. We cannot allow that to happen. We must stop them now while we have the chance."

Cassidy heard a faint rustling coming from behind her, from Quinn, and raised her voice to cover it, to buy time. "What makes you think we can ever stop them? Fanatics have been preaching about monsters since the dawn of humanity. If we stop the Light of Truth, another sect will just take its place."

"Ah, but what truly defines a monster, my dear? Am I a monster? Are you? Are Mr. Ngala and Madame Touleine?" He gestured to the demon. "Is my other friend here a monster? Who gets to decide?"

Cassidy bared her teeth in what might have passed for a smile, but wasn't. "I'm probably not the best judge of that. I tend to get the impulse to call anyone who lifts me up by my tail and then beats the shit out of me a monster. It's this little quirk I have."

"If I had beaten the shit out of you," the demon rumbled, sounding amused, "you would still be unconscious. At the very least."

"You sweet-talker," she snapped. "I didn't quite catch your name before. What did you say it was?"

The demon laughed, and if possible the sound was even more grating than its speaking voice. "I didn't say, little girl. That would be telling. But you can call me Amon."

"I believe you should be listening to Mr. Leonard's request, Miss Poe." Ngala's low, melodic voice came from the dais and drew Cassidy's gaze. "It could prove to be quite important to your future."

Cassidy suppressed a shiver. What was it with these guys? Were they charter members of the Creepy Voice Society, or what? "I'm listening. But I still don't get why you think the Council would be particularly inclined to listen to me."

"We were surprised by it, as well. Your grandmother is, of course, a force to be reckoned with in our community, but we felt fairly confident she would be on our side. You, however, were a bit of an unknown, as was the reason behind the fact that De Santos chose to consult with you on this issue."

Leonard couldn't even say Rafael's name without spitting it. He probably wouldn't appreciate it if she pointed out that it made him sound almost like a were-cat himself.

"Gee, all that praise will go to my head. I don't know if you were listening at the Council meeting that night, but I'm emerging as one of the most respected scholars in the field of the interaction between cultures and fringe groups. It says so right in my faculty bio. You can look it up online."

"You must view this from our perspective," Madame said. "Folk such as we become unaccustomed to asking the opinions of anyone, let alone girls who were unknown to us a few days ago."

Cassidy turned her gaze on the voudun and let it harden. "And I'm unaccustomed to doing favors for people who kidnap my relatives and hold me prisoner."

"We had hoped you would be reasonable, Miss Poe." Ngala stood and crossed his arms over his chest. She could see his medicine wand cradled in the crook of one elbow.

"I don't think I am being unreasonable. You hurt my grandmother, you hurt my friend, and you hurt me. Am I supposed to brush it aside and pretend it didn't happen and do you some big favor? I don't think so." Especially since Adele still hadn't stirred in the arms of the golem. "Why would I help you hurt people? It doesn't matter if they're homicidal lunatics who probably deserve it, they're still conscious beings and I won't be responsible for their deaths."

Cassidy risked a glance down at the floor to Quinn's

prone form and felt a swell of relief when one eye winked open and closed just fast enough for her to see. She used all her self-control to keep the reaction from her face.

"If you are unwilling to cause the deaths of the humans," Leonard said flatly, "you will be causing the deaths of those considerably closer to your heart."

As he said it, the golem stepped forward and tightened his hands on Adele in menace.

Cassidy leaped forward one more time, only to be stopped once again by Madame's magic around her throat.

"Ah-ah," the woman scolded. "Do not be foolish, *'tite*. Is what we ask really so unreasonable?"

The pressure at her throat eased and Cassidy fixed the bayou bitch with a hostile glare. "Gee, I don't know. Is it unreasonable to kill off an entire group of people based on the principle that if we don't, they might make things inconvenient for us? Why don't you go to hell and ask some Nazis?"

This time Madame didn't strangle the little doll. She took a pin from the sleeve of her dress and jabbed it into a cloth-covered leg. Cassidy screamed in pain and dropped to her knees.

She was going to *kill* that bitch in another minute.

"I can see you're going to require a bit more persuasion. I wish you hadn't made this necessary." Leonard's face froze into a mask of cold hatred as he beckoned the golem forward. "Give the old woman to me and kill the werewolf. Make sure it hurts."

Quinn's eyes popped open at that, and his voice rang out clear and strong in the bare room. "I was hoping she wouldn't make it necessary, either, but you know women. Can't tell them a bloody thing they won't argue with."

Before she could look down to see what the lunatic Lupine might have planned, she felt his hands close around her ankles, yank her to the floor, and send her skidding across the polished wood toward the other side of the room. She scrambled for purchase on the slick surface, her skin making a ragged squeaking noise as it scraped and slid along.

But the noise didn't drown out the sound of his voice growling, "Tell the cavalry I said they'd better have an excuse for their piss-poor efforts at punctuality."

Then he stood in a rush, loosened coils of demon rope sliding off him like water, and stretched. She saw his bones shift, his skin ripple, and the light bend around him, and then all of a sudden the man was gone and a seven-foot-tall werewolf was leaping straight for Francis Leonard's pale, maniacal throat.

Damn. Things were going to get messy.

Twenty-nine

Cassidy's skid ended just far enough from the door that it didn't smack her in the head when it blew open with the force of an invading hurricane. That seemed like cold comfort when the heel of a woman's shoe stabbed her hard in the ass.

"Oh, gods, I'm so sorry! Did I hurt you? Oh, I swear I didn't mean to hurt you. Here. Let me help you up."

Small, delicate hands closed around her wrists and tugged ineffectually, but it was the large masculine one hooked in the back of her jeans that ended up hauling her to her feet.

"Forgive my wife," a deep voice said as the scenery flew by. Cassidy was lifted up so fast, she felt as if she should be worried about the bends. "She means well, but she sometimes loses track of where her pretty little feet are going."

With both of her own feet planted back on the ballroom floor, Cassidy had about three seconds to recognize Tess and Rafe De Santos standing in front of her. She didn't bother with friendly greetings, just stuck out her bound hands and snarled.

"Untie me! They have Nana!"

Tess already had the first knot free when an invisible force closed around Cassidy's ankles and jerked her to the floor. She scrambled for purchase against the slick wood, but there was nothing to grab hold of. She felt twin lightning bolts of pain in her hips and saw the world tilt crazily off its axis. Across the room, Madame used that fucking doll to jerk Cassidy up by her ankles and dangle her eight feet off the floor before sending her slamming down with brutal force. She landed directly on her side as Madame had intended and cried out when she felt two of her ribs give way with a snap.

Tess shouted her name over the ringing in her ears, and she struggled against a wave of nausea. The other woman knelt by her side and ran quick hands over her limbs, searching for injuries. Cassidy groaned and opened her eyes just enough to look into Tess's. "Did I mention Madame has a voodoo doll with my hair on its head?"

"No, you forgot to mention that little fact," Rafael growled, rolling his shoulders as if to ease away a knot of tension. "But it won't be an issue for long."

For the second time in as many minutes, Cassidy watched as a man shifted and disappeared, changing into something else right before her eyes. Unlike Quinn, though, Rafael left behind not a werewolf but a sleek, deadly jaguar with fangs like razor blades. He also had a very irritated look in his eyes as he sprang with lethal grace across the floor toward the dais.

Powerful as Madame Touleine might be, her human reflexes were no match for those of a shifter, let alone a Felix. She yanked the black-headed needle from the Cassidy-doll's leg and raised it high above the center of its chest, but her hand never got the chance to fall.

She was too busy screaming and tumbling to the floor beneath the weight of a snarling seven-hundred-pound feline with a temper.

"Don't hurt the doll!" Tess screamed. "You have to get it away from her!"

Cassidy thrust her hands back at Tess and shook them. "Untie me! Hurry up! I don't see Ngala. Where did Ngala go?"

She felt Tess attacking the knots again and turned back to scan the chaos in the room for signs of the animus. She didn't like the idea of him being out of her sight, but all she could see were piles of struggling fur and flesh as Quinn and Rafael kicked some insane Other ass.

A hideous screech from the other side of the room whipped her head in that direction. The demon had risen from his seat on the stage and was currently hovering just below the ceiling, his huge, batlike wings creating a foul wind as he kept himself aloft. On top of that, he looked kind of cranky. Cassidy saw his head turn and his eyes focus on Quinn, and panic flooded her. She remembered how helpless they'd both been against him before, and all she could think about was getting to Quinn's side and doing whatever she could to protect him. Forgetting all about Tess, she took one lunging step forward . . .

. . . and landed back on the floor, flat on her face once again. Only this time, Tess's knee was digging into her spine.

"That time I did it on purpose," the witch grumbled, "and I don't intend to apologize. Stop being an idiot. That's a demon, in case you hadn't noticed. You guys have about as much chance of kicking its ass as I do of keeping a pint of cream in my refrigerator for more than an hour before Mr. Puss-in-Boots over there drains the damned thing. Let me handle the demon."

Cassidy might have wondered how a hundred-and-some-pound human planned to deal with a seven-foot-tall demon, but she didn't have time to worry about it. Before she could even blink, Tess De Santos climbed up on a chair she'd dragged into the middle of the room and shouted, "Hey! Tall, dark, and accursed! Over here! C'mon and show me what you got!"

Shaking her head at the idiocy of humans, Cassidy hunkered down against the floor as the rush of wind from Amon's beating wings threatened to send her sailing. She wanted to see what exactly Tess intended to do with a huge, angry demon who outweighed her by a metric ton and made Charles Manson look like a good-tempered fellow, but she had other things to think about. Like Thabo Ngala and the fact that she didn't trust him farther than she could throw him. Then one quick look across the room drove every single solitary thought from her mind except one.

NANA!

Ngala had reappeared from behind the dais accompanied by the golem. The mindless creature scooped Adele up in his burly arms and turned to follow orders.

Screaming in wordless rage, Cassidy scrambled to her feet and threw herself forward into a shift. Her broken ribs protested as her flesh reshaped itself around them. She felt the searing pain of her body clicking into overdrive, knitting the bones together at an unnatural pace, but she didn't care. She ignored the pain and dove for her grandmother's side.

Her paws searched for traction on the slippery floor

and found just enough to keep her in motion. Her strides ate up the distance between herself and her target, but she knew it wasn't enough. She wasn't large enough or fast enough to reach them in time. She howled in pain and rage and threw on a final, frantic burst of speed.

"Be still!" Ngala roared, raising his medicine wand high and pointing it directly at Adele. "Do not take another step, Miss Poe. And tell your pets to back away from my associates. Do it now."

Cassidy skidded to a halt, her nails carving deep grooves into the wooden floor. Her eyes widened and fixed on the threat poised above her grandmother's head, and she shifted back to her human form on a curse.

"Quinn! Rafael! Tess!" She shouted to be heard over the din. "Back off! Please."

Her voice broke as the room quieted, snarls and roars and howls falling silent. "Please. He has my Nana."

Quinn felt his heart breaking at the pain in his mate's voice. He withdrew his teeth from the vampire's throat and looked up, snarling under his breath at the raw agony on her face. She looked vulnerable and shaken and he never, *ever* wanted to see that look on her face again. Not as long as they lived.

Cautiously and reluctantly, he stepped back from the vampire's limp body and crouched there, licking his chops, his gaze fixed on the animus and the frail old woman in the golem's arms.

It was funny, he thought, that a woman who looked as strong and indomitable as Adele Berry did when she was conscious, could be reduced to something so small

and fragile simply by removing the force of her personality. It shook him. What would his Cassie look
like, he wondered, if she were unconscious and helpless in the clutches of a villain?

Covered in blood, he reassured himself. Because
anyone who laid a hand on his mate, be he man or
beast, would lose that hand along with his life the
minute Quinn got a hold of him.

"All right," Cassidy said, watching the animus and
the golem warily. Her body looked tense and her hands
were half-raised, palms down, in a calming gesture.
"They've backed off, see? They're not hurting anyone."

The animus looked around the room and frowned.
"Where's the demon?"

Eyes wide, Cassidy turned her head, and Quinn followed her gaze. He saw Tess sitting cross-legged on
her chair in the middle of the ballroom floor, her hands
folded in her lap, her big, blue eyes wide and innocent.
The floor and walls around her were charred, and she
had a smudge of soot across one cheek.

"Sorry," the witch said, shrugging. "You were too
late for the demon. Next time, give a girl a little warning, will you?"

There was a moment of stunned silence.

Ngala's mouth twisted in a snarl. "It is of little matter. Why should I need the aid of a demon?"

Cassidy turned back to him and nodded. "You don't
need the demon. And we won't touch Madame or Mr.
Leonard again. I swear. Now tell the golem to put my
grandmother down."

Ngala laughed, a low, harsh, evil sound that had
Quinn's hackles rising. "Why would I do something
like that, you foolish little girl? Do you think I wouldn't

realize that Adele Berry is the key to bringing all our plans to fruition? After I worked so hard to prepare the humans and whip them into the frenzy that would force them to take actions the Council could no longer ignore? Her death will be the impetus the Russian woman's should have been. It will be the final straw that forces the Council to take action against the Light of Truth."

Quinn felt a sickening wave of hatred for this man. He had been the "Damned Soul," and he was the one responsible for the pain of so many in the community. Quinn's rage astounded him, but he knew it would be nothing to what he would feel if the animus succeeded in causing Cassidy the pain of her grandmother's loss.

"The circumstances will, of course, be tragic," Ngala continued, his voice turning falsely regretful, a parody of grief. "As the only survivors, Leonard and Madame Touleine and I will explain how we discovered the Light of Truth finally gone out of control. First they took Ysabel Mirenow, tortured and killed her. That was bad enough, but now we discover they have come to America and settled in our very midst! They arranged an automobile accident that killed the daughter of the governor of New York, and then they kidnapped the most respected member of the Council of Others and used her to lure the head of the Council, his wife, the head of the European delegation, and the poor old woman's own granddaughter to their deaths. Of course, we tried to stop them, but there was nothing we could do."

His stomach rolling with nausea, Quinn marveled at the African magician's level of insanity.

"Clearly, though, this means the Light of Truth must be destroyed," Ngala said, and his eyes blazed with malevolent glee. "You can see how dangerous they are. They are madmen! They will stop at nothing to destroy us. The only way to protect ourselves is to destroy them first. The Council will see. *It is the only way.*"

With a ululating shout, the animus drew back his arm and prepared to deliver his wand's death blow to the unconscious old woman before him.

As one, Quinn and Cassidy launched themselves forward, intent only on preventing the blow from falling, but they were too late. With a sudden jerk and twist, Adele Berry shifted forms and threw herself out of the golem's arms, darting through the legs of the unsuspecting animus.

Ngala whipped around, roaring in fury. He tried to track Adele's movements, but surprise threw him off balance. He discharged the wand into a multipaned window, shattering it with seismic force and sending shards of glass and wood spraying out in all directions like shrapnel from a grenade.

Quinn ignored all of it. With a glad howl he slammed into Ngala and sent the man sprawling. He opened his mouth and prepared to clamp down hard around the bastard's throat when he felt slim, angry fingers tangle in the fur at the scruff of his neck and haul backward with great force. It wasn't enough to move him, but it was enough to get his attention. He looked back over his shoulder and saw Cassidy staring past him at Thabo Ngala, a murderous look on her face.

"No you don't, White Fang," she snarled. "This one is mine. Go disassemble the golem."

Thirty

The feelings of rage and hatred, fury and loathing, crashed through Cassidy like a tsunami, threatening to overwhelm her. They certainly terrified her. She'd never felt this way before, not about anything or anyone. Not even toward the vampires who had murdered her parents. Of course, she'd only been six at the time, and if a six-year-old could have felt what Cassidy had felt, there would have been one more child killer in the world.

She waited while Quinn stepped back off her prey. Ngala lay on the floor, staring up at her with an expression of mad defiance, but his eyes also held terror. She looked into those dark brown eyes and wondered if she should be feeling something like sympathy for him. She couldn't do it. This man had nearly killed her nana. And on top of that, he had planned to kill her and her mate, as well. He didn't deserve her mercy.

Lips curving into a snarl, Cassidy leaned slowly down over the prone form of the animus until her face hovered only inches from him. She inhaled deeply and could smell his fear.

"Cassidy."

At first, she didn't hear the soft voice behind her.

Her fingers curled into fists and flexed, as if she imagined curling them around Ngala's throat. The voice spoke again, more insistently this time.

"Cassie."

Startled, Cassie jerked upright and turned her head. Behind her, Adele stood, as proudly straight as ever, silk back on and barely mussed, without even the pretense of a cane to support her. She looked unharmed, but somehow older than before.

"Let him be, Cassidy. If you kill him now, he will win, in his own way. The Council will deal with him perfectly well."

The older woman turned and gave Rafael a regal nod. The Felix stepped forward from where he'd been standing near Madame Touleine's unmoving form and quickly bound Ngala in a length of shed demon rope. Then he stuffed a wadded-up handkerchief in the man's mouth for good measure to muffle his curses.

Making a soft noise of mingled worry and relief, Cassidy forgot all about the animus, the Felix, and the rest of the world and threw herself into her grandmother's arms.

"Nana! God, Nana, are you okay? Did he hurt you? Do you need a doctor? We should get you to a hospital. We've already been to the hospital. It looked nice. They'll take care of you there—"

Adele laughed softly and stroked a slender hand over her granddaughter's hair. "Hush, kit. I'm fine. Just fine. Don't you worry about me. I don't need any doctors."

Cassidy shook, a great shudder that trembled through her from head to toe, and took a deep breath. "I thought I was going to lose you, Nana. I thought you were going to die and leave me alone again."

"Never," Adele said with a smile. "Even if I did leave you, Cassidy, my darling, I have a feeling you won't ever be alone."

The older woman turned to Quinn with an arch look and beckoned to him. He jerked as if surprised, then started forward. He took two steps before he seemed to realize he still had a dismembered golem hand clutched in his fist. He dropped it as if it were on fire and closed the rest of the distance, shifting back to his human shape.

With one arm still around Cassidy's shoulder, Adele looked at the Lupine before her and gave a small smile. "Well, I can't say you're anything like the man I had envisioned for my Cassidy."

"No, ma'am. I imagine I'm not."

"You're also naked."

Quinn blinked and looked down at his own bare skin. His clothes had been left behind when he'd shifted. *Bloody hell.* "Yes, ma'am. I am."

"And can you give me one good reason why I should give you my approval?"

Cassidy started and shot her grandmother a wide-eyed glance, her voice ringing with shock and amusement. Now that she could begin to see the danger was over, all her other emotions felt heightened. "Nana!"

"I can think of several," Quinn said, both of them ignoring her. "But the first that comes to mind is that if you don't, I might come to regret saving you from that madman over there."

Adele sniffed indignantly and raised her chin several notches. "I'll have you know, young man, that I saved myself."

"Actually, I'm going to say it was a team effort,"

Tess called from her chair in the center of the room. "We all did a pretty good amount of saving. Not to mention ass-kicking." She grinned at her husband. "The ass-kicking was my favorite part."

Cassidy took another look at Tess, peering past the heap of golden curls and the sweet, ingenuous features to the power below. She had forgotten that the Felix had married a witch. Still, she didn't look like the kind to go *mano a mano* with a demon and come out smiling. "You handled the demon?"

With an expression that said she'd had her fill of doubting Thomases, Tess rolled her eyes and pointed to a spot in the middle of the ballroom floor. "Who else here could have done that?"

"That" turned out to be a circle drawn on the wood with fine black line. Parts of the outer edges seemed to glisten as if they were wet, and at the center lay a small copper disc.

Cassidy's eyes widened. "You bound the demon? But that takes salt and a circle and some kind of object to bind him to. I didn't see you carrying anything but your purse! How on earth did you manage to bind a demon with no supplies?"

Tess grinned smugly and held up her tiny handbag. "Eyeliner pencil, saline solution, and a Canadian penny. A good witch never leaves home unprepared."

"Just your routine day at the office for us brave cavalry soldiers," Rafe laughed. He walked over to where his wife sat, usurped her place, and settled her petite form in his lap. "You can thank us for our timely arrival later, by the way. When Quinn didn't call to check in after you reached the hospital, we became concerned. I don't like losing contact with my people."

Cassidy took in the rips and stains on Rafe's usually immaculate clothing and the quickly healing scratches on his face and hands and raised an eyebrow. "Clearly."

"He'll never be the one to admit it, but he's an overprotective worrywart," Tess broke in, smiling at Cassidy. "He insisted we follow you up here and figure out what was going on."

"I insisted that *I* follow them," Rafe growled, scowling down at his wife. "As you might recall, I wanted you nowhere near us when this all happened. You put yourself in danger, mate, and you may rest assured we will discuss that at length when we return to the city."

Tess just rolled her eyes. "Sure we will. Are you forgetting there was a demon here to deal with, buddy? Just what would you have done without me to handle him?"

Rafe laughed ruefully and turned to look at Quinn. "Well, Quinn. Is it your turn to join the brotherhood?" he asked, grinning. "We've had jackets made, if you'll tell me your size."

Cassidy, Adele, and Tess all rolled their eyes. Did men really think women couldn't decipher that testosterone-laden code of theirs?

Adele cleared her throat with excessive volume. "Before you boys proceed with your male bonding rituals, I believe there are one or two loose ends we need to discuss."

Quinn flicked a glance in the direction of the Terrible Trio and sneered. "I say we put them out with the trash."

"No," Rafe said. "As appealing as that idea might be, the Council will deal with them better. They have a lot to answer for, including that demon my wife so ably took care of."

Tess gave a regal nod at his acknowledgment of her assistance.

"You're right. There hasn't been a confirmed demon sighting in centuries. Rumors here and there, but nothing concrete. And summoning was outlawed in the treaties at the end of the Fae-Demon War." Quinn frowned. "They have a lot to answer to the Council for. And when you're done, I believe the European High Council might like a crack at whatever is left over."

The Felix nodded. "Done."

"Gentlemen," Adele interrupted. "I said one or *two* matters to deal with."

"She's right. She did."

Cassidy nodded, following Tess's train of thought. "Handling these idiots is the least of our worries. There's still the matter of the Light of Truth to deal with. Even if they weren't the ones who kidnapped Nana, they still killed Ysabel Mirenow, and might have killed Alexandra Thurgood. Who at the very least is still missing and in imminent danger of being exposed."

"Well, you're almost right," Tess said. "We found her. That's why we were a little late getting here. Once we checked for you at the hospital and found out what had happened to you, Rafe beat the information on where they were hiding Alexandra out of that slimy little orderly. She's safe with a doctor we can trust, and her father's plane landed an hour ago. In fact, he's probably with her by now. But there is still the matter of her hospital admission records."

Quinn nodded. "And we do know the Light of Truth was behind that and that they're already active here in America. That problem hasn't gone away."

"Nor will it."

Cassidy turned and saw her grandmother watching her with an odd expression on her face.

"We can't go back," Adele continued. "A brilliant scholar who specializes in this sort of thing has recently shown me that we can't ever go back. As much as we might like to continue hiding in the shadows and preserving the status quo, it is much too late for that. I think the Europeans are right. The truth is going to come out, and it is up to us whether we control it, or let it control us."

Cassidy felt her heart expand at her grandmother's words. She had never doubted that Adele loved her, but there had been times in her life when she had doubted that her nana had truly respected her. In an instant, all those doubts were erased.

With her arms wrapped around Quinn's waist, Cassidy snuggled close to his side and drew comfort in his strength as she echoed her grandmother's sentiments to the head of the Council.

"This is the beginning of a new era," she said quietly. "Humans and Others are going to have to learn to live together if we're all going to make it through. And I don't want my children to grow up thinking they have to live their lives in secrecy until the end of time. That's not a status quo I want to preserve. That's just another kind of prison."

Rafe nodded, his mouth curving up at the corners in the hint of a smile. "I agree. Well said, Cassidy. Now, let's leave the garbage here for my men to clean up and get back to the city so you can make your final report to the Council."

The group made its way slowly out of the ballroom and into the early sunshine that had just broken over the treetops to illuminate the crisp Connecticut morning. The Others took a moment to stretch and enjoy the fresh air before beginning their journey back to the real world.

Cassidy had her head tilted back, her face raised to the gentle rays of sun, when a shadow fell across her. She opened her eyes to see Quinn staring down at her with the oddest look on his face.

"What you said a few minutes ago," he rumbled, placing his warm hands on her hips to hold her in place. "The part about your children. Would you be interested in a further exploration of that topic? With me? Perhaps later today? And quite possibly for the rest of your natural-born life?"

Cassidy just stood there in the sunshine feeling as if the entire world were glowing with her happiness. "That depends. I couldn't possibly have that sort of discussion with a man who didn't love me."

Quinn wrapped his arm around her shoulders and tucked her tightly against her side. "Then have it with me, darling, because I love you madly, Cassidy Poe. Always will. Lupines mate for life, you know."

"I know this one had better," she said, smiling sweetly. "Because if he tries to mate with anyone else, I'll kill him till he wishes he were dead."

Her mate threw back his head and laughed. "What do you say, Cassie love? Are you going to make me a happy man, or doom me to a lifetime of torment?"

She looked up at him with sly challenge. "What makes you think I plan to only do one?"

Quinn laughed again, loudly and heartily, before he seized a grinning Cassidy around the waist and lifted her into the air.

"That's my girl," he said, spinning her around until she laughed along with him. "Now give us a kiss, love of my life. I haven't had a taste of honey in much, much too long."

Turn the page for a sneak peek at the
next thrilling novel in the Others series

She's No Faerie Princess

Coming Fall 2006
From St. Martin's Paperbacks

"You're three hundred and thirty-seven years old. That's a bit late to be running away from home."

"I'm not running away from home. I'm taking a vacation."

"It looks a lot like running."

"So help me, Babbage, if you don't shut up in the next five seconds, I swear to the stars I will take you with me."

Fiona listened to the resulting silence with grim satisfaction. The pixie continued to flutter beside her head and cast disapproving glares in her direction, but disapproval didn't bother her. If it did, she'd never manage to wake up in the mornings. Babbage, on the other hand, lived in mortal fear of the Queen's disapproval, which was why the threat of bringing him with her to the human world had shut him up in such a hurry. Ever since an incident a few years ago when her nephew had been spotted by several humans as he gallivanted around New York, Queen Mab had gotten a lot tougher about enforcing the ban on travel between Faerie and the human world. Most people tried to stay away from upsetting Mab.

There hadn't been much chance that anything would come of the sightings, considering most humans had stopped believing in the existence of her kind many human centuries ago, but Mab did not like to be thwarted.

Fiona didn't see how anyone could consider her quick little vacation to the human world as "thwarting," though. After all, it wasn't like any of the people there would be expecting to see a Fae walking among them, and with a little glamour—the smallest form of Fae magic—she could make sure all they saw when they looked at her would be a perfectly normal human woman. Humans, in her experience, were not that tough to fool. And while they went about their business in blissful ignorance, she'd be able to do some shopping and take in a few concerts. She'd done it before with no problems. She didn't foresee any this time either.

"I'm telling you, I have a bad feeling about this," Babbage grumbled, apparently unable to keep silent a moment longer. He'd lasted longer than Fiona had expected. Pixies were not well known for their taciturn natures. "If you step through that gate, you'll be sorry."

"The only reason why I would be sorry would be if the Queen found out. And the only way my aunt could possibly find out something like that would be if you told her. Which you're not going to do, are you, Babbage?"

The pixie remained stubbornly silent. For once in his life.

Fiona's hand darted out, pinching his gossamer tunic between her thumb and forefinger and hauling him right up to her face. "Are you, Babbage?"

He glanced from her to the gate on the other side of the clearing where she stood, and back again. His wings drooped at the edges. "No, Princess Fiona. I will not tell the Queen of your rash and ill-advised excursion into forbidden territory."

"I've asked you not to call me 'princess'," she said and released him with a flick of her fingers.

He flew back a couple of feet and gave a wounded sniff. "You *are* a princess."

"Sure, along with ten of my female cousins, and that's not counting the other cousins who happen to be princes."

She peered around the trunk of an old oak tree and scanned the clearing for any signs of movement. Just because she wouldn't let the fear of getting caught stop her from going through the gate didn't mean she wasn't going to try to avoid it.

"None of them are in line to inherit both the Summer and Winter thrones."

"Babbage, do you *want* me to take you with me?"

The renewed threat shut the pixie up, but the damage had already been done. He'd reminded her of something she spent a great deal of her time trying to forget, and now she'd spend at least the rest of the day with it hanging over her head. Pesky pixie pest.

Fiona knew that ignoring the truth wasn't going to make it go away, but it didn't keep her from trying. On a daily basis. She despised court life, whether it was her aunt's Seelie Court or her Uncle Dionnu's Unseelie Court, and the idea of taking the throne of either made her break out in hives, which was exactly the reason that she needed to take a vacation. She didn't have the patience or the deviousness required to be a successful leader of the Fae, and she had no intention of developing either. Her parents might both have been sidhe—the noble race of Faerie—but she swore that sometimes she wished they'd been goblins or trolls or pixies or sprites or even a dryad and a satyr. Any type of Fae under the sun or moon would have been fine with her so long as it wasn't a member of either high court. Sometimes, she reflected, life as a Faerie Princess pretty much sucked.

Thinking about it only steeled Fiona's resolve to screw the rules and seize the opportunity for her much-needed vacation. She took one last careful look around, shouldered her small travel bag, and flicked Babbage a jaunty wave.

"Take care, little friend," she called, hurrying toward the shimmering Faerie gate and into the simple, predictable world of the humans.

Tobias Walker hadn't gotten laid in at least three months. He knew very well that this hardly qualified as an emergency, but he did consider it symptomatic of a larger issue. Not only had he not had sex in all that time—which was not inconsequential for a bachelor werewolf in his prime—but he also hadn't gone on a date, gotten an uninterrupted night of sleep, watched an entire ball game, or taken a day off. Considering all that, was it any wonder that his mood edged toward cranky as he stalked through his three A.M. park patrol?

Technically, this wasn't even his patrol, a fact that only contributed to his case of the grumps. Tonight should have been his night to get a decadent five hours of sleep after a double shift on his regular beat down through Central Park, but the packmate who had been assigned up here in Inwood had come down with a raging case of pregnancy and her mate had refused to let her out of the house. Tobias could sympathize with the sentiment; his own Lupine instincts would have driven him to react the same way if he'd had a mate, but he didn't. What he did have was an entire city to patrol and a force that was already stretched thin to cover it.

He stuffed his hands in his pockets as he stalked through the park, his sharp gaze constantly sweeping the surroundings for anything unusual. You'd think by now he'd be used to the whole thing. It had been like this for nearly six months, ever since the Council of Others and its equivalents from around the world had entered into secret negotiations with the humans. The delicate nature of the talks necessitated an atmosphere of peace, no matter how tense, if the two sides were going to reach an agreement that didn't lead to bloodshed on either side. And when you were negotiating with vampires, shape shifters, Others, and human politicians, Tobias reflected, bloodshed was always a possibility, no matter how hard he and his pack worked to prevent it.

These negotiations would alter the course of the future, for both the Others, who had finally taken their first step out of hiding, and for the humans, who now needed to acknowledge that so many of the things they believed to be safely fictional actually did walk among them. It meant asking the humans to discard centuries of fear and superstition to allow what many of them considered to be monsters to enjoy the same rights and legal protections as anyone else. So in contrast, beefing up Other security to be sure no one got out of line and did anything to frighten the humans into another Inquisition seemed like a wise course of action. As beta of the Silverback Clan and head of security at the largest private club for Others in this half of the world, it fell to Tobias to coordinate that security force. Which was why he was currently on his third patrol in twenty-four hours instead of face-down in his mattress.

Heading north at the fork in his path, Tobias considered all the changes he and his kind had faced over the past months. No one had really been prepared. Sure, Others had been debating about the Unveiling on and off for most of the last century, but that had been a theoretical sort of thing, an "imagine if " approach to the future. It hadn't prevented the shock of learning a few months ago that a radical sect called the Light of Truth had gathered enough evidence to take the decision out of their hands and reveal their existence to the humans whether they were ready or not. That news had convinced the Council of Others that the time had come to take the first steps in claiming an open place in the world around them, hence the secret negotiations. Even the most optimistic members of the Council knew better than to break the news to the human public without first gaining some assurances from their governments that the rights of the non-humans would be preserved. Optimistic did not equal foolish. For their part, the Others were prepared to do their best to keep from doing anything to frighten the humans into abandoning the bargaining table. Tobias figured he was currently doing his best, and the best of at least three other people to boot.

Thankfully, things were staying pretty quiet—quiet enough that twenty-four-hour patrols probably weren't strictly necessary, but you just never knew when that one problem you wanted to avoid would rear its ugly head.

Or scream bloody murder.

Before a sharp, feminine cry had even faded to an echo, Tobias had whipped around, pinpointed the source of the sound, and launched himself toward it, sprinting through the trees in a blur of speed and swear words.